THE LAST S

To Hannah

With best wishes

Roy Berry

Printed in Great Britain & USA and distributed globally by Lightning Source UK Ltd,
Chapter House, Pitfield, Kiln Farm, Milton Keynes, MK11 3LW
www.lightningsource.co.uk

Cover image: The storming of Bristol 26th July 1643 © istockphoto

Published by Rover Press

THE LAST STRONGHOLD

A Romance of the English Civil War

Roy Berry

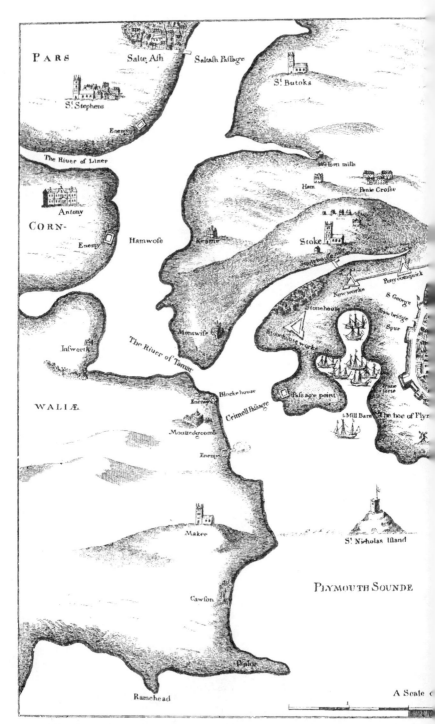

Plymouth in 1643 By kind permission of Plymouth Library Services

A TRVE MAPP AND DESCRIPTION OF THE TOWNE

of Plymouth and the fortifications thereof, with the workes and approaches of the Enemy, at the laſt Seige *A°* 1643

AUTHOR'S NOTES

The main events depicted in *The Last Stronghold* happened. Nowhere are they distorted or transposed, nor are timescales compressed, except that I extended Henrietta Maria's stay at Pendennis beyond the one night that, in, truth, she spent there in her flight to the Continent.

Likewise, the principal characters were real people, only Juliana, Nicholas and his close companions were conceived in my imagination. The other Arundells, the Grenvilles of Stowe and the Carews of Antony, lived and died as the story tells. In the household of Sir Richard Carew there was a senior servant named Nicholas Skelton, as F. E. Halliday reveals in ' A Cornish Chronicle', his history of the Carew family at that time. The clairvoyant, Joan Lobb, was also a real person.

In recreating the main characters, I have tried to depict their appearance and personality as accurately as often scant information allowed, sometimes helped by a portrait – Lord George Goring in Plymouth Art Gallery, Sir Alexander Carew in the library at Antony. Regarding lesser persons, I have to confess there is no evidence that Robert Baker, lace merchant, held Royalist sympathies, but Captain Peter Mundy of the East India Company did describe the Taj Mahal in his journal as he told it to Nicholas.

The present Antony house postdates the one conjured, but Antony parish church, scene of the extraordinary thunderbolt incident, still stands above the village. Trerice continues to nestle ,benignly, in its valley and ancient Lanherne has been a Carmelite nunnery for two centuries. Sadly, Stowe and the later house built by John Grenville, Earl of Bath, after the Restoration, are both gone.

Now as then, Pendennis Castle, witness to Sir John Arundell's gallant obstinancy, dominates the Carrick Roads, in company with its smaller neighbour at St. Mawes, but the secret of the passage between Pendennis and Arwenack House seems to have died with a local estate agent.

For the history of the period, I relied heavily on Mary Coate's scholarly work, 'Cornwall in the Great Civil War and Interregnum'. For pictures of life in Jersey for the Royalist exiles, I turned to the diary of that inveterate chronicler of Channel Islands' events, Jean Chevalier, held by Jersey Museum. A contemporary leaflet in the Bodleian Library, Oxford, describes the interception of the ship, *Doggerbank*, by two Parliamentary frigates, off the coast of Brittany, and the sea fight that followed.

An original letter held in Truro Record Office and written from Pendennis to the commander of the investing Parliamentarians disclosed conditions in the castle late in the siege.

Guidance regarding Grenville heraldry was given to me by the curator of the Royal Institution of Cornwall, but I transposed the Grenville crest – the golden griffin – to Sir Beville's standard, though in fact this bore three rests. I hope that the Sealed Knot and other societies dedicated to the truth will forgive this expedient.

The Civil War was Cornwall's greatest era and its greatest tragedy. When the magnificent Cornish infantry followed the standards of the Grenvilles, Slanning, Trevanion and others to the walls of Bristol and up the slopes of Lansdown, above Bath, gentry and common men died together, in a feudal bond which survived in their county into the 17th century.

The mystery of that bond is the inspiration and theme of *The Last Stronghold*.

For Esme

AUTHOR'S FURTHER ACKNOWLEDGEMENTS

In addition to the references to persons and sources of help in AUTHOR'S NOTES, I also acknowledge the assistance and encouragement given to me by my late wife, Esme, by Marc Danbury, Anne Bassett, Peter Michael, Suzanne Rowles and Michael Berry. Invaluable information was also obtained from:

LONDON, A Concise History, by Geoffrey Trease

The Trial of Charles I, by C. V. Wedgwood

Various material issued by The National Trust and English Heritage

My thanks to them all.

BIOGRAPHICAL NOTES

Roy Berry was born in Bristol and educated at Queen Elizabeth's Hospital and Bristol College of Advanced Technology.

During a career in the aerospace industry, he was variously assistant to the director of administration of the Concorde project, director of a printing and graphics company and manager of departments which produced publications for operating,, maintaining and overhauling helicopters and aero-engines. He held membership of the Royal Aeronautical Society and retired from Rolls-Royce senior management.

In earlier days, he was very involved in theatre and featured in numerous radio drama productions, including 'The Mayor of Casterbridge' and Westward Ho!, which stimulated an interest in writing for radio.

For many years, he and his wife had an apartment in an artillery fort overlooking Plymouth Sound and St. Nicholas Island, near the National Trust property of Antony. From there, they explored Devon and Cornwall extensively, leading him to research and write *The Last Stronghold*.

Daphne du Maurier's *Vanishing Cornwall*, which evokes the spirit and history of the county, contributed to his inspiration and he confesses admiration for her period romances set in the South West.

CONTENTS

CHAPTER 1

The Nestlings

Absorbed by the vista of coastline and ocean, he failed to notice her coming down from the moor, through tawny bracken and yellow gorse. Nor did he see her check the stallion and eye the dry-stone wall which barred her path to the headland. But he heard the pounding hooves and watched the powerful creature breast the wall like a black arrow. It landed, surefooted, on the soft turf, but the slight figure had lost her seat. With a shrill cry, she pitched from the saddle, in a flurry of white lace and plum velvet, and lay winded and shaken. Swinging down from his cob, he ran to her and raised her, 'Are you hurt?' he enquired, solicitously.

For moments she fought for breath. 'Certainly not!' she gasped, pushing him away. Reaching beneath her gown, she removed a muddied stocking and he turned away blushing furiously. He looked back to meet her amused gaze.

She was about 13 years of age, but so self-possessed he longed to impress her. Removing his doublet, he made to drape it over her shoulders, but she brushed him aside, disdainfully. 'Fetch my horse!' she ordered. 'His name is Bellerophon and you will be hard put to catch him.'

He set off towards the glossy thoroughbred, but when he whistled it pricked up its ears and trotted away into the gorse. Gradually, he gained its confidence, until he was able to grasp its bridle and lead it back, triumphantly, to its young mistress.

She had risen and was testing an ankle. 'Help me to mount.' As he raised her on to the stallion's broad back, her amber hair brushed his cheek and he saw there were freckles on her nose. 'I want you to come with me to Trerice, where my guardian, Sir John Arundell, will, no doubt, wish to reward you.'

1

He followed her over the moor and into shadowed lanes, deep between hedges of turf and rock. Scrolled gables showed above a perimeter wall and they rode up to a house of silver-grey limestone.

A maid ran from the porch and two grooms appeared. 'Oh, milady, what has befallen you?'

'Do not fret, Meg! Has Sir John returned?'

The maid looked apprehensive. 'Aye, not a half-hour since and he knows you were riding Bellerophon.' She eased her mistress to the ground and the girl whispered, 'I must dissemble if I am to be spared his wrath, so I have brought this boy along to distract him.' Her rescuer edged towards his mount, but she took his arm. 'Stay and help me inside!' She hobbled along a screens passage and into the great hall, her limp now much exaggerated.

He had a moment to note a full-length portrait of King Charles lit by a vast mullioned window, then the latch clicked and a voice boomed, 'Are you alright, Juliana?' A gentleman in grey velvet crossed the chequered floor, his shoulder-length hair silver, his manner brisk and authoritative.

'Yes, guardian, thanks to this boy.'

'Then you have earned my gratitude.' Sharp eyes appraised him. 'Do I not know you?'

'I think not, sir, though I have seen you at Antony, where my father is steward to Mr. Richard Carew. He has sent me to Trewhella Barton to take over, in due time.'

'Is Jacob Penwarden contemplating his pantables and pipe, then?'

'Not yet, sir.'

The stern face showed a flicker of amusement. 'Tis as well, for you look a mite young for the task. How, old are you?'

'Sixteen, sir.'

'Mm.' Arundell addressed his ward. 'Now, young lady, away to your chamber and we will find out what has happened to you. We will speak of horses, later.' He added, severely. 'What is your name, boy?' He continued.

The girl on the stairs paused and cocked her head, answered, 'Nicholas, sir.'

'So you have your sire's name as well as his likeness.' The craggy brows contracted, as he perused the boy's coarse shirt and stockings. 'Yet, you seem more gentleman than farmer, Master Nicholas Skelton. How has this been accomplished?'

'Mr. Carew saw to it that I was schooled with his son, John, before he went up to Oxford University. He taught me to love books and gave me the freedom of Antony's library.'

For a moment Arundell fingered his beard, deep in thought. Attracted by a movement, above, Nicholas glimpsed the girl's small face peeping through the fretting of the minstrel gallery. 'Tis cruel to confine a young woman of spirit to riding a palfrey,' her guardian continued, 'but she outdistances her maid if she rides the stallion and roams the countryside alone, with what result you have seen today. What say you to serving her as escort and companion, when the opportunity permits?' As Nicholas hesitated, he added, 'I am sure my nephew of Antony will be amenable, when I approach him.'

'Very well, sir.'

'Good, then you will wish to be on your way. Let us say a week today, in the forenoon.'

Back on the moor, he gave vent to his exhilaration and, with a jab of the spurs, he sped across the Bodmin road into the fertile hollow where Trewhella Barton nestled from the Atlantic gales. In the yard, he gave Matthew Tremain, the cowman, an effusive wave. In the kitchen, Dorothy Crabtree, the housekeeper, was stirring broth and he kissed her as he passed. She paused in astonishment. 'My, but you'm in a rare mood, Maister Nicholas, anyone would think you'd met the Queen of England, with your gallant air.'

'Mayhap not a queen, but a princess, Dorothy.'

She shook her head at such levity. 'You'd best get straight out to the byre. Mr Penwarden's not best pleased at having to fetch them cows in alone.'

He smiled. How would they understand, anymore than he, why a brief meeting with a haughty freckle-faced girl had so elated him?

▣▣▣

Next week she was waiting before the friendly house when he arrived, noticeably more agreeable than at their first meeting.

'You are to choose a falcon from our brood and we will train it, together,' she told him. She led him to the stable block, where the birds of prey were housed. Fierce, unwinking eyes regarded him.

'My guardian has taken to you,' she added. He thanked her and chose the most aggressive fledgling. Juliana cut a slice of flesh from a rabbit carcass and passed it to him. 'It will take time and patience before he accepts you as his master.' She looked up and smiled, and he saw that her eyes were hazel-green. 'I will make him a hood and jesses, when we are ready. But come, I am going to play you a piece of music that I learned, specially.'

They crossed the courtyard and hall, and climbed the stairs to the solar, whose great, semi-circular window flooded the room with light. The plasterwork of a fine barrel ceiling was cast into relief and a coat of arms, above the frieze, caught his eye.

'Those are the arms of Henry FitzAlan, Earl of Arundell, K.G.' she explained. 'Sit you beneath them.' Taking a lyre, she plucked a melody from its strings, before laying it aside, ruefully. 'It was not well done.'

'It was beautiful, but sad. I recall my mother singing it, when I was a child,' he told her.

'How fares your mother?' she asked.

'She died when I was six.'

'Methinks you are an only child.'

He nodded.

'I too. My parents died of the smallpox, nigh on a year ago. Sir John took me into his household, but I have been somewhat lonely since, for he and his sons, John and Richard, are much away.'

'I miss my father and the Barton seems a God-forsaken place, after Antony. Though I have much to learn from old Penwarden, he cares for nothing but the land and I long for books and discourse.'

She pressed his hand. 'Then you and I shall have discourse – about books and music and poetry. And we will fly our hawks and ride the moors, together!'

'But not often, I fear, for Penwarden is a hard taskmaster.'

'Then as often as we may.' She rose and he followed her to the door. 'It must be nearly noon and Meg is arranging a "pique-nique" in the orchard.' They descended to the library beneath the solar and she opened doors that gave way to the south lawn. It was late May and every tree in the orchard was festooned with delicate blossom, like clouds of lace suspended from a flawless sky. The maid had spread blankets upon the grass and was laying out sliced mutton and cheese, sugared pastries, a flask of wine and pewter cups. As Juliana arranged her skirts, he watched a pink-tinted petal drop into her hair. 'Meg will be displeased if you leave even one crumb,' she warned him.

He returned the maid's shy smile.

'How came a steward's son to cultivate a taste for books and discourse?'

Thinking she was teasing him, he bridled. 'Mr Carew saw to it that I was schooled with his son, John, who was ever a disputatious fellow and would argue on almost any subject under the sun. I missed him very much when he went up to Oxford University. As for books, Mr. Carew taught me to love them. Perchance, it is difficult for a girl to comprehend the desire for knowledge.'

She regarded him, haughtily. 'You think me, then, ignorant of all but

4

needlework and music?'

'No, forgive me.'

'You are too sensitive, Master Skelton. You are afraid that I think you a bumpkin. I do not! You speak like a gentleman and your words are well chosen. Tell me what subjects you studied in the classroom?'

'Mathematics, Latin, some French, geography and history. I think I learned more outside the classroom, from Mr. Carew. He is a kindly man, very knowledgeable in the growing of apple and pear trees and he keeps a salt-water fishpond down by the river. He also has remedies for all ills and a liking for Socratic argument.' He glanced up from the slice of cheese he was quartering. 'I could tell you much more, but I may weary you.'

Her eyes searched his face. 'I do not think you will! How will you use this education at Trewhella Barton?'

'I am not educated, merely schooled, for I shall never go to Oxford or attend the Inns of Court like John or his stepbrother, Alexander. Although I love the land, the farm is only a stage in my life and, some day, I will succeed my father as steward, at Antony.'

'Would that content you?'

'It is all I may hope for.'

'Were I a man, I would seek some great office of state, like Chancellor of the Exchequer. Would that not be a fine thing – to serve His Majesty and so influence the affairs of the realm?'

'I think it would. Were I Chancellor, methinks I would advise the King to lift the imposition of Ship Money, for it is a matter of great discontent in these parts.'

'Yet the King must raise taxes somehow, while he is at odds with his Parliament,' Juliana retorted.

'I know not the right of it,' he responded. A clock struck the hour and he stood up and brushed loose grass from his breeches. 'It is time for me to go.'

'When can you come again?'

'In about a month I think.'

◫◫◫

Jacob Penwarden applied a taper to his pipe and settled back in his hard chair, in the parlour of Trewhella Barton. A cloud of blue smoke drifted over the remains of their meal. 'So you'm real smitten wi' this young 'oman?'

'I wouldn't say that, but she is unlike any girl I've ever met. Some were silly and a few were tomboys; she is neither, but very intelligent.'

'Is she comely?'

'When she is older I think she will be very beautiful.'

Penwarden puffed meditatively. 'You mark me well, take care that wilful thing in your breeches don't lead ye into no trouble. The Arundells be the powerfulest family in Cornwall not excepting the Grenvilles of Stowe. If one of theirs is defiled, 'twill take more than Mr. Carew to save yer skin.'

For a moment he hated the crude old man with the stubbled chin, the white hair sprouting from nostrils and ears, and he came to his feet sending the chair crashing to the slate flags.

'It's not like that! I wouldn't do that.'

'Steady on! Sometime, 'tis more than flesh and blood can stand to let a maid be when you'm that smitten.' Penwarden came to him and laid a horny hand on his shoulder. 'Besides, she be too 'igh for 'ee lad.' The shoulders trembled beneath his touch. 'Walk with me to the top of the rise and I'll tell ye how to set about training a falcon.'

But Nicholas shook himself free and stalked from the room.

◻◻◻

Juliana led Nicholas around the Bowling Green, to view the vista of meadow and woods, with the tower of Newlyn East Church showing above the trees.

'I have not seen you at worship on the Sabbath, yonder?'

'That is because my branch of the family is of the Catholic faith, like my kin at Lanherne.'

'Are you not fined for failing to attend church?'

'Aye, it is the price we must pay. But that is nothing when compared to the penalty my ancestor, Humphrey Arundell, paid for he was hanged, drawn and quartered.' Juliana shuddered. 'Poor Humphrey! Even so we are ever staunch for our faith. And you are a Puritan?'

'I was raised a Puritan.' This was the first time that he had equivocated about his faith, though, in truth, he had no liking for the suffocating moral diet of the Carews of Antony. 'They say that the Queen practices Catholicism, while the King is an Anglican, yet their bond grows ever stronger.'

She nodded. 'This is weighty discourse on my 14th birthday, is it not? Tell me, do you not think that Trerice is beautiful?'

They were standing level with the first floor of the house, looking obliquely at the E-shaped front. The porch almost hid its great eye – the mullioned and transomed window – but the decorative scrolled gables with their carved mask corbels could be seen to advantage. 'It is, and I see why you love it.'

'Now,' Juliana said, mischievously, 'I have perceived that you are knowledgeable in the arts and I would test your mathematics.' She led him down to the lawn and they stood before the great window. 'While I count the seconds, you must calculate the panes of glass.' She stamped a foot. 'Begin!'

His eye ran, methodically, over one section of the glass, and then he counted the sections across and down. 'Five hundred and seventy-six.'

'That is absolutely right! Eleven seconds. How came you to be so quick?'

He smiled ruefully. 'What use is a steward who cannot add?'

She was looking up at him, the hazel-green eyes wide. Her gown was brown satin, snowy lace at shoulder and wrist. A necklace of pearls, given to her by Sir John, circled her throat. She drew him to where roses glowed red on the orchard wall and picked a bud. 'There is your prize.' Securing the flower in his doublet, he bowed gallantly and kissed her hand. 'Oh, Master Skelton, I do not want this day to end. Yet I know you must depart within the hour. Will you come again, soon?'

'If you will have me?'

'Do you doubt it?'

▣▣▣

It was the Sunday of Harvest Festival. Nicholas rode with the groom, a respectful distance behind Sir John, as they made the short journey from Newlyn East church to Trerice. He had been invited to dine at the house. Arundell beckoned to him and, as he drew alongside, he enquired, 'How is Jacob?'

'Not well, Sir John. The leg where the horse kicked him is badly gashed and contused and I worry for him. Mindful of my patron's treatment of applying elder leaves to swollen flesh, I have done likewise, but the lower leg and foot are blackening.'

'It seems you are right to be concerned. I will have my own physician go over to the Barton to see him, and will send a groom to Antony to inform my nephew of the situation. It amuses me to call Richard Carew nephew, for he is only four years younger than I. Now he has purchased a baronetcy to boost the King's revenues. Did you know that he was born at Trerice to my sister, Juliana's namesake?' Nicholas nodded. 'His father was, of course, a distinguished scholar and author of the Survey of Cornwall. Indeed he died in his library, which seems an agreeable way of departing this life. It is one of my deepest regrets, Nicholas, that I have not had the time for books that I would

7

have wished, since leaving Oxford. At 20, I was Member of Parliament for the Borough of Michell and MP for the county seven years later. Mine has been a busy life.'

'I remain grateful for the opportunity to borrow your books, Sir John.'

'Your life must be as full of labour as mine is of the affairs of the county, so when do you find time to read so much? Juliana tells me that you have devoured nigh half my library, in the past two years.'

'I am profligate with candles into the small hours of the night.'

'Enjoy books young man, but do not burn out sight or mind in the high season of your life.'

They were into the sunken lane leading to Trerice, where two horsemen could scarce ride abreast in comfort. Overhead, the elms were gently shedding their leaves and the old man looked down at the dank carpet muffling their mounts' hooves. 'Like this year my life is into its fourth quarter, and I imagine what little God has given me to accomplish is done. Bye-the-bye, my other guests today are Sir George and Lady Mary Chudleigh and their son, James. Sir George was brother to Sir Richard's late wife Bridget. They are en-route to George's brother-in-law, Sir Reynold Mohun, at Boconnoc.'

They found the Chudleighs with Juliana, before the fire in the great hall and Arundell presented Nicholas. James Chudleigh was about five years older than Nicholas, muscular and of striking vitality and it was apparent that he enjoyed an easy informality with Juliana.

'Dear James is a soldier, lately returned from Ireland. He has been telling me what a strange and beautiful land it is, and how strong are the Irish in their faith.' Juliana informed Nicholas.

'That is but one side of the medal, sweet cousin. On balance, I think it is a benighted place and am well pleased to be back in Devonshire. Yet many fear that Archbishop Laud's High Anglicanism is but a prelude to the restoration of Catholicism in this realm.'

He smiled, deprecatingly, at Juliana. 'But the Commons are right in demanding that the King acknowledge the power and privilege of Parliament, and the lawful rights and liberties of the subject.'

Arundell called them to table and Nicholas studied the intriguing young man, uneasy at Juliana's animated response to him. But Chudleigh drew him easily into the conversation and he consoled himself that Chudleigh would soon rejoin his regiment and Juliana would, again, be his alone.

A week later, Nicholas followed the wagon bearing Jacob Penwarden to his last resting place, in Newlyn East church. At 18, he was master at Trewhella Barton.

CHAPTER 2

The Fledglings

Nicholas crossed the impacted flints of the road, thrusting the cob into knee-high bracken. It was mid-morning and the land was bathed in sunlight, the air rapturous with the song of birds. He smiled, for he was on the way to Trerice – though it had been an oddly-couched invitation. "My master bids you attend upon him at two of the clock," the messenger had said. Anxious not to be late, he heeled the cob to a canter.

At the house, he was led straight to the great hall and left alone. Fine dust hung in the sunlight streaming through the vast window on to the chequered floor. The door latch clicked and he turned, eagerly. 'Good day to you, Master Skelton.' Arundell drew out a chair and sat down. He was clearly in no mood for pleasantries and Nicholas felt a twinge of apprehension. 'You are a worthy young man and my nephew tells me that you have done well in your first year as tenant at the Barton. You have also been a good friend to Juliana and a welcome visitor to my house, but Juliana is 17 and must soon be betrothed. It is, therefore, not meet that this association should continue and I wish it terminated, forthwith.'

'But Sir John…!'

Arundell raised an imperious hand. 'Do not make this more painful for us both. Return to your farm and prepare for the harvest, before matters between the King and his Parliament overtake us all. Sir Richard has given you a good start to your life, continue to serve him well.' Rising, he summoned a servant. 'God go with you!'

Unmindful of everything but the old man's peremptory dismissal, Nicholas allowed his mount to plod unguided back to the high land, ere he bestirred himself. Never again to ride the uplands or fly a hawk with her? Never to see her again? With a cruel jab of the spurs, he brought the cob to a gallop and rode wildly towards the sea. As the cliff edge loomed, he veered away and rode along the coastal track, till the animal was spent and he flung himself from the saddle. It was here they had met, three years ago, and begun that easy friendship which had brought him to this anguish. He should have remembered Jacob Penwarden's words, "She be too 'igh for 'ee lad." Was it only a week since he had poured into verse all that was in his heart and Juliana had kissed him?

And from that moment he was lost – hopelessly in love with her. A curlew cried into the wind, but he did not hear it; nor did he notice the small clouds drifting in from the sea, till they obscured the sun, and he raised his head. How well the weather matched his mood, for now there was a portent of rain and coldness, like the chill in his heart. He called to the grazing cob and together they turned homeward.

❑❑❑

May came and went as the land held him in bondage, for there were late lambs to be reared, crops to be hoed, ditches to be cleared, but Juliana was never out of his thoughts. Juliana betrothed, and to someone of rank, assuredly. Would it be strong, genial James Chudleigh to whom she confided her thoughts and feelings? Mayhap, she was musing, even now, who would come riding to beg her hand, no longer mindful of him. He pictured the hedgerows around Trerice, white with cow parsley and bright with the harmony of red campion and bluebells. He should ride to Arundell's door and bid for her hand, but he could not for he was unworthy.

❑❑❑

From a window of the solar, Arundell watched his ward languishing among the blossoms in the orchard below, the book in her hand unread. It was two months since he had sent her companion away and he had not ceased to regret encouraging the childhood friendship, which had plainly deepened into love. He could give no other name to the sensitive evocation in the young man's verse and he doubted not that his passion was reciprocated by his ward.

All would be well when she was betrothed. But whence should he look for a suitor – to the Grenvilles or the Godolphins? Perhaps another Trevanion or one of the Killigrew brood from Arwenack. It would not be easy for, in truth, he was as constrained by politics and religion as Skelton was by station. How beautiful she was, the perfect oval of her face framed by chestnut curls and little ringlets along her brow. He loved her like a daughter and cared for her happiness above all else – save for his duty to his King, whose business he must be about, even now.

Picking up his papers he went down to the hall, calling for his sons, John and Richard. Hearing the commotion through the open doors, Juliana came into the library to kiss them goodbye and watch as they rode away to Bodmin. The moment they were gone, she sent Meg over to Trewhella Barton; if her love would not come to her because of that dear, intimidating, old man, she must go to him.

By early evening Meg was back.

◘◘◘

The wind was boisterous as they crossed the uneven turf of Trevologue Head and a great swathe of cloud hung over the sea, like a trawled net. He was waiting in the shadows of the tumuli and dismounted, as she slid from the saddle and pushed back the hood of her cloak. They walked towards the cliff edge without speaking, while he marvelled again at the delicacy of her profile, the neat head set upon the long neck.

Turning to him, she demanded, 'Why had I to contrive this meeting?'

For a moment he watched the pulse in her throat; then, recovering his wits, he replied, 'Your guardian has forbidden me to see you.'

'Am I to be surrendered so meekly?'

Hazel-green eyes challenged him and he coloured. 'There are too many barriers between us.'

Such was the anguish in his voice that she relented. 'They are not insurmountable, please God.'

'Are they not? You are soon to be betrothed and may have the pick of the county.'

'Do not despair! My betrothal is not imminent! Had not your verses been disclosed to my guardian, by a servant seeking favour, our association might have continued. But your sentiments alarmed him and he resolved to end it. From whence have you conjured me suitors? My guardian is ambitious for me, but I am a lesser Arundell – not his direct issue – and my marriage portion will be small. And if he would have me matched with another Catholic, he must look to the North Country, for he will not find one suitable in Cornwall.'

Nicholas smiled thinly. What man smitten by such grace would give a fig for her dowry or even her religion? 'If it suited your guardian's book, he would marry you to a wealthy landowner, regardless of creed.'

For a moment she was silent. 'Why did you dedicate those verses to me and then remain tongue-tied, before him?'

'I am a steward's son and he is what he is.'

'Did my guardian not declare you worthy?'

'You are well informed of what passed between us.'

She bit her tongue. 'I eavesdropped from the gallery.'

He flushed again, knowing that she had witnessed his capitulation.

'Did your verses speak truth? Do you love me?'

⊡⊡⊡

Humiliated and without hope, what purpose was there in declaring himself, further? He shrugged and turned away. Sensing his despair, Juliana touched his arm. 'We will speak no more of it, now. I must return, for the light is fading.'

Remounting, they coaxed the horses down a long slope to the beach and into the gentle surf. Without his customary mount from Arundell's stable, he was no match for her thoroughbred and she sped off in a turmoil of spray, the black cloak streaming. At the Beacon, she turned to wave before setting the stallion at the path which rose from the beach, where Meg waited.

He rode home deep in thought. Perchance, the issue of religion was not exclusive, for Sir Richard's mother had come as a Catholic to Antony, but now the Carews were Puritans. Yet what did that avail? Long hours in the classroom and longer in the library had made him acceptable as Juliana's friend, but they had not qualified him as a suitor.

⊡⊡⊡

Juliana was content. She had longed for Nicholas to declare his love on the headland, but his verses would suffice for the present. Her guardian's now-frequent absences gave opportunities for precious, stolen meetings.

It was on such a day, as they walked along strands where shimmering pools waited to be reclaimed by the parent tide, that Nicholas mused, 'We could sail for one of the settlements in the New World.'

'It is a little late for that. Events are overtaking us, my sweeting. My guardian and Sir Bevill are even now issuing commissions in the King's name at Lostwithiel. Both sides are seeking control of the County militia. Have you considered where you stand?'

He regarded her, anxiously. 'My thoughts have been all on you and the farm, but I will follow Sir Richard.'

'Then please God politics will not compound our situation.'

The wind tousled his hair as she studied his face, the straight well-formed nose and firm chin, the harmony of features. Dissatisfaction and ambition were there, too. Sir Richard had shown him wider horizons and he would not be at peace until he had tested himself beyond present confines. Doubtless Sir Richard had imbued a proper respect for the monarch in his protégé, yet his eldest son was one of the Members of Parliament who had voted for the impeachment of the Earl of Strafford, the King's friend. Antony was, therefore, not a household where loyalties could be presumed.

Determined not to show her growing fears she kissed him lightly and said, 'Let us go, for it is getting chill.' They made their way back to the firm sand and walked hand-in-hand along the deserted beach.

▣▣▣

In late August, news reached Cornwall that the King had raised his standard at Nottingham. The Civil War had begun. Thereafter, it mattered little whether the tenants, estate workers and households of the landowners regarded the King as a despot or a man misled by his counsellors, they simply rallied behind their masters; only the tinners and fishermen remained indifferent to the gathering storm.

At the end of the month, a rider clattered up to the farmhouse and Nicholas heard a rich, Devon voice ask for 'Maister Skelton'. He came into the hall as the outline in the doorway resolved into John Gendle, Sir Richard's groom. Gendle was enjoying himself. With a flourish, he drew a sealed letter from his boot and thrust it towards Nicholas. It was from Alexander Carew.

He broke the wax and read, 'Under the powers vested in me by the Parliamentary Militia Ordinance, I summon you to report at Antony on the 1stOctober, 1642, for service with the army of the Parliament…...' He stared at the last phrase – Alexander issuing orders and for the Parliament?

He looked up to find Gendle regarding him. 'I will give you a reply to this letter, John. Go to the kitchen and have a pot of cider and a slice of Dorothy's game pie. I am sure they will be welcome after your journey.'

Gendle smacked his lips. 'They would, Maister.'

15

Nicholas returned to the letter, concerned not to estrange himself from Alexander, the heir to Antony, for might not the King , even now, be reconciled with his Parliament? In penning his reply he played on Alexander's certain concern for his family estates and asked for deferment until arrangements could be made for the management of the farm. The letter finished, he recalled the groom and questioned him about affairs at Antony. Apart from learning that Sir Richard seemed frail, Gendle told him that a portrait of Alexander, commissioned for his coming-of-age, had been mysteriously slashed in its frame and removed.

When the groom had goner, Nicholas remained preoccupied. Alexander was a Member of Parliament – but so was Sir Bevill Grenville, who had been driven to oppose the King, for a while, by the imprisonment and death in the Tower of his great friend, Sir John Eliot. But now he was four-square for his sovereign. Alexander had suffered no such experience. Was it, then, not conviction, but merely prudence that persuaded him to his position. Plymouth, a Parliamentary stronghold, was almost within sight of his home. But to serve Alexander was to bear arms against the King; to become implacably opposed to the Arundells!

But, for the present, the rye and barley stood full and golden, awaiting the sickle. Matching his labourers, he sweated and strained, bundled and bound until the barn was full. Now there was time for other matters and he sent a message to Juliana, through Meg's mother at St. Mawgan, proposing a rendezvous on Tregurrion beach.

When they met he was ill-at-ease, for Alexander had not replied to his letter, but Juliana was bubbling with good spirits and had much to tell him. While she drew breath, he said. 'I am summoned to the Parliamentary colours.'

She gasped. 'But your patron is a Royalist!'

'Is he? In any event Alexander is issuing the orders and he is a Parliamentarian.'

She sifted sand aimlessly through her fingers as he told her of his visitor. 'It is unthinkable that we should be on opposing sides,' she responded.

'Yet I am bound to the Carews, for I am nothing without them. Sir Richard is an old man, probably disinterested in wider events. How may I fare when Alexander is master of Antony, if I disregard him now? Hopefully, we have a little time, for I have begged deferment till the spring, arguing that there is no one at the farm capable of running it. Matthew is a good man, but he is unlettered and could not handle the accounts or buy and sell. Alexander must find a new tenant and that will not be easy.'

She was silent and they watched the tide running in like molten pewter tinged red by the westering sun. 'There will be little opportunity to meet when winter comes,' she said, at last, 'but we must keep in touch through Meg Collins.'

Shivering, she stood up and they walked to where the horses fretted in the fading light. For a moment they clung together, then he helped her into the saddle and she cantered slowly away and was soon lost to sight.

▣▣▣

Michaelmas came and went as the Cornish winter closed about the farm. Raging storms lashed the windows, forming rivulets of water on the leaded panes, obscuring the world outside. When the rains ceased, horizons came briefly into view, to disappear again as mist formed and hung wraith-like in the still air. Now it was the turn of tempestuous winds which tugged at the shutters and flung sparse saplings and shrubs into frenzied jigs.

At each day's end, Nicholas came in from the outbuildings, chilled or drenched, and spent shrouded evenings before the turf fire, boots thrust towards the warmth, a pot of cider at his elbow. Sometimes, he read or re-read his treasured books or wrote verse, lost to the gloom beyond the guttering candle.

At Christmastide, the low room and hall were decked with evergreen for the entertainment of his household and farm workers. Matthew Tremain, his cowman, daughter Janet, Dorothy Crabtree – dark widow of a fisherman – and a dozen other folk made up the small community. As the cider and barley mead flowed and the cheeks of his labourers grew ruddier, he recalled past Christmases at Antony with his father. Then the Carews had been a happy family, united in joy, with Alexander's growing brood of children scampering about the great house and Jane, his wife, presiding over the decorations, supervising the provisions, dispensing mulled ale and punch, while the Yule logs sizzled and spat in the cavernous fireplace. What would be the mood this year, in the divided household? How different it would be with Juliana, for the Arundells of Trerice were gathered in unity among their kin at Lanherne.

His reverie was broken by one of the rowdy farm workers staggering against him, and he went to the fireplace and prodded the turf into brightness. It was time for his guests to partake of the seasonal board Dorothy and Janet had prepared. He beckoned the younger woman to him, admiring – not for the first time – her golden hair and rounded body, the divided fullness of her breasts. What pleasure and comfort she could offer a man! But the capable hands were square and red, while Juliana's were all elegance and grace.

Towards the end of January, as he sat at his accounts, the door was flung back and Janet burst in, greatly excited, 'Oh sir, come quick, there be a soldier asleep in the barn!'

Nicholas leapt to his feet and followed her to the doorway of the outbuilding. In the morning light, he made out a figure recumbent in the straw, as if it had fallen where it stood. A horse, fully harnessed, holstered pistol and sword hanging from its saddle, nuzzled the straw. The man was unshaven, a rough, bloodstained bandage around his head.

As they knelt beside him and raised his head, he opened his eyes and gazed at them, dully. 'Fetch your father,' Nicholas ordered.

They carried the man into the kitchen and laid him on the table. Removal of the bandage revealed a deep scalp graze, which they bathed and dressed. Then they eased him into a nightshirt and carried the semi-conscious figure to bed. Nicholas turned to Dorothy, who hovered in the doorway. 'Sir Richard is a great advocate of a warming stone at the feet of a sick person. Heat one as quickly as you can, 'twill comfort this poor fellow.' These ministrations revived the soldier enough for them to feed him broth, after which he slept for 24 hours.

When Nicholas looked in upon him, the next morning, Janet was sitting watching at the bedside. As the door creaked open, the patient's eyes opened, rational and questioning. 'Good morning! I am Nicholas Skelton, tenant of this farm. We found you in the barn, yesterday. You are quite safe.'

The man raised his hand and felt the bandage about his head. 'Yes, I think I remember.' When they had lifted him on the pillow, Nicholas called for Dorothy to bring food. Presently, he told them. 'My name is James Salter. I was a forester on Lord Robartes' estate before he recruited me into his regiment. We were in battle at Bradock Down. Sir Bevill Grenville led a downhill charge against us, with a giant of a fellow behind him carrying a standard with a golden dragon – a griffin they said – upon it. They came at us so fiercely we were overcome. A musket ball, I suppose it were, grazed my forehead and I pitched into a ditch. I must have lain there unnoticed or been taken for dead. When I came to my senses, I stole a horse from the Royalists' lines and rode, always by night, in a great loop westward to avoid the enemy patrols. I was making for Lanhydrock, but exhaustion overcame me and I sought refuge in your barn.' His words were well formed and he spoke crisply, but the telling of his tale had tired him and he lapsed into sleep.

Within a week, under the devoted care of Dorothy and Janet, he was sufficiently recovered to be on his way. Nicholas smiled to see that Janet had burnished his boots and accoutrements to perfection. Donning the old cloak they had given him, he stepped out into the freshening air of late afternoon. Nicholas, Dorothy and Matthew followed, while Janet held the bridle of his horse.

Salter grasped Nicholas's hand, his smile encompassing the little group about the door. 'My thanks and God's blessing to you all.' Taking the reins in one hand, he slid the other around Janet's waist and kissed her full on the mouth. She yielded compliantly and her lip trembled as he released her. Then he was in the saddle and away, with a last wave to his young nurse as she ran to the gate and watched him disappear from sight.

▪▪▪

In February, the first lambs were born and, before long, the daffodils raised golden trumpets in fanfare to spring. John Gendle came back with another letter from Alexander Carew, which charged Nicholas to leave the husbandry of the farm in Matthew's hands and report to Antony, within the week.

He sent a hurried note to Juliana and, on the blustery morning following, Meg Collins came to the farmhouse. Nicholas opened the door to find her standing in the yard, the wind plucking at her garments, her sharp features agitated, 'My mistress wishes you to come to her at the house, tonight.' She spoke in a harsh whisper.

Nicholas stooped to catch her words. 'Tonight? But what of Sir John?'

'He is away about the business of the war. My lady is alone, with a few servants.'

His heart leapt. Before he could reply, the maid said, 'You are to come to the postern in the south wall and I am to take you to her.' She clasped his arm, 'In the name of Heaven, be careful, sir! If we are discovered I am done for and God preserve my lady if the master should learn of it.'

His throat tightened as he comprehended her meaning and he muttered some sort of reassurance. After she had ridden from the yard and across the meadow, he stood in the chilling wind, letting it tear at his shirt. Juliana's message was clear. She acknowledged his dilemma, understood he must obey Alexander's summons, yet would affirm her love.

Dusk was falling as he went to the stable, harnessed the cob and set off on the route taken earlier by Meg. The wind had dropped, though there was still a chill in the air, but he did not notice it for his mind and body were on fire. At length, he came over the downland and into the lanes, thinking of that last visit to Trerice, almost a year ago, when he believed that he had lost her. Were they, now, to seal their love, irrevocably?

At a discreet distance from the house, he dismounted. Night had fallen, but the moon shone blue and fitful, masked now and then by slow-moving cloud. He hid his horse in a clump of trees and threw his cloak over it. Leaving the cover of the trees, he followed the lane until the wall surrounding the house came into sight. Stealing along its contour, he arrived at the postern and settled down to wait. Somewhere over the wall a hound bayed and a woman's voice silenced it. If it were Thor, Arundell's wolfhound, he hoped that Meg had the dog under control. In the wood behind, there was a beating of wings and the hoot of an owl. Some way to the left, a small creature screamed, then there was silence, broken by rustling and other, nocturnal sounds. As the night cold began to permeate his bones, the postern was quietly slid and he rose stiffly.

The door opened, a shadowy figure appeared in the aperture. 'Are you there, sir?'

'Aye, good Meg.'

Without another word, she beckoned him inside, re-bolted the door and took his hand. Following a path through the garden, she led him to the library door, which stood ajar, and into the house. They tip-toed into the hall, deserted and lit for a passing moment by the ghostly moonlight. Up the staircase he followed her, along the gallery and up another flight of stairs until they halted at a door. Meg pushed it open and, in response to the pressure of her hand, he stepped inside. The door closed, noiselessly, behind him.

The chamber was lit by a single candelabra and a log fire flared brightly. An essence of femininity hung in the air and his senses reeled at the invitation of Juliana's outstretched arms. He went swiftly to her. She was warm and supple against him, her hair fragrant as he buried his face in its russet fullness.

Easing herself gently away, she searched his face. She must be sure! There was devotion in his eyes and sensual awareness, but he was uncertain. She drew him towards the fire. 'I do not know what may become of us, ere this war is ended, but do you pledge that this night shall bind us, forever?'

'I swear it.' Puritan cropped and homespun, he regarded a goddess of whom he was not worthy, whose hair shone lustrous in the firelight, whose body was highlighted and shadowed by a silken robe. She let the robe slip to the floor and, untying the bed gown, guided his hands inside the soft, warm linen. Her breasts were small and firm, the nipples hard to his touch, and a quickening urge possessed him. Tearing the garment from her shoulders, he looked upon her naked beauty, for one awed moment, but the need to possess her was now overwhelming and he lifted her in his arms and bore her to the bed.

Hours later, in sheets scented by her presence, he watched her draw back the heavy window-curtains and the moon light her slim body. She was porcelain, she was perfection and he had possessed her. She returned to the bed, a dark outline now against the thin light from the window, and drew her dressing robe about her. 'It is time you were gone, the servants will soon be stirring.'

He rose and dressed, while Juliana fetched her maid from an adjoining room. Meg led him back the way they had come the previous evening, lifted the latch of the postern with painstaking care and swung the door quietly open. He squeezed her hand and was gone.

Juliana slid back between the sheets stained with her blood, her maidenhood sacrificed in secret betrothal. She had offended all dictates of church and family, and could never belong to another man. 'Holy Mary, Mother of God. Forgive me, forgive me!'

CHAPTER 3

The Blooding

O n the morning of departure, a sense of foreboding hung over the farm. The usual sounds were hushed as Dorothy and Janet fussed about, uneasy for him and apprehensive at the disruption to their lives.

Dorothy came in with a plate of hog's pudding, determined that he should set out on his journey with a full belly. The evocative smell of baking bread wafted in from the kitchen behind the stout figure, her black hair crowned by a white cap. 'You get that across your chest, Maister Nicholas, and you'll come to no 'arm.'

He smiled, affectionately, as Janet followed with a pair of bulging saddlebags. 'And mind you stop on the way and take these victuals. Us have made you a special bacon pie – your favourite.'

It was time to go. Freeing himself from the embraces of the two women, he shouldered the saddlebags and crossed the farmyard to the stables. The fingers of a March dawn were spanning the horizon, as Matthew led out the cob and laden sumpter. He stood on the uneven cobbles, wet with dew, and looked, reflectively, at the dark outline of the Barton, before taking the strong hand of his cowman. 'It rests with you now, Matthew,' he said simply. 'God be with you all.'

He rode through the gate to the south-east, taking the route he had planned, to avoid towns and villages, for he had heard that the Royalist were recruiting men and he had no wish to be called upon to join them, or to account for his journey, as the bearer of a Parliamentary summons to the colours, in Royalist-dominated Cornwall.

His spirits were low as he contemplated the unknown, separated from Juliana and uncertain of Sir Richard's grasp on affairs. The sun appeared, tentatively, behind the distant hills and the sounds of a spring morning filled the pellucid air. As it climbed higher, his spirits rose and he began to respond to the challenge that lay ahead. Mayhap a soldier's life was more befitting to a young man than farming. Could he hope that Sir Richard would countermand Alexander's orders? He tried to imagine himself as a trooper – the traditional role of yeomen and men like himself, who owned a horse. Perhaps he would become a sergeant, for was he not already used to directing men?

These thoughts continued to occupy him until he reached the flat desolate landscape beyond the village, of St. Columb. There he coaxed his mount to a canter, the packhorse with his worldly goods keeping pace behind. By late morning, the familiar beacon of Bodmin was behind him and he was into undulating country close to Lord Robartes' great, new house at Lanhydrock. In the wooded valley of the River Fowey, the winking water invited him to tarry and he reined in and dismounted, stiff after the long ride. Standing in the sandy shingle the horses nuzzled the bubbling water, while he laved his face and hands.

The thud of hooves and clink of harness alerted him to the approach of a body of orange-sashed cavalry. The young cornet at their head halted his men and eyed Nicholas and the sumpter. 'Where are you heading, traveller?'

The troopers watched him, ominous in steel and leather, as he straightened his back. 'About my business.'

The other's face tightened. 'And what is your business?'

'That is between me and my landlord.'

'You are an uncommunicative fellow.' The cornet signalled to his sergeant, 'Unpack those panniers!'

This arrogant sprig was overreaching himself. 'I doubt that Commissioner Carew of Antony will appreciate such zeal touching his affairs.'

The cornet hesitated, unsettled by the self-possession of the plainly-dressed traveller. 'Wait!' he ordered the soldiers unpacking the panniers. 'Show me that you serve the Commissioner!'

Nicholas drew out Alexander's summons from under his saddle and handed it up to his adversary. 'You may examine the seal, but the contents are confidential.'

The cornet glanced at the broken wax. Satisfied he returned the letter with a curt, 'Be on your way!' While Nicholas restored the letter to its hiding place, the cavalry wheeled and disappeared into nearby woodland.

Ignoring the order, he took the victuals from the saddlebags and sat down on the bank of the river. As he ate, he mused on what had just passed. It had been a fatuous battle of wills, but it pleased him to have triumphed and he compared the shallow bravado of the cornet with the iron authority of Sir

John Arundell. To challenge him had been unthinkable. Authority had an aura, which men recognised and accepted; it came with birth and was rooted in confidence, but perhaps it could be acquired with experience.

Refreshed, he followed a route over the downland between Lostwithiel and Liskeard, skirting Boconnoc, scene of the battle two months earlier. In late afternoon, he rode into the yard of the Lanreath Inn and handed the horses to an ostler.

Bearing his packs, he entered the hostelry, its interior dim and smoky, the ceiling uncomfortably low for his tall figure. A man came forward wiping his hands on his apron. 'Good evening, sir, and welcome.'

He smiled at the first friendly contact of the day. 'Good evening, landlord, I seek lodging for the night.'

'Of course, sir, follow me.' They climbed dark, narrow stairs to a room with leaded windows dominated by a four-poster bed; the landlord informed him that food would be ready soon.

When he descended to the taproom, the smoking fire had been coaxed into flame and he seated himself at the hearth, calling for a pot of ale.

The room was empty except for two men seated on a settle in blue and silver livery. Recalling Salter's tale of the Royalists' charge at Bradock Down, he ventured, 'Do I recognise the Grenville colours?'

They eyed him with a mixture of caution and pride. 'You do,' one replied.

'It is said they were much in evidence at Bradock Down.'

'Colonel Ruthven 'll never forget us, I'll be bound.'

'The Parliamentary commander?'

'Aye! We sent 'im back across the Tamar quicker'n 'e come into Cornwall.'

Warming to his audience, the second man took up the story. 'Ruthven's advance guard come through Liskeard to Bradock church and our commander, Sir Ralph Hopton, decided to attack afore the main force arrived. Sir Bevill led us foot through their line and the cavalry on each side of us finished 'em off. We drove them that were left through Saltash and over the river. Their losses were terrible to be'old.'

'Was there a giant of a fellow who carried the Grenville colours?'

'That's Tony Paine. Over seven feet tall, 'e is.'

The first soldier returned to the narrative. 'We weren't so lucky last month, though, when we tried to take Plymouth, for they were too strong and we were pushed back beyond Tavistock. Now they've agreed to a truce.'

'We could use a young man like you, sir,' his companion remarked.

'I shall be seeing Sir Richard Carew of Antony, tomorrow, and he may bid me join you,' he said lightly.

'Sir Richard be dead.'

Nicholas leaned back heavily on the settle. 'Two days ago I believe t'was,' the speaker continued, looking to his companion for confirmation. The other nodded.

Nicholas sat as if struck by a thunderbolt. Sir Richard dead! He had loved him like a second father, that complacent old Puritan, so sure of his place in heaven; that self-taught physician with a treatment for all ills. Dead! It dawned upon him that all hope of avoiding service with the Parliament had died with his patron. The landlord called him, cutting short any further discourse.

Next morning he was astir, betimes, and heading for Antony. Before midday, he breasted the ridge before its south face and saw the Tudor pile of the house below, with the park running north to the Lynher River. His approach observed, he was met and ushered into the presence of Alexander.

The new baronet was 34 years of age and had a delicate, clever face set in a small head. He was dressed entirely in black, save for the fashionable deep lace collar and cuffs, and wore a sword. The new dignity cloaking the familiar figure discomfited Nicholas until he took the chair Alexander indicated, and felt the snake's head carved into the arms, which his fingers had so often caressed.

'I have to tell you that my father died just before you set out,' Alexander said quietly.

'I had already heard and am deeply grieved. Sir Richard was dear to me as my own father.'

Alexander nodded gravely. 'And he held you in great affection. It is sad that you did not arrive before he died.' He spoke for a while of events culminating in his bereavement and of John Carew, his half-brother, but there were other matters on his mind. 'Parliament is strengthening the fortifications of Plymouth and I have been appointed Governor of St. Nicholas's island, which holds a key place in its seaward defences. Following his successes in Cornwall, Hopton is full of confidence and we need every man we can muster to contain him.' He looked hard at Nicholas. 'When my father has been laid to rest, we will speak again of your military service. Meanwhile the library is at your disposal.' He allowed himself a small smile. 'I prescribe Caesar's campaigns in Gaul – in the Latin.'

Nicholas withdrew to find his father waiting in the hall. 'It is a joy to see you, again, my son. Would that it were a happier occasion,' he said, as they embraced.

'Amen! Will you take me to Sir Richard?'

His sire quietly opened the door of the solar and led him across the room to where the old man lay in the open coffin. The face was thinner than he remembered and there was more grey in the beard, but the expression of his patron and benefactor was tranquil and benign. Tears started to his eyes and he went to a window and eased aside the curtain.

In the parkland sweeping up to the ridge, Sir Richard had taught him the pursuits of peace. Soon he must master the arts of war, in this land which had not stood to arms since the Spanish Armada swept along the coast, beyond, near 60 years ago. Then, Cornishmen and Englishmen had won a never-to-be-forgotten victory over the Queen's enemies. Honour and glory were theirs! But what business was he about for Alexander, alienated from his King, the Arundells and even, in part, from his beloved? If only he could have spoken with Sir Richard, to ask where his duty lay. In his confusion, he was sure of only one thing – his loyalty to the Carews, for that was how it had been since feudal times, this side of the Tamar.

He felt a hand on his arm and allowed his father to lead him from the silent chamber. While his father went to his duties, Nicholas remained in the hall, feeling the house around him like an old gauntlet on the hand. There was the arch of Pentewan stone framing the front door, the linen-fold panelling of the walls, the grilled gallery where hidden musicians played in happier days, the ornate newel post of the staircase lit by a window ablaze with armorial bearings.

Slowly he walked to the rear of the house and entered the little schoolroom, still faintly acrid with the smell that boys implant upon their habitual environment. Here, he and John Carew had bent to their studies, under the stern eye of the dominie, before John had followed Alexander to Oxford University and the Inner Temple and the void had opened between gentleman and steward's son.

'Good day, Nicholas.' Lady Jane Carew stood in the doorway. 'It is a day for reflection, is it not, with those we love departed or estranged?'

'I perceive one who is constant, Your Ladyship.' He bowed, deferentially, to the mistress of the house.

Jane Carew smiled acknowledgement of the gallantry. She was almost twice his age, the daughter of Robert Rolle of Heanton, in Devonshire, still graceful and refined, despite bearing seven children. 'I fear that John is much changed since he espoused the Parliamentary cause with such fervour. Did you know he is a Fifth Republican, believing that Christ Jesus is coming to rule over us in place of our King?' The gentle voice was more sorrowful than bitter.

'How fare the children, Your Ladyship? They are much grown I have no doubt.'

Jane Carew's expression lightened. 'Indeed they are. Come you shall see them.'

When his father had been laid to rest among his ancestors, Alexander sent for Nicholas. 'Because you have always been adept with weapons, I commended you to Lord Stamford, the Parliamentary commander in Devon and he has commissioned you lieutenant in his regiment of foot.' He indicated a document on the table.

An officer! He recalled the cornet on the fine horse in the red of Lord Robartes' Regiment, knowing that he had envied him. Yet, he hesitated. How could he tell Alexander that he loved a staunch Royalist, ward of his kinsman? And had he dared, it was too late to say that he wished only to be a farmer. If only it were the King's commission. 'Thank you, sir,' he heard himself say.

'Tomorrow you will cross to Plymouth, to begin your training, which will not be as full as one might wish, for we are desperate for men under arms.' His new patron took his hand. 'Serve us faithfully and may God go with you.'

The next morning he descended to the Lynher River, to where a boat bobbed at the river's edge. Across the water, on the Devon bank, stood Trematon castle, home of Alexander's Parliamentarian neighbour, Sir Richard Buller of Shillingham. Down river lay Sutton Hoe, his destination. He clambered aboard and the boatman pushed off. Antony disappeared behind the mass of Mount Edgcumbe, on the western flank of the Sound. Soon, the great mansion of the Edgcumbes showed among the trees. Resolutely he turned his back on the familiar landscape. Ahead, the Barbican steps loomed and he came ashore beneath the crenellated walls of Hake Castle.

The fledgling had taken wing.

◫◫◫

Juliana hurried into the solar at Trerice and closed the door. From her bodice she drew out a letter, which Meg had brought from her mother and tore it open. One sentence riveted her attention. 'Sir Richard is dead and I am commissioned lieutenant in the Earl of Stamford's foot, a Parliamentarian.' She sank into a chair before the fireplace. In her heart she had believed that Sir Richard would reprieve Nicholas; now she knew the worst, the final blow to their hopes. Beside her, the caryatids supporting the overmantel looked on cold and indifferent.

She rose, ran through the gallery up to her chamber, and flung open the door. 'Oh Meg, Nicholas is a Roundhead! Will I ever see him again?'

Meg Collins' comforting arms enfolded her. ''Tis no good asking me for I cannot say, but there is one who could for sure!'

'Who might that be?'

'Joan Lobb!'

'Mother Lobb? Oh, wist, Meg!'

'People come to her from all over Devon and Cornwall to have their ailments cured and ask about their lovers. Mind you not, 'twas you that told me of a visit Sir Richard Carew's cousin made to her, to have a sore leg cured?'

'Yes, I recall. Joan asked her why she was so sad, then without waiting for an answer said, "I know the cause, for you love one whose name is Thomas. Set your heart at rest, for you shall have him." And it came to pass. Joan even told her that he would sit in his father's seat, though he was then a younger brother, and that came true as well.'

The eyes of mistress and servant were shining with excitement, for they were Cornish and everyone believed – or half-believed – in conjurors and calkers able to invoke the Devil, and old wives like Joan Lobb in league with the fairies.

Meg took her hand. 'Trust me, my lady, she will tell you true!'

Oh, to hear that, one day, Nicholas would return. 'We go tomorrow.'

As daylight invaded Juliana's chamber to end a troubled night, Meg tapped at the door and entered. She rose and went to the window. In the garden, below, mist hung dank and still, shrouding the clipped yews. She shivered.

Meg had been watching her. 'There's nothing to fear, milady, Joan never did anyone harm.'

'I do not fear Mother Lobb, only what she may foretell.' How incongruous! A devout Catholic hurrying to a prattling crone for comfort. Better to pray to the Holy Mother for intercession. 'Oh ye of little faith!'

By the time they set out, the mist had lifted on the lower ground, but wisps still hovered about the hills, and globules of moisture sat upon the twigs of the hedgerows and leaves of the evergreens. After riding for an hour they came to a tinner's cottage, a disused mineshaft, nearby. The earth track they were following ran across the front of the cottage and over the rock-strewn moorland, to disappear among a great outcrop of granite on the skyline. It was a lonely place.

The door of the dwelling stood open and, from the doorstep, a black cat observed them with yellow eyes.

They reined in and Meg said, hesitantly, 'Wait here, milady, I will see...'

'No, Meg, I will go alone.' Juliana slipped from the saddle and went to the door. There was no response to her knock, 'Is anyone there?' she called.

A woman came from behind the cottage wearing a hessian apron over her gown and bearing faggots of wood. She was plump and apple-cheeked, about 50 years of age and gave them a ready smile. 'Good morrow, mistresses, what seek ye of Joan Lobb?'

'Good day, Mother Lobb. I hope that you may foretell an affair of the heart.'

The woman regarded her with bright, penetrating eyes. 'Well come along in.'

Joan led her into a small room of rough-hewn stone. One wall was breached by a fireplace, in which white ash smouldered, with piles of turf neatly stacked alongside. From the ceiling beam hung bunches of drying herbs, their aroma heavy on the air. On the shelves of a dresser stood little earthenware pots and, on the flat surface, beneath, a wooden plate, a black leather jug and a drinking vessel kept company with a pestle and mortar.

'Sit ye down,' Joan invited, drawing out a bench from the table. She closed the door and Juliana was alone with the prophetess.

As Joan took her place across the table, Juliana extended her hand, instinctively, palm upward. The woman did not examine it, but instead took it in a firm grasp. For moments, the now-strange eyes held hers and she felt anxiety surrender to a sense of peace, as if a soothing balm had been applied to a wound. Compelled by that gaze, her innermost thoughts surfaced and were mirrored in her eyes.

'An affair of the heart, is it, lady?' Joan repeated her phrase, reflectively. 'Tus that and more. 'Tus the love of your life and you have sealed the knot.'

Unabashed, Juliana asked, 'And how will it be with us?'

The eyes were compassionate now, their power extinguished. 'The road ahead is hard and I will not speak of it. Suffice that you know how it will end.'

Outside, Meg caressed the horses' muzzles and watched the door, anxiously. Aware of the dangers on the road, she had slung a brace of pistols across her saddle; now she loosened one in its holster. She did not know what effect a pistol ball might have on one in league with the fairies, but, to the best of her ability, she would protect her young mistress from mortal and immortal alike. Time passed. Surely they should be finished by now. She drew and cocked the pistol. The door opened and Juliana appeared. As she came towards Meg, her face composed, the faithful maid released the hammer and slid the pistol back into its holster. Juliana turned and waved to Joan Lobb, smiling on the doorstep, then she kissed her servant on the cheek. 'Thank you, dear Meg,' she said.

◫◫◫

From the craggy heights of Okehampton castle, Nicholas gazed towards the headquarters of the Parliamentarian army. Hours since he had ridden in from Plymouth, bearing a letter of introduction to Lord Stamford, keen to become a fighting, infantry officer.

Having subdued his unease at serving the Parliament, he had embarked cheerfully on a course of instruction in the wheellock and flintlock pistols, the matchlock musket and the cavalry carbine. A row of musketeers had primed, loaded and fired their cumbersome weapons, at his orders. He had commanded pikemen to advance, shoulder, port and charge pikes, as they moved forward, wheeled and retired. It had been a heady experience.

But his arrival at Okehampton had caused barely a ripple. Stamford lay sick and Major General Chudleigh, his second-in-command, was out inspecting the positions held by his forces.

The light was already fading when the clatter of hooves rose from the streets below and he saw a group of officers enter the headquarters. Hopefully, Chudleigh was among them. He picked his way down the steep, uneven motte and made for the town.

James Chudleigh put down the document he was reading, as the new lieutenant was ushered in. 'I believe we have met before.' Nicholas nodded. 'Lord Stamford is at Exeter, abed with gout, so I welcome you on his behalf. Had you arrived two days earlier you would have seen action, for we attacked Launceston, when the truce expired, and would have carried the day had not Hopton been reinforced. But many of our troops are raw and were unsettled by the retreat. Your first task will be to instil discipline and...' He broke off and looked past Nicholas, as an officer burst into the room.

'What is it, Quartermaster?'

'I crave pardon, sir, but I have vital intelligence. While I was riding two miles west of the town, I espied three Cavalier scouts upon Sourton Down. They are like to be the advance guard of Sir Ralph Hopton's army.'

Chudleigh leapt to his feet. 'Damnation,' he exploded. 'Require my senior officers and every cavalry officer to assemble here, immediately. Order the troopers to saddle up and have my horse and the lieutenant's ready!'

Chudleigh unrolled a large map of the area and perused it intently, while the room filled with men. Then he turned to his expectant audience. 'It is probable that General Hopton is advancing upon us from Launceston. His numbers will be much superior to ours, and we need cannon to halt him, but, unhappily, they have been despatched to Crediton. I, therefore, propose to lead our cavalry on to Sourton Down and devise some means to delay him, while our foot stand to at the entrance to the town. How many horses have we, Captain Drake?'

'One hundred and eight, sir.'

'So few.' Chudleigh's eyes sought Nicholas. 'Lieutenant, you shall be my liaison officer. Mark well the route, for you may return alone. Come, gentlemen!'

With his officers at his heels, Chudleigh hurried into the stable yard, where the troopers were checking their saddle-girths. Mounting, they spurred westward, in a ragged file. It was now quite dark, the night air was sultry and their nostrils were assailed by the stench of sweating horses as they toiled up the steep ascent from the town and surged on to the open down. Lightning jagged, exposing hills and hollows in eerie blue light, as Chudleigh led his force into a depression and halted. With thunder rolling about them, he called, 'Mark me well! I plan an ambush, so let no man show himself until I order the charge. The first troops in contact with the Royalists will cry, "Fall on, fall on! They run, they run." Do your work well. Create the maximum confusion and remember only we stand between Hopton and Okehampton!'

He had scarcely disposed the horsemen along the depression when they heard the first distant sounds of the approaching host. A knot of apprehension gripped Nicholas's stomach. He had heard some of the tales about Chudleigh – how the 25-year-old general had distinguished himself in the recent retreat from Launceston, when he had saved his men and all the guns, by masterly generalship. But could even the brilliance of Chudleigh succeed in this desperate recourse? In the flickering light he watched him as, head cocked, he sought to separate the sounds of men and nature.

Soon, they heard the clop of hooves, tramping feet, the murmur of voices and, distinguishable now from the muttering thunder, the rumble of wagons and cannon. Over the hill came the vanguard of dragoons, then the tall pikes and fluttering banners, stark against the electric clamour of the sky. Emerging from the blackness of the down, the column seemed endless. On they came, breastplates glinting. Chudleigh's sword slid from its scabbard with a metallic hiss. In another moment they would be seen!

A single shot rang out, discharged by a nervous trooper and Chudleigh, his advantage forfeit, roared, 'Charge!'

Out of the depression they surged, firing their carabines and shouting their exultant battle cry. The Royalist dragoons bunched, tentatively, and then reeled back before the desperate Parliamentarians. A second wave reached the cannon, but Lord Mohun and Bevill Grenville rallied their men about the precious guns and fierce hand-to-hand combat ensued.

Chudleigh pressed towards the melee, Nicholas close behind. Turning in the saddle, he pointed towards the cannon. 'See over there, a portmanteau on the ground. Get it!' While Chudleigh grasped the bridle of his horse, Nicholas drew his sword and ran to the fringe of the flailing, fighting men and thrust among them. The flank of a plunging horse struck him to the ground;

tramping hooves straddled him and passed on. Rolling over, awkwardly, in his body armour, he regained his feet and dodged back into the fray. As he reached the case and plucked it from the ground, a dark figure loomed above and slashed savagely downward. Parrying the blow, he cut his way out and ran towards the general.

'Twas nimbly done.' Chudleigh declared, as he scrambled back into the saddle. 'Now ride with all speed, keep the valise safe, and have the foot sent to reinforce me.'

With the flat of his sword, he struck Nicholas's mount and horse and rider galloped wildly from the field. Nicholas wiped earth from his eyes and peered anxiously into the blackness, for landmarks, while the din of conflict faded into the distance. He was trembling with excitement.

Chudleigh and his troopers dashed once more along the Royalist column, before fading into the night. The glimmer of smouldering matches signalled the arrival of his infantry, but lashing rain and two rounds of shot from the Royalists' cannon discomfited the drenched Parliamentarians. Chudleigh was obliged to mount another cavalry charge, which broke at the bristling wall of pikes the Royalists had implanted. But he had done enough. Withdrawing to Okehampton, he left Hopton to assess his losses and retire to Launceston.

Back at headquarters, Chudleigh sent immediately for Nicholas and the portmanteau. The dangers of the night seemed only to have stimulated the young general and he eyed Nicholas's bedraggled appearance with some amusement. 'You acquitted yourself well in your first affray, Lieutenant, but I see you've paid a price.'

Nicholas looked down ruefully at his sodden, earth-stained doublet. 'The theme of last Sunday's sermon was Pride and Vanity, sir, and I felt both in this uniform, but now I am purged of my sin.'

Chudleigh's eyes twinkled. He had released the straps of the portmanteau and was spreading the contents out. 'What have we here? Muster rolls, a list of contributors to the Royalists' funds? And something more interesting.' He opened out two rolls hung with red seals. 'I swear we have General Hopton's orders!'

He went to the door and ordered a clerk outside to decipher the documents, before returning to stand before the window. 'What is Ralph Hopton concocting to dismay me now, I wonder?' he mused, elbows on the sill. 'Remind me of your Christian name, Lieutenant!' he demanded over his shoulder.

'Nicholas, sir.'

'In war, Nicholas, it is paramount to study your opponent – the way he thinks, the pattern of his actions. Know him like a brother. Indeed, in this unnatural war, he may be your brother. Hopton is my enemy, yet I bear him no malice and respect him as a soldier and a man.'

'What kind of man is he, sir?'

'A professional soldier of middle years, who fought in the Continental wars for the Queen of Bohemia, the King's sister. Hopton is a Puritan and a Constitutionalist. He is quick-tempered, resolute, a man of honour, not a self-seeker, dedicated to the King's cause. What is more, he is supported by a likewise, doughty conglomerate – Grenville, Slanning, Mohun – admirable men all.'

It was such a neat portrait, painted almost wistfully, yet with authority – that quality which Nicholas had recognised as setting some men above their fellows. Chudleigh spoke without condescension and he relished their brief intimacy.

'What qualities make a good soldier, sir?'

'A broad question that, I warrant.' Chudleigh looked at him, thoughtfully. He had taken a liking to the naive, young man, only a few years his junior. 'Strive always for the regard of your men, care for them, and do not squander their lives. Seek also to be on good terms with the local populace, wherever you are, for it is from them that your best intelligence comes. If you command cavalry, exercise tight control over them. Commanders who allow their horse to gallop from the field in pursuit of the enemy usually rue the day, for while they are away that same enemy may be destroying their foot.'

Before he could develop his theme, further, the clerk brought in the decoded texts and he seized them eagerly. As he read he chuckled in triumph. 'I want you to carry a despatch to Lord Stamford. Report here within the hour!'

When he returned, Chudleigh gave him a document and the repacked portmanteau. 'Go straight to his lordship and submit my despatch. I promise you will be well received,' he added wryly, 'for 'twill effect instant cure of his gout. In fact, meaning no disrespect to your regiment, I think your encounter will give Stamford's Foot new meaning.'

His sleepless night forgotten, Nicholas hurried out to the stable yard. Chudleigh had entrusted him with an important mission and he would not fail him. Cantering from the town, he rode hard through the rolling Devon landscape, until the red sandstone walls of the city of Exeter came into view. At its south entrance, he presented his papers and was admitted through the massive gatehouse and directed to the domicile of Henry Grey, Earl of Stamford. There, an aide took the despatch and he was shortly brought before the earl. Stamford sat awkwardly at a desk, wearing a dressing gown, with one bandaged foot supported upon a low table. Two senior officers stood behind his chair.

'So you are my newest officer, eh, Lieutenant, commended by Sir Alexander

Carew, as I recall?'

'That is correct, my lord.'

'And Major-General Chudleigh requires me to study some papers you have brought.'

Nicholas handed over the case and Stamford glanced briefly at the original contents. Then he began to read the deciphered text. Suddenly, with a cry of excitement he leapt up, the table fell over and his foot struck the floor. Oblivious of his infirmity, he waved the texts at his aides. 'Hopton is ordered to advance into Somerset to join with the Palgrave Maurice. We shall deny them that conjunction, gentlemen. At eight in the morning we hold a Council of War. See to it!'

As they hurried away, Stamford gave his attention to Nicholas. 'Report to my quartermaster for overnight lodging and return here at first light.'

Once outside, Nicholas gave way to pent-up amusement; it was uncanny how Chudleigh had foreseen that encounter with his commander. Later, fed and simply accommodated, he set out to see the city, following narrow streets overhung by the upper stories of timber-framed houses. Near the city walls roofs had been stripped of thatch, which a sentinel told him was a precaution against fire-raising by anyone besieging the city. Turning back, he came to the open space before the cathedral. The afternoon sun had brought the myriad carved figures covering the west front of the cathedral into sharp relief. Mitred, crowned and armoured they stood or sat, mute testament to the skills of stonemasons long dead. Inside, he gazed in wonder at the fan-vaulted roof, held aloft by tall columns, which strode majestically to the high altar, dominated by a massive cross. He was drawn towards the crucifix and felt an impulse to kneel before it. God was in this place. But the fall of his boots and the clink of spurs drew covert glances from the silent worshippers. He halted and retraced his steps into the temporal world, outside.

Next morning he reported to the earl, finding him a more imposing figure fully accoutred. Stamford handed him a document, commenting dryly, 'General Chudleigh has shown great confidence in you. Return with all haste bearing these orders.'

▣▣▣

Brimming with confidence Stamford crossed the Cornish border with 6,000 troops at his back, having despatched Sir George Chudleigh on a diversionary raid upon Bodmin. Having arrived at Stratton, he established his army on the lozenge plateau overlooking the town and sent horse and dragoons to harass the advancing Royalists.

On the Monday evening they appeared below, half his number and with a supplies position so desperate that every soldier had been issued with one dry biscuit only, early in the advance. With Chudleigh beside him, Stamford weighed his own position – ample provisions and ammunition secured behind barricades.

'They will come at us up these western slopes,' he surmised, 'for on the east the hill is precipitous and inaccessible to cavalry. Our 13 guns should wreak havoc upon them.'

Chudleigh did not reply. Through a spyglass, he was studying Hopton and the general officers about him, as they assessed their task – Mohun, Slanning, Colonel Trevanion, Sir John Berkeley and Grenville, hat in hand, the dying rays of the sun catching his auburn hair. What were his thoughts, this chevalier *sans pareil*, as he looked up into the snouts of the cannon – reflections of mortality? But they were everyone's unspoken thoughts at this hour. Were they also of his delicate and beloved wife, at home at Kilkhampton, just a few miles to the north? One thing was certain, Sir Bevill would fight fearlessly tomorrow, for he was a grandson of the redoubtable Sir Richard Grenville of the Revenge.

The sun dipped into the sea behind Bude, signalling each side to its final dispositions.

Nicholas and his musketeers lay in an ancient earthwork, on the lower slopes of the hill, facing approximately south. They had not moved all night and he was stiff with cold and soaked in dew. As first light revealed the prospect below, he raised himself, cautiously, and saw the enemy, half a musket shot away. A ball whined over his head, presaging a heavy volley of small arms fire and cannon shot. Orders were shouted, as the Parliamentarians prepared to return the fire. Then the Royalist infantry commenced to jog ponderously upwards, a solid, hostile phalanx. From a throat suddenly dry, he cried, 'Give fire!'

Deafened by the crackle of shot from the troops on either side, he saw figures in the foreground crumble like rag dolls. Others began to converge on the gaps in their thin cover; another line of attackers followed and another. But he had seen the seemingly inexorable advance falter and was master of himself.

There were further orders from behind and he shouted, 'Fall back and reload!' As his men rallied about him, the probing, thrusting pikemen and flailing musketeers came on up the slope towards them.

'Give fire!'

More men were struck down, but the rest came on and into them, bearing them backwards up the hill. With the musket butts of his men whirling around him, he laid about with his sword and, once, deflected the hard point of a pike from his vitals. A face appeared briefly, fiercely contorted, a sword slash exposed its cheekbone and it was gone, like something from a nightmare. Men were falling on all sides and his feet sought solid ground, between the prostrate forms, the bloody slime and the tangle of discarded weapons. The rat-tat-tat of a drum was sounding the advance and he felt the press behind and a yielding in front, as the Parliamentary line swung and the Royalists, fearing to be outflanked, fell back.

Through the acrid smoke of cannon and small arms, Stamford and Chudleigh watched the ebb and surge of the struggle, below, as the ranks of bristling pikes and clubbing muskets recoiled and countered. The attack on the south side was led by Hopton and Mohun and, to their left, the blue and silver of Grenville's men combined with Berkeley's colours.

By three o'clock, the hail of shot from the Cornish army had almost ceased and there were obvious preparations for an assault with sword and pike. The attack was pressed forward so remorselessly, by Grenville and his comrades, that Chudleigh found himself in imminent danger, as the triumphant Royalists struggled over the lip of the hill. He glanced about for Stamford, but he was nowhere to be seen. Matching Grenville's resolve, he rallied together a stand of pikes and counter-attacked so vigorously that Grenville was borne to the ground, as his Cornishmen fell back in disorder.

Driven yet again up the hill by the pressure from below, Nicholas joined the counter-attack and found himself shoulder-to-shoulder with the gallant Chudleigh, amid a sea of pikes. After the cold fear and exhaustion, the downhill charge was heady, exhilarating, but progress slowed and halted as Sir John Berkeley came to Grenville's aid. The Cornish pikemen, in helmets, leather buff coats and body-armour formed a veritable wall of steel and, as the din subsided, the order 'Charge your pikes!' The steel-shod shafts were presented and surged menacingly up the hill with the indefatigable Grenville out in front. Close behind strode the giant figure of Tony Paine, bearing the standard of the golden griffin.

With the tattered remnants of his men at his back and the charismatic Chudleigh at his shoulder, the raw lieutenant of foot gripped his sword tighter. Chudleigh grinned encouragement, 'Sourton Down was but an apprenticeship. This is your blooding. Stand firm!'

On the flank of the Royalist attack, a musketeer, with powder still in his flask, blew on his match, aimed at Chudleigh and fired. A searing shaft of pain drove into Nicholas' chest, the griffin's head grew larger until its blood-red background diffused and exploded in his brain. His knees buckled and he fell back upon the cluttered ground.

CHAPTER 4

The Turncoat

'Holy Mother, grant me glad tidings, I beg!' Juliana prayed silently, where she stood under the archway of the perimeter wall at Trerice and watched the approach to the house. It was an overcast morning, in early June, and the hem of her gown was soaked with dew, for she had remained rooted to the spot nigh on half an hour, afraid to leave.

At last, the sound of a cantering horse. She ran forward to meet the rider and grasped the reins, as Meg slipped from the saddle and stood, dejectedly, before her mistress. In answer to the unspoken question, she shook her head. 'I fear not, milady, my mother has neither news nor letter.' The foreboding which Juliana had fought for the past two weeks tightened its grip. 'Why do you not send to Antony for tidings; the Carews are your kin?' Meg suggested.

'The Carews are enemies of the King.'

'I cannot believe that, milady.'

'It cannot be denied.' She began to pace up and down, arms stiff, small fists clenched, then halted, her decision made. 'We go to Stowe!'

Meg was nonplussed. 'To Stowe? But why?'

'Nicholas' regiment is the Earl of Stamford's Foot and there has been a great battle at Stratton, against Stamford. The Cavaliers were victorious and Sir Bevill was one of their leaders. From the victors we may gain news of the vanquished.' The logic was undeniable. 'We depart immediately. Go, pack a valise and tell William Jennings and John Hocking that they are to escort us!'

Juliana would brook no delay and, by noon, the group were on their way. That night they lodged at a modest country house, the owner and his spouse honoured that an Arundell should seek shelter beneath their roof. With the early sun giving promise of a fine day, they took to the road, next morning, and some hours later were through Kilkhampton and before the gates of Stowe.

The lodge-keeper led them along an avenue of beech trees, smooth and grey as the piers of a cathedral. In the park, on either side, rhododendrons bourgeoned and fallow deer raised their heads, as they passed by. The house came into view at the head of the combe, magnificent upon its knole – part machiolated and ringed by terraces ornate with statuary. Above them, clipped yews circumscribed the seat of the Grenvilles.

As they drew rein, the front door was opened by the steward, grooms came running from behind the house.

'Greetings, Master Phillips. Is Lady Grace at home?'

'Her Ladyship is in the rose garden, milady.'

'I would take it most kindly if she would receive me.'

He nodded. 'Please to follow me.'

Juliana was led to a walled pleasance on the south side of the mansion, where Lady Grace Grenville was feeding a flock of white doves. Seeing Juliana she rose, the doves fluttering around her, and came forward with a warm smile. 'My dear, dear child, how wonderful to see you.' She took her visitor's hands.

'Lady Grace, 'tis joy to see you again. I beg pardon for this intrusion and trust that you do not judge it improper.'

'Why should I do that? I see so few of our friends, nowadays, and, with Bevill away, I am much alone.' She indicated the stone bench where she had been sitting. 'Come, tell me all your news.'

'I have journeyed here in the absence, from home, of my guardian and without his knowledge. Were he to know, he would be gravely displeased.' She hesitated, searching for the right words. 'There is someone of whom I seek news. I have reason to believe that he fought at Stratton.'

'That information should not be difficult to gather. What is his name and regiment?'

'Lieutenant Nicholas Skelton of the Earl of Stamford's Foot.'

'But that is a Roundhead regiment, surely?' Grace Grenville's eyes were questioning.

'Yes.'

The older woman waited a second for Juliana to continue, her gaze troubled. 'Bevill remained at Stratton with the prisoners. I will send to him.' Juliana encompassed Lady Grace's hands with her own, not trusting herself to speak. 'You and your servants shall stay here until we have the information you seek,'

Lady Grace added, soothingly. 'Wait here awhile, and be at peace, child.' She rose and walked towards the house, her gown brushing the lavender which grew among the flagstones.

Alone in the quiet of the garden, Juliana felt her composure returning. Grace Grenville was so kind; would that she always had such a friend to turn to.

Her thoughts were broken by the steward, inviting her to take refreshment, but, later, she and Lady Grace returned to the warmth of the pleasance, to draw strength from one another, for each loved a soldier and each feared for him. The night she faced alone, with a dread that stood by her pillow, brooding, tangible.

She awoke with a start, as the first hint of daylight invaded the great Red Chamber. She slipped into her dressing robe and went to the window. At first there was absolute silence beyond the casements, but, as the sky lightened, the park came gradually to life. Birds rose from the distant beeches and the deer were revealed grazing the mist-strewn grass of the combe. On the terrace, sparrows hopped busily among the statuary. Nicholas loved life as did these creatures; Holy Mother, grant that he is still of this world and whole.

This must be Lady Grace's constant prayer. She recalled the picture that she had drawn of her Lord – not of a fearless leader of infantry, but a beloved country gentleman concerned for his tenants and servants. In her mind's eye, she saw him reading poetry in his great chair at the day's end and studying designs for mullioned windows, to beautify his home. Grace had spoken of their early life – how Sir Bevill served at Court after taking his degree at Oxford, and how he had been elected MP for Launcesten. When she told Lady Grace that her guardian had, recently, been cast down by the death of John, killed skirmishing with a Roundhead patrol at Mount Edgcumbe, she had been all sympathy, for she had lost two of her own sons before the war.

Drumming of hooves, far off! A horseman was riding along the avenue. When he was clearly visible, she discerned that he wore the broad red sash of the Cavaliers and her heart almost ceased its beating. Clattering up to the front door, he swung down from the saddle and the bell jangled in the hall below.

Hurrying across the chamber, she eased the door ajar and, through the balustrade, watched a servant open the door. Her straining ears caught a reference to Sir Bevill and information for Lady Grace. The messenger was admitted and the servant began to ascend the staircase. Retreating, she discarded the robe and climbed between the sheets, her heart pounding. After an eternity of waiting, there was a gentle tap at the door and Grace Grenville came in, her face solemn. Taking Juliana's hand, she murmured, 'I have news of the lieutenant. He is alive though gravely wounded.'

Juliana drew in a sharp breath, which caught in her throat and she found herself crying. Lady Grace sat on the bed and enfolded her, tenderly, as her mother had once done.

☐☐☐

James Chudleigh sat at table with his captors, a ring of faces amber in the light of a candelabra. This was a goodly fellowship, in contrast to that false rogue, Stamford, who had avowed to Westminster that his deputy had deserted to the enemy, on the field of Stratton. In truth, he had been taken prisoner in the heart of the Royalist army, while Stamford had left the field. Damn Stamford for a dog!

Hopton rose and surveyed the scene – the beards wagging above white lace, claret glowing red in the cups. The discourse stilled, instantly. 'Gentlemen, we have the honour to entertain one whose dash and initiative, at Sourton Down, I have come to rue and whose courage, in our recent, great victory, we can only admire – especially you Bevill – for he enjoys the rare distinction of bringing you to your knees.' As the shout of endorsement died, he continued, 'Let us drink the health of Major General Chudleigh.'

Their regard was the final persuasion James needed. 'General Hopton, gentlemen, tonight you honour me with your kind reception and usage and, for my part, I cannot conceive of finding myself in more gallant company. You toast me as a soldier, but how much more apt that I should toast you – for your courage and resolution against great odds. Stratton was a notable victory and it confirms that you are worthy men, dedicated to your cause. With your inspiration before me, I declare to you in good conscience that I accept the pardon His Majesty has promised me, and declare myself of your number, henceforth.'

A great roar of approval met this statement and he sat down, well content. As conversation resumed, Grenville leaned towards him, 'I crave a few moments of your time, in private.'

They bowed to Hopton and went into their host's study. 'Know you Lieutenant Skelton of Stamford's Foot?' Grenville enquired.

'I do. He rode with me at Sourton Down and fell at Stratton.'

'How do you value him?'

'I declare him a young man of wit, valour and ambition.'

'Ambition?' Grenville mused. 'That does not reassure me. I am concerned for a lady who sustains an attachment to this officer of which her family would not approve, were they aware of its continuance. Charity has dictated that I ease her anxiety, yet I cannot be indifferent to my responsibilities to her house.'

'No harm can come of it, presently.'

Grenville nodded. 'It would seem an enduring problem, though, for she is of strong character and passion, methinks – not giving her heart lightly. Her house is dedicated to the King – Skelton is a Roundhead.'

'As was I, but lately!' Chudleigh smiled. 'I shall seek to bring my officers into His Majesty's service and, perchance, this is the moment to influence Skelton, for 'twould remove the obstacle to their happiness.'

'I fear there are others, but we shall have been diligent in the King's cause if we persuade him to join us.' Grenville was amused by the hint of match-making in their conversation. He ought to advise his confrere, John Arundell, of the situation, for he knew no more of Juliana's suitor than Chudleigh had told him. But he would not do so. Juliana may be headstrong, wayward even, in her persistence, but her strength of character was his guarantee.

'How fares the lieutenant and what do you intend for him?' Chudleigh enquired.

'We are confident of his recovery. As soon as possible, he will be moved here under Edward Gilbey's care. As you know, Gilbey was disabled fighting for the King at Bradock Down. He is a compassionate man and Skelton will be in good hands.'

Chudleigh nodded approvingly. 'My thanks for your kindness , Sir Bevill. Perhaps you would be good enough to keep me informed regarding all my wounded officers. With Sir Ralph Hopton's permission, I will visit each one.'

▣▣▣

In an upper bedroom of Gilbey's house, James Chudleigh looked down at the drawn face of his lieutenant of foot. 'How is your wound mending?'

'Well, thank you sir.' A grimace of pain, as Nicholas shifted position, belied the cheerful statement.

'Nevertheless, I will not tire you, but you should know that I have declared allegiance to His Majesty the King and intend to serve him, henceforth. Should you do likewise, you may hope for preferment, through me, for you have acquitted yourself well. When you are convalescent, we will speak further of the matter.' He stooped and pressed Nicholas' shoulder. 'Think on it!'

Weakened by pain and fever, and overwhelmed by Chudleigh's decision, Nicholas lapsed into troubled sleep. As his mind cleared, he realised that he had been offered the prospect of full reconciliation with Juliana and of winning Arundell's regard. The price was estrangement from Alexander.

43

Days later, he heard the noise and bustle of the Royalists preparing to depart from the courtyard, below, and the scourged parkland, beyond. Easing himself from his cot, he tottered to the window. This was the army, these were the men, that he had fought against so lately; not Continentals, not even English, but Cornishmen, like himself. The florid wagon-master, the artillerymen struggling to harness oxen and horses to the guns, the chirurgeon packing implements and ointments, while his assistant stamped their camp fire into extinction. There was the tall-hatted chaplain stuffing a bible and crucifix into his saddlebag, equipped, equally, to lead his flock in worship or prepare the casualties of the next encounter to meet their maker.

For every pikeman there were two musketeers in homespun coats, breeches and stockings. A variety of headgear was in evidence, but all wore a sword and carried a matchlock musket and rest.

Dawn had flown before order emerged from the chaos. Commands were barked and the creaking line of wagons and cannon, the porcupine of soldiers, moved off into the narrow Devon lanes. Dust rose, pikes bobbed and regimental standards, each bearing the cross of St. George with the colour and device of its colonel, fluttered above the hedgerows. The Cornish army, marching to its destiny, was a brave sight, and he returned to his bed chilled and perplexed.

But as the memory of the agonising probing for the musket ball faded, he awaited Chudleigh's return, clear in his thoughts. This time, the general settled in a chair and stretched out his legs before enquiring what he had decided. Nicholas wanted Chudleigh to understand, for he could wish nothing better than to serve him.

'You have shown me much kindness, sir, and I wish to make you recipient of a confidence. For generations, my family have been bound to the Carews, and I am personally obligated to them for educating me and appointing me tenant to a farm. I am also to receive an emolument in the will of Sir Richard Carew, it seems.'

'So? Your obligation was to my uncle, and he is dead.'

'The bond is to the family. It is feudal and I cannot break it. As Will Shakespeare has it, "This above all – to thine ownself be true!"'

Chudleigh smiled. 'Do not confound a rude soldier with quotations. The bard also declared, "Homekeeping youth have ever homely wits". I commend you for your loyalty, but self-interest must weigh with you. I have but lately begged my own father to change sides, so that I may not confront him on some battlefield.'

'You may best appreciate the strength of my conviction, sir, if I tell you that I love a lady of quality, known to you, who would be greatly pleased by my conversion.'

The general raised his eyebrows. 'May I know who the lady is?'

'Juliana Arundell.'

James hissed through his teeth. 'Juliana! Jack-for-the-King's ward! Does the lady return your feelings?'

'She does.'

Chudleigh regarded him with compassion, for he knew, as Skelton must, that a change of allegiance to the Royalists would not persuade John Arundell to give his beloved ward in marriage to a likeable nobody. Not in itself, but...! As he contemplated the stricken figure, Chudleigh evolved an ingenious plan. 'I see you are resolved, but for cousin Alexander's sake, and because we have been comrades-in-arms, I will leave money for you to be cared for, until you are fully restored to health. Do not despair, for I believe you may yet serve the King with honour.'

James grasped his hand and walked away, waving aside his expression of gratitude. This was how Nicholas would remember Chudleigh, for he never saw him again. Some weeks later, he died from wounds received at Dartmouth, fighting for his newly-espoused cause. His fear of confronting his father never materialised, for Sir George resigned his Parliamentary commission and defected to the Royalists, at about the time of his son's death.

▣ ▣ ▣

After the army moved out from Gilbey's home, only a handful of wounded officers remained and their number diminished till only he was left. In convalescence, he was cared for by Letitia Gilbey, the daughter of the house. Each day, the fair, gentle girl brought him posies of flowers and they would sit in the window of his room, basking in the sun which streamed through the glass, conversing in great contentment. When he was able to descend to the portrait-hung drawing room, he would stand beside Letitia, as she played the clavicord, admiring the supple fingers and the curve of shoulder and neck. The ethereal sounds from the instrument, blended with the scent of pot-pourri, were a balm, which expunged violence and death from his mind.

Mr and Mrs Gilbey observed, uneasily, their daughter's attraction to the tall, dark, Parliamentary officer, an enigmatic presence in their house.

He was perfectly fit now, yet nothing was demanded of him. Gilbey seemed content to discuss agriculture and listened, attentively, as his guest talked of such matters as denshiring the soil and the breeding of sheep and cattle.

Each day he walked or rode in the surrounding countryside, often with

Letitia, who would turn to him, the sun in her hair, freckles on her tip-tilted nose, and regard him tenderly. And he was becoming overly fond of this buttercup girl, though it was only brotherly love, he told himself, for he was bound to Juliana.

Towards the end of July, Gilbey asked him to his study while he took a pipe of tobacco. Painfully extending his game leg, Gilbey began, 'I received momentous news, this morning. Bristol has fallen to Prince Rupert!'

Nicholas regarded him, incredulously. 'It is not possible! It is not possible!'

'Believe me, it is.'

'It is the second city in the kingdom, with a great castle. The Parliament would have defended it to the death.'

How strangely impersonal was that reference to 'the Parliament' and the absence of dismay at their defeat, thought Gilbey, as he continued. 'Methinks, Colonel Nathaniel Fiennes was not the man for that dour task, being lawyer before soldier, and no match for Rupert and the Cornishmen.'

'How fared the Cornish Army?' Nicholas enquired.

'Decimated I fear. They fought on the south-western side of the city, from dawn and needs must cross a great ditch to assault the ramparts. So large was this ditch that their scaling ladders were too short and even wagon-loads of faggots failed to reduce it, sufficiently. After three hours of the most desperate endeavour they retreated, with a third of their comrades dead, and fought their way back through the outlying districts. When Rupert called for a thousand men to support his attack on the northern side, the Cornish were hard put to muster half that number, though they shared in the final assault.'

'Have you news of their leaders?'

Gilbey perused a document on the table at his elbow. ''Tis a tragic tale I fear. They scorned to take cover and were picked off by sharpshooters from the ramparts. So many gone – Sir Nicholas Slanning, Colonel John Trevanion.'

'And what of Sir Bevill Grenville ?'

Gilbey regarded him with infinite sadness. 'That flower of chivalry died early in the month, pole- axed at Lansdown, near Bath.'

Nicholas closed his eyes. Sir Bevill gone, too, the best-loved gentleman in Cornwall. How bravely they had marched away, so short a time ago. He had not foreseen this carnage when he became a Roundhead lieutenant. Those fine men believed, passionately, in their cause and had died for it; James Chudleigh, recognising their conviction, had joined them – had pressed him to do likewise. He had declined, because of Alexander; he was a Roundhead, because of Alexander. Arundell may regard him as an inferior, but he had respected him;

now he despised him for serving the enemies of his anointed King. How could he endure?

Leaving Gilbey's study, he sought out Letitia, and they went to tend the graves of two of his brother's officers, in the little churchyard near the house. On the way back, he was assisting her over a stile when two riders appeared round a bend in the road, one a captain the other a sergeant. The captain elegantly doffed his hat to Letitia, his smile revealing strong, white teeth. 'I am come for Lieutenant Skelton of the Earl of Stamford's Foot,' he said to Nicholas.

'I am he.'

'Captain Knollys of Sir John Berkeley's staff. Yonder is Sergeant Hanniford. I am charged to bring you to Sir John's headquarters before Exeter.'

Letitia tightened her clasp of his hand and he felt his own heartbeat quicken. 'May I ask why, captain?'

'I cannot tell you. As I have business with Mr.Gilbey, we will ride ahead and await you at the house.' With a further flourish of his hat, Knollys and the sergeant cantered off.

Back at the house, Nicholas found his valise packed, and took an improvised meal with the soldiers. When it was time for farewells, it was apparent how attached to one another he and the Gilbey family had become and Letitia was near to tears. But soon they were away and on the road, the high-summer dust rising about them.

These past weeks had been an idyllic time, in some ways, but now Nicholas was glad to be back in the company of soldiers and he glanced at the refined features of the captain riding, silent, beside him. Knollys knew nothing of the mission upon which he was engaged, but was intrigued to be escorting a junior Parliamentary officer to a general of the King's western army. His charge was more than curious. Having no idea of what lay ahead, he reflected yet again upon his erstwhile host. Gilbey was no ordinary country gentleman. How had he come by the detailed intelligence to which he referred, when they spoke of the capture of Bristol? Who were the lone horsemen who arrived at all hours, to be hurried into his study? What were the documents he had seen recently being unloaded from a coach – a rare sight in these parts? Who and what was Edward Gilbey and why had he remained so long in his charge?

Walled, embattled Exeter came into view, below, the cathedral dominating the houses clustered about it. At the headquarters of the investing Royalists, on the outskirts of the city, Nicholas was left waiting in an anteroom by Knollys, but was soon brought before Sir John Berkeley. The general studied him carefully.

'How old are you, lieutenant?'

'Twenty, sir.'

'General Chudleigh informed me that you are bound in loyalty to the Carews of Antony!'

'That is true, sir.'

'You persuaded him that the bond is unbreakable. Do you confirm that?'

'I do.'

'Excellent, for I propose to disclose something touching the safety of Sir Alexander. Will you swear not to reveal it to any man, regardless of what you may decide?'

'I so swear.'

'Sir Alexander has let it be known that he might be persuaded to surrender his command to us.' Nicholas gasped, as Berkeley continued, 'We won great victories in Somerset and Bristol, but at a terrible price. While I am confident that Exeter will fall to us without undue bloodshed, Plymouth is a vastly different undertaking. Bastions have been added to the medieval walls and linked with a bank and ditch and it will be resolutely defended. On the seaward side, St. Nicholas Island is the prime guarantee for the safety of the castle and town. If Sir Alexander were to yield it up, we might effect an onslaught from the Sound, with much enhanced prospects of success. Unfortunately, he is a devilish wary fellow and wants nothing less than that the Great Seal of England should be appended to his pardon, before he will commit himself.'

'He is a lawyer, sir.'

'Aye, there you have it! I cannot avoid delay in accomplishing his wishes and can only return him ample assurance of His Majesty's pardon and full remission of his offences. In the meantime, he is in grave danger of discovery. From his first intimations, it has been foreseen that you could play the key part in his conversion. The time is now ripe and I put it to you that you make your way to the island, contrive to be alone with him and give him my best assurances, on behalf of Prince Maurice. Then urge him, with all vigour, to delay no longer.

'Your uniform should serve as passport to him and I am hopeful that contact with someone he trusts will bolster his flagging confidence in the King's intention. I need not tell you that the enterprise is hazardous for you and your patron, but the rewards will be commensurate. Success will much advance His Majesty's cause in the west and you will be released from your obligation to him. Consequent upon its accomplishment, I will appoint you captain of a troop of horse or a company of foot, as you choose. What say you, for I believe that would suit your purpose?'

What said he, indeed! His mind had sketched a plan even as Berkeley was speaking. It should be easy for a Parliamentarian officer, mustered at Plymouth, to gain a foothold on the island and, thence, an interview with Alexander. Armed with the general's assurances, he was confident that he could suborn Alexander and so do him true service. Juliana would be delighted and Arundell could hardly remain indifferent to him, were he to become the instrument which unlocked the gates of Plymouth.

'I will attempt, it, sir.'

'Bravo! Evolve a plan and submit it to me for approval. I propose that you work in conjunction with Captain Knollys, who will be made party to our intentions and Sergeant Hanniford. But do not delay! You and the sergeant will cross the Tamar at its upper reaches and travel through Cornwall. The necessary passes will be provided. Captain Knollys will await you with a boat at Millbrook Lake which, as you know, issues into the Sound.'

Berkeley's pompous manner had eased with the acceptance of his proposal and he regarded the small beard and curled lovelocks, which Letitia had persuaded Nicholas to grow, with some amusement. 'May you be successful, not least for your own sake, for methinks you make an indifferent Roundhead.'

᳁᳁᳁

From the musket walls of St. Nicholas Island, Sir Alexander Carew, Governor, looked across the water to Mount Edgcumbe house, home of his Royalist neighbour and kinsman. Beyond the Mount, in the twilight, lay Antony and his wife and family, some of whom had made their displeasure at his Parliamentarian sympathies painfully apparent. Now the Royalists were ascendant in Cornwall and much of Devon, such that only Plymouth seemed truly secure.

What had shaped his judgments? Assuredly it was the Petition of Rights and opposition to the royal tyranny while he was a student at the Middle Temple. He had rejoiced that the birds had flown when the King came to the Commons to arrest the five Members, including his relative, William Strode. He had been so sure of himself! When Grenville sought to dissuade him from voting for the Act of Attainder to impeach Strafford he had declared, 'If I were sure to be the next man that should suffer upon the same scaffold with the same axe, I would give my consent to the passing of it!' So he contributed to the death of the King's friend.

What had happened to those certainties, now that events were shaping against him?

CHAPTER 5

Betrayal

The peacock strutted among the apple trees in the orchard at Trerice, inspecting the rough grass for titbits and relishing the warm sun on its back. On the capped wall, separating the orchard from the front lawns, a blackbird watched the perambulation with a beady eye. Indifferent to its presence, the peacock strutted purposefully towards the wall. Resentful of this incursion into its territory, claimed so vociferously at dawn, the blackbird fluttered down and confronted the intruder.

Contemptuous of its sober-suited adversary, the peacock spread its tail feathers into a rustling fan, a hundred blue eyes on a sea of luminous green. Stiff with self-esteem, it revolved slowly, so that not one iota of its magnificence should remain unseen.

Juliana smiled; such vainglory and all for one blackbird. What a blessed thing it was to smile again, for Trerice was a sombre place, its grieving master absent, his son and heir dead. The aura of John's vanished presence seemed to await her in unexpected corners of the house, to remind her that another among that small company who had shown her regard and affection was gone. First John, then Sir Bevill – and what of Nicholas? She had left Stowe for Trerice the day that Sir Bevill sent word of him, for she had not dared to ask if she might see him. Then came the news of Sir Bevill's untimely end and she had hurried back to Stowe to comfort Grace Grenville, to find that her family had rallied round her and she was not needed.

There had been one letter from Nicholas, telling of his recovery and reaffirming his love. But since then, nothing! She made towards the door of the library, to prepare for the return of Sir John and Richard.

⊞⊞⊞

Shorn of tonsorial extravagance, Nicholas lay on his bed and watched the outline of the canopy sharpen, as early light filtered through the window of the inn.

Growing stronger, the August sun climbed above the surrounding rooftops. Today, he must ride for Plymouth to the lonely man on St.Nicholas Island. Trewhella Barton and the simple people who had once shared in his life seemed distant and unreal. Only Juliana remained clear in his thoughts.

As the sounds and smells of early morning emerged from the buildings around the courtyard below the open lattice, he bestirred himself and called for the simple repast he had ordered the previous evening. Scarcely had he finished it when Sergeant Hanniford, plainly attired like himself, cantered in beneath the stable arch, holding his mount on a lead rein. Hurrying down the stairs, he tossed coins for his board to the innkeeper and joined the soldier, outside.

'Good morning, sergeant. You are betimes.'

'Aye, sir, needs must, for 'tis far to ride and no time to spare.'

Nicholas swung into the saddle and hauled his horse about. Then they were spurring towards the upper reaches of the Tamar, over the river at Polston Bridge, and making for the familiar country around Antony. That night they bivouacked in the open and late on the second day saw them reconnoitring the banks of the Gannel Estuary, on the outskirts of Millbrook. Ahead, in the gathering dusk, Captain Knollys stepped from a clump of trees and Hanniford, his duty done, turned back whence they had come. 'The tide is on the turn and there is plenty of water running down the Tamar,' Knollys said. 'The wind is coming briskly from the south-west, so you should have no difficulty making the island. There is a small boat awaiting you on the silt.' He looked sharply, at Nicholas, 'You can handle a boat?'

'You ask that of a Cornishman?'

Knollys gave a short laugh.

Back among the trees, Nicholas donned his uniform, while Knollys eyed him, critically. 'You look damnably neat for a fugitive,' he declared, rubbing earth into the tunic. Once satisfied of the erstwhile Parliamentarian's appearance, he led the way quickly to the boat.

'These are your last instructions. A small force of infantry is standing-to in Millbrook, in case there is an opportunity to take over the island. An attempt

52

has been made to intercept a Royalist privateer returning from St. Malo to Falmouth. It is intended that it should stand off Plymouth Sound, in the event that Sir Alexander Carew resolves to abandon his command and depart by sea. Should the tide allow you to re-enter the estuary, remember that it is patrolled by the Parliament. I will give you what support I can from the shore of Mount Edgcumbe park, in case you come ashore along the coast.'

They waded into Millbrook Lake to the boat and hoisted the sail. Knollys gripped his hand and, with muttered good wishes, launched him on the tide. A fresh wind filled the canvas and bore the small craft along. For a while, he heard only the slap-slap of water under the hull, saw nothing. Round Devil's Point, the stern lanterns of ships showed, riding at anchor in the Sound, the pale light casting wavering reflections on the inky depths and transforming the lower rigging of masts and yards into threads of gossamer. His ear caught the creak of timbers, a thin snatch of a ballad, distant commands. Coming close under the lee of a man-of-war, he saw that her gun-ports were cleared for action, their cannon pointing towards the open sea. Even with St. Nicholas Island in his hands, Berkeley would not find Plymouth a plum ripe for picking.

The outline of the fort loomed and he hauled down the sail. From the walls a voice challenged. 'Who goes there?'

'An officer of the Parliament requesting permission to land.'

A kettledrum beat the alarum and flaring torches bobbed along the slipway. The sergeant of the guard and six musketeers, weapons levelled, awaited him. As the boat lurched against the slip, he leapt ashore. 'Lieutenant Skelton of the Earl of Stamford's Foot.'

'Where are your papers?' The sergeant demanded.

'I have none, for I am an escaped prisoner with vital information for the Governor.'

The sergeant was strangely hostile. 'What is the nature of this information?'

'That is for the Governor's ear only.'

He was led under a stone arch into the heart of the fort, to a small room in the Governor's house, and held under escort. For several minutes, the sergeant was absent; when he reappeared, Nicholas was taken, immediately, to an office, where Alexander awaited him. Not until the door had clicked shut behind the departing soldiers did Alexander speak. 'I am relieved to see you, having been concerned for your wellbeing. How come you here?'

'I bear a message from Prince Maurice, through Sir John Berkeley, expressing his good intentions towards you, if you will surrender your command. He entreats you to delay no longer, for you are in imminent danger of discovery.

If you agree, a Royalist force will occupy the island.'

Alexander's small face was pinched, his eyes suspicious. 'How come you to be playing envoy?'

'I have been under persuasion to join the Royalists. When it became apparent that my commitment to you and your house was unalterable, Sir John Berkeley entrusted me with this mission. My loyalty to you will be unaffected by your decision,but I beg you to hesitate no longer, for it is a fragile secret known to too many.'

Reassured, Alexander began to pace, slowly, up and down. 'I would require certain guarantees regarding the well-being of my wife and family and the de-sequestration of my estate.'

Jesu, did he think he was in a court of law! 'I can offer nothing but guarantees of good intentions...' was all he was able to say, when the door burst open and the guard commander strode in, with a black-garbed stranger and six musketeers at his back.

Alexander spun round. 'What is the meaning of this?'

The dark stranger stepped forward. 'Sir Alexander Carew, I arrest you in the name of the Mayor of Plymouth and the Committee of Public Safety, acting for the Parliament.'

Alexander blanched. 'On what charge?'

'Mayor Francis will acquaint you better when you are arraigned before the Committee. Your sword to Sergeant Hancock, if you please.'

Alexander ignored the request. 'Who has levelled these charges?'

'A servant has spoken against you and others will add their word.'

Recognising the hopelessness of his position, Alexander gave up his weapon, 'I cannot conceive what may be behind this, but it can, in no manner, concern this officer,' he said, indicating Nicholas.

'Nevertheless, I must detain you, Lieutenant, awaiting the pleasure of the Mayor and Committee.' The stranger gestured, brusquely, 'Confine them to the cells!'

Flanked by the escort, the two prisoners were conducted along a dimly-lit corridor, down a flight of steps into a narrow cell. The door was slammed, a key grated in the lock, and the footfalls of the guard retreated and died. They were alone. A guttering torch cast their shadows upon the sweating walls.

Alexander coughed in the smoke and grasped Nicholas arm. 'I am undone, betrayed. They will come, shortly, to take me into the town and God knows what will befall me. Take what opportunity you can to escape and offer comfort to my wife and children. Thank Sir John Berkeley for his kind intentions, as I thank you for your devotion. From now on make what shift you can. I believe you would do best to serve the King.'

He drew Nicholas down onto the cold flags. 'Will you pray with me?'

How often, thought Nicholas, had he knelt in prayer with this man and his family at Antony house or in the quiet of the village church? A great affection welled up within him, mixed with pity. He had done his best and delivered the message – albeit too late to save his patron. Was this, then, to be the end?

Their prayers concluded, they sat in stunned silence, until footsteps echoed in the passage outside, a key turned and the guard commander entered. 'You will come with me, Sir Alexander.' Alexander made to embrace Nicholas, but drew back, not wishing to implicate him further. As the door clanged behind him, the torch spluttered its last.

Hours later the blackness was relieved, when a corporal and a soldier came to bind his wrists and march him along the passage, up into the night air. He was halted at the slip, by the corporal, while the soldier went to draw in a boat. Across the narrow water, on the shoreline of Mount Edgcumbe, Knollys waited; he might as well have been a thousand miles away. The corporal was whispering at his shoulder, 'Be still, while I loosen your bonds. You must tip me and the musketeer overboard, but do it well for Janet would not wish her husband punished for failing in his duty.'

Nicholas turned his head and recognised the soldier they had nursed back to health at Trewells Barton. 'James Salter, praise be to God!'

Salter prodded him forward with his sword, while his fingers sought the slack knots. He had very little time. Salter set the sail and took his place in the stern, arm across the tiller. Nicholas sat amidships and the musketeer stood holding the mast, watching the way ahead. As his hands came free he leapt up, grabbed the mast with one hand and,with the other, seized his guard's locks and threw his weight to the left. The boat heeled and he yanked painfully at the musketeer's hair. With the heavy musket, bandolier and powder bag adding to his imbalance, the soldier pitched overboard. Salter stood, staggered convincingly and followed him over the side.

The sail jibbed before Nicholas grabbed the rudder and turned into the wind, which blew briskly offshore. There was no possibility of getting back up the Gannel Estuary and he must keep his distance from the island. It had to be the open sea. He would set course for the Great Mew Stone and come around towards the west, once clear of the Sound. The cries of the floundering Roundheads grew fainter, as the wind bore him along , but the sky was lightening to a pale turquoise and he had become visible from the fort.

In confirmation, a fusillade of musket fire crackled from the ramparts and whined around him, while, astern, a patrol ship hauled the soldiers from the water and turned in pursuit. A second volley from the island fell short, and he had cleared the Sound before the outline of his pursuers began to resolve in the uncertain light.

Two balls struck the sail, a third hit the gunwhale and a flying splinter drew blood from his temple. There was no chance of reaching the friendly shore and it would be a matter of minutes before he was either overhauled or shot. He crouched in the bottom of the boat, taking what cover he could.

An explosive roar rebounded from the land and something struck the water behind. A cry or alarm from the pursuit vessel encouraged him to peer over the stern and, there, bearing down upon them, was an armed merchantman, the Union flag flying from its masthead, a swivel gun still smoking in the bow. The ship was coming in from seaward and slicing across the bow of his adversaries – the forgotten ship from St. Malo!

A spread of canvas, the tracery of rigging, open gun ports – the ship was almost upon him. He dropped the sail and swung the tiller hard over, as a looped rope arced down. The bow wave struck and he steadied himself in the bucking boat thrusting his arms through the loop. In an instant, he was jerked from the craft, trailed briefly in the water, tossed against the hull and hauled, rudely, aboard. Two seamen heaved him to his feet and half-dragged him onto the quarterdeck. With lolling head, he contemplated the deck planks, fighting for breath.

'These Parliamentarians are wanting in hospitality,' a voice remarked dryly. He looked up at the captain, then over the bulwarks, where the patrol vessel was turning shorewards, in the wake of the ship.

Poor James Salter! The captain's comment could hardly be applied to him. Ducked, shot at, and due to be called to account for losing a prisoner – to repay one week's care and lodging. The strain of the last, several hours lifted as he began to laugh. 'On the contrary, they were most reluctant to see me go.' He straightened. 'I am greatly obliged to you, sir. Who have I the pleasure of addressing?'

'Captain Wilkins, master of the privateer, Goshawk. Need I ask if you are the officer with whom I was to rendezvous?' Amusement at their exchange lingered in his eyes.

'I am he, but I fear I am unaccompanied. Now I must hasten to Exeter. Where may I be put ashore?'

'Carrick Roads is my destination. I cannot change course. With this wind, we should be there in about seven hours. In the meantime, victuals and a hammock await you.'

Nicholas watched the friendly coast fall astern, as Plymouth Sound, Penlee Point, then Rame Head crowned by its tiny ruined church, were lost in the sea mist. Had Knollys been a frustrated witness of his pursuit and rescue? What ordeals awaited Alexander? Gone was his dream of unlocking Plymouth's seaward gate and becoming the suddenly-eligible suitor of Arundell's ward.

Soon after midday, Wilkins sent for him and they stood on the quarterdeck, in warm sunshine, as Goshawk entered Falmouth haven, guarded by the twin fortresses of St. Mawes, to the east, and the much larger pile of Pendennis Castle, to the west. Goshawk slipped past the Pendennis promontory and weighed anchor under the protecting guns of the castle.

When sails were furled amid the unloading of muskets, cannon and ammunition was under way, Wilkins joined Nicholas at the rail. 'I will take you to the castle governor, Sir Nicholas Slanning.'

'Sir Nicholas died last month, from wounds received at Bristol,' Nicholas informed him.

'I am grieved to learn that, for he was a very fine gentleman.' Wilkins paused .'Then we will meet his successor.'

A cutter was launched and the pair were rowed ashore. They climbed the long, steep hill to the gatehouse, where Wilkins presented his credentials. Then across the ward and into the keep. At the entrance to the guardroom, a tall, powerfully-built officer with flaming red hair and beard greeted Wilkins. 'A pleasure to see you, Phillip, I trust you found space for a few bottles of claret among the weaponry?'

'Have I ever failed you, Robin?'

The smile was broad and affable. 'Never! You wish to see the Governor?'

Wilkins nodded. 'With all haste, I beg.' The officer was back within minutes to lead them into an office at the head of a narrow stair.

The figure seated at a table looked up as they entered and an astonished Nicholas endured the scrutiny of Colonel Sir John Arundell. Wilkins handed over his papers and began to introduce his companion. The Governor cut him short, 'We are acquainted, I thank you.' He regarded the orange sash Nicholas was wearing with distaste.

Shaken, Nicholas stammered, 'I beg leave to account for my presence to you alone, Sir John – with great respect to the captain.'

Arundell's brows contracted. 'Very well! Please leave your manifest Captain, we will discuss it later. And now Lieutenant?' he enquired, brusquely.

Nicholas decided to declare the purpose of his mission. Starting with his association with James Chudleigh, he unfolded the story of his undertaking and escape. By the end of his narrative Arundell's hostility had vanished. 'My kinsman has been greatly misguided and I fear for him,' he said, sadly. 'My concern, now, is for Lady Jane and the children. I must afford them what succour I can.' 'He rose and came to stand before Nicholas. 'You have been constant and courageous, and it was no fault of yours that the enterprise failed. Sir John Berkeley made you a proposition, contingent upon your success, but I believe you still merit the reward. 'With the suspicion of a smile, he added, 'I think he will be receptive to my view. Now that you are released from your obligation, take whatever opportunity General Berkeley offers.' He pressed his fist against Nicholas's chest. 'Honour and serve the King!'

He stepped past Nicholas to the door, 'You will start for Exeter, shortly; my aide, Captain Smythe, will ride with you.'

'Thank you, sir,' Mustering his courage, he continued, 'May I enquire after Juliana's health?'

Arundell opened the door. 'She is well. Be so good as to wait here.'

Nicholas spent the minutes admiring the view from the narrow windows. Across the glimmering waters of the Roads, St. Mawes Castle squatted on its low promontory; westward, a jagged flank of coastline ran away to the southern horizon, where land and sea diffused to an azure haze.

Pendennis was an artillery castle with none of the pinnacled romanticism of a medieval fortress. Henry VIII had planted the sturdy keep and curtain walls at the seaward end of the dog-leg promontory and Elizabeth had enclosed the plateau on which it stood with embrasured ramparts and a stone-revetted ditch. The shape so formed was approximately that of a seven-pointed star, elongated between its northern and southern extremities, and pierced on the western side by the gatehouse. Across the enormous ward, remote from the keep, stood a complex of domestic buildings – barracks, kitchens, a hospital.

He scarcely heard the door open, but turned when Juliana ran to him with a cry of joy. He clasped her to him. At last she drew away, 'I have been so anxious for you.'

'Did you not receive my letters?'

'I received one and knew that you had survived the battle and were recovering, that is all.'

'Then be at ease, for I am well.'

Taking his hand, she led him through a small door on to the battlements. It was mid-afternoon and the promontory, the sea and the distant hills were bathed in sunlight. He leaned on the warm granite and breathed the tangy air.

'How did you know I was here?'

'My guardian sent a message that you were waiting for me. Perchance I should not ask why you are here, but tell me how you have fared since we were together.' She looked at him and he reached towards her, but a sentry appeared on an embattled look-out, above, and he curtailed the impulse. Instead, he told her how Alexander obtained his commission, of James Chudleigh and Sourton Down, and how he fell, wounded, at Stratton. She ran her hand, gently, over the shabby uniform where the musket ball had entered, as Arundell stepped through the low doorway with his aide.

'This is Captain Robin Smythe, your guide to Exeter.' The big man took his hand in a grip of iron. 'Other garments have been found for you and I wish you to carry this to General Berkeley.' Arundell passed a letter to him, as he continued, gravely, 'The flower of Cornish manhood has been cut down in our cause and other young men, of courage and resolution, must take their place. I would see you among that number. Be on your way and God speed!'

He returned with Smythe through the doorway and, before Nicholas followed, Juliana stole a quick kiss. As she hearkened to their footsteps descending the stairway, her spirits sank. Yet, there could be no doubt of her guardian's newborn regard for her lover. Mayhap, the letter to Berkeley might lift Nicholas over one of the obstacles between them.

Had Mother Lobb spoken truth? Was this a turning point?

CHAPTER 6

Royal Intercession

Nicholas sat, his restless horse, outside Bedford House, Exeter, waiting to escort the Queen to Pendennis Castle, en route to the Continent. Immediately in front of him stood the litter and, behind, the section of troopers he commanded. These surroundings had become so familiar – the imposing residence of Hannah Antony, the goldsmith's wife, his quarters for the past 10 months and, beyond, the crowded houses, the pinnacled towers of the cathedral, whose bells had been the accompaniment to his life, since he returned from Pendennis.

There was movement. Prince Maurice and Lord Jermyn, who were to lead the column, appeared at the entrance to the Queen's lodgings. Conversation ceased as they waited upon the woman whose Catholic faith and French associations had alienated her from the people, exacerbating her husband's problems. A ragged and uncertain cheer rose from the burghers standing by, as Henrietta Maria was borne out in a chair, her ladies following. On one side waddled her dwarf, Hudson; on the other came the Countess of Dalkeith, holding the Queen's two-weeks-old daughter. Before she was lifted into the litter, the Queen gave her child a last, anguished look.

With Maurice and Jerymn now mounted, the column moved slowly forward, through the narrow streets, past the cathedral and porticoed Guildhall, beneath the south gatehouse and into the countryside, beyond. Purple foxgloves,waving in the hedgerows, reminded Nicholas of those days on the moors, above Trerice, when he had ridden with the Arundells, hawk on wrist, and believed that he was one of them. Then, bitter rejection. Yet, in some measure he had been rehabilitated. Thanks in part to Arundell's letter, Berkeley had awarded him a captaincy in the Royalist army and appointed him to his staff. Weeks after, Exeter fell and Berkeley became Governor of the city, now a Royalist mint. It had been a period of privilege and comfort, soon to end, for they must face the army of the Earl of Essex, advancing through Somerset. In the meantime, he would be Arundell's guest, again, and in such company.

The royal litter swayed, ceaselessly, as the frowning heights of Dartmoor were skirted and Okehampton and Launceston fell behind. What misery must the prostrate refugee be enduring, within its narrow confines. Her flight from Essex would give little encouragement to the common people of Devon and Cornwall to join the ranks of those who would oppose him. The craggy contours of Bodmin Moor appeared, were traversed and the column descended to the flat land towards Truro. On the fourth day, they crossed the Pendennis headland and passed under the royal arms in stone surmounting the castle gatehouse.

The litter came to a halt before the waiting Arundells. Sir John and Richard bent over the Queen's hand and stepped back. As Juliana rose from her curtsy, the Queen held on to her hand and tried to leave the litter, but her legs would not support her and she crumpled to the ground. Nicholas reached her first and he and Juliana raised and held her till others came to her aid. Faced unexpectedly by her lover, Juliana gave a little gasp of delight.

After that encounter, there was no time for Juliana to think of anything but Her Majesty's care and comfort. When the Queen had retired, she spoke at length with her ladies. They told her how the war was sweeping back into Cornwall and how dangerous was the position in the north, where the Fairfaxes, father and son, had joined with the Scotch army to pen-up the Earl of Newcastle, in York.

Next morning, Juliana sent her maid to Nicholas and she found him in a sparsely-furnished room studying a provisioning list. 'Oh, sir, 'tis lovely to see you, again. My, but you are a fine gentleman, I'll be bound.'

Nicholas took her hand, affectionately. 'And what of your mistress?'

'She longs to be with you, sir, but has many duties. My lady asks how long you will remain here?'

Nicholas shrugged. 'That is uncertain. A few days at most, for we are ordered on to Okehampton. Tell her I will come to her tonight.'

'No, sir, you mustn't do that. The guards have been reinforced, because of the Queen's presence, and you would be apprehended. Think of our lady's reputation'

'Then tonight I will find a way and tomorrow I will come to her.' Nicholas took her gently by the arm and led her to the door. 'Tell her!' he said firmly.

Having resolved to see Juliana, Nicholas searched for a way to achieve his aim. Earlier he had learned that Robin Smythe was guard commander that very night – a stroke of good fortune. A firm friendship had been forged between them during their hilarious progress to Exeter, last summer, with frequent stops at taverns along the way and frantic gallops to make up lost time – a welcome antidote to his sorrow at the arrest of Alexander. But would Robin, a responsible officer, help him? No, not while the Queen's safety rested with him, for sure! He would persuade Smythe that he should walk his rounds with him, in preparation for the night his own troops were to provide the guard. Thus, he would learn the layout of the apartments and the position of the sentinels and, thereby, come to Juliana.

▨▨▨

Abed in the silent castle, sleep eluded Juliana. It had been an eventful day, but she had done everything a loyal subject should to make the Queen's stay restful. Her Majesty had been kind and appreciative and she was well content. It was of Nicholas that she was thinking, now. His sudden appearance at her side was like a miracle.

How he had changed since last summer. Then, he had been a shabby youth, tense from the attempted subornment of Alexander Carew. But it was a man who had looked into her eyes, today – the epitome of a Cavalier, in lace collar, black doublet and silver-braided sleeves. His plumed hat was worn at a jaunty angle and, most agreeable of all, a red sash was about his waist. His proposal to come to her was rash to the point of madness, but she longed for him. If he would brave detection in the royal apartments, she would risk disgrace, so that they might be together again. With a sigh, she thrust the foolish thought from her mind, but she would see him though she served the Queen.

The following morning she went to the Queen's bedside, to determine the royal pleasure. Henrietta Maria lay propped up with pillows, a small pale doll. Dark eyes regarded Juliana. 'Did I detect an amour between you and the officer of my escort, Mademoiselle?' Juliana flushed. 'He must be quite a man to distract you from your duty to your Queen!' The eyes belied the severity in her voice.

'I crave Your Majesty's pardon, I was taken by surprise.'

'Do not apologise, child, I am a Frenchwoman and love love.'

She patted the bed. 'Sit here and tell me about yourselves.'

Juliana hesitated at the proposed intimacy, but the Queen folded her hands, expectantly. 'Begin at the beginning.'

To her surprise, she talked as easily to her royal audience about her lover as she had to Grace Grenville, and found relief and tranquility, thereby. When she had finished, the Queen thought for a moment. 'This indisposition, which has plagued me since the birth of *ma petite* Minette, confines me to this chamber and I have grown weary of the same few faces. Bring your captain to supper. Methinks, 'twill do him no harm with your guardian to have supped with the Queen of England, and Harry Jermyn is brother-in-law to Sir John Berkeley – he shall be our fourth. Should your lover acquit himself well, be sure his general will hear of it, likewise, be warned that Harry is merciless with men of lesser wit than himself.'

'Your Majesty is most kind.'

'We shall see about that! Command him – invite him – to my table at the hour of eight.'

Meg laughed at Nicholas' foolish surprise, when she delivered her message. Afterwards Nicholas sought out Robin. 'Gad, Nicholas, you are privileged indeed. Be sure your linen is clean and do not speak till you are spoken to. When you are first presented to the Queen, address her as "Your Majesty"; 'twill then suffice to call her "Madame"'.

'It will be my only opportunuty to meet Juliana and I must find her a gift. How may I accomplish that?'

'By taking horse to Penryn, forthwith, where you may purchase nigh on anything your fancy conjures – French fripperies, rings, jewels. I will come with you.'

They rode down the hill from the castle and across the neck of the peninsula, following the sea's edge. A great mansion came into view, castellated amd gabled.

'What is that place?' Nicholas asked.

'Arwenack House, home of the Killigrews, a rumbustious family withal – pirates, lighthouse builders and past governors of Pendennis castle among them. King James held one of them in the Fleet prison and a Lady Jane was sentenced to death for raiding a Spanish ship, as it lay at anchor in the Roads. She gained release and went to live in Penryn. She may dwell there, still.'

Beyond the mansion, some cottages and sail-lofts, cellars and alehouses clustered about a quay from which a long, wooden jetty projected. The stink of fish hung heavy in the air. 'And here we have Smithick or Pennycomequick, as you will,' continued his guide. 'The Killigrews have long wished to establish a port here and call it Falmouth. Is it not a magnificent haven? From here, ships may sail east to the Orient or west to the New World. Men could make fortunes from such an enterprise.'

'You are a fount of knowledge, my friend.'

'Aye, 'tis my inquiring mind, Nicholas. I have never stayed long anywhere, but I must know all about it.'

Ahead of them, the town of Penryn climbed the hill from the river's edge. As they rode in, Nicholas noted the plentitude of taverns and alehouses. 'I see it was not altruism alone which prompted this excursion,' he remarked, dryly.

Robin shrugged his shoulders. 'Well, it does rank second only to St. Ives as a place to slake the thirst. Is your fancy for wine or ale?'

'Neither in great measure, methinks.'

Robin grinned. 'Oh come now, I would not deliver an inebriated guest to Her Majesty. We will take a quiet flask, here, at the sign of the Dolphin.'

Inside the spacious taproom they called for the potman. 'A flagon of Rhenish, I pray you, and some of your excellent lobster,' Robin demanded.

A man leaned out of a shadowed alcove, 'For one not of these parts, you have a discerning palate, sir.'

Robin cocked an eyebrow, as the man came over to them. 'Allow me to present myself. Captain Peter Mundy of the East India Company, at your service.'

'Robin Smythe. This is my good friend Nicholas Skelton. We are captains in the King's service and delighted to make your acquaintance. Pray tell us more of this monarch of the sea.'

Mundy nodded. 'I endorse the appellation, for I once traded in the Cornish lobster, ere I was drawn back to sea.'

'You are travelled?'

'I have sailed the world these 30 years, to Europe and Far Eastern climes – to Java, Malay, China and Japan.'

'And have seen many wonders, I doubt not?' Nicholas enquired, intrigued by this outgoing man.

'You cannot imagine some of them. Yet I have seen nothing, I vow, to equal the Taj Mahal.'

'What is that?'

'A great mausoleum at Agra, in India. It has been nigh 20 years in the building and is the tribute of a king to the memory of his dead wife – a fretted thing of pure gold, engraven, enamelled and set with jewels.'

His taste for travellers' tales blunted by campaigning, Robin interjected, 'Speaking of jewels and knowing you to be a seafaring man, I wonder if you might assist my friend, who seeks a bright bauble for his love.'

Mundy reached into the pocket of his coat and brought out a soft, leather pouch. 'Gladly would I aid a swain to find favour with his lady.' Unlacing the neck, he spilled four rings on to the table before them. 'What is her colouring?'

'Her eyes are hazel-green, her hair is ripe chestnut,' Nicholas told him.

'Then it is the green of the emerald for her. What think you of this?' He held up a luminous stone, which winked and glittered in the light.

'I declare it a beautiful thing, but too rich for my purse.'

'But you like it?' Mundy persisted.

'It would complement her beauty to perfection.'

'Then it is yours!"

Nicholas stared at him in astonishment, prompting Mundy to add, 'I promise it will not ruin you. These rings were given to me by an Oriental potentate, for services rendered. He did not value them as highly as you.'

'What am I in debt to you?' Nicholas enquired anxiously.

'Join me in a flagon of wine and we will discuss it.' He signalled to the potman , before placing a small, leather-bound volume on the table.

'I surmise you are not a widely-travelled man, Captain Skelton, and may find my diary of interest, while you have the look of a man-of-the-world, Captain Smythe.'

'Hardly the world, Captain Mundy, but I have seen much of the Continent and have no great hankering to roam further.'

'Ah well, each man to his taste, though I confess I am never happier than at home in Penryn.' His companions' voices faded as Nicholas began to read the diary and was transported to another world, far removed from the cliffs and moorland of his native county. He was recalled, some time later, by Mundy preparing to leave.

They bade him farewell and were returning to the castle, when Robin said, 'You had a rare bargain from the good captain. Methinks, he is a romantic and you caught his fancy.'

Taking the ring from his pocket, Nicholas held it between thumb and forefinger. 'I know not what impression I shall make upon the Queen, but I believe I shall please Juliana.'

'Mayhap, but to influence Her Majesty you must first win over Lord Henry Jermyn, for his opinions carry much with her. In truth, he cares only for the influential and exalted and will show you a fine disregard.'

They were passing through Smithick and Robin drew rein at the jetty. 'Let us walk out along there and I will tell you more of Jermyn,' Robin said as they slid from the saddle. 'He is the son of a Suffolk knight, Sir Thomas Jermyn, and has caused great distress to his sire, having been imprisoned for carrying a challenge to a duel, then banished for seducing one of the Queen's ladies-in-waiting. Sir Thomas was so overborne by these events that he left court and retired to the country. In due course, Henry succeeded to the title and, in four years, had so rehabilitated himself as to become Secretary to the Queen and, through her influence, Baron Jermyn of St. Edmunsbury.'

The two Cavaliers had reached the end of the jetty and stood looking across the water to the castle, on its promontory. Nicholas, conscious that the hours to his appointment were shortening, had listened carefully; it was apparent that his main concern was not Royal protocol. As if reading his mind, Robin put a heavy arm about his shoulders. 'Do not be lulled into one unguarded moment, this evening, my friend.'

◼◼◼

Henrietta Maria sat at table bolstered in an armchair, her neat feet resting on a footstool. She was dressed in a gown of lemon satin, trimmed with lace, and a necklace of pearls encircled her throat. Behind her in the small room, overheated by a blazing fire, Juliana and Lord Henry Jermyn awaited the arrival of her guest. There was a tap on the door, Hudson opened it and, with a stubby bow, announced, 'Captain Skelton, Your Majesty.'

His tall figure filled the doorway. 'Good evening, captain.'

'Good evening, Your Majesty.'

'You know this lady,' the Queen pronounced, with a tiny smile. 'I present Lord Jermyn.'

Jermyn nodded coolly. Pursed lips showed that he was not pleased to be burdened with the young soldier's company. The Queen indicated their places at the table – Nicholas to her left, Juliana to the right and her Secretary facing his royal mistress. During the simple repast, conversation was stilted until the Queen spilt her glass of wine. 'I was exhausted before the birth of "*ma petite* Minette,"' she sighed. 'Now I am part-paralysed and my sight is impaired. Indeed, how could we endure, were it not for the loyalty of our Cavaliers – gentlemen like yourself, Captain.' Her eyes closed and her head drooped, disconsolately.

Jermyn broke the uncertain silence which followed. 'Are you a gentleman Captain?'

Nicholas hesitated and Juliana interjected, sharply, 'Captain Skelton was the protege of Sir Richard Carew of Antony!'

'And what has accrued from that patronage, Mistress Arundell?'

'He became responsible for Sir Richard's farm, in the Hundred of Pyder, three years before his majority.'

Jermyn tilted a sardonic eyebrow and Juliana flushed. 'Splendid! But I asked the Captain if he were a gentleman. 'Tis one thing to till the land and quite another to own it. The former affords small leisure for that learning which marks the gentleman.'

'That is a premise worth testing, my lord,' Nicholas responded.

'So there is mettle here,' Jermyn mused. 'Indeed? Ambition will not avail a landless blade who lacks knowledge and wit.'

The queen opened her eyes and smiled gently at Juliana. 'What is ambition and learning? Only love is all! I know not if I may see my husband, again, yet I know our love will endure till death. Was there not an earlier King of England who so loved his wife that he raised a cross at each place her body rested, on its last journey home?'

''Twas Edward I, Madame,' Nicholas informed her. 'And only now, in Agra, India, a Mogul has built an exquisite tomb of pure gold, enamelled and set with jewels, in memory of his departed wife.' He glanced towards Jermyn, who was observing him intently. 'You will know of it, my lord.'

'Indeed.'

Nicholas frowned. 'But I have forgot its name.'

Jermyn fingered his glass. 'It seems we have both forgot,' he said, at last.

'Now I remember – it is the Taj Mahal.'

Juliana had feared that Nicholas would not long play mouse to Jermyn's cat, but he had thrown down his gage with a vengeance. Jermyn's face was a thundercloud, as he glanced at the Queen.

Hudson came to clear the table, halting the Secretary's attack and Henrietta Maria's eye ranged over the tapestries, hastily hung to obscure the bare walls. 'Did you know my husband acquired the finest collection of paintings in Europe, Captain? They illuminated the walls of every palace – Whitehall, Richmond, Nonesuch, Windsor. I even had a number at Somerset House.' She turned to Juliana. ' Sir Anthony Van Dyck depicted the King, most handsomely, as "Charles the First a la Chasse", it was a great favourite of mine.' At the recollection of those gay, distant days, her voice faltered.

'I trust that Your Majesty is not overtaxing her strength?' Jermyn enquired solicitously.

'No, Harry, I draw strength from these young people.' But she closed her eyes and lay back in the chair.

Nicholas remained silent, suspecting that Jermyn was preparing new bait.

'What think you of our Cavalier poets, Captain?' he demanded suddenly.

'I like them well, my lord.'

'How would you rate them?'

The Queen's heavy-lidded eyes opened an instant to appraise the combatants.

'Their inspiration is Sir Phillip Sidney's ideal of poetic chivalry, of course, and to that extent I could not separate them.'

Jermyn's languid tone sharpened. 'What of their style?' he pressed.

'Sir John Suckling's apparent spontaneity is most to my liking, I find Sir Edmund Waller too studied. But Richard Lovelace has perfectly captured a soldier's emotions, in "To Lucasta on Going to the Wars".'

'Perhaps you could quote it to us?'

Nicholas glanced towards the Queen. Without opening her eyes, she said 'Pray, continue, Captain.'

He cleared his throat.

Tell me not, Sweet I am unkind,
That from the nunnery
Of thy chaste breast and quiet mind
To war and arms I fly.
True, a new mistress now I chase,
The first foe in the field; And with a stronger faith embrace
A sword, a horse, a shield.
Yet this inconstancy is such
As thou too shalt adore;
I could not love thee,
Dear, so much Loved I not honour more.'

'What fine sentiment,' the Queen murmured.

Suspecting that Henrietta Maria was relishing the contest, Jermyn sought to recover the initiative. 'You spoke of the ideal of poetic chivalry, but do you not find the poet's view of woman somewhat earthy?'

'Woman is a creature of flesh and blood, my lord. To eulogise her as such lends sincerity to the verse.'

Jermyn stroked his fair beard for a moment, before reaching for the wine. He filled Nicholas' glass before his own, and Juliana sighed with relief, at the tacit gesture.

It was apparent that the Queen was exhausted. 'I would retire, Harry.' Extending a limp hand to Nicholas, she murmured, 'Thank you for entertaining us so admirably, Captain. You have a sharp intellect. Take care where you unleash it.'

Nicholas bowed, 'I shall remember your words, Madam.'

'Walk with the captain, Mademoiselle, but come to me before you retire.' When the door had closed, she smiled saronically at Jermyn. 'Still you cannot resist a duel, Harry, and again you have paid the price. Write to Sir John Berkeley and commend that young man. Meantime, I will speak in his favour to Sir John Arundell. Now, send my ladies to attend me.' As Jermyn turned away, she smiled again. *Cette soirée etait très agréable.* She had never forgiven Harry Jermyn for seducing one of her ladies.

In the corridor outside, Nicholas was contrite. 'I cannot conceive why the Queen invited me to supper, and now I have offended her.'

Juliana took his arm. 'I think not. I grant that you were treading a narrow path, but, methinks, you kept your footing. Who knows why she invited you. Mayhap, she fears her own thoughts and we distracted her from them.'

They passed the two sentries and were halfway down the spiral stairway, to the guardroom, when he paused, 'I have something for you.' Reaching for her left hand, he slid the ring along her third finger.

'Oh, Nicholas, it is beautiful!.' The emerald stone sparkled in the weak light from below the stairs. 'Every time I look at it I shall think of you. I cannot wear it, openly, I shall put it on a chain and keep it hidden, next to my heart, until we are together again.' No other words were necessary, as she pressed against him and he held her close. She drew away, reluctantly, 'I have to return to my royal mistress.' With a quick squeeze of his hand she turned back up the stairs.

▯▯▯

It was Sunday – service time. The Arundells had bade their royal guest farewell and watched her embark, with her retinue, aboard a Flemish man-of-war. Ten other vessels lay about the Queen's ship and a swift galley of 16 oars stood with them, in case of emergency during the voyage to Brest. From the quarterdecks, anxious eyes scanned the exit from the Roads, where three Parliamentary warships under the orders of Robert Rich, Earl of Warwick, lurked to secure the Queen's person.

Juliana listened to the anchors rattle up from the sea bed, watched the bustle of busy mariners in the rigging, the cream sails shake clear of their lashings and belly out before the wind. The party assembled on the quay-side raised their hands, in farewell, as the ships, gun-ports cleared for action, turned towards the open sea. Her feelings at this moment were mixed – relief that her responsibilities were at an end, apprehension for the royal charge's safety on the voyage and sadness at the departure of the woman who had shown her much kindness. That sadness would have been deeper had she known that Henrietta Maria would never see her beloved husband again.

She turned from the moving scene to her concern for her lover, who was, even now, riding towards the Parliamentary army heading into Cornwall. Surreptitiously, she drew out the ring and regarded the bright emerald. It was fit for a princess. With a sigh, she returned it to its hiding place.

'Juliana!' Arundell called from the waiting coach, but she did not respond. Sensing her melancholy, he came to her and they watched the ships sail out into the hostile waters beyond the head. Choosing his words carefully, he said, 'A certain personage has been at pains to impress upon me the worth of Nicholas. I respect that opinion, but our personal happiness must wait upon a victorious conclusion to this struggle.'

CHAPTER 7

Dark Episode

Encamped with his army at Tavistock, Robert Devereux, Earl of Essex, sat before his maps in the fading light of a July evening, patiently listening to his general officers arguing the wisdom of pressing forward into Cornwall.

He was a melancholy man, unlike his rash father, favourite of Elizabeth. His reluctance to engage his sovereign in battle had allowed the King to leave Oxford and slip between him and Sir William Waller and head for the West Country. Thus, the Committee of Both Kingdoms had favoured Waller to relieve Lyme and Plymouth but Essex, ignoring their wishes, had continued to move through Devon, pursuing the King and his army.

Lord Robartes of Lanhydrock was holding forth, 'Surely, Lord General, it is our duty to clear Cornwall of Royalists and settle it in peace, and you can be assured of my personal influence, in this aim.'

Sir John Merrick's mouth curled at Robartes claim. 'I trust, my lord, that this advice is not coloured by self-interest, as providing the opportunity to recover your sequestrated estate and collect your rents?'

'Come now, Sir John, there is weight in the argument,' Essex interjected, soothingly. 'Occupation of the western ports would deprive the King of the munitions he imports in exchange for Cornish tin.'

Major-General Skippon leaned forward, 'Our army has already been weakened through supplying garrisons at Lyme, Weymouth and Barnstaple and the troops are in ill-humour for want of pay. Behind us are two large armies holding the option either to engage us or pen us up in this narrow county.'

'But our rear has been secured by the capture of Taunton Castle and

Barnstaple has foresworn its allegiance to the Royalists,' Essex reminded him.

'It must be appreciated that the Cornish are inately conservative and will respond to the King's presence among them, my lord; I council prudence,' Merrick urged.

Essex rolled up his maps, 'Gentlemen, I believe that we have no choice. We go forward into Cornwall, and to the relief of Plymouth, putting our trust in Almighty God.'

As the divided council broke up, Essex lit his pipe and went to the window, to watch the sun set. It was blood red.

◘◘◘

With other cavalry officers, Nicholas squatted on the slopes of Boconnoc park, awaiting their newly-appointed General of the Horse. It was good to be back on Cornish soil, after the noise and bustle of the King's state entry into Exeter and his conjunction with Prince Maurice's army. Thereafter, they had moved south to occupy Launceston and contain Essex, who had forged across the river at Horsebridge and on into Bodmin.

George, Lord Goring, limped towards them with his secretary, Sir Richard Bulstrode. Hitching himself on to the barrel of a cannon, he grunted with relief as the weight was taken off his smashed ankle, memento of the Seige of Breda. Nicholas was fascinated by the 36 year-old general. Goring was not conventionally good-looking, the features were lean and foxy, but the tall figure exuded elegance.

The General of the Horse leaned towards his officers, buff-coated, helmeted and corsleted for the foray he was about to launch. 'Lord Essex has blundered into a fine predicament, gentlemen. If he fails to command the hills above Lostwithiel, or loses the harbour of Fowey, he will be trapped, for he has precious little hope of being relieved by Waller. He is already outnumbered and has four armies bearing down upon him – the King's, Prince Maurice's, Sir Richard Grenville's and Lord Hopton's. Already he is short of victuals and will be denied replenishments, if we can secure the east bank of the River Fowey and, thereby, command the harbour entrance. With this objective, I am despatching a force of cavalry to seize the ford over Penpoll Creek, and capture Lord Mohun's house, "Hall", near Bodinnick Ferry. Thus, we may seize the peninsula at the mouth of the river. Captain Skelton's troop has already reconnoitred the area and will form the van of our force, the others will be as follows...'

So this is to be my re-baptism of fire, Nicholas mused, running the rowel of his spur along the hard earth.

Within the hour, they were moving through the sun-dappled woods along the south bank of the Lerryn River. At the village of St. Veep the main force halted, while Nicholas and his troopers moved forward to overlook the ford, at Penpoll Creek, and the Parliamentary troops encamped about it. Once over the creek, the Cavaliers could drive south to master the eastern shore.

Drawing his sword, Nicholas signalled the cavalry to extend into a broad line. Sensing the impending action, a horse whinnied, alerting the Parliamentarians, who ran to their weapons and began to form the familiar, defensive formation, their backs to the ford. Before their pikes could be presented, Nicholas cried, 'Charge.'

A hundred throats echoed the cry as spur struck flank, the chargers threw up their heads and the line moved forward from trot, to canter, to gallop. Dust rose in clouds from the thin grass, as they descended the slope and swept along the foreshore, carabines crackling. Into the half-formed defence they thundered, driving the enemy foot into the water. A pike head grazed Nicholas' side and caught in the swinging baldrick. Unhorsed he fell, heavily, into the shallow water, as the pikeman drew his sword and lunged, awkwardly, towards him.

He was still grasping his own weapon, and swung upwards as the infantryman thrust down at him. The hostile weapon drove into the silt and he rolled aside and on to one knee. The armoured man spun, swinging his blade in a great arc, but the impetus of the attack unbalanced him and he pitched forward, under the hooves spattering the water. Surrounded by his own men, Nicholas turned back into the fray, but the Parliamentarians resistance was crumbling and they were throwing down their weapons. The ford was theirs. Detaching a group to secure the opposite bank, he climbed on to his horse, wet and dishevelled, his side oozing warm blood. He was alive and victorious, a soldier again.

Prisoners and casualties counted and cared for, they crossed the ford and pressed on south and lay, that night, in open bivouac. The prospect of further action on the morrow denied sleep, so Nicholas rose and walked, silently, among the recumbent men, checked the sentinels and horse lines and returned to his place on the cold ground. His wound felt stiff and sore, but he warmed his spirits with images of Juliana. In time, a grey dawn drew back the shutters of the night, a trumpet sounded and the camp began to stir. Rising, he looked towards the outline of Polruan Castle, where the Fowey spilled into the sea.

By nightfall they had possessed it.

███

With the left bank of the river secured, Charles Stuart commanded the entrance to the harbour of Fowey and had all but severed communications between Essex and Warwick's fleet.

When Nicholas arrived back at Boconnoc park, he learned that Geoffrey Knollys was in camp and awaited him. They had become firm friends through their service together on Berkeley's staff, during which time Nicholas had learned that the aristocratic Geoffrey was, in fact, the youngest son of the Earl of Thurston. Nicholas sought him out immediately. 'What brings you this far south-west?' he enquired.

'My troop is part of Lord Goring's reinforcements for containing Essex in the river valley. When orders for the day were issued, I requested that our two forces form one of the afternoon patrols. It was agreed.'

Nicholas grinned, appreciatively. 'I always did admire your staff work.'

By noon, their force was filing through the narrow lanes towards the high ground. As they breasted the slope, a knot of peasants came into view on the verge of the track. At their approach, the jostling, homespun group clambered over a stile and disappeared into nearby woodland. Nicholas and Geoffrey dismounted to inspect the objects of their attention, the broken bodies of two pikemen with throats cut and blood running along their armour like claret spilled from a goblet. So muddied and stained were their uniforms that the orange sashes were barely distinguishable. Nicholas gazed at the savagery. 'Never have I seen the like of this.'

'You will, again,' Geoffrey replied somberly, 'for the Cornish have good reason to hate the Roundheads. They say they have despoiled land and livestock everywhere. Many houses in Lostwithiel have been pillaged and, hereabouts, the Rashleighs have suffered grievously, for their own house in Fowey and all 60 rooms at Menabilly have been plundered.'

Remounting, they rode on to the crown of the hill and looked down on the valley between Lostwithiel and Fowey. Ten thousand Parliamentarians were pent up there – in a killing-ground. From the Royalist guns, iron-shod death rained into the packed formations, at musket shot range, and in the fields and lanes around, opposing groups engaged, reformed and locked again in bloody combat. Exhausted by unremitting assault for eight days, the Parliamentarians were in an appalling condition and the stench of defeat seemed almost tangible. It must end soon!

▣▣▣

Late that night, as they sat drinking with Goring and his officers, in their headquarters at St. Blazey, Nicholas asked Geoffrey his opinion of their general.

Refilling their cups, Geoffrey replied, quietly, 'The gentleman has a dangerous air and his troops are as wild as he. They are a greater liability to the King than half Essex's army, with their habit of living off the country. And they do not want for other consolations! While they were in Lancashire, they carried along with them a bevy of strumpets called the Leaguer Ladies and pleasured themselves whenever the fancy took them.'

Nicholas laughed and regarded Goring with renewed interest. Peering at the flushed faces, through the haze of tobacco smoke, Goring caught his eye. It was time to test the mettle of some of his officers.

'You're a devilish good-looking fellow, Captain Skelton. Tell us what ye look for, first, in a woman. Is it a firm arse or a fair face?'

Taken aback by the sudden attention, Nicholas hesitated. 'I cannot conceive that my views would engage your lordship.'

'What a damnably prizzy answer! They engage me! Let us hear from you – or have we a Cavalier who has never mounted a charge upon a two-legged filly?' He reached for a flask of brandy as a dutiful gale of laughter greeted this sally.

Geoffrey raised his cup to his lips. 'Do not cross him a second time. Be bawdy, cynical.'

The laughter died as Nicholas eyed Goring. He had probably drunk twice as much as himself, yet his speech was crisp, his eyes alert, but the mouth, which had earlier seemed drawn in pain, was relaxed. 'Strong flanks are essential to any good mount, my lord, yet I could not abide a woman who looked like my horse. Methinks, I rate face and form equally.'

'How, then, would you rate pleasure in women against the bottle?'

The company was still. 'Well, my lord, I must stand firm for women. Would I not be dependent – on the bottle?'

'You are a credit to us, captain! And would you marry for love or money?'

A dangerous man, Geoffrey had said, and he was being led into perilous waters, for all present knew that Goring was heavily subsidised in his lifestyle by his wealthy father-in-law, the Earl of Cork. 'I hope for the best of all worlds, Sir – a treasure strong in both quarters, one might say.'

A burst of merriment had acknowledged each double-entendre. Goring smiled, appreciatively. 'Well said, captain. Keep all your weapons as sharp as your wit and we will make a general of you, yet!' He turned his attention to Geoffrey. 'Captain Knollys, pray pun for us the sentiments of a cavalryman contemplating matrimony.'

Geoffrey sipped his wine, coolly, for a while. 'It is the vogue to express one's sentiments in verse, my lord. Perchance, I should follow the fashion:

A Cavalier must surely falter,
Ere he is led before the halter,
No more to tumble in the hay,
As he was wont, sweet yesterday.
But, saddled now with house and wife
He may prefer the stable life,
And gallop in from park and spinney,
At every stimulating whinny.
Yet those who'd tread the bridle-path,
Should contemplate the aftermath,
When once those frisky calls to play,
Become a disenchanting 'Neigh!'

As his quick-silver mind honed the next verse, the Earl of Cleveland hurried in and Goring held up his hand. 'A palpably sharp performance, captain.'

Cleveland engaged him in brief animated conversation and Goring levered himself to his feet. 'It seems, gentlemen, that the King issued orders that our forces should stand to arms, tonight. I did not receive them. In the meantime, Essex's cavalry have broken through our screen of musketeers covering the road from Lostwithiel to Boconnoc, and are riding pall-mall for Plymouth. You will give chase, Lord Cleveland.'

While the earl hurried away, Goring continued, 'Essex's foot are making for Fowey and the small ports nearby; we must see that they do not escape. To arms then!'

The company tumbled unsteadily into the darkness, where the smoke of torches mingled with the mist. Trumpets and brazen throats brought the cavalry into orderly lines, and Cleveland's force rode away in pursuit.

It began to rain. Soon the narrow road from Lostwithiel to Fowey was a quagmire and almost impassable. Daylight revealed the desperate Paliamentarian foot struggling to keep their cannon and wagons moving. Horses strained and slipped, as whips cracked about their backs, but when rotten harness snapped, equipment was abandoned at the wayside. Before the Royalists' attacks, the infantry were driven from hedge to hedge and, finally, defeated in the ancient entrenchments of Castle Dore, above Fowey. By evening, Essex's left flank was turned cutting him off from Golant, Fowey and Menabilly and, next morning, he fled to Plymouth in a fishing boat, with Robartes and Sir John Merrick. But his cavalry crossed the Tamar and, like himself, found sanctuary in the beleagured port.

It fell to Skippon to make what shift he could for the surrender of his forces. The King's terms were honourable and generous and, on 2nd of September, the slightly-wounded Skippon conceded to him, at Fowey. The defeated army began the long trek home to Portsmouth, threatened and abused as it went.

Two days later, an aide to the King summoned Nicholas to attend upon his royal master. They crossed the River Fowey, to rein in before Lord Mohun's house at Bodinnick Ferry. Nicholas waited, apprehensively, before a pair of doors leading off the great hall and guarded by two motionless Life Guards. Then, he was ushered before a group of three persons. The diminutive centre one, seated, was the King. Attending him , on one side, was his nephew, Prince Maurice, and on the other, Robin Smythe!

Nicholas made a deep bow to his sovereign.

'A good afternoon to you, Captain Skelton. Please to come forward.' The pleasant voice was pitched low to control a stammer.

Nicholas advanced into the room, his eyes on the King. The face was harder and manlier than in the portrait at Trerice, but the aloofness remained. He wore a moustache and narrow, pointed beard, slightly fairer than his hair; his doublet was of royal blue velvet trimmed with gold, the sleeves slashed to reveal a pounced white shirt, beneath. A diagonal sash of lighter blue was overlaid by a deep lace collar and on his breast blazed the star of the Order of the Garter.

'You will recognise your commander, Prince Maurice, but you may be surprised at the presence of Major Smythe.'

Nicholas inclined his head to Prince Maurice and glanced at Robin, who smiled, wryly.

'Sir John Berkeley has vouched for your ability and loyalty and I would have you serve me in a matter requiring courage and discretion.'

'I am Your Majesty's servant.'

'Then know that we are in hope of entering London, on our impending move eastward. There have already been bloody demonstrations in my favour, at Clerkenwell, and we intend to exploit all support from the citizens, by forming a network of sympathisers. The task has been assigned to Major Smythe, who has requested that you work with him.'

'I would be honoured to serve Your Majesty, so.'

'I understand that you may expect short shrift if you are apprehended, having been concerned in the affair of Sir Alexander Carew, while in the service of the Parliament.'

'That will not influence me, Sire.'

'Then, Sir John Berkeley will be instructed to allocate funds from the Mint, for your endeavour. You will first undergo a course of instruction in matters pertaining to your mission, at the home of Edward Gilbey, Esquire.' Briefly unmindful that he had signed away the life of his loyal minister, Thomas Wentworth, Earl of Strafford, to appease the Parliament, the King added, 'You will find that I am not ungrateful to those who serve me well. Go with the Captain, Major Smythe, and may Almighty God favour our endeavours.'

The two soldiers backed to the door, bowing. Outside Robin tried to deflect Nicholas' questions, by drawing a sealed envelope from his buffcoat. 'A *billet doux* from your lady,' he said, grinning broadly.

Nicholas's heart leapt as he touched the envelope, but he looked questioningly at Robin.

'Do not concern yourself, my young gallant, I am in the confidence of Mistress Arundell. She sends you her devoted love, which doubtless she affirms, therein. Away with you to read it. I am lodged at Lord Goring's headquarters and will join you there, later – thence to find a good hostelry with a private room, plenty of ale and a full-blown wench to serve it. There you shall learn what I have planned towards making you a Major.'

Nicholas laughed as they walked to where a trooper held his horse, delighted as always by the bouyant good humour of the big man. Mounting, he spurred back across the River Fowey, uplifted by the prospect of the adventure before them. In his room, he broke open the letter and read eagerly.

'Dearest Love,

I trust that Almighty God is preserving you in health, and safe from injury. For my part I am well and happy, for you should know that Her Majesty the Queen spoke to my guardian concerning us, though he will say only that we should wait upon the conclusion of this war.

We have learned that Her Majesty, although fired upon, reached safety in France, thanks to the speed of her Flemish ship, which sailed two leagues to the Parliamentarians' one.

How I wish hostilities would end and that the King might, once again, assume the position to which God has appointed him.

I yearn for you and will love you always,
Juliana.'

He read the letter twice more, kissed it and placed it inside his tunic. He was under no illusion that the wily old man had blessed his candidacy, but he thanked the royal Frenchwoman who had brought his dream a step nearer fruition.

Early that evening, he and Robin arrived at the Frances of Fowey, for their supper, together. Robin called forth the landlord, his presence dominating the room, ' I am entertaining a senior officer of the King's army. What is your best fare?'

The innkeeper eyed him shrewdly. 'I recommend the goose, followed by apple pie and cheese and accompanied by a bottle or two of burgundy.'

'Have you a private room?'

'That I have, sir.'

'Then show us to it and send up a bottle straightway – your Cornish roads are devilish dusty. Have you a comely maid to serve us?'

'I think I can promise that.'

He led the way up a staircase of black oak and admitted them to a room overlooking the harbour. Within the oriel window stood a heavy table and chairs. Robin looked out at the ships rocking at anchor. 'Admirable, landlord.'

As the innkeeper hurried away, Robin drew out a chair, divesting himself of hat and sword. 'What does it feel like to be an important officer?'

Nicholas grinned. 'I wish you had called me "General", for age seems to pose no obstacle to rank.'

'Be patient, I have no plans to advance you beyond Major.'

They watched a girl enter with wine and goblets. Her skin was smooth and olive, the bone structure of face and nose delicate and proud. Black hair fell in ringlets about her shoulders. She smiled, gravely, poured the wine and left, without speaking. Robin stared after her. 'God's wounds, what a beauty!'

Food was brought in by a mature woman in the same image as the girl. When they were alone, Nicholas surmised, 'Perchance, they are mother and daughter, and of Spanish descent – from a survivor of the Armada or a raid on the coast.'

'If they are typical daughters of Spain, 'tis a pity so many ships were blown up to Scotland.' Robin feigned apprehension. 'I doubt my customary slap on the buttocks would have been appreciated.'

Supper concluded, Nicholas raised his goblet. 'God save King Charles for not living off the land and depriving us of this pleasure. And congratulations on your promotion to Major.'

The girl came back with brandy and Robin's brow furrowed in concentration. 'Now, m'lad, for the serious business. I believe 'tis a forlorn hope that the King may enter London – the capital is strong for the Parliament. Be that as it may, our task is to identify his support and mould it. It is a long-term objective, permitting us a month in the country to equip you for your part. 'Tis my task to make a swordsman of you! You will also acquire some ability in the French language which is more than I could hope for, being no scholar. And you must learn coding and markmanship, not forgetting the geography of London.'

'Excellent accomplishments for a gentleman,' Nicholas reflected. 'You seem only to have overlooked dancing lessons!'

'Be sure you master them, for they may stand you in good stead.'

Robin called for the account. While paying the innkeeper, he idly examined a crown in his hand. 'Under Christ's protection I rule,' he read aloud. 'His Majesty is in no doubt of his divine right. The pity is his subjects are not all of like mind.'

Outside, as they turned for St. Blazey, the big man said, 'Tonight, I shall dream of that beautiful girl, but I fear it will not be long ere some gentleman wins her hand.'

'A gentleman would not be likely to court an innkeeper's daughter and, no doubt, she is a Catholic.'

'Give me but half a chance! Could you picture me wed to her and host at the inn?'

'You as landlord, I see clearly. The rest is not so easy.'

Robin bellowed with laughter as they set their mounts along the road back.

CHAPTER 8

The Aftermath

As they crossed the brown wilderness of Bodmin Moor, on their journey to Gilbey's house, the first survivors from Essex's army appeared ahead of them. The thin straggle of men spared no glance for the passing horsemen, but shuffled on, shoulders bent, eyes downcast. There were men with nothing but torn remnants of clothing girding their nakedness; others were unshod – feet rent by flints. A woman exposed to the waist, her back livid with wheals, dragged a soldier along till he pitched forward, dragging her down with him and they lay together, in abject despair. Ahead there were hundreds more, wet hair clinging to their faces and necks, white flesh glistening under the rain, which had begun to fall again. There were saturated bandages, suppurating wounds and, occasionally, a still figure, face down in the mud.

'Savage vengeance for savage spoilation,' Robin observed morosely. 'Truly an eye for an eye.'

The moor left behind, they came towards a large barn, set back from the road and approached by a narrow track. From it, there came a faint cry of anguish. Glancing at each other, they spurred up the track and across the dung-slurried cobbles of the yard. Suddenly, the postern was flung open, four roughly-clad men emerged and made for the fields behind.

Inside, a hulking fellow stood in the straw, hauling up his breeches. At his feet lay the body of a woman, the ivory orbs of her breasts exposed, her skirt flung carelessly across her thighs. Drawing his pistol, Robin demanded, 'What Devil's work is this?'

Nicholas went to a second figure sprawled on the earth floor, turned it over and groaned with dismay. It was James Salter, and he had been killed by a terrible blow to the head. Numb with foreboding, he went to the woman. She was young and her loose clothing showed she had once been buxom. Matted, fair hair obscured her features. He gently brushed away the hair, revealing an ugly contusion on the left temple. 'Dear God!' He rose and turned away.

Robin struck the man in the face and he dropped, senseless, blood and saliva trickling from his mouth. 'Nicholas!' Robin was shaking his shoulder. 'Do you know the young woman?'

'Yes.'

'She has been used like a camp follower. Who is she?'

'Wife to James Salter, there, who gave me my freedom on St. Nicholas' Island. She is – she was – Janet Tremain, the daughter of my cowman at Trewhella Barton.'

Robin stooped to look at her wedding band. 'I swear she is not dead!' he cried.

Nicholas dropped to his knee beside the girl. She was unconscious, but a small pulse beat in her neck. 'Praise be to God.' He drew the tattered blouse together and covered her with his cloak.

'Stay with her while I find transport.' Robin pointed to the black-bearded man. 'Brook no dispute with him – spit him if needs be.'

Nicholas remained looking down at the motionless girl. Sweet Janet, you were already in love with James when he rode away from Trewhella, healed by your gentle hands. Did you tramp behind him all the way from Plymouth? What drabs and harlots have you consorted with? So many questions to be answered.

He began piling straw at the entrance to the barn, to cushion Janet's journey. Hearing movement behind, he went to the felled man. Although snoring obscenely, he showed signs of returning consciousness. A wave of hatred swept Nicholas and he drew his blade as the man coughed, opened his eyes and spat blood. Nicholas presented his sword to the stubble at his throat. 'What is your name?'

Blackbeard stared up at him without replying, till he applied pressure and drew a thin ooze of blood. 'Bartholomew Grimes', he answered, thickly.

'Named after a saint were you? An irony, that! Now the names of your accomplices in this perfidy?' He prodded harder with the steel and the man muttered four names, which Nicholas committed to memory. 'Are you Roundhead deserters?' he demanded.

As Grimes appeared to be lapsing into unconsciousness, he released the sword from his throat. Immediately, the eyes opened and a hamlike fist shot upwards and struck him on the cheekbone, as he bent forward for a closer look. Lights exploded in his brain, as his attacker hooked one foot around his heel and jerked. He staggered backwards against a stall as the man leapt up and closed with him. His sword arm was clasped, fiercely, and a palm thrust under his chin. Slowly, he was bent backwards over the stall rail until his spine seemed about to break and breathing became impossible. His senses reeled; there was an explosion in his mind. The hand slid from his face, the grip on his arm relaxed and the heavy body slid to the floor. Robin, a smoking pistol in his hand, bent over the body.

'Is he dead?' Nicholas croaked.

'Yes.' Robin straightened and pointed outside, where a cart was waiting with two Royalist soldiers sitting on the box.

They wrapped Janet in the cloak and laid her gently in the wagon. With James's body at her feet, they rumbled downhill, through the buttresed Southgate, into Launceston. 'We are going to the castle,' Robin explained. 'It is mostly in ruins, but some houses in the ditch survive, as makeshift accommodation for the garrison, and there are women there.'

They jolted through the market square and passed under the jagged remains of the south gatehouse, to a line of timbered-framed houses, where James' body was removed. Robin hurried away, to return with two capable-looking goodwives and they carried Janet into the sick quarters. When that was done, Robin went to make peace with the Constable and ask for a surgeon to examine her. Nicholas waited in a small garden till he returned, accompanied by an army surgeon, who told him that Janet's only serious injury was the head wound. 'Her skull is not broken' he added, 'and when she recovers consciousness we will move her to more suitable quarters at Madford House. It will distress her further to learn of her husband's death. It would be best if you broke it to her – I understand she knows you.'

Nicholas nodded. 'I must also bury her husband.'

Robin had arranged overnight accommodation at the Bell Inn. At supper, he grew impatient as his friend lapsed into drunkeness and tried to goad him out of his mood. 'After we have done at Edward Gilbey's, I swear you will never again fall victim to such crude oafs as today's specimen. That villain was unconscious when I left you – when I returned you were near to having your back broken. At the first sign of trouble, you should have spitted him.'

'You are right. Should I ever come across his companions, I will not be caught so.'

Robin slipped an arm through his and heaved him to his feet. 'Be that as it may its bed for you, my lad.'

Next morning, with throbbing head and sour stomach, he went down to the stableyard and found a groom to pump water over him. As he pulled on his shirt, he noticed that the sky above the weathercock was showing patches of blue. A musketeer hurried across the cobbles. 'The young woman 'as come round sir.'

At the sick quarters he was met by Janet's nurses. At the sound of his step, in her whitewashed room, Janet opened her eyes, recognition dawning. 'Oh, Maister Skelton!'

He took her hand. 'How are you feeling, Janet?'

'Well enough, I thank ye.'

There was silence between them. How could he tell her? Should she ask first, how would he answer? He patted her hand self-consciously.

'Don't 'e fret,' she said, 'for I know about James, I saw it 'appen.'

'Who did it?'

'One of five villains – they called 'im Zeb. James tried to stop another, black-bearded devil from takin' me in the straw, while t'others stood around urging 'im on. This Zeb 'it James with an axe.' She shuddered.

'James will be avenged.'

She lowered her eyes. 'That villain never 'ad me, sir. Nobody's ever 'ad me, but my James.'

'How came you to be there and to get that bruise on your head?'

She hesitated, as if reluctant to begin. Then, she said, 'James were demoted for letting you escape from St. Nicholas Island. Then, later, 'e were sent to join the Earl of Essex's army and I followed 'im. We saw terrible things in that valley near Fowey. Them Royalists 'ad us like rats in a barrel, but we survived, some'ow After the surrender, we joined the stragglers going east, afeared to be on our own. But after a time anything seemed better than that misery, so we turned north, thinking to go back to Llandhyrock over Bodmin Moor, away from people. We was sleeping in that barn when them renegades come upon us.'

'And the bruise?' Nicholas repeated

'I tried to save James.' She turned her head away and closed her eyes. As he watched, a tear ran along her nose and on to the white pillow. She looked back at him, 'That villain never 'ad me, sir.' Nobody's ever 'ad me but my 'usband.'

He nodded. 'James will be avenged.'

Gently releasing her hand, he crept from the room. Recognising the nurse as one who had taken Janet into their care, the previous day, he asked, 'Do you know if she has been ravaged?'

The woman looked at the floor before answering, quietly, 'She has.'

As he left the sick quarters, Robin arrived with his horse and troopers at his back. 'How is she?'

'Conscious.'

'Good. We are going hunting.'

'Hunting? I have a burial to arrange.'

'Tis all in hand. A chaplain will visit Mistress Salter and establish her husband's creed. The burial is tomorrow. Meanwhile, we command 20 men to search for the creatures who ran from the barn.'

'When we find them, leave the one called Zeb to me.'

From the barn, they followed the direction the men had taken, across the wet fields. The air was warm and humid and thin mist hung in the hollows and around the boles of the trees. After about four miles, the ground rose and lush pasture gave way to moorland turf.

Robin halted and leaned towards Nicholas. 'Now, my apprentice agent, how shall we proceed from here? How far? Which way?'

Nicholas was thoughtful. 'We last saw them 16 hours since. If they have progressed three miles in each hour, rested, foraged and moved on they will not be more than 15 miles away. '

'In which direction are they heading?'

'Essex's troops were recruited in the eastern counties, but these are footloose deserters, intent on survival and spoilation, not on heading homewards. They have ravaged the south-west and will fear to return there. Let us continue in the line they have taken, thus far, and sweep west and north-west of it, in two groups.'

Robin nodded agreement. 'We will extend each group to the limit of man-to-man contact – 'tis not too difficult over moorland. Ride for an hour, then turn back.' He paused and heeled his horse closer to Nicholas. 'Should you find them, do not take upon yourself the role of judge and jury. That is work for the county justices.'

They rode on through bracken and rock, climbing steadily, until Nicholas, in the centre of the line, arrived at the foot of the tor called Brown Willy. Below, the moor ran away to its western extremity, the River Camel and, to the north, he made out the stone huts and circles of a pre-historic settlement. Shadows of cloud scurried across the landscape as the sky cleared. Then the sun burst out, sharpening the greens and russets and yellow gorse. Along the De Lank river, four figures were moving.

Signalling his party to close up, he advanced at a canter until the group ahead saw them and broke towards a towering outcrop of rock – a natural fortress – and disappeared among its craggy contours.

Nicholas cursed. On the open moor, they were no match for cavalry, but, among those rocks, they were a different proposition. Encircling the outcrop with his men, he tightened the ring till a first musket ball sang past his head and he ordered the troops to take cover behind the scattered boulders. With carabines at the ready, they ran from rock to rock till they reached the base of the upward slope.

'I order you to surrender!'

His challenge was answered with another shot. A further advance evoked a fusillade of shots, but, now, they were among the lower rocks of the stronghold and into the fissures above. Nicholas looked upward, at the instant a man stepped into his path and levelled a pistol. He saw the finger crooked around the trigger begin to squeeze. There was a shot.

The man stared at him, dully, as his knees sagged and the pistol discharged into the thin soil at his feet. Nicholas glanced over his shoulder, to where one of his troopers was preparing to reload his carabine. He began to climb, again, over the motionless figure and upward. Other shots sounded among the rocks and twice he heard a cry.

Ahead the granite opened out into a small arena of grass, in which one of the fugitives was standing. A trooper appeared on the rocks above and leapt down, sword in hand. The man fired the pistol he held and the soldier landed and pitched forward, his blade falling at the other's feet.

Nicholas scrambled out of the confining rock-cleft, drawing his sword, ducking as his adversary hurled the empty pistol. Scooping up the cavalryman's sword, his quarry stood poised as Nicholas came at him. He was broad-shouldered, powerful, with a fierce scar spanning cheek and forehead and his swordplay was crude but robust. The sheer ferocity of the attack drove Nicholas backwards until he felt the unyielding rock face behind. Believing his victim to be, virtually, on a chopping block, his assailant made a wild sweep with his blade, as Nicholas lunged forward and pierced his heart.

With his force reassembled he found that he had suffered one fatality – the trooper who had saved his life. Of the renegades, one was dead and three were captured. He approached the prisoners. 'Is one of you called Zeb?' They pointed to the body of the man Nicholas had spitted and for the only time in his life he took cold satisfaction from the act of killing.

◘◘◘

When the simple coffin had been lowered into the grave, Nicholas took a handful of brown earth and sprinkled it, reverently, into the shallow pit, then he drew the chaplain aside and asked him to take Janet to Antony House, with a letter for Lady Carew.

Later he told Robin, his tone inviting comment, 'I believe it best that Janet should go to Antony rather than return to the Barton'

'Do you not think that she should return to her father?'

'I am not sure. Matthew Tremain is a simple man, not equipped to deal with a problem of the mind, and I fear for her reason, if she returns to the place where she met James. Jane Carew is a sensitive, compassionate lady and I believe Janet will fare best at Antony.'

Robin nodded. 'One day, men may draw fear and horror from the mind as we draw blood with the leech or poison with the poultice. Till then, compassion and understanding must suffice.'

He left Robin and walked to the infirmary. Janet lay motionless, but she stirred as he entered. 'How are you today?' he whispered.

'Right enough, sir. 'As my man been decently buried?'

'Yes, it was properly done.'

'May the Lord receive 'im into 'is Kingdom.'

'Amen! Zebediah Lambert is dead.'

She was thoughtful for a moment. 'God's will be done.'

'I cannot stay longer, but the chaplain will take you to Lady Carew, when you are able to travel. She will care for you till you are fully restored – unless you prefer to return home?'

'Oh no!' she responded, emphatically, 'At Antony 'er ladyship and I will be two lonely souls together. Mayhap we shall draw comfort from one another.'

He nodded. ''Tis true she needs comfort, at this time.'

The merest glimmer of a smile lit her eyes. 'You'm a good man, sir, and I 'ope you win your lovely lady for you deserve 'er.' He pressed her hand, much moved.

'She is going to be alright,' he told Robin, as he threw his saddle bags across his horse. They mounted and rode out under the stableyard arch towards the home of Edward Gilbey.

CHAPTER 9

The King's Agents

They sat at board with the Gilbeys, Robin dressed in a suit of maroon velvet, with snow-white lace at throat and cuffs. He was in his element, as he regaled the company with stories of London life before the war, occasionally glancing at Letitia, to be sure he held her attention. He need not have feared, for she was spellbound. But her eyes twinkled mischievously, as she said, 'Major Smythe, you are either a very wicked man or you have an artist's gift for adding light and shade in the telling of your tales.'

Her mother laid a reproving hand on her sleeve, but the raconteur beamed, affably, as he reached for the pewter cup at his elbow. Gilbey's silver had long since gone to finance the King's cause. 'My reputation for telling stories is well-founded, Mistress Gilbey, I confess, but tomorrow I shall write a new chapter in the life of our farmer, as I make a swordsman of him.'

Gilbey caught Nicholas' brief frown and understood. Smythe was a delightful fellow but he was a little overbearing in drink and had no cause to patronise his companion, whose manners were perfect, his mind sharp and informed. Bluff and blunt, Smythe was a broadsword of a man, his companion a rapier. It was this antithesis which draw them together. As the King's spymaster in the west, Gilbey had to be a shrewd judge of men and the dark Cavalier was well suited to the task ahead. So different from the confused, young Roundhead of a year gone. Though intellectually superior to Smythe, he would be hard put to it in physical contention with his doughty friend and Gilbey quietly relished the prospect of observing their encounters, as sconces of candles were brought in to hold the lengthening September shadows at bay.

Master and pupil were astir early. As they stepped on to the terrace, in shirt and breeches, the morning air struck dank and chill, but somewhere above, undaunted, a lark was in song. Robin tossed a blunted practice sword to his pupil. 'This is the on-guard position. Before we begin your instruction, show me if they taught you anything at all in the Parliamentary army. On guard!'

Nicholas circled the big man, noting his poise and balance. Suddenly, he mounted a compound attack with a series of reprises, swiftly executed, which brought an expression of surprise to Robin's face. From a first-floor window, Gilbey watched with interest. At the edge of the steps from the terrace, Robin halted the attack. Cat-like, he turned Nicholas, counter-attacked and drove him back. The cadence of Robin's attack was infinitely varied and difficult to counter, but a trompement deceived his opponent's parry and Nicholas came at him again, with a series of swift skips and runs. For several minutes, the duel continued – feint, parry, reprise, riposte – until with a swinging circular movement, Robin sent his adversary's sword arcing over the balustrade into the roses below.

The victor mopped his brow, 'Zounds, but you are a deep one, my Cavalier. The Parliamentarians did not teach you those tricks, I'll be bound. Confess your secret!'

Nicholas laughed, 'You have the secrets,' he called ruefully, from the flower bed, 'but what skills I have were learned from the fencing-master at Antony.'

'Then I am resolved that all future lessons will be held in the stableyard, away from the house. I will not have the fair Letitia see me chased around the terrace like a scalded cat.'

During the next fortnight, the two men were in daily contention, with lunging, flicking blades or locked together in wrestling holds. Nicholas's skill in the latter had been non-existent, when they began, and he retired to bed each night strained in every muscle. Gradually, the aches eased and the bruising became less frequent, but he concluded the instruction without regret, for the brutish art was not to his taste. Skill with the sword, however, was deeply satisfying, as it had been at Antony, but, there, the live steel had held no connotation with sudden death. The remaining hours were spent practising markmanship with musket and pistol, and Gilbey's quiet parkland echoed with the roar of exploding powder and the cries of flighted birds.

The evenings were a congenial climax to the day, for his friend's fund of yarns never failed and, whenever he paused to quench his thirst, their host was ready with some topic of discussion or observation. His wife proved an unfailingly gracious hostess and Letitia, who had grown even prettier and more poised since Nicholas' earlier sojourn, basked in the attention of their guests.

While the two stood on the terrace, the night sounds of the country about them and the smell of Robin's pipe in the air, the big man observed, 'This is preferable to being pent up in Pendennis or hounding Essex through the lanes of Cornwall. And what a splendid girl Letitia is – somehow like a bowl of cream. You know, Nicholas, I may make a declaration of my feelings to her before we depart this house.'

Nicholas regarded the profile of his friend against the light from the house. It was apparent that, at 32 years of age, he was experiencing a deep-felt urge to settle down, after years of professional soldiering and adventure. It was also evident that he interested and amused Letitia, but he had seen no sign that the girl held more tender feelings for him. He hoped that he would not be hurt, for he was a proud man. Receiving no response Robin glanced at him, but he remained silent.

The next day Geoffrey Knollys arrived. Edward Gilbey asked Robin and Nicholas to join them in the study. Nicholas greeted his comrade-in-arms enthusiastically, but Robin, outwardly cordial, viewed with misgiving the arrival of this stranger with the sharp, refined features and composed manner. 'Captain Knollys is to be the third man in your triumvirate gentlemen,' Gilbey told them. 'He is fluent in French and an expert in coding – he will be responsible for the other half of your instruction and will accompany you on this mission.'

With Geoffrey's arrival, the pattern of the evening entertainments changed. Letitia played the clavichord and accompanied Knollys, as he sang in a pleasant baritone voice and, sometimes, Nicholas spoke verse. Robin continued to amuse them with his irreverent humour, but he no longer held the stage and seemed positively subdued when Latitia's gentle eye rested upon Geoffrey.

One morning, Nicholas found Robin unusually aggressive in practice and, when they had concluded, he smiled, apologetically. 'You have been the undeserving recipient of my ill humour, engendered, I confess, by base jealousy. Glad I am that I said nought of my feelings to Letitia, for I perceive that she is greatly taken with friend Geoffrey. God's teeth!' he exploded in frustration, 'I long to take a young woman to wed, but I lack the graces to make a conquest.'

Nicholas nodded sympathetically, 'You are an honest fellow, Robin and have the great gift of humour. It will stand you in good stead at the right time.'

'Would that I had Geoffrey's manner. He is such a self-effacing fellow, one can only guess at his accomplishments.'

'Then mark him well, for he has the style of a gentleman.'

▣▣▣

In late September, the adventurers bade farewell to the Gilbeys and called upon Sir John Berkeley, at Exeter, to obtain bills of exchange for the financing of their enterprise. As he handed the documents to Robin, Berkeley said, 'You are to join up with the King's army and travel with them till they turn for Oxford. Thereafter, you must ride alone.' He singled out Nicholas. 'My information is that Sir Alexander Carew will come to trial, shortly. If he is condemned, you will bear witness to his last hour and report back to me. If his family eschew him right to the end, you will offer what consolation you can to Lady Jane Carew. I wish you all good fortune and God's protection.'

The possibility of further involvement in Alexander's personal tragedy sobered Nicholas and both friends were sympathetic of his mood, particularly Geoffrey – conscious of his own involvement in the affair. During a meal of cold victuals at the Ship Inn, he said, jocularly, 'Twas here those two strumpets seduced you, the day you were made captain.'

Nicholas flushed, for was not Robin the confidante of Juliana? But the big man's eyes immediately kindled with mirth. 'What's this? First I am surprised by your prowess as a swordsman, now I learn of unconfessed cut-and-thrust with taproom whores. You are a bold fellow to pleasure yourself so.'

Nicholas was spared a reply, for Geoffrey continued, 'They were no whores but the daughters of a Welsh goldsmith who was visiting Sir Richard Vyvyan.'

Robin slapped his thigh. 'In mint condition, then!'

Their roar of merriment caused the merchants and lawyers about the room to smile, indulgently, at the three roisterers. 'I must not deceive friends – as a seduction it was a failure,' he confessed.

'How so ?'

'We were celebrating my appointment, when my funds ran out. I went to my room to find a crown or two more. In a drunken error, I entered the room next door and beheld two black-haired witches in their petticoats, preparing for an evening engagement. With senses aflame, I swept across the room, encompassed one in each arm and fell upon the bed with them. Their giggling enthusiasm matched my own, which was nothing lacking, for I encountered their undraped buttocks clefted and smooth as a peach. Unhappily, while attempting to consolidate my position upon one of them, I fell from the bed with the damsel atop me and my head made the first contact with the floor.

This sobered me, somewhat, and allowed their Welsh Puritanism to override their natural inclinations. I came to my feet ensnared by baldrick and sword and made an apologetic exit, in some trepidation. Fortunately, they did not make issue of the matter, but they gave me a very knowing look as I swept them a flourish upon their departure, the next morning.'

'A knowing look?' Robin mocked. 'A poor reward for such enterprise!'

'And no basis for your subsequent reputation as a philanderer *par excellence*,' Geoffrey added.

Robin looked benignly upon the young Cavalier, bound in honour to the exquisite Juliana. 'Come,' he said, rising from the bench, 'we ride for His Majesty.'

They met up with the King as he left Chard and integrated with the marching column. Robin soon had news of events. 'George Goring has taken Barnstaple, but Plymouth, Lyme, Taunton and Weymouth remain loyal to the Parliament,' he told them. 'This army has transportation problems, for people along the way oppose the requisitioning of their oxen to draw artillery and baggage trains.'

Nicholas was sympathetic. 'Who can blame them – they are needed for autumn ploughing.'

'I trust that we shall not be deprived of our funds, for the King also lacks money for horses and clothing and has been dependent upon the Commissioners of Devon to provide both.'

Geoffrey turned in the saddle and surveyed the banners floating over the long line of horse and foot. 'Where are the Cornish?' he asked.

'Some are here, under Prince Maurice, but more are west of the Tamar, I wager,' Nicholas replied. ''Tis devilish difficult to lure a Cornishman far from home. They will follow only their traditional leaders, and then mainly in defence of their families and acres.'

□□□

Nights were spent in the open and, when the sun had set, they sought comfort from the chill air around the camp fire, where Robin never failed to produce a flask of wine. It was at South Pernot, west of Sherborne, that they watched Prince Rupert of the Rhine ride in at the head of his escort. Sitting tall and erect in the saddle, he looked sternly handsome, yet there was an expression on his face that was both gentle and melancholy.

As the column passed through the ranks of cheering troops, to halt before the house of Lord Paulet – the King's lodging – Rupert dismounted and knelt at the feet of his uncle. Charles Stuart embraced him, affectionately, for he was the son of his sister, Elizabeth of Bohemia, and they were devoted to one another.

'You are looking at the most successful cavalry commander of this war', murmured Robin, 'though 'tis said that, with the death of his white dog, Boy, from whom he was inseparable, his familiar spirit has left him and his luck with it.'

'He fought with George Goring at the Siege of Breda,' Nicholas volunteered.

'That shared experience hardly seems to have endeared the one to the other,' Geoffrey commented

'What age would he be?'

'About 25' said Geoffrey. 'If you seek to equate age with responsibility, Sir Bevill Grenville's son, John – knighted at Bristol last year – is with the army, here. He is only 16!'

Rupert turned to dismiss his force and the dark cloak swung aside, revealing breeches and doublet of rich turquoise. The King moved into the house, Rupert following hat in hand, to report on the state of his forces at Bristol.

□□□

The Royalist army tramped on over undulating downs, chalk-scarred and sparse of trees – much as Roman and Saxon had done before them – until they came to the flat land around Salisbury. Guided by the slim spire of its cathedral, they trudged wearily into the city for a brief respite. By late October, they were north-east of Newbury, where the King took quarters in the great mansion of Shaw, its park littered with the dead brown leaves of autumn. The house was within shot of Donnington Castle, held stoutly for his monarch by Sir John Boys, for over a year.

The King's potential adversary, Sir William Waller, had eluded him and joined with the Earl of Manchester, coming from the north, but it was clear that action would not be long postponed. With Maurice and his Cornishmen, the three friends took position on a rise just west of the village of Speen and watched the clamour and bustle of an army preparing for battle. To their right lay the town of Newbury and the River Kennet, while their left flank rested upon the River Lambourne, which ran across the northern outskirts of the town. In the centre, Shaw House served as a formidable strongpoint. North-east lay Donnington Castle and, beyond Newbury, the village of Shaw.

The day had advanced to mid-afternoon, when Waller struck with 800 musketeers of Essex's army and four regiments of Aldridge's brigade. As the shadows lengthened, pressure on Maurice increased, for the Parliamentarians, recognising the Cornish who had plundered and tormented them on the retreat from Lostwithiel charged furiously up the slopes.

'Gad,' shouted Robin, 'see how they attack the cannon.'

'Small wonder,' Nicholas yelled, 'they are the same pieces we captured in the Fowey valley.'

Robin did not reply for a musketeer, physically almost his equal, was upon him, slashing viciously. Parrying the blow, Robin drove his swordpoint under the enemy's chin and he fell. Another surge of Parliamentary infantry broke through to the cannon and covered the touch holes with their hats. Then, they were through the guns and upon them. From the corner of his eye, Nicholas saw Geoffrey's swordarm moving swiftly and expertly, as the desperate onslaught drove them out of their redoubt and back into Speen. The London Brigade stormed after them, sending them reeling down Shaw Road and away from the village.

With the capture of the village, Skippon busied himself with repossessing his artillery and the pressure eased, briefly. But the guns of Donnington pounded on and Goring, at the head of 800 troopers, dashed at Oliver Cromwell's leading squadrons so fiercely that he sent them back in confusion. With the light failing, Maurice drew in his survivors and the Royalist army marched away through a gap between Shaw House and the Castle – bunching dangerously as they poured over a small bridge spanning Lambourne – and slipped away to Wallingford, the battle undecided.

Geoffrey looked at his friends, drawing breath and cleaning their weapons. Like himself, they had suffered superficial wounds, which he dressed. 'A hot action,' he commented, as he tied the last knot and repacked his saddlebags. 'What think you of my Lord Goring's charge?'

'The gentleman has panache! But what a paradox – one moment dynamic, the next wayward and idle. He cuts a better figure astride a horse than he does with a bottle,' Nicholas replied.

Geoffrey moved to the far side of his horse, to check a girth, and Nicholas murmured to Robin, 'Our friend is a fine swordsman.'

Robin grinned wryly. 'It had not escaped me and we may again be grateful for it, as we were today.'

'How did we extricate ourselves?'

'We may thank Goring, Donnington's guns and the defenders of Shaw House, who repelled a late attack from the Earl of Manchester.'

A stocky foot soldier in the Grenville livery came to Nicholas, tears in his eyes. 'Begging a word wi' ye, sir.'

'What is it, sergeant?'

'As you'm a Cornishman, sir, we thought ye should know that Sir John Grenville be dead.'

Nicholas stood quite still, the levity born of survival drained from him, 'How came he to his end?'

The soldier swallowed. 'Killed in the field, sir. They'm bringing his body in, now. We'll be taking it back to Stowe, like we did his faither's.'

'Thank you for telling me, sergeant. I share your grief.'

Flicking the brim of his hat, the infantryman made towards his lines and Nicholas turned to Robin, 'I mind Juliana saying that Sir Bevill was the glass wherein youth did dress themselves. Now his inspiration is no more and neither is his son's. Poor Lady Grace.'

Robin pressed him gently towards his horse and, from the saddle, they watched the rear of the Royalist army disappear along the road to Oxford.

On 23rd of November, the King re-entered his temporary capital, in triumph. His agents, meanwhile, journeyed on to London – the true seat of power.

CHAPTER 10

Capital Investment

From a window in one of the tall, newly-built houses lining Piccadilly, Robert Baker watched the street scene below. As a mercer, grown wealthy from trade in the fashionable ruffs and collars – piccadills – he had an eye for style. For this reason, he looked again at three, approaching horsemen. Their apparel was quite unremarkable – like any moderately – successful merchants – but it would have been a bold footpad, indeed, who demanded their purse. The big man with red hair and beard was the most flamboyant, but the lean-featured, elegant one would have graced any soiree. The youngest, who looked Celtic,was strikingly handsome. Most curious!

Unaware of this appraisal, Robin gazed, nostalgically, about him. He was home!

They came into The Strand and the press of people swelled. Huge wedge-shaped coaches, ornate and tassel-hung, lumbered by. Stage-wagons sought openings in the traffic, but each space that appeared was, immediately, filled with sedan-chairs, carts and horsemen. Their nostrils were assailed by the myriad smells of the city – the stink of humanity, of dung, sweating horses, baking bread and, as they passed the open door of a hostelry, of meat pies cooking. A barefoot child darted from the curb to beg a penny, skilfully dodging the hard hooves of coach horses. A girl stooped to don a wooden yoke from which two pails depended and her creamy breasts and shoulders reminded Nicholas of poor, voluptuous Janet. He looked at the great square bulk of Northumberland House, a tower at each corner, tall chimneys soaring above the gables. Robin's hand gripped his arm. 'There is Arundell House, town home of the Earls of Arundell.' He grinned, sardonically. 'A prospective relative, mayhap!'

Nicholas laughed. 'It's true that the Arundells of Trerice are related through marriage to the Fitz-Alans.'

'London looks much bigger than I remember it,' Geoffrey remarked. 'It seems to have spread westward.'

'The smoke has become unbearable in the city and the nobles have been leaving it in favour of these outlying parts,' Robin replied. 'Besides the nobility prefer not to live cheek by jowl with the merchants – though they need our money,' he concluded with a great bellow of laughter.

They turned towards the Thames, drawing aside as a detachment of London Grey-coats marched past followed by one of the trained bands. 'All this soldiery makes me nervous,' Robin declared. 'Let us to the Swan inn on the river bank, it shall be our headquarters.'

◘◘◘

For the next month, the Cavaliers busied themselves establishing a network of Royalist sympathisers and contacts. Down river, they built on the rudimentary organisation which the King had confided to Robin, through which he identified sea captains willing to bring in cargoes of weapons and munitions, if the price were right. Such men were not difficult to buy, for these were hard times and there was little foreign trade to occupy and reward them. But the work was dangerous and the possibility of discovery, by spies and informers for the Parliament, ever present.

One dark evening in early November, with smoke-laden fog hanging about the Thames, Robin and Nicholas made their way towards a French barque moored below the Tower at Wapping. Robin had arranged a meeting with the captain through the English mate, who he had met in a nearby tavern, the previous day. Fearing the contact unreliable, the big man had charged Geoffrey to follow them as rearguard. 'I like not this assignation,' he had said. 'Last year, the Londoners built 18 miles of defence works and forts, running from the river's edge, upstream of Horse Ferry, through Pimlico and around the north of the city to meet the river again, at Wapping. It follows that any escape route, east along the river, is completely blocked by this wall.'

'Then we must pray there is no treachery,' Nicholas commented.

'Pray by all means, but be prepared.'

With the fog muffling all sound, they stole along the wharf until the barque loomed above them. At the foot of the gangplank leading to its deck, Robin turned and peered into the grey gloom behind. There was no sign of Geoffrey.

As they came aboard, the burly figure of the captain materialised and beckoned them towards the stern cabin.

'My friend will stay on deck,' Robin said.

'There is no need. The ship is deserted.'

'Nevertheless, he will stay here.'

'*Ça no fait rien!*' The captain shrugged.

Nicholas waited at the head of the plank, in the eerie pall. The fog clawed at his throat and he coughed quietly. There was movement ashore! He listened, intently, as the sound increased, the hollow ring of boots on timber. Breastplates and casques gleamed, dully, as a body of troops appeared out of the murk. 'Halt!' An officer stepped forward, a seaman at his shoulder. 'Whoever is aboard, come ashore, in the name of the Parliament.'

'Hold on, sir, I'll fetch the cap'n,' Nicholas feigned.

'Hurry, then, and no trickery.'

He strode towards the cabin as Robin and the captain emerged, alerted by the voices. 'The mate has betrayed us,' Nicholas whispered.

'Over the port side, there is a boat. Take lt! Go, quickly!' the master urged.

Footsteps on the gangplank drew them to the starboard bulwark. As the officer appeared, Robin placed the sole of his boot in his midriff and pushed. The soldier staggered, lost his footing and pitched into the dark water between wharf and ship. The splash animated the group, below, and someone yelled, 'Get a rope, a net, anything.'

'Grab this and heave!' Robin indicated the heavy plank and between them they pitched it into the water, after the Roundhead.

The captain urged them towards the port side. 'Into the dinghy, I will cast you off. *Allez'vite!*'

Their searching hands found the mooring rope and while Nicholas half-slid, half-climbed, down, Robin whisked a purse from his doublet and scooped a handful of coins from it. 'Payment for the dinghy,' he said, thrusting the money into the Frenchman's hand.

As he straddled the rail, the other man grabbed his arm. 'I am still at your service.'

'But you have been exposed.'

'Captain de Vries was not born yesterday, *mon ami. Allez!*' He released Robin's arm and began shouting, 'Quickly, come aboard, they are escaping!'

Robin dropped into the boat as Nicholas deployed the oars. 'The tide is coming in.'

'Then head up river.'

Nicholas pulled strongly away, as a shot hummed, overhead, and they slid into the swirling fog. For several minutes, Robin cogitated in silence. 'He's a Breton and a cool one at that. I am minded to take him at his word and contact him again.'

'When he comes out of gaol.'

'It's his word against the mate's and he is a foreign national, so they must tread warily. I think the good captain will weather the storm.'

'And I think we are putting our heads in a noose working with such people!'

'You are probably right, but we have no choice.'

He rowed cautiously on, Robin watching the way ahead, until the water grew increasingly agitated. Nicholas ceased rowing. 'What is that?'

'It must be Morice's water-wheel, by the first arch of London Bridge. Go carefully!' Almost at once they were engulfed by the span and great piers of the bridge, while the nearby wheel rumbled, alarmingly, in the stygian darkness. Then they were through and into the lighter darkness beyond.'

'What is Morice's water-wheel?' Nicholas asked curiously.

'It was devised by Peter Morice, a Dutch servant of Sir Christopher Hatton, to pump piped water over the steeple of St. Magnust Church, at the north end of London Bridge, and through the streets to Leadenhall, the highest point of the city. When the tide rises, the water issues from four spouts, one in each direction, to serve the houses in the adjoining streets and swill the channels through Bishopsgate, Aldgate, the bridge and the Stock's market.'

There was a long silence while Nicholas conserved his energy. When Robin judged that they were in the area of Westminster stairs, he instructed him to ease the boat towards the Thames' northern edge and they drifted gently along, straining to read the names of the moored ships.

'There she is,' said Robing at last, 'the Shadwell. I watched her moor from the inn, this morning. Pull across her bows, we are nearly there.'

'And glad I am to leave this stinking river.' Nicholas pulled a face.

'Aye, 'tis a festering place, but even worse at low tide, in summer.' The stairs appeared and Robin held a finger to his lips. 'We will land if all seems clear and cast-off the boat.'

As the small craft brushed the stones, they came ashore and fended the boat away. For a moment they waited, listening, before cautiously climbing the steps. All was well! Back at the Swan, they found no sign of Geoffrey and nearly an hour passed before he arrived, the smell of fog still on his clothes. 'Gad, the things I do for you varlets, but I am relieved to find you safe, home,' he said, drawing off his gauntlets and rubbing his hands. 'Your horses are stabled near the Tower.'

'Now that they have wind of us, we must move on,' Robin replied. 'We are, anyway, the subject of increasing curiosity to the landlord and his customers.'

'And where shall we go?'

'We will put the Thames between us and the Parliament. I have a fancy for the Tabard at Southwark.'

'That pleases my fancy – 'twas from there that Chaucer's pilgrims set out for Canterbury,' Nicholas commented.

'Our pilgrimage will take us no further than its taproom, for I believe the landlord brews a fine ale.'

They continued, painstakingly, to identify Royalist sympathisers and gradually obtained promises of money and support for the King. Shortage of food, sea coal and other commodities, and the efforts of religious extremists to eradicate all pleasure, had curtailed social life and made people conspicuous on the street after dark. But, often, a master would not trust his servants and the Cavaliers were obliged to keep assignations at night, sometimes on foot. There were visits to the city and to fine houses in Lincoln's Inn Fields and Covent Garden. When the household was abed, the master would admit them, with lighted candles held aloft, and lead them across chequered floors into empty rooms, where the feeble glimmer of light scarcely reached the walls. Their affairs concluded, they left as furtively as they had come.

One night, Robin and Nicholas received an invitation to supper from a more confident host. When they arrived, Robert Baker regarded his guests with astonishment, recognising the horsemen he had admired from his window. Small wonder he had noted them, for they were men of purpose, like himself. During the repast, conversation was tense and brittle, but, when the ladies had departed, their host enquired, soberly, 'What think you of His Majesty's chances of regaining London?'

Robin examined the fine Venetian glass between his fingers. It was his duty to sustain the morale of Royalist supporters in London, but Baker was a hard-headed merchant, concerned as much with the return of fashionable society as the restoration of the King to the capital.

'There are difficulties,' he said carefully. 'As with many of the nobles and gentry, the common people seem strong for the Parliament. There is also a widespread wish to remain aloof from the struggle and pursue normal life.'

'What are your lordship's views?' Baker enquired of another guest.

Like Robin, the nobleman was thoughtful. 'It is a political truth that he who controls the capital controls the country and His Majesty missed his great opportunity after Edgehill, when three of his armies could have converged on the city. Now, with the defences strengthened and the trained bands enlarged, I fear there will not be another.'

'Then we must make one!' Baker interjected stoutly. 'There is much that loyal subjects can do.'

'Indeed!' Robin's resolve matched his own. 'But it will need organisation and discipline if the King's will is to prevail.'

'I pledge my ships and warehouse for the importation of munitions,' Baker assured them. 'What better hiding place for weapons than a bolt of cloth or a crate of Breton lace.'

'Aye, and, likewise, I pledge my support,' the nobleman vouched. 'Better to pass one's taxes to the King, any day, than these damnable killjoy Roundheads, in their tall hats.' He stood and raised his glass, 'Here's health to His Majesty.'

Rising, they joined him in the now-traditional toast.

When, later, they headed across London Bridge for Southwark, Robin declared. 'We are making progress, at last.'

'Aye, and need have no more truck with DeVries and his kind,' Nicholas replied.

Robin gestured towards the exclusive shops and houses of the wealthy, which lined the bridge, and raised a cautious finger to his lips. As they approached the southern gatehouse, Nicholas glanced up at the poles bearing the heads of offenders against the state, but night hid their ghastly pinnacles.

At the tower of St. Mary's Church, Overy, a mounted figure emerged from the shadows and barred their way. Robin's pistol was half-drawn before Geoffrey called, 'Stay!'

'What ails?' Robin demanded.

'We are discovered! A party of Roundheads came to the inn not half-an-hour since, asking for three men fitting our description. The landlord earned your bribe by feigning confusion, while I ran along the yard gallery and dropped to the stables. I had my horse saddled and away before they found their way to our rooms.'

'Where are our documents and funds?'

Geoffrey patted a valise at his saddlebow. 'All here!'

'That was cool. What a shame that such an elegant fellow had to abandon his best velvet.'

Geoffrey flashed a broad smile. 'All here!' he repeated. 'I shall not be outshone.'

'It would be folly to stay together after this,' Robin said. 'Tonight, we will go to ground in Bankside, where I doubt they will come looking for us, but, tomorrow, we must go our separate ways. Come, we have dallied too long.'

He thrust his pistol into Geoffrey's hand. 'Where we are going, we shall need all the protection we can muster.' Appraising Nicholas' black doublet and flawless lace, he shook his head in mock despair. 'And we have to be wearing our Sunday best!'

They turned off the main route from the Bridge into the area which lay along the river, between Southwark and Paris Garden, a maze of narrow streets and tall tenements, cheap taverns and whore-houses. Robin drew rein before a small squalid inn, with a narrow arch leading to a stableyard, behind. A boy loitered at the door beneath a dim lantern.

'You!' Robin beckoned. The lad's head cocked alertly and he came to them. 'Follow us to the stableyard and watch our horses. If anyone tries to steal them, shows any curiosity about them, fetch me. Fail me and I'll skin you alive.' He tossed him a coin.

'Leave it to me, me lord.' The urchin described a courtly bow.

Robin led them out beneath the arch, to find three women waiting, their faces painted, hair henna-dyed. 'Hullo luv! My, but you're a nice-looking boy,' one of them said to Nicholas.

One of her companions took Geoffrey's arm, while the other addressed Robin. 'How abaht a drop of gin and a tumble in the feavers, then.'

Robin beamed, warmly. 'Mayhap later, sweetheart, but first some ale for we have ridden hard.'

'You could ride even harder wiv us, dearie?' They shrieked with laughter.

'We shall see! Where may we find you?'

'That's my young brother looking after yer horses, he'll bring yer to us!' She leered, grotesquely, 'You'd be better off with us than in a place like that.' She pointed to the inn. 'Cut yer throat for tuppence, in there, they would.'

'Thank you for the warning.'

'A pox on that invitation!' Geoffrey exclaimed.

'Aye, it would be. But you must agree she has an original wit,' the big man replied dryly. 'And who knows where we may end this night.'

'Meantime, let us into this den of thieves and find a corner to protect our backs.'

A foetid, animal stench affronted them as they entered and all conversation ceased, abruptly. In the half-light about a dozen faces turned towards them. Robin ushered his companions towards a vacant bench, near the door and looked around amiably. 'Good evening.'

Someone belched.

'Now then, Thomas, watch yer manners. These gentlemen ain't used to that sort of behaviour. 'A four-square fellow looked, severely, towards someone hidden behind a pillar, before fixing them with a baleful eye.

'Three pots of best ale, landlord!' Robin called. The innkeeper did not move.

'You heard what the gentleman said, Barnabus.'

The landlord drew the ale and thumped the brimming vessels on the table. 'Thank you.' Robin, the soul of courtesy, handed over some coins.

In the silence Nicholas surveyed the dirty, pocked, greasy, hostile faces; the matted hair and beards; the moist, slack lips; an eye-patch; a squinting, wispy-locked cripple who grasped his crutch like a giant mallet. The walls behind them were black with smoke, the plaster broken and cracked.

'We'd be happy to drink with you, masters, wouldn't we lads?' The heads nodded agreement.

'Ale all round, landlord,' Robin demanded.

Bloodshot, watery, bemused eyes watched them over the rims of the ale pots, as the burly man came towards them, feet swishing the straw covering the earth floor. He was about 40 years of age, perhaps a seaman or a casual river-side worker, bargeman even. He was certainly held in some respect by the clientele. From under the crinkled brim of his hat, he surveyed Robin, 'We are highly honoured by your visit, sirs, I must say. Might I enquire the reason for it?'

'We are awaiting the arrival of a ship in which we have an interest.'

'On this side of the river and it can't wait till morning? My, my, it must be important business. I expect you're carrying quite a bit of money, then?' His tone was wheedling, with a hint of menace.

'Very little,' said Robin, patiently. 'We deal in bills of exchange.'

'Oh, I doubt that! I doubt that very much, if you does your business in the small hours of the night. However, I'll take your word for it, but how would you like to hand over what you have got – to me and these poor lads!' The eyes of the watchers sharpened.

'I wouldn't like that at all, my friend!' Robin said evenly.

'Oh dear! That is unfortunate!' He looked over his shoulder. 'Ain't that unfortunate, lads?'

His cronies laid down their pots and Nicholas felt like a stricken lamb, the carrion crows hovering darkly around.

'I would like to buy you and your friends more ale, though. Better than this unseemly talk of money.' Robin smiled again.

The man laughed, uneasily. These were strange merchants; he wished he had looked at their faces before their clothes, but he could not draw back, now. 'I see you ain't takin' me serious,' he complained. Reaching into his gaping doublet, he drew forth a double-barrelled pistol, and levelled it, unwaveringly, at Robin, 'Hand over your money, all of you, starting with you, redbeard.'

Robin sitting at the end of the rough table responded, instantly, by raising it in front of him like a shield. His opponent, taken by surprise, hesitated, then fired one barrel – too late. As the roar of the explosion filled the room and the bullet richochetted into the ceiling, Robin toppled the splintered table, sending the man staggering back in the confined space. Geoffrey and Nicholas cocked and fired their own pistols, stupefying the clientele. As choking smoke almost hid the Cavaliers from view, Robin called, 'The door!'

Nicholas pulled up the latch and wrenched the door open. They tumbled out, slamming it behind them. Across the cobbles, under the arch and into the yard. Unhitching the patient horses, they swung into the saddles.

'Up behind me, boy, and take us to your sister! 'Robin extended an arm and hauled the skinny, agile boy on to his horse. They careered into the narrow street fronting the tavern, leaving the landlord and his customers standing about the door. The burly man was not among them.

Their guide led them westward, towards the Thames, until the ruins of the Globe Theatre showed dimly on the left. Soon they arrived at the remains of a great house on the river's edge, its tall chimneys stark against the sky, and passed between two pillars, the gates long gone. The emerging moon revealed a paved court, cracked and uneven.

'What of the horses? 'Robin asked the lad.

'Through that arch is what used to be the stables. A lot of people live there, but there's a bit where the roof's fell in. You can hide them there.'

They hesitated.

'It's live and let live here. They'll know you're visiting my sister and her friends.'

Nicholas smiled at the euphemism, but glanced, doubtfully, at Robin. The big man nodded. Leaving the horses in the ruined stable, they followed the boy into the tenement. He lit a small lantern and, by its light, led them into a vast, vaulted hall, where sleeping figures lay around the walls. They ascended a great, rickety staircase. Off the gallery, above, there had been a bedchamber of some splendour. Its mullioned windows were mostly broken and boarded, but, through one, Nicholas saw the moon-bathed river and the outline of the northern skyline of Blackfriars.

Robin sank into a wooden armchair, while Geoffrey looked around at the rough plaster and brick, the small remnants of linen-fold panelling, which had once graced the walls, the broken moulding above .

'Shall I fetch my sister and her friends, guv'nor?'

'No, no, they will return in good time, I am sure.'

'I'm going off to bed, then.'

'Where do you sleep?'

'In a closet along the gallery.'

'Listen, boy, what is your name?'

'Miles, my lord.'

'Now, Miles, you look a bright lad. Can you get us some clothes – not plague-ridden rags, mark you ?'

'I swear it sir. I helps out at the Globe.'

'It was destroyed last year.'

'That's true, but there are still some theatricals living there and they rent out costumes to other players.'

'Splendid. I want you to take us along to the theatre, just before first light.'

'And we'll see the manager, guv'nor.'

'Now, away to your bed!'

'This is an astonishing place. Why do you think it was abandoned?' Geoffrey enquired.

'Who knows! At the dissolution of the monasteries, the nobles and influential acquired church property and abandoned their old homes. Take the Lord Treasurer of the time – having gained possession of the Austin Friars, he promptly converted them to stables and it was not uncommon to turn places like this into tenements. No doubt, someone is still growing fat from the proceeds. Now let us try to sleep. Set the door ajar and balance the platters above.'

'And when our lady friends return?'

'We will drink gin, play cards and resist all invitations.' Robin grinned wickedly. 'But make sure your pistol is loaded.' He gestured towards a dilapidated four-poster bed. 'Whoever fancies that fornicating pit is welcome. I am for the chair.'

Thrusting out his legs, he tilted his hat over his eyes and was asleep in minutes, but his hand lay lightly on the pistol in his sash. Geoffrey, whose nose had wrinkled, fastidiously, at the offer of the bed, wrapped his cloak about him and stretched out on a bench, while Nicholas chose the table.

Some two hours later, there was a crash of metal and women's voices slurring obscenities. As the trio sat up, the three harlots staggered into the lamplight, eyes glazed, hair awry. 'What in the 'ell are you doin' 'ere?' demanded the one who had favoured Robin, earlier.

'We are here on your invitation, madame.'

'Well y'should 'ave come when we asked.' She gave Robin an unfocused stare. 'I've 'ad my fill of men for one night. I just want my bed.' She swayed a little and Robin took her arm.

'Allow me to assist you.'

She shook off his hand and fell upon the bed. In a moment she was snoring drunkenly. Her companions, nonplussed by her abdication of leadership, made a half-hearted approach to Nicholas and Geoffrey.

'Do you all live in this room, ladies?' Robin enquired.

'No, we sleeps next door and uses this one for business.'

Robin took money from his pouch. 'Here is payment for the use of your room. Leave us now.' Striding to the bed, he lifted the sleeping whore and followed the other two into the gallery. When he returned, he resumed his seat and was soon asleep.

As first light came through the broken mullions, etching the cobweb-hung ceiling, Nicholas turned, stiffly, on the hard table and heard Geoffrey stir, nearby. Robin spoke first. ''Tis time that young scallywag was here and we were away.'

He was straightening his doublet when the boy came lightly into the room. 'Come, masters, hurry, for jocund day stands tiptoe on the misty mountain top.'

Nicholas gaped at the boy. 'Where did you learn those words?'

'Sometimes actors rehearse at the Globe and I watch them, for I would be one, myself.' He flitted from floor to bench to table, seeming to hover in space above them. The light caught the ragged undernourished figure, the wan face. 'I'll put a girdle round about the earth in 40 minutes,' he declared, in a light musical voice.

'Come, boy, enough theatricals.' Robin's voice was brusque, but he laid a hand across Miles' shoulders, as he leapt to the floor.

They walked swiftly along the gallery and down the staircase. Across the weed-infested courtyard they found the horses, safe and impatient to be moving. With the boy up behind Robin, they headed for the spoiled pentagon of the theatre.

'I'll wake the manager,' said Miles. 'Actors drink deep and sleep late.'

'Hurry, then.' Robin chafed, but the boy was soon back and beckoning them to follow – into the ruins and under the partially-reconstructed stage. In a corner the manager, confused and en dishabille, rose from a grubby bed.

'My apologies for disturbing you at this ungodly hour, but needs must, I fear.' Robin doffed his hat.

Mollified by this courtesy, the manager studied the imposing figure. 'Do I understand that you wish to hire costumes, sir?'

'You have it in a nutshell, though not in entirety. We serve one who loved the theatre.' He paused, warily gauging the other's reaction. Satisfied, he continued, 'The truth is, my friends and I wish to re-enter the city as unobtrusively as possible.'

The manager looked at them, undecided. 'Did he whom you serve also love the masque?'

'That he did, right royally – he has scant time for such fancies, now.'

'Then we who tread the boards must serve him, for we have been little encouraged in our craft, of late. This day, I am to send costumes and properties to the Swan, but I want for pack-horses and drivers. Do you follow me?'

Robin's eyes lit with inspiration. 'Aye, 'twould be a capital investment.'

'I find, sir, that you have what we, in the profession, term "presence". As it cannot be disguised, it must be exploited. Know you the character Falstaff?'

He turned to Nicholas, who laughed, 'I do and he stands before us.'

'Your figure, sir, is powerful and needs to be paunchy. Your hair and beard are red and arresting – they need to be grey and shall be, by the application of Fuller's earth.'

He transferred his attention to Geoffrey. 'I perceive in you, sir, elegance and poise. It shall be disguised by leaping and gesticulation. 'Tis a fool's costume for you, sir, the cap of bells drawn about the head – an excellent disguise. We will dim that smile, which must have charmed many a lady, by discolouring the teeth.'

The manager was now absorbed in a major theatrical production. He regarded Nicholas, 'As for you, sir, I cannot recall seeing a more comely countenance upon a man. We shall simply give you the head of an ass. Can you bray sir?'

'I will learn,' Nicholas assured him.

'There is naught to it! See!' He threw back his head and, with a great inhalation and exhalation of breath, produced a sinusitic 'hee-haw.'

'Oddsfish, but you are a tonic, after a cold, hungry night.' Robin's eyes twinkled with delight at the overblown personality.

'Hungry say you? I am sure a poor actor can find sustenance for such an appreciative audience.' He looked towards the boy. 'See to it, Miles.'

As the lad scurried away, Robin said, 'Our mounts are a little overbred for packhorses.'

'Then they shall be disguised like yourselves.' He cogitated, ample chin in hand. 'They shall earn their oats advertising the Swan and will be led, together, in a line. The leading animal shall bear a flag draped around its withers and all shall be caparisoned with bright curtains. 'Twill make a fine sight – all of you on the Bridge. Miles shall go with you, as a guide, and two of my good fellows will accompany you with pipe and tabor. In an hour, the market folk will be pouring into London. Mingle with them, bellow, make music, dance my friends, 'tis your surest disguise!'

███

The south gatehouse of London Bridge appeared, ahead of them, and Nicholas, peering through the eye-slits of the ass's head, shivered. They were surrounded by people walking, people staggering under yokes and panniers, draymen, carts, horses, even an occasional coach. And they were the centre of attention. Ahead, in a red and yellow fool's suit, tinkling bells on his cap, Geoffrey capered and grimaced like a madman. Behind him strode Robin, decked in a great, padded doublet and ruff, his trusty sword at his side, two loaded pistols hidden in the folds of his sash. His hair and beard were grey, the cheeks padded from within, his nose a bucolic red. Nicholas half-walked, half-trotted, his arms arched like a rearing moke. Miles brought up the rear. All the while the tabor thudded, rhythmically, in time with the high, light notes of a pipe.

As they passed under the arch of the gatehouse, they were confronted by three pikemen each side of the narrow thoroughfare. A captain, feet apart, barred their way. 'How now! You will wake every burgher still abed.' He indicated the tall merchants' houses.

'Pardon our exuberance, captain,' Robin bellowed.

'Where are you bound?'

Miles came to his side. 'The Swan, sir. The party is in my charge.'

The officer was amused by the assurance and authority of the tousle-haired boy. 'Well, no one has denied it, so say on, lad. You actors are a rum lot.'

'We're taking costumes, drapes and properties to the theatre, for a new production, sir.'

The soldier eyed them, dubiously. 'Methought all theatres were closed. Speak a piece from the bard of Avon!' he demanded of Robin.

Nicholas saw Geoffrey stiffen. Robin was a resourceful man, but no patron of the arts – an actor without recall! They were lost!

Robin struck a posture, a macrocosmic parody of Miles' earlier performance. 'I'll put a girdle round about the earth in 40 minutes,' he boomed.

'Who is that?'

'Puck, sir – a sprite,' Miles interjected.

'Zounds, as a sprite you are grotesque.'

'Come, 'tis my finest role, you slight me.' Robin gave a little skip and twirl.

The Roundhead looked at him, severely, 'Your days are numbered, my friend.' Robin thrust his hands into the folds of his sash, feeling for the pistol butts. 'Unless you lose a ton of weight.' He laughed. 'Methinks, the Royalists' blockade will attend to that.'

Robin was irrepressible. 'May we be on our way then, captain, for jocund day stands tiptoe on the misty mountain top, and there is much to do?'

The officer moved aside. 'Aye, on your way!'

As they moved forward, the tabor and pipe struck up and, from within the claustrophic head, Nicholas peered through a gap in the houses, where turgid water had been visible the night before. Today, the Thames winked gaily back at him.

CHAPTER 11

The Punished and the Profane

The three had separated. Nicholas went to the Boar's Head, his task to discover the date of Alexander's trial and to follow the proceedings. On a murky, November morning, he set off along Cheapside, the great artery of the city. At the squat tower of St. Mary-le-Quern Church, he stepped around the osier-hooped cans of house servants and water carriers, waiting to draw water from the Tyburn conduit. The cobbles, wet and greasy with soot, led into Paternoster Row, where smoke swirled about chimneys and gables. Pushing on through jostling porters and boisterous apprentices, he came to the environs of the Palace of Westminster.

Dwarfed by the massive hammer-beam ceiling of Westminster Hall, he paused to take his bearings. The walls were lined with shops, almost devoid of goods and, at the far end, a flight of steps rose to the entrance to St. Stephen's chapel – the House of Commons. A porter was seated at the doors. 'Good morrow! I am a scribe for the *Weekly Intelligencer*, charged to report the trial of Sir Alexander Carew. It is my first, important assignment and I am at a loss where to begin.' Nicholas smiled artlessly. 'I would be happy to pay for any help you could give me.'

The ferret face was hostile. 'I doubt they'd try him here.' His eyes narrowed. 'Meet me in The Pheasant, t'other side of Old Palace Yard at noon, and have some silver with you.'

The nondescript figure, with mousey locks and shabby, green-black clothes, looked shifty and unreliable and he regretted that he had agreed to this *rendezvous*, so close to the Parliament. Tankards of ale were set before them;

the porter drank, greedily, and wiped his mouth with the back of his hand. 'I needed that! Been thirsty work, it has, sniffin' out this and that on your worship's behalf.'

'What have you learned?'

'Sir Alexander Carew is to come before a Council of War, at Guildhall, charged with treason.'

Nicholas leaned forward. 'When will it begin? How may I witness it?'

The man studied him; he met scibblers every day and this one was out of a different mould. 'Most scribes is interested in the big debate on the New Model Army that Cromwell says will mark the end of the Royalist cavalry. Nobody else has given a toss for Sir Alexander Carew. I can't help you no further. It ain't healthy to sniff around them that's threatened with the block, so I reckon I'll take my money and be on my way.'

Nicholas slid some coins across the table, which the man pocketed, with a curt touch of his forelock. He rose and edged through the noisy drinkers; a shaft of light probed the smoky interior, and he was gone. Nicholas followed, and made his way to the Thames embankment. From Westminster stairs, he watched the royal swans glide by, on the dark water, filled with foreboding for the future of both his patron and his King.

□□□

Alexander Carew looked, frantically, around his cell in the Tower of London. Those suffocating walls! He seized a bench and climbed towards the only source of light, gaining a narrow view of a snow-leadened sky. With the cold air caressing his face, he conjured a vision of freedom and space. He was astride his horse, nearing the end of the long journey from the House of Commons to Antony. The sea was rolling into Plymouth Sound and a blanket of vivid snow lay about the shoulders of Mount Edgcumbe. His lips were salt and the breeze was on his cheek. Hurry! He would soon be with his beloved Jane and the children, around the great fire in the solar.

The ecstatic moment passed and he fell back into his cheerless prison. Dear God, everything was lost – honour, the regard of his family, soon, life itself! Yet, he was resolved to make a good end. But first there was his will. Shuffling to a small table, he took up a quill and eyed the grimed, chapped hand which held it 'Jane must have custody of John, my son and heir,' he began. Jane! She had won him a further month of bleak life by pleading his distracted state of mind to the Commons... 'and two parts in three of all my lands, tenements and

114

hereditaments which my wife shall hold.' He paused and saw Jane pregnant, again, with his child... 'till that there be raised thereout the full sum of £500 apiece for each of my daughters, and younger children born and to be born...' Would they restore his portrait to the wall, when he was dead. 'And I desire said dear wife to remember her promises concerning my children both before our marriage and often since.' Anticipating the inability of his wife, or other executors, to carry out his will, 'because of the violence of the present war,' he added a codicil. He would also leave two rings to his uncles, George and 'One-handed' Carew. Such a legacy to a man with one hand!

□□□

Monday, 23rd of December, 1644 – almost Christmas. Nicholas waited in a stand above the noisy crowd surrounding the scaffold, on Tower Hill. It was nearly 10 in the morning and he had been there two hours, absorbing every detail of the scene – the casements of the Tower of London, the Beauchamp Tower right of centre, the Byward Tower beyond, with the tall masts of ships visible in the distance. And there, over a huddle of roof gables, dominating and four-square, the White Tower, its turrets capped with lead.

The weather was seasonal – cold and overcast – and he was numbed by the wind and the horror of the event he had come to witness. Arriving, betimes, he had bribed his way to this premium position, level with, and a few feet from, the scaffold. Below was a sea of hats, bonnets and hoods, stretching as far as the moat, then north to Legges Mount and south to the Bulwark Gate. It seemed half London was here. As the crowds assembled, the hum of conversation had grown until it filled the air – excited, tense, lustful for the spectacle to come.

A roll of drums, down by the barbican, stilled the babble. Two companies of the London Trained Bands were approaching, swathing a path through the crowd. In the centre walked the Lieutenant of the Tower and his officers, with Alexander – a sick old man. They mounted the scaffold, followed by the attendant clergy and members of his family, but his half-brother was not among them.

One of the ministers urged him to defend his conduct, but he cried out, 'My greatest enemy can lay but the suspicion of the fact against me. I desire but to be at my period.' The Lieutenant took up the interrogation, but Alexander replied that he took all blame upon himself. When it was clear that he would admit no political error, the minister returned to the spiritual theme. Nicholas could not bear to look at the tormented man, but watched the executioners, black-hooded like monstrous ravens, the honed axe in the straw at their feet.

Alexander began to speak. 'I have surveyed myself with indignation for my sins, especially pride. I'll do that duty which I came here for.'

'Sweet Jesus, make them stop!' As if in response to his breathed prayer, the minister abandoned his harassment and asked Alexander who he would have on the scaffold with him. He turned towards his half-brothers. 'These are my kindred – my ancestors were counted honest men.'

Around the scaffold, the motley crowd called for an address and Alexander was pushed to the front of the platform. Nicholas smelt the stale breath of his neighbour, as he leaned towards him. 'One fing 'e won't know much abaht it, when young Gregory tops 'im.'

'Young Gregory?'

'That's what we call 'im. Richard Brandon's 'is real name – took over from 'is father, Gregory Brandon. Lives just dahn there in Rosemary Lane,' the man gestured towards the nearby houses. 'E's already done the Earl of Strafford and like to do the Archbishop o' Canterbury, the way fings is goin. Never needs to strike twice.'

'Praise be to God for that.'

'Will you join with me in singing the 23rd Psalm?' Alexander asked the crowd and began to sing. Nicholas heard his own voice joining in the familiar words.

Brandon stepped towards Alexander and craved his pardon. His victim gave him money and said, 'I forgive you and thank you,' as he laid his head on the block, murmuring, 'Lord, into thy hands I commend my spirit.'

Nicholas' neighbour was right; Brandon struck once and there was a souging gasp from the multitude, like wind rustling trees, before they erupted into excited chatter. The commander of the troops about the scaffold eyed the people, nearest, warily. When his eye fell on Nicholas, he pointed and shouted orders. There could be no doubt of his intention, as a half-dozen pikemen broke ranks and shouldered into the throng, behind their captain. Nicholas was trapped from behind by the crowd and, in front, by the soldiers. Fighting his way to the northern edge of the stand, he swung over the balustrade and fell, awkwardly, among the people below, striking his head against the rough planking. Back on his feet, he stumbled towards the houses at the western extremity of Tower Hill, into the dispersing throng behind the stand.

There was a shout from the top of the structure. 'Stop that fellow!'

He was among the market stalls of the street traders drawn there by the execution, when a pistol was discharged, somewhere behind. He entered a warren of mean streets. A montage of houses, gables, leaded windows, and decaying brickwork, bobbed before him. Staggering into a doorway, he leaned back and drew air into his bursting lungs. For some half a minute, there was no other sound but his rasping breath, then running footsteps. Suddenly, he remembered the officer who had tried to apprehend him. It was the erstwhile Sergeant Hancock, who had arrested Alexander.

A high window opened, opposite. 'Come on up, handsome, the door's open.' He looked up at a woman who was listening to the sounds of pursuit.

Drawing on his last reserve of energy, he crossed the road and climbed a dark staircase, as the soldiers pounded past. Taking his arm, she helped him into her room and pushed him on to a bed. When the pain in his chest eased, he took stock of the woman standing over him, the raddled cheeks, the flesh beneath the chin already slack, the overblown figure exuding a powerul sensuality.

'Thank you.'

'For what, dearie? You've had nothing yet.' She lifted her skirt, displaying a plump thigh and placed one foot on the bed, in clear invitation.

He struggled to rise from the bed, but she pushed him back. He remembered Robin's remark, 'You are a bold fellow, pleasuring yourself with whores.' This time he swung his legs, resolutely, to the floor, obliging the temptress to draw back.

'So you don't fancy me! Well, perhaps the military will reward me, at least.'

She turned towards the door and he grabbed her wrist. 'Not so, but I have to attend a burial.'

'Lord love us, and you was in a rare hurry to get there.' Cockney humour bested her anger.

'They are interring Sir Alexander Carew, executed an hour gone, but I do not know where. If you will go to the Tower, and discover this for me, I will pay double your fee.'

'Treble,' she said, quickly.

He held out a handful of silver. 'Show me!'

With a plump finger, she selected some coins.

'Half now, the rest when you return. Come back, alone, or your bedding shall burn.'

'There's no call for that! She gathered up a heavy cloak and went off down the stairs.

Moving quickly to the lattice, he watched the woman emerge, below, and set off towards the Tower. Satisfied, he left the window and looked about him. It was a mean chamber, the wall plaster cracked and broken, the hearth blackened by soot. But the fire burning in the grate cast reflections in a warming pan and added lustre to a tasselled, red shawl lying across a chair. On the mantle stood two figurines – bucolic, mischievous – one male, the other female. He examined the latter; it was damaged, but some of its beauty and colour remained – not unlike its owner.

Till now, he had seen the woman as a mere receptacle, a creature, yet her shabby home – her workplace – was warm and flushed with colour. He pictured her clientele – seafarers, bargemen, market traders with silver to spare, garrison troops from the Tower. What a fool! He was waiting to be trapped in a small room at the head of a narrow stair, where a pikeman could spit him like a chicken.

In a curtained alcove, he discovered a grubby, brown cloak and a shapeless, felt hat. Donning them, he left the house and waited in the doorway, opposite. When the woman reappeared she was alone. Seeing him, she thrust hands on hips. 'What the hell d'you take me for? I told you I wouldn't let you down.' He followed her back to the chamber. 'The gentleman's family have put his remains in a box and they're on their way to St. Augustine's, Hackney.'

'Will you take me there?'

She laughed. 'Not if you're going to wear that hat. It don't suit you no better than my fishmonger friend.'

'Your friend shall have mine, then.' He gave her a slow smile.

'Come on, then.'

When they arrived at the lych gate of the church, she pointed to a small knot of figures in the graveyard. He took her arm. 'What is your name?'

'Connie.'

'You have been true, Connie. One more service, I beg. Go to the Bull inn, at Bishopsgate – ask for the large gentleman with the red beard and tell him that Nicholas recommends a change of address. Say that I am retiring to the country, as arranged.'

She nodded. While he counted out the money he owed her, she said, half-tenderly, half-bitterly, 'You're almighty prizzy for a young blade, ain't you. You'd have come to no harm with me, you know.' She cocked an eyebrow. 'Who is she? Some high-and-mighty lady, I'll be bound! Got you tied to her proper, ain't she?' She shrugged and gave a weary smile. 'You've spoilt me for the fishmonger and them others - ugly devils.'

He stooped and kissed her rouged cheek. 'God go with you, Connie.'

He watched her disappear around the churchyard wall, then he moved slowly to the graves, looking cautiously about him. The quiet ritual of commitment was in progress and was soon done. The figures moved away and melted into the December haze, leaving the gravediggers sole occupants of the scene. As they bent to their spades, he took the final steps forward, stooped and tossed a handful of dank earth into the open pit.

Skelton had kept faith with Carew.

CHAPTER 12

Oxford Aberration

Waiting passengers stamped and shuffled their feet around the Oxford coach, while the horses, equally impatient, scraped iron-shod hooves upon the cobbles. Away from the wind, Nicholas stood by his mount, which was secured to an enormous basket at the rear of the coach.

'All aboard!' the guard called.

His three fellow travellers climbed in and settled into their seats, and, with a last glance along the Strand, Nicholas followed. Where were they? A street gamin had brought a note to him at the Boar's Head, the previous night, in which Robin told him to repair this morning to the coach terminus. Knowing Robin had gone to meet Geoffrey from one of Robert Baker's ships, he feared something had gone amiss.

The driver and guard had mounted to their box when he heard a clatter of hooves and a voice bellowing. 'Hold, there!' Nicholas listened to the familiar voice. 'Hold, I say. Give us a moment to tether our horses and we'll be aboard.'

In no time, the remaining space outside the coach was filled, a whip cracked and a voice cried, 'Hi up!' Hooves scraped, resolutely, on the cobbles as, with grating wheels, the cumbersome vehicle moved forward.

'Gad, 'tis cold as chastity out here!' Robin's face appeared at the window. 'Your pardon, ladies, will you take a little brandy to ward off the chill?' He presented a flask at the aperture.

Three heads were shaken in dissent, but Nicholas accepted. 'That is most civil.' With the fiery spirit burning his throat, he looked through the window at the leaden sky above before securing the leather curtains against the wind. But the blast, not to be gainsaid, searched and moaned through the gaps between curtains and frames. After a time, the warmth of the close-packed bodies afforded a little comfort but Robin, always one to brighten a journey, remained silent on his chill perch, with Geoffrey.

As far as the dimness of the interior and their heavy garments would allow, Nicholas carefully observed his fellow travellers. On the same side as himself sat a plainly-attired woman; opposite, was a gentleman of obvious quality, judging from his beaver hat and kid gloves. Alongside him was a lady, richly-attired and masked against the cold. It was apparent that the three were travelling together.

At completion of the first stage of their journey, the coach rumbled into the courtyard of an inn, and it seemed natural that Nicholas, Robin and Geoffrey should coalesce into a group, as they entered the welcoming warmth. 'I do not think we can relax, yet,' Robin declared, as they drank mulled ale before a blazing fire. 'I suspect this route is subject to particular surveillance by the Parliament and we shall not be in Royalist terrain till we are on a line with Reading. I know you are anxious to be back in the West Country, Nicholas, but it would be wiser to stay together, till the next stage.'

Nicholas was eyeing the lady and her gentleman companion, standing about a second fire at the opposite end of the room. As the mask and hooded cloak were removed from her shoulders, the lady turned, revealing ringlets of black hair, finely-boned features with a slight arching of the nostrils, and a full mouth. Her eyes met his and he experienced a disconcerting excitement at their dark intensity.

His appraisal was interrupted by the noisy arrival of a group of drovers, stamping and beating their arms, and commenting on the conditions outside. 'Anyhow, it ain't as bad as 'tis beyond Newbury,' one of them was telling the landlord. 'Road over Wiltshire Downs into Somerset be blocked with snow drifts, they d'say.'

Overhearing this, Robin said, 'It would be folly for you to ride on, alone, into such weather. Postpone your journey. Tomorrow, we will abandon that creaking boneshaker and all take horse for Oxford, ere the snow closes in.' It was prudent advice and he might hope to travel on west after Christmas.

'All aboard,' a voice called from the door.

While the Cavaliers stood aside for the ladies and their escort to enter the coach, Nicholas attempted a closer look at the raven-haired beauty, but she was again swathed in her cloak, with the hood raised, and he could see little. It was obvious that the second woman was her maid. When the gentleman in the beaver hat followed, a sword-scabbard showed beneath his cloak. Geoffrey leaned in through the open door, 'Your pardon, sir, but do I address Lord Henry Warburton?'

The man in the beaver hat paused, 'What led you to that conclusion, sir?'

'I recall you visiting my father's seat at Thurston Park. I am Geoffrey, Lord Knollys' second son.'

'Why yes, I remember. How is my old friend?'

'Well, but impoverished, through the sequestration of his estate by the Parliament.'

''Tis a common enough tale and he was ever staunch for the King,' Warburton replied.

'I remember him saying the same of you, my lord.'

Seeing Warburton's cautious glance at his two friends, Geoffrey introduced Robin and Nicholas.

'Are you travelling to Oxford?' Warburton asked and when Robin replied that they were, he seemed well pleased, but confined himself to introducing the lady opposite him as his travelling companion.

During supper, together, at their overnight stop, the beautiful woman's voice revealed intonations similar to Henrietta Maria's and Nicholas surmised she was French. The dark eyes continued to disconcert him.

In such company, Robin did not pursue his intention to proceed on horseback and they departed the inn, together, at first light. They were over the southern flank of the Chiltern Hills and about 10 miles south-east of Oxford, when Warburton gesticulated towards the land north of the road. 'It was near here, at Chalgrove Field, that John Hampden was mortally wounded in a skirmish with Prince Rupert, in the summer of last year,' he informed them. 'How differently events might have shaped, had he not died. His moderating influence was a loss to all good men, not merely the Parliament,' Looking out of the other window he continued, almost to himself, 'And below these hills, beyond the Thames, poor Falkland charged to his death at the first battle of Newbury, borne down by his despair.'

They came to the outer defences of Oxford and Warburton and Robin presented their documents. In each case, they were accepted without hesitation by the guard. Warburton pointed out their first view of the city – the pinnacles and parapets of Magdalen College rising from the trees bordering the River Cherwell. At Magdelen Bridge, transformed into a drawbridge, they were again halted, only to be passed through with the same alacrity as before. Warburton nodded towards the passes which Robin was tucking back into his doublet, and said, 'It seems I may set aside my earlier caution and present you to my "travelling companion", Madame La Comtesse de Turville.'

The Frenchwoman expressed herself fortunate to have encountered the Cavaliers on their journey and enquired if they would be staying in Oxford over Christmas.

'I think it is possible Madame, for Captain Knollys and I must gain an audience with the King.'

'Then you must be patient,' Warburton told them. 'The Court will celebrate with masques and revels, as if Christ Church were Whitehall, and it will not be easy to gain the attention of His Majesty. We anticipate less difficulty, for the Comtesse bears letters from his beloved wife.'

The Frenchwoman looked steadily at Nicholas, though she addressed Warburton. 'I wish to invite these gallant officers to the divertessements, milord, while they await the King's pleasure.'

'It shall be done, madame.'

'When the coach arrived at the Mitre Inn, Warburton told them, 'I always lodge here, gentlemen. It is newly-built and you will find it comfortable, though you must lie three in a room, for Oxford is bursting at the seams. The cellars are very old and cater for the most discerning palates.'

Robin smiled appreciatively, 'I am glad to hear it.'

When they had descended, the Comtesse waved an elegant hand, '*Au revoir et bientot*,' she said, as the coach drew away.

Warburton was right; only one room was allowed to them. Robin looked about it. 'I need space to compose my report to the King, so go you, both, and explore the city. When you return, we will sample those celebrated cellars.'

Nicholas and Geoffrey stood at the door of the hostelry. 'Well, my friend, I know this fount of learning as I know my face, for I graduated here,' Geoffrey informed him. 'Where do you wish to start?'

'Gad, Geoffrey, you are a deep one! In one day I learn that you are heir to a barony and a graduate of this university. How I envy the latter, as I envied Alexander and John Carew when they came up. Show me Exeter College, I pray.'

They followed Somnour's Lane to Palmer's Tower, alongside the city wall, and stood before the embattled entrance to the college. Like a man on a pilgrimage, Nicholas studied its two stone-vaulted arches carved with foliage, heraldic shields and corbels of angels. Through this gateway, Sidney Godolphin, Nicholas Slanning and Bevill Grenville had passed to gain their education. Their bright lights were extinguished, while he still lived. He returned to where Geoffrey waited and they retraced their steps to the Mitre.

Robin brandished three handsomely-penned invitations to a masque and revels in Christ Church Hall, the following night. 'The Comtesse's maid brought them while you were out,' he explained.

The prospect of such an evening, in the company of the Frenchwoman, induced a boyish excitement in Nicholas and he circled the small table at which Robin still sat, doffing his hat and bowing extravagantly. Robin regarded him, severely. 'I trust you number dancing among your accomplishments? Court revels are no place for a gallant with two left feet.'

'I will contrive well enough, for I had ample practice at Exeter,' Nicholas assured him.

'I am relieved to hear it, because I wager the Comtesse has marked you as her partner. What say you, Geoffrey, will you take me?'

'Assuredly not!' "Odds on" are too short for my purse.'

Nicholas flushed at his friends' raillery, disturbed by their predictions. 'Methinks, Warburton is assigned that role.'

'If I judge the situation aright, his lordship is but polite host to the Queen's agent. Think on't, my friend, a beautiful adventuress invites you to masked revels – do the possibilities not excite you?'

'You misread the situation,' he responded, lamely.

Geoffrey sought to spare him. 'Will you attend service with us,. at midnight, in Christ Church Cathedral?'

He hesitated a moment»,for it was not meet that a Puritan should take part in such a ritual. 'I will,' he said.

Robin put his papers away. 'Christmas begins as from now.'

Rime shone like mother-of-pearl on the footpath and breath smoked in the crisp air, as the three companions made their way from the Mitre to Christ Church. Climbing the vaulted staircase they entered the Hall, to find a world of colour and gaiety, from which the Court seemed resolved to exclude the war for the festive season. Among the animated groups of Cavaliers and graceful ladies, Warburton stood beside the seated Comtesse. With a small gesture, he invited the three to join them.

The Comtesse extended a hand to each, in turn. '*Bon soir, mes chevaliers et Bon Noel!*' Her gown was of pale cream satin, the neckline cut low and laced with scarlet ribbon. A large pearl, complementing the roundness of her breasts, hung from a fine, silver chain about her neck.

'We understand that His Majesty is detained, but will attend the masque later in the evening,' Warburton told them.

'It is said that Mr William Dobson, the court painter, has excelled himself with this production,' the Comtesse added.

Robin smiled mischievously, 'I look forward to it, particularly, Madame, having been a thespian, myself.'

The Comtesse's eyebrows lifted in polite surprise. 'I would not have marked you as an actor, Major Smythe.' She indicated a chair beside her. 'Please tell me about it.'

As he launched into an account of their adventure on London Bridge, Warburton turned to Nicholas and Geoffrey. 'Would you not judge this a splendid venue for a Court in exile. Whitehall could scarce provide a finer setting for these coxcombs.' He nodded towards the centre of the floor, where courtiers and their ladies danced to the music of flute, tabor and vial.

'Yes,' said Geoffrey. 'It has always delighted me.'

They looked about at the fine proportions, the carved and gilded roof, the heraldic badges in the windows. 'Wolsey's grand design,' Warburton commented. 'How are the mighty fallen.' He began a conversation with Geoffrey about student life at the university. Conscious that Nicholas was not truly encompassed by it, he suggested that he invite the Comtesse to dance. In some trepidation, Nicholas broke in on Robin's further reminiscences and led the smiling beauty on to the floor, to join in the graceful, rhythmic movements.

On returning to their friends, the Comtesse enquired, 'Are you comfortably accommodated at the Mitre, Captain Skelton?'

'Indeed I am, Madame, thank you.'

'I am in the Warden's Lodgings, near Her Majesty's old apartments in Merton College.' Something in her dark eyes made him reach for his wine, to relieve a sudden dryness of the throat.

A fanfare of trumpets announced the arrival of the King, sumptuously attired in silver satin, a group of adherents about him. It was the signal to begin an elaborate theatrical production. Against a backdrop of ornate pillars, scrolls, arches and statuary, garlands of flowers were trailed and draped by gauze-clad nymphs, thunder rolled, lightning flashed, pyrotechnics flared. Lute-playing gods and goddesses of mythology appeared and vanished, to be followed by Titania, Oberon and all the dipping, flitting, soaring company of fairyland. It was a magical experience and, when the last firework had died, the final chords were struck and the smoke had rolled into the roof high above, Nicholas gasped with wonder.

'I perceive that you enjoyed the diversion, Captain!'

'Indeed, Madame, 'twas wondrously contrived.'

'Now, methinks, we may follow the King to supper.'

While the entertainment was proceeding, what appeared, at first sight, to be a great feast had been laid. Tables bore fare of all kinds, laid around elaborate centre-pieces of boars' heads – glazed and piped with lard – which lay on bright salvers, wreathed with bay and rosemary. There was partridge, pheasant, plover, snipe and duck; there were game pies, jugged pigeons, roast chestnuts, sauces, sweetmeats – and more wine, brandy and cordials. But in truth, the displayed victuals were thinly spread and generously interspersed with evergreens and bright baubles, for there was little food to spare in the King's capital.

Nicholas felt a strong hand on his elbow. 'Take care, my friend, for I think you do not have the celebrated Smythe capacity for strong drink. Be sure your legs do not fail you.' Robin gave him an enormous wink. 'And keep your tinder dry.'

Wiping his fingers, fastidiously, on a kerchief, Geoffrey added, 'And your pistol primed.'

Nicholas laughed. His senses were aflame, his sensuality stirred by the raven-haired Frenchwoman, who watched them, amusedly, from across the hall. Two points of colour burned in her cheeks and he had noted how her bosom rose and fell as he took her slim hand in the dance. The hand was raised now and she beckoned with one finger. 'You will not desert me, Captain' – it was more order than question – 'the revels are about to begin and you must take a mask.' She held up her own gilded disguise, 'Be sure you do not mistake me!'

'Have no fear of that, Madame. Should I do so I would not rest till I found you again.'

'That is well said.'

The Master of the Revels was calling for attention and the most robust part of the evening's entertainment began. At about two o'clock in the morning, the King withdrew and the revelling crowd began to thin.

'I would take it kindly, if you would join with Lord Warburton to escort me through Corpus Christi College to my lodgings,' the Comtesse said.

Nicholas stole a covert glance at Warburton who waited, nearby, but he seemed not to be party to what passed between them. The Comtesse lowered her voice until it was just audible above the chatter around them. 'Wait beyond the stairs leading to the rooms above Fitzjames Gateway when you leave me.

Disguise your intentions from his lordship, if you wish, but you need not dissemble, unduly.'

Robin and Geoffrey came to thank their hosts for the evening, their final 'Goodnight' taking in Nicholas, as they departed. With the Comtesse between them, Warburton and Nicholas walked through the college, pausing while Warburton opened a door into a garden. 'This door was put here so that His Majesty might visit the Queen at Merton, without disturbing the porters,' he explained.

May I go equally unnoticed, Nicholas thought. Towards relieving the embarrassment he felt at Warburton's presence, he said, 'Methinks Oxford will never be the same again, when the Court has gone.'

'It will, for in some ways it is timeless. Now, 'tis true, all the young blades and some of their tutors think only of drilling and soldiering and all study is forgotten.'

They climbed a staircase and the Comtesse halted at a dark door. 'This is my lodging. I thank you for bearing me company.' Warburton opened the door and she stood framed, dimly, in the entrance, '*Bonne nuit, dormez-bien, Milord, Capitaine.*'

As they descended the stair and emerged into the bitter night air, Warburton indicated the general direction of High Street and the Mitre, 'I do not think you will encounter any barred doors,' he said dryly. 'I bid you goodnight, Captain Skelton.'

'Goodnight to your my lord.' He stood in the frost-laid quadrangle, bathed blue by the moonlight, and watched Warburton disapear from view. He was cold, tired, guilt-ridden, yet lustful for this unusual woman who had conveyed her desire so plainly to him. She would be abed soon, waiting, the black ringlets spread upon her pillow, the white breasts and the dark mystery betwixt her thighs ripe for his caresses. He shuddered and returned to the staircase. One sentry called to another and the quadrangle glowed red, as someone on the ramparts fed a brazier. He hesitated a moment longer, before turning on his heel and striding, purposefully, towards the Mitre. In High Street, he was obliged to step aside to avoid groups of carousing soldiers and women of the town as they swayed past. It may have been the season of goodwill, but there was an underlying aggression to the bawling staggering revellers and he was unarmed.

Gratefully, he reached the Mitre and eased open the door of their room. The narrow, truckle beds were empty. Striking his tinder, he lit the single candle, drew off his boats and lay on his bed. He should feel overwhelmed with virtue, instead of merely flat and empty. What would the brotherhood of the Ship Inn think of him, at this moment? A French noblewoman had offered herself to him and he had hurried away, like a nervous schoolboy. Gad, he was tired! Not even the strident sounds from the street below could keep him from sleep.

He awoke. Robin stood framed by the doorway and Geoffrey stirred in the bed next to his. 'What, home before me!' Robin gasped in astonishment. 'I expected you about midday, a worn shadow of your former self. Was that Amazon too much for you?'

Nicholas searched for words, 'I did not stay,' he admitted, finally.

'It is the truth,' said Geoffrey. 'He was sleeping like a babe when I came up from the taproom. And what of your night of love?'

'Ah, that surprises you, eh, Nicholas? You were so fascinated by the mistress you did not appraise the maid. I made certain arrangements' – he ran his finger along his moustache in a characteristic gesture – 'that have been implemented. But this is a bad business! One does not scorn such an invitation from such a lady with impunity. It is a bracing morning and they tell me the grove of Trinity is an excellent walk. There, you shall tell me all.'

Nicholas rose, stiffly, and drew on his boots. As they left the inn, Robin said, 'So Mistress Juliana came between you and the Comtesse, eh?'

'That is about the truth of it.'

'But you are not betrothed, whatever is in your heart. I would not be impertinent enough to say Geoffrey and I would have made a man of you, yet we suspected you were a virgin – an unthinkable state for a Cavalier. Mistress Arundell will prove a demanding wife, I wager, and would not appreciate a bumbling, fumbling fellow in her marriage bed.'

The sky was lightening and the air felt warmer and Robin's cheerful philosophising dispelled Nicholas's gloom. He continued, 'She was widowed six months since, when she and her husband brushed with Roundhead agents, while they both served the Queen. She saw in you only a balm, a brief easement to her pain.'

'I did not know. Then, where stands my Lord Warburton?'

'He is her new partner, not of an age to be her lover, but close and loyal. You have affronted her and may yet face him for it on the banks of the Cherwell. Duelling is quite the vogue, I understand,' he concluded, lightly.

Nicholas laughed, uneasily. 'Love is a dangerous game, it seems.' 'Aye, but you will not play at it. Be on your way home to your light-of-life,' He shook his head sadly. 'Geoffrey told me how you wish you had attended the university and we vowed you should become a Bachelor of Arts, this night, but you have failed, miserably.'

Nicholas smiled in amused disbelief, 'So that is why you encouraged me. I vow you are Oxford's most incorrigible Fellow!'

Robin's bellow of mirth flighted the rooks in the elms.

CHAPTER 13

Touching the King's Honour

New Year's Eve, the threshold of 1645. Sir John and Richard Arundell relaxed before the dying fire, at Pendennis Castle. Outside, the night wind howled, fiercely.

Their distinguished prisoner, James, first Duke of Hamilton, twirled his goblet, reflectively, reliving the events which had brought him to this pass. Unable to support Montrose, the King's lieutenant-general in Scotland, in plans to attack the Duke of Argyll and his party, he and his brother, the Earl of Lanark, had left Scotland for Oxford and presented themselves at the feet of their monarch. But the King had chosen to mollify their enemies and despatched him, captive, into the West Country.

'You know, Arundell, I am not a violent man, preferring the political to the military solution. Were my countrymen not driven by the Devil to interfere in England's affairs – like Argyll's resolve to impose Presbyterianism on the country, in return for his support of Charles Stuart – I might not, now, be entering another year of imprisonment. Where shall we stand, at the end of it?'

'Come, Your Grace, this is no time for low spirits!' Arundell rose and held up his cup. 'Shall we toast His Majesty and wish success to his arms?'

'With all my heart. Here's health unto His Majesty!' Lifting his goblet, Hamilton encompassed them with his smile. 'It is nigh on a year since my confinement, here, and I count myself fortunate you have made it bearable. God grant I celebrate next Hogmanay a free man, in the service of the King. Now, if you'll excuse me, I'll be away to my bed.'

John Arundell summoned an escort and, when the door had closed, said sadly, 'What a lonely man – the Duchess dead these seven years, separated from his children, alienated from the King to whom he is devoted.'

Richard looked fondly at his father. 'Yet, unlike 'Jack-for-the-King', his commitments will never extend to hazarding his possessions, methinks.'

The old man patted his son's hand. 'And praise be to God, we Arundells are all for one and all for the King.'

◙ ◙ ◙

Hamilton and the eager girl harkened to the approaching horseman, not yet visible on the climb to the gatehouse. The Duke smiled, gravely, accustomed to this daily vigil, in the biting wind from the sea. The courier appeared, astride a steaming horse, tawny boots spattered with mud, face taut with cold.

Juliana stepped forward and Hamilton moved away, aware that his presence unsettled the sentry. 'Good day, corporal, have you anything for me?'

'Yes, but my orders are to deliver all I carry to the Governor, milady.' He touched his helmet, apologetically.

'I am sure that does not include my personal letters. ' She dazzled him with her smile.

'Perchance not, Ma'am.' He thrust a stiff hand inside his buffcoat and drew out a sealed paper. Leaning down, he handed the letter to Juliana and, with a shake of the reins, rode on to the keep.

She rejoined Hamilton. 'In the circumstances, Mistress Arundell, I suggest postponement of our game of *picquet* until this afternoon.'

'Your Grace is most understanding.'

'Who knows better than the prisoner the joy of receiving a letter from a loved one.' He bowed and made towards the ramparts. Juliana watched the solitary figure; he was friend to all the Arundells, but to herself, particularly.

In her room, she opened Nicholas' letter.

Written at Exeter, 2nd of January 1645.

'Dearest Heart,

I love you! How long it has been since we were together.

There is much to tell, but I will save it, for I am in great hope that I may see you ere another fortnight has passed.

Suffice to say that Alexander was beheaded on 23rd of December last, and that I am charged to visit Lady Jane and offer what solace I can. Thereafter, I am granted seven days leave-of-absence.

132

Pendennis seems a grim trysting place at this time of year. Can you contrive a visit to Trerice, about your domestic duties? If so, would Widow Collins accommodate me at St.Mawgan?

Trust Corporal Harding, he will relay your answer.

Your devoted Nicholas.'

Hamilton saw that her mind was not on the cards that afternoon, though he was unaware of her preoccupation with how to meet Nicholas. She decided to plead homesickness to her guardian and, when courtesy to Hamilton allowed, sought him out. 'The castle begins to oppress me and I long to see Trerice, again. It seems an eternity since we were there.'

'But it is midwinter and the roads are nigh impassable! The house will still be there in the spring.' Arundell looked at her sternly. 'The truth is, my dear, that Captain Nicholas Skelton has returned to Cornwall and you, somehow, plan to see him. I have just read his report to Sir John Berkeley, concerning the execution of Alexander and he is charged to give an account of it to Lady Jane, at Antony.'

Juliana flushed at the emphasis her guardian placed on the truth. 'Forgive me, I should not have dissembled, but the castle is not congenial, in winter, and I would gladly brave the roads to be at home for a while.'

'Lanherne is only five miles beyond Trerice. If you so wish, you may visit the family and I will ask John to receive Nicholas.' He paused. 'Let there be no subterfuge, Juliana. We Arundells are not creatures of milk and water; when we love we give our all. Do not dishonour us. Promise me that.'

Juliana held the shrewd eyes. 'I promise!' She kissed him and hurried away to find her maid.

□□□

Though Lady Jane Carew had received details of her husband's end through the family, she listened intently to Nicholas' account, seemingly comforted that Alexander had borne himself well. When Nicholas came to the last minutes on the scaffold, she moved to the window – her pregnant figure silhouetted against the light – and watched the children playing with Janet on the terrace, seeking to temper the horror his words evoked. The family relied on her and she must remain strong, for the sake of the baby to come. 'Please God, this vile conflict will be ended before young John has to make the choice of King or Parliament, for 'tis one that has cleaved this family in two.' She paused, struck by the bitter irony of this last phrase. 'You have served my late husband well and for this I thank you.' She struggled for composure before asking, 'Would you like to have words with Janet?'

'Indeed, yes, for I hope she has found new happiness here.'

'I believe she has, for she loves and is loved by the children.' Reaching for the chatelaine around her waist, she tapped with a key on the window and beckoned. A few moments later, the door burst open and the excited, chattering children tumbled into the room, their dogs slipping and scampering before them, on the polished floor. Janet came last, her face glowing with pleasure at the sight of him. He was gratified by her appearance. The light-golden hair, he had last seen foul and matted, was burnished and disciplined and her gown seemed hard put to contain the ample figure. Her smile was a little secret, serving to enhance its attraction.

They talked easily, until it was time for the children to be taken to the nursery, and Nicholas and Lady Jane were left alone. Having noted his appreciative assessment, Jane remarked, 'Janet does not lack admirers among the men of the household and estate, yet she seems indifferent to them.'

'Perchance, time will resolve that. She would, certainly be a catch for any of them.'

'Her most ardent admirer is John Gendle – a man of compulsive appetite. His wife died in childbed, three months since, bearing their ninth.'

'I am sorry to hear that. Though he is a great procreator, he is a kindly man withal.'

'True, and Janet might do worse, but his family would be a great burden to shoulder.' She rose, to be about her household affairs. As he was leaving, she reached up and kissed his cheek. 'Thank you.'

Picking up a fowling piece from the hall, he set off across the park. As he neared the cottage, he heard his father calling from the doorway. 'A trooper from Edgcumbe has delivered a letter for you.'

Seizing it, he read, eagerly, 'Juliana is visiting Sir John Arundell of Lanherne and I am invited to call upon them. I must be on my way.'

The older man put his arm about his shoulders. 'So be it.' He did not voice the fear that his son might be hurt by this ambitious relationship.

Nicholas turned his horse on the high parkland above Antony House and looked back at its tall chimneys and glinting windows. As a boy, the mansion and its inhabitants had been a whole world of security and stability, now all was changing – Sir Richard and Alexander dead, the King's rule in jeopardy. His mother had died when he was eight years old. He remembered how he had missed her and the assurance of her arms about him, when the candle flickered in his little box room at the cottage, and he imagined the ghosties abroad in the park, outside.

But, along the road from Truro, Juliana would be waiting for him. He drew the animal's head around and urged it to a canter. Soon, the bucketing saddle and the wind streaming his hair dispelled his sombre mood and he sang one of the airs he had learned from Geoffrey.

By evening, he arrived before a hostelry in Lostwithiel, cold and hungry. Next morning, he crossed the River Fowey and rode due west.

☐☐☐

From a small wood on the edge of the road, four men, dirty and unkempt, without cloaks against the sharp frosty air, watched the approaching travellers – the auburn-haired lady, her maid, four stalwart retainers and two trailed pack-horses.

'What d'ye think, Sergeant?'

Their leader licked chapped lips. 'Nothing to think on. We got no hosses, no money, precious little raiment and 200 miles to travel.'

'The odds ain't good, they'm strong and fully armed.'

'And the best chance we'll have of four suits of clothes, this winter, on this road.' He eyed his gaunt band and they returned his gaze, irresolute. 'Three months we've lived like animals on these damned uplands, half-starved and frozen. Ye can chance dying be cold steel or face certain death on the cold ground. I've made my choice!' As the advancing party drew level, he emerged from the wood, the others following, and levelled a pistol at Juliana. 'Hold, there!'

She reined sharply. 'What is the meaning of this?'

'Not wishing yer ladyship no harm. Just the hosses, weapons and top clothes of yer men, and what money and food ye have, if ye please.'

Juliana heeled her horse forward into the eye of the pistol. 'You'll surely hang for this outrage.'

'We'll die, anyway, if we don't help ourselves so we've nothin' to lose, ye see.'

'Who are you?'

'Stragglers from Lord Essex's army.'

'But the retreat was last September.'

'We left the column and hid out for fear of the Cornish. Now, we've a mind to be home. Come!' He took a pace forward, aiming the pistol at Juliana's heart.

From somewhere behind her, there was a sharp crack and the sergeant staggered back and fell to the ground. Juliana's bodyguard surged forward, drawing their weapons, leaving Meg staring, motionless, at the prostrate form. A smoking pistol was in her hand, a smouldering hole in her cloak. Juliana hurriedly dismounted and beat at the charred fabric, before gently persuading the stunned maid from her horse. As she slid to the ground, Meg put her arms about her mistress's neck and burst into tears. Juliana took the pistol and sat her upon a nearby rock. The renegades had, meantime, yielded, meekly, to the Arundell retainers.

Leaving Meg to regain her composure, Juliana gave her attention to the wounded man. 'See how badly he is hurt.'

A servant picked up the sergeant's pistol and bent over the prone figure. 'He doesn't look too bad, milady – been hit in the shoulder. They're a poor- looking lot – a puff of wind would blow them over.' He examined the pistol. 'And this is not loaded, milady.'

Juliana knelt beside the sergeant and drew back the tattered doublet. There was much blood, but the ball appeared to have furrowed what flesh remained on his shoulder and passed on. Nauseated by the alien gore upon her hands, she tore her petticoat and formed a pad to staunch the flow. She looked around at the others. They had been musketeers and still wore the bandoliers which had carried their twelve apostles – the cartridges for their firearms. Each man had surrendered a rusty sword, their only weapons.

'Give the wretches bread, meat and cheese,' she ordered.

'Milady, there's a rider on the hill!' A young retainer was pointing to the ridge above them, where a horseman cantered against the sky. The youth at her side had already sighted his weapon when the rider turned towards them, doffed his hat and waved. It was Nicholas.

'Stay, all is well.' She ran towards him, as he leapt from his horse and swept her up into his arms. 'Oh dearest Nicholas, I am so glad to see you.' She buried her face in his chest, scenting leather and the cold, clean air of the moor. He pulled back her hood to kiss the chestnut locks.

'What is afoot, here? I thought I heard a shot.'

'We were held at pistol-point by footpads, till Meg shot their leader.'

'God's peace, an Arundell accosted on a Cornish road?'

'They are not locals, but Essex's remnants.'

Nicholas walked to the prisoners and looked down at the sergeant, still but conscious. 'What game is this you play, villain?'

The prone man looked up at the stern face. 'No game, sir, but a bid for life.'

'Had you harmed this lady, your life would be at its term.'

'We be no villains, sir, though desperate men who've gone in fear of their lives since the defeat.' His teeth began to chatter and Juliana called for blankets to cover him.

'Have you harmed or robbed anyone in that time?'

'No sir, 'cept, mayhap, stole a chicken or two and a pail of milk.' There had been a few more items he would not mention.

'His Majesty gave you a promise of safe conduct he could not keep. I will take you to Truro in hope we may now redeem that promise, in the King's name. Where is your home?'

'Portsmouth, sir.'

'They shall have money to buy a cloak and food on the journey,' Juliana volunteered.

'Christ's blessin' on ye both for yer charity.' His head lolled and his lids closed, but a spark of hope lighted the hollow eyes of his comrades. When a simple litter had been made, the men were directed down the road to Truro, with their burden, and Nicholas prepared to follow.

'This business will deny us a day,' he said, resignedly, 'but I see it as touching the King's honour.'

'It touches the honour of the Cornish people – you must do it. Come to Lanherne as soon as you can.'

CHAPTER 14

The Rift

Truro's garrison commander had not accepted the prisoners willingly, so that dusk was falling when Nicholas arrived before the front of Lanherne. As he approached the ancient house, with the wolf's head crest above the door, it had looked cold and inhospitable, but he received a warm reception from Sir John and his family. 'Welcome to our home, Captain,' the younger Arundell greeted him. 'It is time the shutters were closed and we were becoming anxious for you. Have you delivered your Roundheads?'

'Yes, Sir John, they begin their journey home, tomorrow, under the King's protection.' He bowed to Lady Arundell and two bonneted mites – their daughters Anne and Frances – who held the hands of a glowing Juliana.

Arundell led him to an enormous stone fireplace, ablaze with logs, where he warmed his stiff quarters, under the discreet appraisal of the family, as they settled themselves about the fire. 'Pray Captain Skelton, do tell us all news of the King's affairs,' Elizabeth Arundell requested.

Servants were disposing sconces of candles about the great room as Nicholas took a proffered chair. 'Would that I brought you better tidings, Your Ladyship, for it cannot be said that things are well – defeat at Marston Moor, an inconclusive second battle at Newbury, and the strength of the Eastern Association making repossession of London and the surrounding counties a formidable task. The Parliament are building a New Model Army, more disciplined and efficient than the old, and it will make its impact, soon. I spoke of Newbury – you will have heard that Sir John Grenville died there.'

'Oh, but he did not,' Juliana interjected. 'Though it was first believed he had.

He is recovered.'

'Praise be to God, I rejoice for him and his kin.'

'As do all western Royalists, for he is our natural leader,' Sir John added.

'Indeed, for his uncle is not worthy of that role,' Nicholas ventured.

'Sir Richard is still a Grenville and a Cornishman,' Arundell retorted, brusquely. Such judgements from a worsted-stockinged yeoman were not welcomed.

'Nicholas is right, notwithstanding,' Juliana intervened. 'It was dishonourable of him to accept £600 from the Parliament, for his troop of horse, then bear their plans for a spring campaign to Prince Rupert – in a coach and six and an escort of 30 troopers, what is more.' She could not hide a small smile at such audacity. 'Little wonder they hanged him in effigy.'

Juliana's quick defence of Nicholas was not lost on Sir John. 'Mayhap, but the *Mercurius Brittanicus* got to the heart of it when they described Sir Richard as a red fox, and questioned the sagacity of those who listened to him,' he replied. Juliana may be a minor Arundell – what an appellation for his striking kinswoman – but Jack loved her like a daughter and this was not a match he would approve.

The conversation passed to less contentious matters, until Nicholas withdrew to change from his riding clothes, in preparation for supper, and the children were put to bed.

Under the influence of his best Rhenish wine, Sir John became more liberally disposed to his guest and, when the servants came to clear table, he took him off to his den. In the faint light of candle and fire, they were soon deep in discussion on the management of his estate. Arundell looked fondly about the leather-lined, gold-embossed walls. 'This has been my family's seat since the 13th century and loyal servants of our King are welcome here. We lived at Chideock, in Dorset, until I inherited. The estate lacks timber and will require all my efforts to restore it. As if this were not problem enough, they have published a tract accusing me of harbouring a seminary priest. How much we Catholics suffer from intolerance.' He hesitated. 'In saying that, I presume your own tolerance towards us.'

'I may be a Puritan, but I have no sympathy with those who declare that the theatre, dancing and gaiety are sinful, in themselves. Then, there are the zealots who would destroy what they regard as imagery. Why should we not emulate the beauty God, himself, has created – through great cathedrals, or music or ritual?'

'You may well ask. Does this opinion portend your conversion to a more congenial faith?'

For a moment Nicholas was silent. Again this opportunity to ingratiate himself with the Arundells. 'I cannot proselytise, it would wound my father, and I am not one for theosophy. The road would be too long and difficult, so my conscience and I must make what shift we can.'

'Then I pray we both find our way to salvation.'

'Amen to that.'

Juliana slipped into the room, unseen by her kinsman and dark suitor, who wore green velvet with grey stockings and elegant, buckled shoes. He looked so handsome that her heart fluttered giddily. 'Will you not join us?' she begged sweetly.

Elizabeth Arundell awaited them. Drawing a chair to the blaze, for Juliana, she said, 'Now, my dear cousin, tell us about your friend, His Grace of Hamilton.'

Nicholas shifted uneasily, as Juliana spread her skirts, 'Where must I begin, there is so much to relate.'

'What manner of man is he?' Elizabeth prompted.

'A widower of some 40 summers – an excellent age in a man, do you not think? Save for the Marquis of Argyll, he is the most influential man in Scotland and was close to the King, being a keen art collector and a man of wide culture. Colonel John and Richard regard him as a poor soldier and suspect in his judgements, but it is by reason of his weaknesses that I find him *sympathetique*.'

'While he is attracted by your strength, no doubt,' Elizabeth surmised.

As Juliana continued to speak of Hamilton in glowing terms, Nicholas grew increasingly despondent. The dread that he would be ousted by someone truly approved of by her guardian had never seemed more real than at this moment. The great nobleman was, clearly, an engaging personality and he pictured a mature, self-confident yet vulnerable man of wealth and refinement. Old John Arundelll would not be slow to recognise the possibilities of a union in such an association.

Evidence of the Arundells' ancient lineage and connections was all about him, in this house of Lanherne – the fierce crest, the embossed shields on the fireplace – and, at Trerice, the arms of the 24th Earl of Arundell, K.G., reminded all that Henry Fitz Alan had taken Mary Arundell as his second wife. He, himself, was a nonentity, received among them merely to gratify Juliana and because they honoured those who served their King. Sir John had patronised him when he hinted, earlier, at financial constraints, for they were not evident in his lifestyle.

Silent and glum, he waited, until the last ounce of information concerning the Duke had been gleaned, then he took his leave and rode from the serene, old house to his lodging with Meg's mother, at St. Mawgan. The frost, like powdered steel upon the ground, reached for his heart with an icy hand.

On the following day, Nicholas and Juliana rode for Trerice, where she was to pick up her escort back to Pendennis. She studied his gloved hands on the high pommel of the saddle and felt proud and gratified, for he had won the regard of her kinsfolk.

Her love was in a darker humour; the more he thought of Hamilton, the larger the Scotsman loomed between him and his passion. Except for brief concern over Chudleigh, he had never experienced jealousy concerning Juliana, for no young blades had come to pay her court, as he had, once, feared. Now, the situation had changed with a vengeance.

In an effort to dispel the black mood, he tried to make conversation. 'No doubt the sergeant and his comrades are on the road home. The military commander at Truro will not delay them, for they are a burden on his ration allowance.'

'I declare Cornwall well rid of such footloose men. Come, let us canter. Trerice is but a mile more and I long to be home.' She urged her mount forward and, soon, the familiar gables appeared behind the elms, stark against the sky, as if outlined by a cartographer's pen.

He helped her unlock the door and Meg hurried away to the kitchen. The house smelt cold and musty, but she walked, briskly, into the hall and stood looking about, while he went to shelter the horses from the biting wind.

When he returned she had disappeared. She was not in the library, or the solar, or the bedchambers beyond the gallery. He came to the open door of her room and found her standing at the window, where he had seen her, naked, in the moonlight. At the remembrance, he went to her and sought her lips, eagerly, but she did not respond. He tried to draw her to the bed, but she resisted him.

'Sweeting, I long for you,' he whispered.

'It is a mite chill for such a dalliance,' she said, primly.

'I promise it will not be for long.'

'Please, Nicholas, I cannot!'

'Why, there is no one here but Meg?'

'I cannot give myself to you.' She laid a restraining finger on his lips, but he would not be gainsaid. Kissing her hard, he laid his hands over her breasts and she gasped. Holy Mother, make him understand! 'A gentleman does not force himself upon a lady, so.'

It was an unfortunate choice of words and he cast her, roughly, from him. 'I doubt the Duke of Hamilton needs to force himself upon you – he is gentleman enough for any lady. Last night we heard of nought else save his virtues, ample, I trow, to gain the favours you once bestowed upon me!'

Her eyes blazed with anger.'That is a vile slander!' she said and struck him in the face.

For a moment, he stared at her in disbelief, then he spun on his heel and stalked from the chamber. Juliana stood, rooted, aghast at what she had done. It was like setting a spark to a tinder box! How could she have been so unfeeling? Rousing herself, she ran through the musicians' gallery to a window overlooking the stableyard, in time to see him mounting his horse. She wrestled, frantically, to open the casement, but it would not yield and she watched, helplessly, as he cantered from the yard and disappeared among the bare trees.

He rode until the choler abated. He had been petulant and unreasoning. Juliana had discussed the Scots nobleman, openly, in his presence and had been as affectionate towards him as ever. What more natural than that she and Hamilton should be drawn together – kindred spirits mewed up in Pendennis. She had spoken with equal warmth of her relationship with the Killigrews of Arwenack.

Yet, she had rebuffed him. Perchance, her Catholic conscience had denounced that one intimacy and, at confessional, she had been sworn to chastity. Mayhap, it was merely the time of her flux. Whatever the reason, he had abandoned her in a fit of pique.

Hauling his horse about so hard that it shied, he rode pell-mell back to Trerice. He found the house locked, the stables empty.

Climbing to the high land, he followed the road south beyond Truro, but there was no sign of Juliana and her escort. Wretchedly, he turned his tired mount towards Exeter.

At Mrs. Collins' cottage, Juliana toyed with a dish of soup, while the good widow enthused over her departed guest. She listened numbly. She had struck him intending to hurt, yet understanding his bewilderment, realising, too late, that he had feared her relationship with the Duke. How could she reassure him through letters, which might be opened by the military?

'Will you take another cup of mead, milady?' The kindly voice broke her reverie and she smiled up at the tall, angular figure. 'I thank you, no.'

Through the lattice she saw her escort of four servitors approaching, fetched from Trerice by one of the estate workers. She drew her cloak about her, while Meg slipped a taffeta mask over her face, as protection against the frosty wind.

'You have been fortunate in the weather, milady. Not a drop of rain in a week and the ground firm.'

'Indeed, Mrs.Collins. I trust that it will hold, for we must travel hard till nightfall to make up lost time. Thank you for your kindness and hospitality, to myself and Captain Skelton.'

'An honour and a pleasure, milady.' The good woman bobbed a curtesy, before reaching out to embrace her daughter. The company fell in behind Juliana and they cantered away to her other haven, overlooking the Carrick Roads.

▣▣▣

Two days afterwards, Nicholas rode into Exeter and went, immediately, to his billet to compose a letter to Juliana.

'Dearest Love,
Forgive me! I offer no excuses for my behaviour; it was unforgivable.
Pray God you arrived safely back at Pendennis and that it will not be too long ere I see you again.
Tell me that I am forgiven, I beg you.
Your devoted Nicholas.'

Within a week, the letter was in the despatch pouch of Corporal Harding, as he rode from Mount Edgcumbe park and thrust his horse at the steep climb up to Maker Heights. He saw the church tower with its four distinctive pinnacles and smelt the salt air blowing up from the Gannel Estuary, before three musket balls, fired from ambush robbed him of life. A Parliamentary patrol, in the blue and grey of the Plymouth garrison, emerged from the hedgerow and surrounded the sprawled figure. A gloved hand tore the seals of his despatches. At the bottom of the pouch lay a letter from a repentant lover to his lady – it was not important. The officer tossed the document over his shoulder and, borne on the wind, it lodged briefly in the winter-dry twigs at the roadside, before fluttering into an open grave.

At the gatehouse of Pendennis, Juliana watched the courier, a stranger, ride in under the arch. He shrugged in response to her eager question – there was nothing for her. The Duke of Hamilton took her gently by the arm and led her towards the seaward ramparts.

CHAPTER 15

The Self-Seekers

March, 1645, and the Royalist stronghold of Exeter was abuzz with the news. Within his headquarters at the Deanery, Sir John Berkeley, Governor of the city, looked around the group of officers before him. 'No doubt you will be cognisant, gentlemen, that the King has appointed Prince Charles, as Prince of Wales and Duke of Cornwall, to the titular command of his forces in the west. Negotiations towards the treaty of Uxbridge have foundered, for His Majesty can have no truck with demands for the establishment of Presbyterianism in England, Paliamentary control of the Militia for seven years, or the abrogation of the Irish cessation. He has declared his support for episcopacy.

'We have been fortunate, till now, that this war has been conducted with tolerance and a desire for peace on both sides. I fear that this will change. We have already witnessed the execution of Sir Alexander Carew and Archbishop Laud and it cannot be denied that we, ourselves, have been guilty of cruel excesses.'

He paused, to allow his last comments to register with his officers. Nicholas, among them, took his meaning. Sir Richard Grenville, callous and arrogant brother of the knightly Bevill, was not averse to hanging prisoners, to make a point. When he recaptured Saltash, the previous October, he had threatened to hang 300, in revenge for the execution of his young kinsman, Captain Joseph Grenville, by Lord Robartes. Fortunately, the King's intervention had prevented this crime.

'Be clear that the Prince has been appointed Generalissimo of the Royal forces in the west, based in Bristol, but he will be guided by an ad hoc advisory committee of Privy Councillors. This body will comprise the Princes's Governor – the Earl of Berkshire – the Duke of Richmond, the Earl of Southampton, Lord Capel, Lord Hopton, Lord Culpeper and Sir Edward Hyde, who will retain his office as Chancellor of the Exchequer.'

Toby, next to Nicholas, whispered behind his hand, 'I wager there are the seeds of confusion in that arrangement. As if we did not have enough problems, with commanders jockeying for position and influence.'

'Aye, but we need not fear that petty jealousy and self-interest will weigh with Hopton or Capel – these are dedicated men.'

Nicholas saw Berkeley's eye ranging towards them and laid a cautionary hand on his companion's arm.

'If there are no questions, gentlemen, we will dismiss. Further details regarding your attachments in these new circumstances will be forthcoming shortly.'

As they rose, Nicholas said, 'Let us to The Ship, for a pot or two of ale.'

'Well said. 'Tis an excellent hostelry for solace and relief.' Toby Herrick grinned, wickedly.

Nicholas smiled to himself, remembering the night of carousal when Toby and his other companions believed he had laid the two Welsh damsels.

When they were seated in the familiar tap-room, Toby confided, 'This is typical of my fortune. Just as things begin to look interesting in Exeter I am posted elsewhere, to a God-forsaken spot.'

Nicholas drew from his pot. 'Where is that?'

'Pendennis Castle.'

His interest quickened, 'When do you go?'

'In three days.'

Here was a good friend who might serve as go-between 'twixt Juliana and himself. But, first, he must disabuse Toby of his false reputation as a ladies' man. 'A moment ago, I was thinking of the celebration of my captaincy and the episode with the daughters of the goldsmith.'

Toby nodded, 'I wish it had happened to me. I had a fancy for those black lambs, myself.'

'To be honest, my friend, it didn't happen as I recounted it. I did those ladies less than justice. After a few moments of heavy breathing, when I began to wonder what I had taken on, their religious scruples got the better of their natural inclinations.'

Toby leaned his head against the back of the settle, a smile spreading across his boyish countenance. 'You fraud, Skelton! The times I have lain in open bivouac and warmed myself with thoughts of those two sisters smothering you with Celtic passion. Why, you damned fraud!'

'The truth is, Toby, my true love is at Pendennis, but we have quarrelled and I ask your help as peacemaker.'

Toby looked at him, keenly. 'Then I am permitted to know the name of this lady?'

'Juliana Arundell, ward of the Governor, Colonel Sir John Arundell.'

'Jove!' gasped Toby. 'When I talked to the officer I am replacing, he told me of Mistress Arundell before he mentioned the strength of the garrison or the number of cannon. He said she is bewitchingly beautiful!'

'She is, indeed, and I have foolishly jeopardised my place in her affections. Will you take a letter to her?'

'Yes, but fair game, Nicholas, perchance I may have prospects. Would you have me blight them as a go-between?'

'We are betrothed,' he told him, less than accurately.

Toby was silent. 'I am sorry,' he said at last. 'I congratulate you and dare assure you that I would have no chance with such a lady, for my father's estate in Dorset has been sequestrated by the Parliament. I am not presently eligible, being penniless.' He gave a resigned shrug.

Better a sequestrated estate than none at all, Nicholas thought. 'Will you carry for me, then?'

'Aye, I will.'

They looked towards the doorway. Two men had entered and the larger was demanding ale, in a familiar, booming voice. Nicholas leapt to his feet. 'Robin! Geoffrey!'

They met in the middle of the taproom. Robin held him in a great bearhug, nearly driving the breath from his body, then Geoffrey took him over for a more restrained greeting.

'You're buying the ale, my lad!' Robin gave him a flat-handed blow between his shoulderblades.

'And gladly. Let me present Captain Toby Herrick – Major Robin Smythe. Geoffrey Knollys you know.'

Nicholas signalled for ale and sat down in the midst of his good companions, delighted at the turn of events. 'What news?' he demanded.

'Of the mission, we will have words later. Regarding ourselves, we have been on furlough for two weeks at Edward Gilbey's. Our friend here has become betrothed to the delectable Letitia.'

'My congratulations. You are a fortunate fellow.'

Geoffrey smiled. 'I know it.'

'And what of you, my fiery friend?' Nicholas looked affectionately at the big man.

'Oh, no permanent commitment. Would that I could have sampled big Conny's brand of comfort, before we scurried out of London.'

Nicholas laughed at the outrageous twinkle in the bright eyes. 'Gad, what a union that would have been.'

'And what a pleasure!'

Nicholas remembered the tawny mane, the thighs and ample breasts of the prostitue, and had no doubt that Robin spoke truth.

'And what of life in the west?' asked Robin.

'Prince Charles is our new commander.'

'Aye, we have heard. He left Oxford for Bristol just behind us. But what of the military situation?'

'Not good, I fear. Dorsetshire, except for the Isle of Portland and Sherborne, in the hands of the Roundheads and our forces in Devon and Somerset at the task of blockading Plymouth, Lyme and Taunton. We are bedevilled by quarrels between Goring and Sir Richard Grenville and between Grenville and Sir John Berkeley.'

'These gentlemen had best be alive to the way events are shaping for the Parliament. Next time, they will not be dealing with the ineptitude of an Essex, but with men like Fairfax and the New Model Army – formidable adversaries.'

'Come!' said Geoffrey, 'there is only gloom in this discussion.' He snapped his fingers at a serving maid. 'Will you drink to my fair Letitia?'

'Gladly, for I perceive a truly happy man,' said Toby, till now a silent member of the group. They raised their tankards to the honey-and-sunshine girl who had restored Nicholas to health. Recognising that he was not part of this friendly, but close-knit, group, Toby made his excuses and left.

'How went it 'twixt you and the King?' Nicholas enquired.

'I did not see him for four days, but he expressed appreciation of our loyal service to the Crown, which I, hereby, convey to you. He does not nurture great hopes of reclaiming London, for he has fewer friends there than he would wish. The capital is better informed than elsewhere in the country and people know the tide is turning against him.'

'And will continue so, unless our superiors mend their ways. Ambition and self-interest prevail here in the west. If it is the same throughout the kingdom, the Royalist cause will be lost,' Nicholas commented, soberly.

'Meanwhile, we are met again, Geoffrey is betrothed and the ale is good,' Robin put his hand across the bottom of a serving maid leaning over the bench beside him. 'More ale, my pretty.'

Toby Herrick took Nicholas' letter to Pendennis Castle and he impatiently awaited a reply. Grenville was severely wounded before Wellington House, near Taunton, and brought in a litter to Exeter. His men refused to obey the commands of Sir Joseph Wagstaffe, commanding Goring's foot and cannons and the Prince's Council appointed Sir John Berkeley to their command. The strained relations between Berkeley and Grenville spilled over to their officers and Nicholas found the atmosphere near intolerable.

In May, Prince Charles was counselled to raise a new army of 8,000 men, with the intention of subduing Taunton, and Grenville succeeded in his wish to command these western forces. Berkeley, while retaining his governorship of Exeter, assumed responsibilty for the siege of Plymouth. Unhappily, finance was inadequate to pay the army, discipline began to crumble and desertion was rife. The malevolent spirit of Grenville drove him into another quarrel with Berkeley, who forbade the Cornish commissioners to execute Grenville's orders.

The New Model Army, under Fairfax, was making itself felt and the plan to take Taunton was abandoned. Goring was appointed commander of the western forces, with Grenville as his major-general and Berkeley as his commander at Plymouth.

Before the confusion created by these contradictory appointments could be resolved, the King summoned Goring to Northamptonshire to resist Fairfax's threat to Oxford. But Goring ignored these orders, wishing to stay in the west and reduce Taunton. The Council of the Prince favoured his decision, for he commanded 11,000 troops, though they accepted the problems his presence caused. In any event, they considered, the Prince of Wales would not be safe in the west without this force. So Goring wrote to the King, informing him that he would possess Taunton within three weeks and advising him to stand on the defensive. But the letter fell into the hands of Fairfax, as he prepared to engage Charles Stuart at Naseby, the next day, where without Goring he was disastrously defeated.

Soon it was the turn of the west, as Fairfax swung towards Taunton. The New Model Army was a disciplined force, while Goring's was degenerating into an idle, plundering rabble, their commander a source of inspiration to them. While Goring debauched, the keeping of guard became lax, his troops took free quarter and the Somerset peasantry, subjected to every sort of rapine and deprivation, finally rose in arms in an attempt to protect their homes. The organisation they formed, the Clubmen, grew to between 5,000 and 6,000 men and, instead of assisting the King's cause against the Parliament, as might have been, became a further force with which the Royalists had to contend.

Nicholas watched these failures of leadership with alarm and found himself a forgotten witness at one of the frequent quarrels between Grenville and Sir John Berkeley. Grenville had stormed into his commander's office and, without waiting for the door to close, flung a letter before Berkeley. 'How in the name of thunder am I to hold together an army, when monies to pay them are witheld from me? I will not command men to fight who are not paid. Time was when I received £2,000 a week from Devonshire and £700 a week from Cornwall for my forces before Plymouth. Now that I am the King's General in the west, I am receiving pittances, and they are declining.'

Berkeley flushed darkly, 'You are not the King's General. My commission as Colonel-General of Devon and Cornwall is superior to yours as Sheriff of Devon.'

Grenville, a soldierly and intimidating figure, towered over Berkeley, palms spread on his desk, auburn locks obscuring his profile. 'Damn you, given the chance I can recruit and command a force of disciplined troops as fast as they desert your lewd friend, Lord George Goring.' He growled the consonants deep in his throat. 'But, because you have ordered the commissioners of Devon and Cornwall to disobey my orders, I cannot even round up deserters.'

'Lord Goring is no friend of mine,' Berkeley riposted, vehemently. 'He is a debauchee, you are a sadist. Your supplies are obtained by extortion and cruel excess, while men of substance become your ransom victims. I could forgive your methods of raising finance if much of it were not diverted into your own purse. I am not averse to your hanging plundering troopers, but you enjoy it – you make jest of it. Everything you do is tainted by self-interest, greed and vindictiveness.'

'And, by God, how you yearn to see me brought down. But I am a Grenville. Cornwall is my county. So is Devon.'

Berkeley understood the significance of this remark and was silent. Grenville, still seriously affected by his wound, had exhausted his spleen. He stood upright and drew in a deep breath, 'I am also a better soldier than you or Goring put together, and you know it.' With this final sally, he turned on his heel and stalked from the room, without a glance at the silent captain.

Berkeley caught Nicholas' eye and searched for some comment to relieve the tension, 'How came he from the same mould as the noble Bevill?' He spread his hands, expressively. The question was rhetorical. What should a captain say to the Captain-General of Devon and Cornwall regarding the King's General in the West? And where did that leave Goring, anyway? He regarded Berkeley, sympathetic and despairing, but said nothing.

'Grenville is right, though, to be concerned about the shortage of money.' He eyed Nicholas thoughtfully, 'I will write a letter to Sir Edward Hyde, at Bristol. As Chancellor of the Exchequer and a member of the Prince's Council, he should be able to find means to pay the troops. He sat at his desk and picked up a quill. The letter written and sealed, he passed it to Nicholas, 'Take this to Sir Edward, insist that he receives it, personally, and acquaint him with the special character of the Cornish soldier. Let him see that he will not fight east of the Tamar unless he is paid. Show him that money is the key to the restoration of order and morale in the western command.'

Nicholas left Berkeley's office, excited at his mission. He must pass through Roundhead territory to reach the great port of Bristol, to a meeting with one of the most powerful men in the Kingdom. It would help to dispel the depression brought on by his failure to effect a full reconciliation with Juliana. Through Toby Herrick's good offices, they had begun to correspond, again, but her letters seemed stilted and he knew he must find means to speak with her, face-to-face, to express contrition for his behaviour at Trerice, and swear his undying love.

▣▣▣

At first light, he cantered from Exeter and rode north. The sun, assured of its welcome, climbed steadily into the clear sky. Whenever possible, he travelled off the road, the thud of his horse's hooves muffled by warm turf strewn with myriad daisies – like roseate pearls on a velvet cushion. Before him, the broad panorama of Devonshire unrolled – vistas of shallow, blue hills, swathes of red earth, here and there a copse of trees. Once a wood pigeon broke from a clump of elms, to disappear in a flash of grey and white and he saw a hawk plummet to earth, where its keen eyes had spotted prey. He swept off his hat to feel the sun upon his head.

Near Taunton, still held by the Parliament, he grew cautious. The broad prospects, he had earlier commanded, narrowed and the road climbed gently upwards. Before breasting the slope, he left the horse hidden in a clump of trees and walked towards the skyline. Suddenly, hearing the drumming of hooves and the jingle of harness, he ran back to the cover of a bush and threw himself into a shallow depression beside it. Over the hill came eight troopers, buff-coated, armoured and helmeted, sleeves colourfully ringed, their faces hidden behind protective bars. As they passed by a cloud of dust drifted over him and he choked, conscious that he lay exposed to view. But the hostile group passed on and disappeared.

From the top of the hill, open country swept west to the Quantock Hills, somnolent in the sunshine, blue-hazed and mysterious. Ahead, the road stretched north to Bridgwater and Bristol – empty.

Arriving at Bristol, he passed through the outlying areas to the city walls and drew rein before St John's Gate, straddled by the perpendicular church of St. John the Baptist. While the guard examined his documents, he drank with cupped hands from the conduit which bubbled from the wall, before joining a thin line of people passing through the vaulted gateway, to swell the busy throng within the medieval heart of the city. As he climbed Broad Street, to the street junction dominated by the High Cross, he glimpsed church steeples between the high-gabled, timber-framed houses. There seemed to be churches everywhere, for the peeling of bells rose above the rumble of cartwheels, the clatter of hooves on cobbles and the cries of the street vendors. It must have been a different scene in the grim winter just past, for the city had been stricken by the plague.

Past the cross at the bottom of the High Street, he came upon a wooden bridge spanning the river, crowded with substantial houses. And there, to the left, overhanging the river's edge., rose a massive castle, its keep pierced with quatrefoils, its castellations etched sharp against the blue of the sky. Here was where he must seek Sir Edward Hyde.

Hailing a passing drayman, he asked for directions to the gatehouse and was instructed in a curious accent, which seemed to attach ells to the ends of words where they were never meant to be. Having arrived at the castle, he was informed that Hyde was attending a meeting of the Prince's Council and might be available in about two hours. After being given food, he was left to wait in a small vaulted antechamber.

From a narrow window, he looked down river at the cluttered bridge and the tangled rigging of ships. So this was Bristol, the second city of the Kingdom, which had cost Rupert the flower of his army, the Cornish infantry, and their gallant leaders. He thought of Goring, drunk and indolent, of Grenville, quarrelsome and avaricious, and Berkeley, unsettled by incompatible orders and appointments. What heroism and what folly, what waste this war had evoked!

Voices in the passage outside and the door burst open. Three men swept in, their leader glancing at Nicholas as they passed into the next room. After one of them had left, the second – a secretary – called him. 'Sir Edward Hyde will see you now.'

152

Hyde stood with his back to a great fireplace, a fleshy figure with light locks and a narrow miniscule beard, but his face was square and powerful. 'Good day, Captain.'

'Good day, Chancellor. I have a letter from Sir John Berkeley, Commander at Exeter and before Plymouth, which I am ordered to convey to you, personally.'

Hyde read the letter, 'Yet another demand upon the King's purse,' he said, resignedly. 'It was intended that contributions from the Duchy and from Devon should finance His Majesty's affairs in the west.'

'Indeed, sir, but these contributions are declining. Cornwall has been depleted not least by Lord Essex, but also I fear by the depredations of our own forces. These monies are required to pay the troops and, thereby, to restore discipline and encourage the Cornish infantry to reform and move eastwards, against Sir Thomas Fairfax.'

Hyde laid the letter on a table. 'The state of affairs in the west is a matter of grave concern to us. Lord Capel and I have been discussing it but now. Some of your peers, Captain, are deuced contrary people. As General Berkeley's aide, you will know that Lord Goring was commanded to send his infantry and artillery to Grenville, for an attack on Taunton, and to stand with his horse upon the borders of Dorset and Wiltshire. Although he had proposed the assault, he retired to Bath instead – to recoup his health, so say. Happily, he obeyed my call to return to duty, but I am sorely troubled by such humours.'

The tall personage who had accompanied Hyde reappeared, angrily brandishing a document. 'Now Grenville has returned his commission of Field Marshall, to the Council, and is skulking in Ottery St. Mary.'

'God's teeth.' Hyde exploded. 'Is there no end to this malevolence?'

With an effort at self-control, he introduced Nicholas to Lord Capel. 'Sir John Berkeley will have need of you, Captain, but rest at Bristol overnight. You will find the Raven, in Mary-le-Port Street, comfortable. Thank Sir John for his letter and assure him it will receive every attention.'

The realisation that Hyde and Capel were working with such flawed instruments profoundly depressed Nicholas. Guiding his mount to the quayside, he sat looking at the ships lining the river's edge.What must be the end of this self-seeking? With Fairfax surging across Dorset, the Roundheads could soon be over the Tamar and into Cornwall. What would befall Juliana on the Pendennis headland, from where there was no retreat but into the sea?

Overcoming an urge to hurry south, immediately, he turned his tired horse into the heart of old Bristol.

CHAPTER 16

The Rival

Juliana's agitation was evident as she came into Arundell's office, 'I have heard that the Parliamentary army has defeated Lord Goring at Langport and that the retreat to Bridgwater has become a rout, with many prisoners taken.'

'Two thousand, I fear,' her guardian said, gravely. 'Believing the battle lost before it was begun, Goring dispatched his baggage and all but two of his cannon to Bridgwater and, without artillery, could not hold his line. What is more, the Clubmen joined the Roundheads and intercepted his supplies.'

'Can nothing be done?' Juliana asked, wide-eyed.

'We are calling on the Posse Commitatus on the instruction of the Council, which is now at Launceston.'

'What will militiamen achieve against the New Model Army?'

'They could achieve wonders imbued with the spirit of two years ago. Come child, all is not lost!'

'I fear for Nicholas. What will become of Exeter?'

'Questions, questions! Fairfax is not ready for Exeter. Now away with you to His Grace's good company.'

Juliana reached up and kissed the bearded cheek. 'We must ask God's aid in our prayers.'

'Indeed we must.'

As she emerged into the sunlight, a courier, leading his weary horse, was heading for the Governor's office. 'What now?' she wondered, perching upon the warm stones of the wall to await events.

In a while, Toby came hurrying towards her. 'Bridgwater is taken!'

Her face tightened. 'And what more?'

'That is enough! Bridgwater was our arsenal.' The speed with which these blows had struck the Royalists was stunning. Toby read her mind. 'Do not fear for Exeter!'

Juliana smiled gratefully and Toby's heart leapt. What an adorable creature! He had been her slave from the moment he presented the letter to her, but she was attached to Nicholas and there was no hope for him. The object of this devotion regarded the fresh-faced, young man affectionately. He was a total contrast to the urbane Hamilton, but, between them, they had made her isolation bearable.

'Permit me to take you for a ride,' he proposed, tentatively.

She slipped from the wall. 'I would like that.'

A few minutes later he returned, mounted and leading the black stallion, Bellerophon. Clattering from the castle, they followed the long sweep of the bay west of the peninsula, until they reached the dunes behind a stretch of golden sands. Securing the horses, they climbed a path which rose from the shoreline and wound through gorse and bramble. At a gap in the tangle of foliage, Juliana paused to take in the view, where the coast swung south to the Helford River. Toby studied the perfect parabola of her throat, the swell of her neat breasts above the plum-satin gown. To be so close to her, in this deserted spot. Taking her elbow he turned her to him, then drew her towards him and kissed her. For one heart-stopping moment, she yielded, before pushing him fiercely away. He tried to speak, to apologise, but he could scarcely breathe. Juliana's face was a mask of guilt. 'I am sorry,' was all she said.

A whiff of jasmine deserted his cheek and was lost on the wind. Reaching for her hand, he blurted, 'Forgive me, but you must know that I love you!'

'You do me a great honour, but it is of no avail – Nicholas is my love.'

'Yet you did not repulse me, at once?'

She released her hand, gently. 'It was the response of an affectionate friend.' But in truth, for that small segment of time, she had transferred her yearning to a surrogate lover, seeking its consummation. 'The blame is mine,' she continued. 'It is not meet that a lady should ride out without a chaperone.' The words sounded prim and foolish. 'We should return to the castle, for there are to be prayers for the King.'

The journey back was awkward and silent, awed as she was by the power of her impulse. Would that Nicholas were here with her, behind those stout walls, their estrangement resolved. Would that he had aroused her, for they were bound by true love.

Inside the gatehouse, Toby took the reins of her horse. Despite his professed regret and deferential bow, as they parted, she knew that he was triumphant. Back in her chamber, she prepared for her devotions. Lust was one of the seven deadly sins; must she confess to it?

Toby was in turmoil. To have held Juliana in his arms, their bodies melded, lips in warm contact! Was it an ephemeral moment, never to be repeated, or had he fanned some glow of which she had been unaware? She had avowed her love for Nicholas, but he was miles away, while they were in daily contact – close, communal. Here a spark, carefully nurtured, could become a flame. He was not honour-bound to Nicholas, for he had discharged his promise to serve as go-between. Nicholas had said that they were betrothed; it was not true. He, in turn, had told Nicholas that he was not eligible as a suitor, because his inheritance was sequestrated, but it was redeemable. And what would Nicholas bring to such a marriage? He was precious uncommunicative regarding his background and expectations, but he was a resolute fellow and would not lightly surrender such a prize. Perhaps, at the end, it must be decided with steel.

During a troubled night, Juliana devised a plan and waited, next morning, upon her guardian, who was holding council with his officers. As they left, each doffed his hat and bowed gallantly. Toby held back, but she avoided him and stepped into the Governor's office.

'Ah, it is you, my dear! Not the best of days to be abroad,' Arundell stared through the small, deep window at the sea mist wreathing the keep – a narrow vista of grey walls melting into grey fog.

'Could you arrange for Nicholas to be transferred here?' she asked, abruptly.

'I think not. He is a valued aide-de-camp to Sir John Berkeley.'

She played her second card. 'Sir John must secure his lines of communication with us, lest the Prince of Wales withdraw into Cornwall.'

'Assuredly, and it would advantage me to have his ear, for Grenville is pocketing county revenues which I need for food and pay.' Arundell's shrewd eyes narrowed, 'What game is this, young lady?'

'I perceive the need for a live link – a liaison officer faithful to both parties.'

Her guardian's eyes began to twinkle, 'And your nominee?'

'Why Nicholas!' she declared, triumphantly.

'I will think on't.'

She squeezed his hand. 'Thank you.'

When she had gone, Arundell remained thoughtful, brows furrowed. Fairfax had turned east from Bridgwater to capture Sherborne, giving a brief respite to the west. It was time to prepare for the worst, and he would be ready to serve his Prince and King. Juliana had indicated the need and Nicholas was the ideal choice – though somewhat junior for the task. Pity was it would entail regular visits to the castle, just as Juliana seemed to be forming an attachment with Captain Herrick, a most eligible young man – High Anglican and heir to estates in Dorset. So be it, the task was paramount.

▣ ▣ ▣

Nicholas lay on his cot and wiggled his toes, luxuriously. It was the first time in 24 hours that he had taken off his boots. Berkeley was stretched to breaking point at Exeter and Plymouth, and he ached in every limb from long periods in the pummeling saddle. Gad, he was tired! Worsening quarrels between Berkeley and Grenville had soured relations between their officers and he was weary of animosity and sullen receptions. With mind overwrought, he slipped into uneasy sleep, then deeper unconsciousness and began to dream of Juliana, atop Pendennis keep, the August sun firing her hair, her arms extended, imploring him to come to her. He tried to go, but she came no closer, no closer…

A loud banging on the door. Where was he? 'What is it?'

'Beg pardon, sir, the General wishes you to present yourself at his office.'

He groaned inwardly. Another confounded assignment, before he had recovered from the last. He drew on his boots, smoothed his doublet and slipped the baldrick over his head. Cramming on his hat, he hurried across the courtyard to his commander's office. Berkeley looked up, as he entered. 'I have another task for you,' he declared. Nicholas' tired face was expressionless. 'I am appointing you to liaison duties between me and the Governor of Pendennis Castle – Colonel Arundell.'

Losing the battle to remain impassive, he smiled, 'Yes, sir.'

'You will take up your duties as soon as you have rested. The western forts will increase in significance as our difficulties grow. You will visit Pendennis, monthly, taking in St. Mawes Castle and St. Michael's Mount, and will advise me how to apportion money and supplies between them. Also, I wish to know the destination of contributions paid to our commissioners, how rights over naval prizes are decided, and the legality of licences issued for the export of tin and wool in exchange for munitions – in short, what funds are collected and where they go. Are these orders clear?'

'Quite, sir. Shall I leave at daybreak?'

'The day after tomorrow will suffice.' Berkeley waved a dismissal, but his voice arrested Nicholas, as he reached the door. 'In recognition of your increased responsibilities, you are promoted to Major.'

Exhaustion vanished. Hurrying away, he beat a tattoo on Robin's door. 'Major Skelton is inviting friends to an entertainment,' he called.

The door was flung open to reveal Robin in shirt and breeches. 'Well don't look so damn smug!' he declared. 'It's taken you long enough!' They gathered up Geoffrey and repaired to The Ship. It was a memorable evening.

Two days later he rode out for Pendennis.

◻◻◻

Nicholas warmed the glass of old brandy in his hand. It had been an excellent meal, considering the shortages in the county, and his host had been at pains to honour him, on his first duty visit. Around the table were gathered the Duke of Hamilton, Sir Arthur Bassett from St. Michael's Mount, Sir Henry Killigrew of Arwenack House, Colonel Richard Arundell, Major Hannibal Boynton over from St. Mawes Castle and, luminous in the candlelight, Juliana. The guard captain had just come to escort the Duke to his room and Juliana excused herself from the company.

'Gentlemen, bring your brandy to the fire, 'twill make for more congeniality.' Arundell prodded the glowing logs. 'Major Skelton is charged to determine what funds are available in the county and how they are disposed. Our people protest to the High Sheriff, Sir Richard Prideaux, that they need two summers, two autumns and two harvests in one year to pay the taxes imposed on them, yet this money has been misapplied and no accounts passed. These and other abuses, like free-quartering our troops on the local people, must be abolished!'

Nicholas looked around the company. 'It has been a disastrous August, gentlemen. Even now, a ship lies at anchor at Falmouth, to evacuate the Prince to the Continent, but the Council hesitate to implement the King's command for fear of the dismay it would cause.'

'Aye, 'tis a dreary catalogue. What say we postpone further discussion on it till the morrow?' There was a general murmur of agreement to Richard Arundell's proposal.

Juliana rejoined them and, as Nicholas rose to arrange her chair, John Arundell's watchful eye saw little to encourage his hope that she might look elsewhere, for a husband.

Nicholas followed his orders and returned at the end of each day to Pendennis to sup with Hamilton and the Arundells. One evening, as he rode towards the stables, he found the Duke standing in his path. 'Good evening,

Major. Would you take a turn around the walls with me?'

Handing the reins to a waiting groom, Nicholas fell in at his side. 'I have a high regard for Mistress Arundell and am concerned for her happiness, so I speak freely. She loves you and longs for your betrothal.'

'I wish nothing better, Your Grace, but Colonel Arundell harbours objections to our union. In his heart of hearts, he would prefer Juliana to find a husband among her own kind.'

Hamilton nodded. 'I understand his motives. He wishes to strengthen his family connections – as would I – by an advantageous marriage, and hopes that it might be Catholic, for his ward's sake. But these are unusual times, affording the disadvantaged a chance to rise, while depriving others of their wealth and position. I was a Marquess and am a Duke. I was close to the King. Now I am his prisoner.'

'Colonel Arundell would not allow a formal betrothal, in any event, until this war is over.'

Hamilton stopped, hands behind his back. 'That could be years away, regardless of the present run of the tide. This beautiful lady is a prize beyond value and you must be worthy of her. Go to that redoubtable man and press for her hand. He is a Colonel, but you are a Major with excellent prospects of advancement. He respects you. Do not be overawed by him, exploit the unique opportunity presented to you. As usual, Will Shakespeare has said it for us:

There is a tide in the affairs of men which taken at the flood leads on to fortune;
omitted all their days are dwelt in shallows and in miseries.'

Nicholas finished it, '*On such a full sea are we now afloat and we must take our turns or lose our ventures.'*

'You understand, go to it!' They resumed their promenade.

Nicholas hesitated, 'Know you, Your Grace, that I am a turncoat Roundhead and was a principal in the subornment of Sir Alexander Carew? What would be my fate if I were taken prisoner?'

Hamilton laid a hand on his arm. 'Who knows when the courtier may feel the kiss of the axe? Besides the Roundheads, I have enemies at Court and in Scotland against whom I must guard, yet I have wed and sired six children. Today you live, tomorrow...?' He raised questioning hands. 'Take your sweetheart, for if you do not another may.'

'Your Grace has shown himself a true friend.'

◻◻◻

The logs spat and glowed in the andiron, countering the pervasive chill of the September evening and illuminating the small chamber. It was the first time that the lovers had been alone and there were things to be said.

'I beg you to forgive me for my conduct at Trerice. If ever I doubted it, I know now that I was unjust.'

'You must know that I have done so.'

'Then let us speak no more of it, but, instead, of betrothal, for I am determined that your guardian shall acknowledge my suit.'

'I think that he may, for his objections must seem less valid in these times.'

'You sound like the Duke. '

She smiled, enigmatically, and he wondered if there had been collusion between them. 'Assure my guardian that you will respect my faith, and I believe he may be won over.'

'I will do so, gladly.'

Rising, she came behind his chair and spread her hands on his shoulders. 'Let us ask him, tomorrow.' She leaned down and kissed his locks. 'Oh, Nicholas, let us ask him!'

He took her hand and kissed the slender fingers. 'I am resolved,' he answered.

It was well into the night before she lapsed into sleep, breathing thanks to Mother Lobb for her prophecy, which, she was sure, would now come true.

Nicholas met her as she came from matins and they hurried to the Governor's office. Richard Arundell was seated at the desk. He bade them 'Good morning. My father wishes you *Bon voyage*, Nicholas. He was obliged to go to Truro to seek emergency funds. The master of the ship standing by for the Prince was here, avowing he would up-anchor and sail if payments owing to him were not immediately forthcoming.' Puzzled by their intensity, he asked, 'Is something wrong?'

Nicholas overcame an urge to drive his fist into the door. 'Nothing that won't wait, thank you. My compliments to the Governor and yourself. I will see you in October.' He took Juliana's arm and they walked out to the ward. Were all their days to be dwelt in shallows and in miseries? 'We will have to wait another month,' he told her.

With a sudden return of spirit, she vowed, 'Aye, and if we have to ride all over Cornwall to find him, we will do so.'

'Now, I must leave you, my love. Pray for us.' Her face softened as she took his hand.

They slipped into an empty stall, next to where Nicholas' big gelding tramped, restively, saddled and impatient to be gone. She threw her arms around his neck and he crushed her to him, a desperate urgency claiming them. The long stable building, the balusters, feed racks, nervous horses, diffused and receded until only they remained, disembodied, separate.

He eased her down into the sweet clean straw and began to explore beneath her gown. At the far end of the building, a rake toppled, noisily, on to the cobbles. The sound broke the spell and he rolled away from her and came to his feet. Juliana straightened her gown and plucked straw from its rich surface, while Nicholas peered through the balusters. There was no one there.

'Sweet fury, how long are we to be tested thus?' She turned and faced him. 'I was within an ace of betraying my guardian – the Governor's ward spanning in the stables.' She spat the sibilants in self-disdain.

'I swear we could not have been observed.'

'Shall I tell you who sought us out? Your friend, Toby Herrick.'

'Toby? But I have seen nothing of him since I came here.'

'Be assured, he has seen you and avoided you. I swear it was he who followed us.'

'Why should he do that?'

'Because he has declared an attachment to me and is, no doubt, consumed by jealousy.'

'Then he is a false friend, to become my confidante and intermediary, while seeking to usurp me. If that is his game he shall feel the point of my sword.'

'That would resolve nothing. Since his declaration, I have shown him indifference and he will, no doubt, soon abandon hope. Come, you must be gone. It is a long ride to Plymouth. Do not kiss me, again.' She took his hand, and he brushed her fingers with his lips.

Out in the daylight, he mounted. Juliana kissed the horse's velvety muzzle. 'Carry him safely,' she whispered. She stood back and raised her hand, as he flicked the creature's flanks with his spurs. 'We shall be betrothed next month, I swear it.' He headed for the gate and, in seconds, was gone.

CHAPTER 17

Robin Lovelorn

Berkeley received Nicholas' report before Plymouth, whence he had come to inspect his forces, but his other preoccupations prevented its immediate study and he confined himself to awarding Nicholas two days furlough.

He hurried to find Robin, who had accompanied Berkeley south. 'It is now Friday noon and I am free till Monday morning.'

'And I.'

'What say you to two days with my father at Antony?'

''Twill beat sitting here and staring at Robartes' massive fortifications – they quite depress me,' Robin responded, enthusiastically.

The next morning dawned overcast and a fine drizzle descended, as they crossed the river and headed towards Antony. Robin drew his cloak about him. 'I had hoped for a little fishing and a few quarts of ales,' he commented gloomily, 'but we must rest content with drinking. Ah well, it might be worse.'

'No true fisherman is discouraged by a little rain,' Nicholas smiled. 'I also had in mind that we join in family worship on Sunday. Lady Jane would take it kindly.'

Robin was surprisingly amenable. 'Well my eternal soul stands in need. Besides, I would meet her Ladyship, for I hear she is a woman of sterling qualities.'

'Indeed, she is. Glad I am that you are contemplating redemption. 'Tis not long since you were warning me of the perils of liaison with such ladies as Conny, then you confess to lusting for her.'

'Ah, that is where experience tells, my friend – have no fear on that score.' He grew more serious. 'You know, Nicholas, I could have grown attached to her, for I perceived not only a fine figure but a good heart.'

The escutcheon-crowned gates of Antony loomed, the black ironwork glossy with rain. The lodgekeeper came shuffling out and opened them, with a cheerful greeting to Nicholas, and they cantered across the park to the cottage of Skelton senior, girded in mist. Although forewarned of their arrival, his father was not at home, but they found a fire burning in the hearth, the reek of applewood hanging heavy in the air. Bacon, cheese and bread lay on the table, a small cask of ale with leather pots beside the simple fare.

'Dry your cloak at the fire and draw a measure of Cornish mead, Robin. I will take the horses to John Gendle – he is the head groom – and, if I can stop him talking, will be back, shortly.'

'Well said, and thanks to your father for his foresight.'

As Nicholas entered the stableyard, John Gendle emerged from the building. 'Why, if 'tain't Maister Skelton, and how be you, sir?'

Gendle had never called him 'sir' before. 'Very well, thank you John, and how do I find you?'

'Well enough, sir, but a mite lonely these days. What I need is a guid woman to care fer my young uns and warm my bed.'

'I'm sure you'll find one ere long.'

'I hope so, Major. Anyhow sir, welcome home.'

Leaving the horses with him, Nicholas returned to the cottage, to find that his father had come in and made the acquaintance of Robin. Indeed, Robin appeared completely at home, as he described their experiences in the second battle of Newbury.

'I see that I am spared from introducing you to this redoubtable redbeard, father,' said Nicholas, as they embraced.

'Yes, and I have already learned more of your exploits from Major Smythe than I did from you in the whole of your last visit.' Skelton senior was tall and straight-backed, like his son, but his shoulders were a little stooped and there was a trace of deference in his manner. Yet he was a senior member of the Carew household, a trusted steward who had participated in the inventory of Sir Richard Carew's possessions, upon his death. Comparing father with son, Robin noted the same singularly-handsome features, the same modulation of the voice, the speech grammatical but with a trace of the Cornish burr. He was clearly an intelligent and articulate man, literate but circumscribed.

'Your son has not disgraced you or his patron, Mister Skelton,' Robin assured him.

'I am gratified to hear it, though I would have expected no less.'

Robin was moved by the immense pride in the father's eyes. He looked about the small Tudor room, timbered and plastered, at the open fireplace, the pile of fragrant burning logs, the sturdy bulbous furniture, the slate-flagged floor. It was neat, clean and modest – where it had all begun for his friend.

'I am charged by Her Ladyship to invite you to sup with her. Like me, she is keen to learn how the war goes for the King.'

'That is most gracious of Her Ladyship. I take it we accept, Nicholas?'

'Indeed, with pleasure.'

'I fear, Mister Skelton, that there is little to cheer her regarding His Majesty's affairs.'

'But I would be acquainted of them, nonetheless. Come, let me charge your pots and platters, for I would know what transpires beyond the river out there.'

Nicholas build up the fire and the trio gathered about the hearth – the soberly-dressed host in a straight armchair, his flamboyant guests perched upon the settles flanking the fireplace – while Nicholas smiled upon the two men he loved best in the world. When his father's curiosity concerning affairs in the wider world was satisfied, Nicholas said, 'I believe Robin would be entertained by what transpired at Antony Church, on Whit Sunday – when was it, five years since?'

Skelton's face lit at the prospect of matching the redoubtable raconteur opposite. 'Aye,' he said, ruminatively, 'that was a rare day!'

Robin rose to his cue, 'Tell me!'

'Well, we were attending communion that morning. There must have been nigh on 200 of us in church. Old Sir Richard was sick, but his eldest daughter, Elizabeth, was there. Mr Bache, the minister, was at the table, when a ball of fire shot hissing through the chancel window and burst with a terrible bang. A vile smell of gunpowder and brimstone filled the church and sheets of flame came through some of the other windows. To tell the truth, I have little recollection of it, for ere it burst the ball struck me two great blows, as if t'were a flat stone, first on one side of the head then t'other. They tell me it ran around my seat, then rolled up the chancel, killing a dog before it exploded.'

'How fared others in the congregation?' Robin encouraged.

'I will relate it. But when you take supper, ask Lady Jane if you may examine the testaments given, afterwards, to Sir Richard, by some of the lower servants. I mind well that John Gendle, Nicholas Wilcock, John Hodge and Ferdinando Reep had rare tales for the master. Mr.Bache was stricken on the left side of the head and the outside of the left leg, in such sort that he verily thought that the hair of his head had been burned off and his leg scalded. Were it not that he had, at that moment, stepped to the communion table with the cup, 'tis said he would assuredly have been killed.'

'And did not some of the women parisioners also suffer injury?' Nicholas prompted.

'Indeed! Dorothy Tubbe, who was kneeling to receive the communion, was smitten so that it seemed to her that her knees and legs were stricken from her body. Then, Susanna Collins received a grievous blow. The wrist of her right arm was scalded as broad as a three-pence piece – red and raw for a week. Antony Pike was stricken, as if mortally, in the lower part of his body and felt the water in his bladder boiling hot.'

Nicholas saw Robin suppress a smile as he had himself, many a time, as he listened to the story of the thunderbolt. The villagers of Antony and the Carew servants had certainly spared no effort to give old Sir Richard full value when he had interrogated them. 'Let us not forget William Sargent, father.'

Skelton saw the twinkle in his eye and was constrained to smile himself, 'Aye, William Sargent. Well, he was kneeling a little way off from the chancel window and was stricken so forcibly, on the chin, that it seemed his body was severed in twain and his water violently issued from him. Indeed, for a time he lost his sight and senses, yet, for two or three years before he had suffered pain in his chin, but from that time he was cured.'

Robin slapped his thigh and took a great draught of ale. 'Mister Skelton, I vow you tell as pretty a tale as I!'

'And that, dear father, is no mean compliment, I swear.'

Skelton rose and stooped over the logs piled at the fire's edge, well pleased.

At the appointed hour, Nicholas and Robin presented themselves at the house and were received by Jane Carew. Nicholas bent over her hand. 'It is a great pleasure for me to pay my respects, Lady Jane. May I present Major Robin Smythe.'

Jane Carew smiled, as Robin bowed. 'It is good to meet you, Major Smythe, for Nicholas has spoken much of you.' She summoned a servant.

'I need not ask if two Cavaliers will take a glass of wine before supper.' She regarded the big man in the plum-velvet suit, his powerful, well-formed calfs, the fine shoes with red-edged soles. As for Nicholas, she could scarcely relate him with the gauche, young farmer who had eagerly accepted a Parliamentary commission from her husband, an eternity ago. She raised her glass. 'Health to His Majesty.' Her voice rang clear in the high chamber.

'The King.'

'Is it true that His Majesty would have his son leave the country for France?' She enquired.

Their reply was interrupted by the arrival of Janet, who dropped a deep curtsy. Nicholas, the second person to observe a metamorphosis that evening, surmised that Lady Jane had given her the pale-blue satin gown she wore. Her corn-gold hair was dressed fashionably and the peach-like skin glowed with health. A demure lace collar covering her shoulders failed to disguise the fullness of her figure. The large hands, once red and coarse, were soft and groomed, the once-thick Cornish accent much modified.

'I must thank you, Major Smythe, for your assistance to me after Launceston.' She failed to raise her eyes to him at the recollection of her degradation and loss.

Robin was most attentive to both ladies during supper, charmed by his hostess and fascinated by her companion. Whenever Lady Carew and Nicholas were engaged in conversation, he would lean towards Janet and address her in a close, confidential voice, breathing the fragrance of lavender she exuded. In turn, her attention and readiness to be amused stimulated and flattered him.

As they were leaving, Lady Jane indicated a large portrait on the wall, which showed signs of stitching at top and bottom of the canvas. 'You will observe, gentlemen, that my husband has regained his rightful place among his ancestors and in the hearts of, at least, his Royalist kinsmen. Following the affair of St. Nicholas Island, his family cut the portrait from the frame and consigned it to the cellars. Now that he has paid with his blood, for his aberration, he is again honoured among us.'

Robin, whose eye had been taken by the mutilated picture during the meal, returned to the table for one of the candelabra. Holding it aloft, he studied the painting by the flickering flame.

'It depicts Sir Alexander at his coming-of-age,' said his widow, 'and was commissioned by his father, Sir Richard.'

He saw a young man with a small oval face, full-lipped and moustached, dressed in a buff doublet and red breeches, a ruff at his throat. He was shod in tan funnel boots, elegantly spurred, and held a rapier supported by a decorated baldrick over his right shoulder. Behind him, on a chest, stood a plumed casque and gauntlets. On the floor in the shadows lay a steel corslet. Robin replaced the candelabra. 'I am happy that your husband has regained his place among you, Lady Carew.'

'Would that were true of all our family. Sir Alexander's half-brother, John, is unhappily alienated from us. He declined to be present at my husband's end, being a Fifth Republican and believing that Christ Jesus will return to rule over us, in place of our King.'

'I wonder, sometimes, if the good Lord has not despaired of us all –

brother against brother, blood against blood, people against King,' Robin responded, soberly.

'He will prevail,' said Jane Carew. 'I would be most happy if you would both join us for morning service, tomorrow, at Antony Church, when we may beseech Him to look kindly upon us.'

'Delighted.' Robin took his hostess' hand. 'My thanks to Your Ladyship for your kind hospitality.' He turned to Janet who stood a pace behind her mistress and, taking her hand, kissed it. 'My thanks also to you, Mrs Salter, for the pleasure of your company – a most agreeable evening.'

▣ ▣ ▣

The night air, as they walked across the park, was fresh and, high above, galaxies of stars winked in the black vault of the heavens. Robin slammed his gauntletted hands together. 'What a delightful evening,' he commented, enthusiastically. 'So gracious a lady and so comely a companion. By gad, Nicholas, I would never have known that delectable creature as the same poor waif we found in the straw, by Launceston.'

'Tis not the same for I have never seen such a transformation. Lady Jane has performed a near miracle.'

'You know me, Nicholas, I have a penchant for a well-proportioned woman and, when she is also fair and well conducted, I regard her as thrice-favoured. Do you remember how I would have set my cap at Letitia Gilbey, but I saw she would have none of me and I declared that I would become a gentleman. Well, I know now that I do not have it in me. As you are aware, my father is but a small landowner – a yeoman – and I a second son, so I became a professional soldier, a Continental mercenary. Everything I possess was gained from booty and pillage, through the spilling of blood. I tell you, my friend, I am sick of the stink of powder and the stench of death. I would take that young woman to my heart and cherish her, that she might lie beside me at night, bear me children, keep my home and comfort my old age.'

They reached the door of the cottage and Nicholas ushered his friend inside. He lit the candles and stirred the sluggard fire into life. His father would remain at the house, overnight, and, clearly, Robin had much to say. 'Let us take a glass of your French brandy,' he said. ''Twas your present to my father, but he will not grudge it.'

'Do not deprive the good man for I have another bottle in my room. Wait, while I fetch it.'

Thoughtfully, Nicholas took two goblets from the court cabinet, in the shadows beyond the fire. Was he presumptuous, too immature, to assume the role the worldly-wise Hamilton had played so recently with him – counsellor in marriage to this seasoned, yet vulnerable man, yearning for peace and domesticity.

Robin descended the short staircase and ducked into the room. 'Make it a good measure,' he said, handing him the bottle. He seated himself beside the hearth.

Nicholas had never seen him so absorbed. 'Did you know that Janet's father was my cowman at the Barton?'

'I believe you mentioned it.'

'Would you truly be happy with an unlettered wife, a milkmaid?'

'Would you recognise her as such?'

'Not immediately, thanks to Lady Jane.'

'I describe myself as a Londoner, but I came from Essex and have a yen to return some day. Janet's forbears would not arouse undue curiosity, at such a distance.'

'Mayhap, but you could not escape them. In the long winter evenings, when a wife must be all things to her man – comforter and friend – you would talk of the Court, of countries and campaigns, of alarms and adventures; and she would listen. And what then? You are a natural philosopher, Robin – on what would you sharpen your mind?'

'Is it the role of a wife to sharpen a man's mind?'

There was an edge to his voice. He had presumed too far. "Think you Janet will have you?'

'By God, I will ensure it!'

There seemed nothing more to be said. 'Let us finish the brandy, that you may sleep on it.'

'I have no need, for I am resolved.'

❏❏❏

The Carew coach carried them to Antony Church, the next morning. At their appearance, the villagers and estate workers, waiting among the gravestones, bobbed and doffed their hats. And Nicholas was gratified by the acknowledgements of the local people, who had known him since he was a boy. During the long sermon, his mind wandered to the never-to-be-forgotten incident of the thunderbolt, which had caused such speculation concerning God's wrath. He surreptitiously tested his Latin upon the inscribed memorial plaque, which Alexander had installed in memory of his celebrated grandsire,

Richard Carew, author of the *Survey of Cornwall.*

How strange, he thought, that Alexander should pay tribute to his grandfather, yet there was nothing in the church to recall his gentle father. Perchance, they had quarrelled over Alexander's espousal of the Parliamentary cause, or, mayhap, Sir Richard had alienated his son by his wearisome lectures on moral rectitude, when he was young. He glanced at Robin and saw his eyes upon Janet's hands, lying primly in her lap. There had clearly been no change of heart overnight.

When the ritual ended, Lady Jane left the church with her companions, under the curious but respectful gaze of the villagers. They shook hands with the rector and were soon sweeping through the park gates and along the drive to the house. Near the Skelton cottage, Jane Carew halted the coach and the Cavaliers prepared to descend. 'While Sir John Berkeley is besetting Plymouth, I conceive that you will remain in the locality, gentlemen. You are welcome here, at any time, and it would give me pleasure to entertain you to supper, on any future visits.'

Nicholas spoke for them. 'It has been most agreeable, Lady Jane, and we would gladly do so. Now, if you will excuse us, we must return to duty.'

They stepped down and swept an obeisance. As the coach began to move, Robin's eye sought some communication from Janet, but she was barely discernible inside the coach.

▣▣▣

On the 11th of September, Berkeley assembled his officers and surveyed them, gravely. 'Gentlemen, I regret to inform you that Bristol has fallen. Yesterday, Prince Rupert surrendered the city to General Fairfax.'

There was a gasp at this enormous reverse and Nicholas sprang to his feet in disbelief. 'But we understood that Lord Goring and Sir Richard Grenville had been ordered to march to its relief, sir. Where are they?'

'I fear that His Lordship's sporadic energy has failed him and his army is disintegrating,' Berkeley answered, bitterly. 'However, Sir Richard's forces are intact and ready to defend Exeter.'

Nicholas persisted, 'When I was in Bristol, there were 140 cannon and ample munitions to defend it. A continuous bastion encompassed the castle and a fort at Windmill Hill had been converted into a powerful, pentagonal castle. These are fortifications we inherited from Colonel Nathaniel Fiennes, when we took the city, and we have greatly strengthened them, since.'

The eyes of Berkeley's officers were on Nicholas, numb with apprehension. They turned towards Berkeley, as he replied, 'That is correct, Major. The city was capable of withstanding a three-week siege, but neither the townsmen nor the garrison had the will to defend it. And Prince Rupert, as commander, was not persuaded to rely on reinforcements from Lord Goring or any support from the King's Welsh garrisons. The Prince has, apparently, gone to Oxford to report to His Majesty and I fear that he will be very ill received, for this defeat deprives the King of his greatest port and magazine and frees Fairfax to turn upon Cornwall. You should also realise, gentlemen, that we are now cut off from the Royalist forces in Wales.' He looked about him. 'Are there any more questions?'

The stunned silence persisted. 'Go, then, and make ready for what is to come!'

As the group broke up, Berkeley beckoned to Nicholas, who followed him along the corridor to his room. Berkeley closed the door. 'It would seem that Lord Hopton and Chancellor Hyde are planning to survey Pendennis Castle and St. Michael's Mount and to inspect the magazines of Bodmin and Truro. They will be particularly concerned to find a safe haven'- he smiled grimly as he enunciated these last words - 'for the Prince of Wales. Your work towards fortifying the western forts is now in more influential hands than ours and you will, therefore, relinquish those responsibilities.'

Nicholas, already dejected by the news from Bristol, felt his heart sink. There was to be no second chance, then, to press Arundell for Juliana's hand.

'I will shortly leave the investment of Plymouth to Sir John Digby and return to Exeter, to strengthen its defences. You will accompany me,' Berkeley concluded.

A few days later Fairfax entered Lyme, while Goring sent all but 1,000 cavalry and 200 foot soldiers towards Cornwall, and moved up-country to defend Exeter. As a consequence, Tiverton was left inadequately defended and, on 19th of October, the castle fell. Exeter now lay before Fairfax, its fortifications deficient.

Berkeley stood on the city walls, in the blustery autumn wind and looked to the north-east, Nicholas at his side. Holding on to his hat as the breeze whipped his locks he said, 'Grenville is at Okehampton, Digby stands before Plymouth and Goring has ceased to propound his plan to unite his remaining forces with Grenville and march against Fairfax. The idea of those two, self-centred, incompatibles uniting against anyone is ludicrous. Our chief hope lies in the lateness of the year. Will Fairfax remain in the field and come at us, or will he retire to winter quarters?'

Nicholas pinioned his billowing cloak. 'From what I can see of our defences sir, I think we must pray that the latter will prevail with him.'

Berkeley's face was grave. At last, he said, 'I think a glass of claret may dispel the gloom.'

His hopes were realised. Fairfax retired to quarters at Ottery St. Mary, to restore his tired and sickly troops. His adversary, Goring, declaring that he also was unwell, transferred his responsibilities to Lord Wentworth and set sail for France.

When he received the news, Berkeley asked, 'What think you, Nicholas? His Lordship declares that he will return to resume his command in two months. I pray that we have seen the last of him, for what may we attribute to him? Weymouth, Taunton, Bristol and Tiverton Castle are lost, this city in dire peril and the whole of Devon and Cornwall demoralised by the machinations of Grenville and himself. Ere long, the Council of the Prince will surely retire deep into Cornwall, and Hyde and Hopton will be obliged to obey the King's injunction to despatch the Prince of Wales to the Continent.'

There was a rap on the door and a junior aide-de-camp entered. 'The Lord Hopton to see you, sir.' Hopton appeared in the doorway and advanced briskly upon Berkeley. Nicholas' interest quickened for this was his first sight of the soberly-attired commander, with the small beard, who had so impressed James Chudleigh with his loyalty to the King and lack of self-interest.

'General Hopton, may I present a member of my staff, Major Skelton.'

Hopton regarded Nicholas keenly, as Berkeley prepared to dismiss him. 'No, stay, Major, I have work for you. Your preliminary work prompted the survey of the western forts, which Sir Edward Hyde and I recently undertook. I commend you for the report, which you prepared, and Sir John for his foresight in commissioning it.

'I wish you to organise and lead a train of munitions and provisions to sustain the Mount and St. Mawes Castle, but most particularly Pendennis Castle, for I believe that it will play a major role in impending events - even to providing a haven for the Prince of Wales.'

With a brief glance at Berkeley, for approval, Nicholas assured him that it would be done.

'Good! Here is your authority and lists of the arms and provender you will take. Be about this matter immediately.'

So, the fickle pendulum was swinging in his favour, for he would be well received when he appeared before the gates of Pendennis Castle with a train of weapons, powder, ammunition and provisions behind him.

CHAPTER 18

The Fickle Pendulum

Extracting wagons, horses and all the paraphernalia of war from the quartermasters proved difficult, for everything was in short supply and there were conflicting demands for the little that was available. Grenville reported that he lacked match, bullets, shoes and stockings while Richard Arundell, recently appointed to command the garrison and the trained bands at Pendennis, pressed for every sort of sustenance, declaring that his men were so miserably equipped they deserted daily. In Exeter itself, provisions and funds were so scarce that there was not even £40 available to pay for the intelligence service so vital to the Royalists.

But, finally, Nicholas turned his back on the city which had played such a part in his life and rode towards the Cornish coast, a train of wagons rumbling behind him. Along each flank tramped a file of musketeers and pikemen, while a small body of dragoons protected its rear. Despite their impassive faces, Nicholas suspected that his soldiers were only too pleased to be putting the Tamar between Fairfax's army and themselves.

They had put both the Tavy and the Tamar behind them, when Nicholas heard the thud of hooves, on the soft ground, and saw Robin approaching.

'By heaven, what are you doing here?'

'Seeking the pleasure of your company, as ever. I surmise this column will pass close to Antony?'

'Quite correct! We are moving south-west to Liskeard. So that is it, Lady Jane's open invitations.'

'What say you?'

'I'd say your mouth is watering for the fair Janet.'

'Yet I would not eschew her ladyship's gentle society.'

'Nor I. We halt nearby, overnight.'

Nicholas beckoned to his cornet. 'Jamie, ride to Antony House at Torpoint, present the compliments of Major Smythe and myself to the dame, Lady Carew, and enquire if we may join her at supper tomorrow.'

As the young officer wheeled his horse and galloped away, Nicholas turned to the new arrival. 'How did you contrive to be on this road at this time?'

'Is it not vital that sound liaison is maintained between Sir John Digby at Plymouth and Sir John Berkeley at Exeter, at this dangerous time?'

'Assuredly, for Plymouth will pose an increasing problem as Fairfax approaches.'

'As our commander quickly recognised,' Robin smiled sardonically.

'And he believed you best suited for the liaison task?'

'He appeared in no doubt.'

'Did you put it to him that the best way to Plymouth was by a double crossing of the Tamar?'

'Ah, that required some ingenuity, but he agreed that I should visit Millbrook garrison and Mount Edgcumbe House, strategic points in the siege of the city.'

Nicholas grinned, broadly. He was very glad to see the big man. 'So Janet, like Plymouth, is to be besieged.'

'At the closest possible quarters, for I have not ceased to think about her since we were last at Antony. I would have her,' he declared, fervently.

Nicholas did not respond.

Their steady trek had brought them within a few miles of Landrake when Robin's quick eye caught a glint of metal in the winter sun, on a ridge above the road. 'Beware!' he shouted, pointing.

A group of about a dozen horsemen were bearing down upon the rear of the convoy. The dragoons, inferior to real cavalrymen and taken unawares, bunched tentatively. Nicholas spun his horse and spurred towards them, shouting to the foot soldiers to come to the ready. The enemy horse discharged their carbines at the milling dragoons, adding to the confusion and swept along the flank of the convoy, delivering a fusillade of pistol shots at the draw horses. As the stricken animals fell, the convoy halted.

Isolated in front of his troops, Nicholas faced the marauders. There was only one thing to do. With drawn sword, he rode at the officer leading the attack. As the hurtling figures approached, a pistol ball struck his charger in the shoulder and it staggered and fell. A shaft of pain shot up his leg and he sprawled, pinioned, beneath the dead weight. Lifting his face from the earth, he looked for the enemy. They had swept past and he registered a montage of retreating rumps, swishing tails and flying clods of earth. Now they were turning, discipline and cohesion in the close formation. Beyond assistance from his foot soldiers and the reforming dragoons, he was helpless – in the path of the returning cavalry.

They came on, swords drawn, lobster-helmeted, visored, cuirassed and buff-coated, red-sleeved and gauntleted, wrapped with an orange sash. Every detail was clear – the muscles working in the horses' shoulders, the flared nostrils, bared teeth clamped on iron bits.

A sturdy, black-booted leg emplanted itself before his face, a leather butterfly poised on the instep, a sharp spur spanning the heel. For a second , the hind legs of a horse tramped dangerously near, then the animal started forward towards the looming horsemen, as if propelled. Its bulk caused the tight line to open and, before it could re-knit, the line swept past, shaking and churning the earth. A wedge of turf struck him; at the same instant, he heard a grunt and a sharp exhalation of breath. The leg buckled and a heavy bulk fell across him.

The suffocating weight was being lifted, then more pain as the entrapped foot was released. He looked up into the face of Captain Manton, his second-in-command. 'What has happened?'

'They have withdrawn, sir, but they did deadly work.'

Remembering the figure that had straddled him, he looked around. Robin sat on the ground, nearby, being eased from his buff coat while a chirurgeon laid out the contents of his satchel. Robin's face was chalk-white, but he forced a smile. 'You are a devilish impulsive fellow,' he said, ruefully, glancing from the discarded buff coat to his blood-soaked shirt.

Manton signalled to a waiting farrier. 'We'd best cut that boot away, sir,' he told Nicholas.

He nodded.

When the soldier had sheared the long boot to the ankle and the task of extracting the foot began, Nicholas diverted his mind from the pain by watching Robin. A sword-slash at the base of the neck was being staunched and dressed, but it was apparent that his thick ox-hide coat had spared him from death. Then he saw the farrier despatch his charger with an axe and nausea overcame him. The chirurgeon secured a rough splint to his leg. 'I fear the ankle is broken, sir.'

Nicholas turned to Manton. 'Determine our casualties, free the dead and wounded horses and redispose the stores and munitions. The convoy must move deeper into Cornwall, as rapidly as possible. Send a messenger to Millbrook garrison; ask for reinforcement of the escort and request transportation of our wounded to the garrison or Mount Edgcumbe House. Now, lift me into one of the waggons and make ready to press forward.'

Manton signalled to two musketeers, but, as he was lifted, a sharp twinge shot along the injured leg and he groaned. Robin called to him, 'Major, you will not withstand a journey to Pendennis in that condition. Captain Manton is an experienced officer, trust him to lead the column, while you travel by litter to Edgcumbe'.

Nicholas dwelt briefly on the welcome he would have received at Pendennis, but it was true – the journey would be a nightmare over the rough roads. He sent Manton about his duties and he returned, shortly, with a report of the casualties. It was a sobering catalogue.

'You can do no more here, so leave us and hurry on,' Nicholas told him.

The convoy had gone from sight, before his mind turned upon the events which had, literally, passed over him and he looked to where Robin lay, propped uncomfortably. 'Was it your calf, which obscured my view of the enemy?'

Robin winced. 'Aye, and a mis-timed sword cut that obliterated it.'

'For a second time, I owe you my life.'

'My dear fellow, I was merely preserving my *entree* to Antony House.'

Nicholas dragged himself over to where the big man lay and took his free hand, 'May it prove worth your while.'

▣▣▣

Mount Edgcumbe House sat four-square in its steep parkland, as it had since before the Duke of Medina Sidonia cast a covetous eye upon it, from the deck of his galleon, while Drake issued from the Sound, below, to distract his attention with grapeshot and canister, nigh 60 years before. Vigilant sentries watched the Devon shoreline and were observed, in turn, by Nicholas and Robin, from one of the tower-rooms. There were voices in the hall. Quick footsteps tapped the floor and Lady Carew and Janet looked down at them.

'Oh you poor, dear men,' Her Ladyship exclaimed, pressing Robin gently back into his seat, as he attempted to rise. She indicated Colonel Edgcumbe who stood behind them. 'My good neighbour has told me of your misadventure – and your gallantry, Major Smythe.'

Robin smiled diffidently, pleased by Janet's admiring regard. 'I understand that your injuries are knitting,' Lady Jane continued, 'and I have asked permission of Colonel Edgcumbe to take you to Antony, to complete your recovery.'

'That would be delightful, Your Ladyship,' Robin beamed.

176

Edgcumbe went off to return shortly with two brawny troopers, who made a hand-seat for Nicholas and carried him to the waiting coach, with Robin following. The heavy vehicle rumbled off down the drive and on over Maker Heights to Antony. As Nicholas limped through the great doorway of the house, Lady Jane said to Robin, 'Pray excuse us, Major, I would have a private word with Nicholas. Janet will conduct you to the solar, where a good bottle of madeira awaits you. We will join you there.'

She opened the door of the library and Juliana came towards them, exquisite in a gown of olive silk. Nicholas turned to his hostess, but the door had closed and they were alone. His stick clattered to the floorboards and he waited, unsteadily, for her embrace. She picked up the stick and helped him to a chair, while the silence of the room enveloped them, the rich smell of wood and leather heavy in the air.

'They said you were not badly hurt and that Robin saved your life.'

'Yes, the leg should be mended within three weeks and I owe it to him that I am, otherwise, sound. But how came you here?'

'Jane sent word of you and invited me to stay. My guardian could not deny the widow of his kinsman, for our differences with the Carews, except John, ended with Alexander's death. At that time, I wrote my condolences to Jane, for I have always been fond of her, and we have corresponded since. She has known you longer than I, so I confided our secret and she has told me things about your early life I did not know.'

'You must have astonished her.'

One eyebrow arched, but she did not reply. 'Three weeks together is a heavenly prospect, is it not?' she asked.

'Aye, it is.'

Above them hung the ornate plaster ceiling with its great, globular pendants; behind, rose shelf upon shelf of books, bound in red and green leather, tooled and blocked in gold. Juliana in this room – it was a perfect moment. He took her hand and caressed the long slim fingers. No words were needed till she said, 'I think we should join the others.'

'I can hardly bear to leave. I love this room and you grace it like a jewel.'

'Then, bring me here, often, for I am composing a portrait of a boy – dark, tall for his age and a little gangling, methinks. He sits at this table, beneath the Carew arms, seeking the path to wisdom and understanding.'

'For which he searches still.'

▣▣▣

177

During the next fortnight they were much alone, for Robin was usually in the company of Janet and the children, with whom he had become a great favourite. Juliana – resolved to improve her knowledge of herbs – came often to the library, to pore over hand-coloured illustrations and pages of spidery script. 'Who knows when I may need an apothecary's skill?' she answered, when he questioned her preoccupation.,

Mid-January laid a light mantle of snow upon the park, threatening to curtail the walks that Nicholas insisted upon taking, to exercise his injured leg. Today, as they emerged from the house, snowflakes dusted Juliana's hood and eyelashes and he stooped to kiss away a melting flake from her nose.' What think you of Robin's attraction to Janet?' he asked.

'I am concerned, for he seems much affected by her.' She was thoughtful. 'Her close relationship with Jane must end soon, and she must progress to a new phase of her life. If she is sensible, she will return to her own kind, for though Jane may have wrought a remarkable change in her, in some ways she is already formed and moulded – albeit broadened and uplifted by recent experience – the same person at heart. '

'And what of Robin?'

'He is a powerful presence who draws people of substance and significance to him. He must not tie himself to her!' She took his arm. 'Make him see!'

Shortly afterwards, Robin sought him out as he read in the library. He came in, tentatively, and seemed almost to tiptoe across the floor. 'My friend, I am much preoccupied. I had thought to propose marriage to Janet, as you know, yet your lack of approval occasions me unease.'

Nicholas hesitated. 'Do you love her?'

'Well enough, methinks. 'Tis sure I admire her.'

'Know you her feelings?'

'It is hard to say. She finds me agreeable, for she has said so.'

Nicholas closed his book and laid it on the table. 'What I would say to you, Robin, is not what you wish to hear.'

'Yet say it.'

'I have had much cause to ponder our society – why some are placed high and some low. Is it pre-ordained, as our peers would have us believe, or a mere accident of birth, that some are vouchedsafed all the advantages? What might we have been, given wealth, power and education? This struggle will decide more than the ascendancy of King or Parliament, for within the Roundhead army the old tenets are already being challenged by common men rising through the ranks. And members of the House of Lords and the Commons have, lately, been precluded from holding military or naval commands, through a self-denying ordinance. It is the beginning of a great levelling movement.'

'If it is, it will not be achieved in our time!', Robin interjected, bluntly. 'Whatever men may be in the sight of God, they are not equal in each other's eyes. But we were speaking of matrimony.'

'I had not forgot. Will you agree, then, that nature, as well as society, draws distinctions? Will the lion lie down with the lamb, does the wit drink with the dullard, or the fanciful debate with the prosaic?'

'These are matters for conjecture, Nicholas. Things of the spirit also draw men together. My wits may be sharper than my troopers, yet many times they have borne me up with their stoicism and humour. Fail to understand the human spirit and you will never win the hearts of men.'

'Agreed. But we were speaking of your marriage.'

'My proposed marriage. You are right – wedlock is a union of minds as well as bodies.' He contemplated the floor for several minutes, while Nicholas watched emotions come and go – like shadow and sunlight on a landscape. Then, he fingered a row of books before saying, finally, 'I am not an intellectual fellow like you, nor gentleman-born like Geoffrey, but it would not be a proper match.'

Nicholas sighed with relief. It had been a curiously high-flown and oblique discussion of his friend's dilemma. To relieve the awkward moment, he said, 'Now advise me, Robin, how may I become a less pedantic fellow?'

'Never take yourself too seriously. No man who can laugh at himself will stand so charged.'

With the denial of his hopes, Robin became morose and dinner was an almost solemn occasion, each guest conscious that the house-party was drawing to an end. At a loss to lighten the mood, Lady Jane looked around her board – at Juliana, an honoured guest; at Nicholas, an oddly equivocal presence; to Major Smythe who had been so attentive, even tender, towards Janet. Yes, Janet, brought into the house like many another stricken creature, to be nursed back to health, before being returned to her natural habitat. It was almost time to let her go. How she and the children would miss their gentle companion.

A loud rapping at the door sent sound echoing across the hall and, in a moment, a servant appeared. 'An officer seeks word with the two gentlemen, my lady.'

Cornet Jamie Ross entered. Confronted by the three ladies, he swept off his plumed hat in an elaborate bow. 'My pardon to the company for this intrusion, but I bear orders from Sir John Berkeley to these officers present.' He looked towards his seniors. 'The advance of Sir Thomas Fairfax has obliged General Berkeley to raise the siege of Plymouth and amalgamate his troops into the army now retreating into Cornwall. The General requires that you resume your duties with him, immediately.'

Foreboding showed in the faces around the table. 'What is the broader situation, Jamie?' Nicholas asked.

'We are plagued, as ever, by the ineptitude and rancour of our generals.' He paused, shocked by the impulsive reply.

'In what particulars?'

'Lord Wentworth, commanding the remnants of Lord Goring's army, declines to accept any orders not issued by the Prince of Wales. While he lay in winter quarters at Bovey Tracey, Cromwell unexpectedly attacked his horse, catching the officers at cards, and the force fled in confusion to Tavistock. Despite falling back upon 6,000 of our foot and 5,000 horse, Lord Wentworth ordered a general retreat. This panicked the new levies among the Cornish Trained Bands, although many were prepared to fight for the Prince. In consequence, the opportunity to relieve Exeter and defend Cornwall has been lost.' Jamie regarded his senior officers, resolutely, insensible of the irony of such weighty judgement from a beardless boy.

'Who is now in command, then?'

'Lord Hopton, sir. He has arrested Sir Richard Grenville, for refusing to serve under him, and despatched him to imprisonment in St. Michael's Mount.'

Nicholas shook his head 'These are evil tidings. I much regret, Lady Jane, that we must depart, immediately, for Exeter.' He looked into the desolate face of Juliana. 'Jamie, you will obtain an escort for Mistress Arundell, from Colonel Edgcumbe, and lead it to Pendennis Castle. I place this lady's safety in your hands.'

Jamie bowed. 'It shall by my life before yours, lady.'

Juliana smiled at the boy. 'And my whole trust shall be in you, Cornet.' Jamie blushed at the dazzling response.

'As for yourself, Lady Jane, will you not flee to Pendennis with Juliana?'

'No, I will stay to preserve my son's inheritance.'

Nicholas made to dissuade her from this course, but she was not open to persuasion. An hour later, with a last wave to the womenfolk on the steps of the house, the two Cavaliers rode across Antony park into a blinding snowstorm, for Exeter.

❑❑❑

That evening, while the three women sat again, at board, Jane Carew looked from the portrait of the young man, above her, to her companions. This bloody and unnatural war had robbed her of a husband and her children of a father; Janet's beloved James lay under the snow in Launceston churchyard, and Juliana would not remain unscathed – of that she was sure. There was no doubt of her deep attachment to the landless, almost penniless young man who the Carews had educated, whose only prospect lay in the success of the King's arms. As for herself, when might she hear the clatter of Roundhead troopers in the drive, the rap of a swordhilt upon her door? They would see Antony as a Royalist house, home of the late traitor to their cause.

The room seemed to grow chill and she shivered. Crossing to the bell-rope, she summoned a servant to build up the fire.

CHAPTER 19

Fairfax Ascendant

Sir John Berkeley moved away from the plan of Exeter on his map table and picked up a list of stores. His appraisal of the defences of the city had sobered him, as it always did, and the list did nothing to encourage hope. There was little prospect that Hopton would march to his relief, or even supply the livestock and provisions so desperately needed, but he must urge him to do so. Looking at Nicholas, bent over the table, he recalled that far-off day when he had agreed to further the plan to take Plymouth from the sea – that day he had compromised him with his own side. Well, here was the opportunity to put his loyal aide beyond the reach of a vengeful Parliament – for a while, at least.

Seated at his desk, he wrote rapidly. 'Nicholas, I want you to acquaint Lord Hopton of our plight, here, and beg him to send what succour he can, before placing yourself under his orders.'

'But surely, sir, my place is with you.'

'There is nothing more that you can do here, and the general will value your knowledge and experience.'

Nicholas did not move, till Berkeley placed the letter in his hand and, taking his arm, pressed him towards the door. 'Go now and do me this last service, and may God be with you.'

▣▣▣

Elsewhere, the fate of Devon and Cornwall was being decided. General Sir Thomas Fairfax stood in the doorway of his headquarters, looking towards the village of Chudleigh, 10 miles due south of Exeter. Out there in the night his army lay quartered, while he waited for Skippon's regiment to join him from Bristol and more troops to arrive from Corfe Castle. Ten days ago, they had stormed Dartmouth, in heavy snow and frost, and what a haul of prisoners and artillery that victory had netted.

The tall, raven-haired figure returned, thoughtfully, to his room and dropped into an armchair. With fingers entwined, he reviewed his policy towards the prisoners he had taken. It had been a master stroke, telling the Cornish foot that he had come to save their county, not to ruin it. And the two shillings he had thrust into each man's hand, before sending him on his journey home, had been money well spent, for 3,000 Devonshire men had joined his colours at Totnes and Powderham Castle had surrendered, the next day.

Yes, events were shaping well, yet there was one point of concern. A letter, intercepted at Dartmouth, revealed that the Queen and Jermyn had received authority to raise troops in Brittany and Guise, for immediate service in England, and this potential threat obliged him to act now. But what to do? Sir John Berkeley had rejected his summons to yield up Exeter, so seemingly he must storm the city. But when? Perhaps it would be prudent, in face of this confounded weather, to retire back into winter quarters and wait for the spring. Alternatively, he could march northward to Torrington and engage Hopton, who was reportedly advancing from Launceston.

He stretched and consulted his timepiece; it was midnight, time for bed. As he rose, Commisary-General Ireton burst into the room brandishing a document. 'Tom, see you this letter. It was brought to me by a Devonshire Justice, named Davies, and purports to come from Robert Love, the Prince's Secretary in Truro. It tells that Hopton and Grenville are at odds, that there is a rift in the Council of the Prince and that he is planning an early departure from the Kingdom. It urges us to advance, speedily, to gain advantage from these distractions.'

When he had read the letter, Fairfax asked, 'Henry, be so good as to ask Oliver to join us.' Ireton hurried off to return several minutes later with Lieutenant-General Cromwell, shirt unlaced, doublet loose, sandy hair awry. Fairfax proferred the letter. 'Read this, Oliver, I doubt not 'twill interest you.'

As Cromwell absorbed it, a broad smile lit his blunt features, emphasising the wart beneath his lower lip. 'Let us rejoice, if it be true. I suggest you convene a Council of War to consider it.'

Fairfax nodded.

The Council regarded the letter with some scepticism, arguing that it would have been an act of folly for the author to send such a self-indictment through Royalist territory, particularly as such information could well have come to Fairfax's ear through his excellent intelligence service. Nevertheless, it was decided to move towards Torrington.

Fairfax's advance was delayed by violent storms, which smashed the bridges over the river Torridge, but he pressed forward to Ring Ash, five miles from Torrington. There, as the weather cleared bright and dry, Nicholas saw him from the neighbouring hills.

Hopton had moved towards him, equally resolute, covering the 18 miles from Stratton to Torrington in one day. But his troops were dispirited and he was unable to order them to fortify the town or keep the guard. It was into this shambles that Nicholas rode, to be welcomed by Hopton as an officer conversant with the strength and disposition of the western forts, his last line of retreat. Hopton listened, attentively, as he warned of Fairfax's approach and the strength of his force.

'I am obliged to you, Major, for my neglectful scouts have observed nought.' He sent for his senior officers and ordered that earth barricades be erected at every entrance to the town and flanked by cavalry. Then he despatched 200 horse, under General Webb, on a reconnaissance to the east, and sent a further 100 to take up a position in Stevenstone Park.

When these dispositions had been made, Nicholas presented him with Berkeley's letter. After reading it, Hopton said, 'I regret that I am unable to assist General Berkeley and will send him word to this effect, for he is adamant that you should not return to Exeter.'

So Nicholas awaited the coming of Fairfax.

Their adversary could brook no delays, for the sparsely-populated country offered neither quarters nor provender. Thus, he struck swiftly. Hopton's dragoons, at Stevenstone, took the first shock. By early evening, they had been driven back to the town and the Parliamentary foot had reached the barricades. Nicholas held close to Hopton, hoping to be of some service, but, as they drew back into the town and darkness fell, the Parliamentary assault faded.

For about an hour the Royalists busied themselves loading waggons and coupling gun limbers, in preparation for retreat. At nine o'clock Fairfax, recognising these intentions, launched an all-out attack. With Hopton, Nicholas faced the onslaught, the crisp and continuous rattle of musket fire, the flashes of exploding powder lighting the tired, anxious faces of their troops. In the bright glow of fires, men reeled and fell, pikes and muskets cast asunder. He heard the scream and clatter of horses, and through the hedges came the awesome pikes, as he remembered them above Stratton. Hopton's soldiers fought doggedly, but the pikemen and flailing musketeers pushed them from one hedgerow to the next, on to and over the barricades and into the town.

Hopton spurred forward to hold the line, but his horse suddenly pitched and toppled, killed under him. Nicholas pushed his steed into the melee, his naked sword cutting a path towards Hopton. He half-saw a pikeman thrust his weapon into Hopton's face and the general disappeared, temporarily, from sight.

'Rally round General Hopton!' came the cry. A senior officer, whom he recognised as Lord Capel, was brandishing his blade to draw men about him. They were hacking at the Roundhead foot obstructing their path when, without warning, a fierce orange glow fused the scene into stark delineations, unreal in their intensity. There was, instantaneously, a gigantic roar and the church, in which 50 barrels of Royalist gunpowder had been stored, disintegrated, devastating the town. Slates, stones, baulks of timber and the mutilated remnants of the two hundred prisoners incarcerated in the shattered building rose high in the air and rained down upon the struggling men.

For a brief instant, friend and foe alike were transfixed with shock. Royalist infantry streaming out of the town towards the Tamar halted aghast, as did Cleveland's brigade pressing to re-enter it. No one was immune from the bombardment; a sheet of lead struck a man dead in the street beside Fairfax.

Despite his wound, Hopton rallied support and he and Capel fought with the rearguard until their broken army had withdrawn across the river. Even then, he would not abandon his men. When it was suggested that he and Capel should break out east with the horse, to join the King, he refused. 'I prefer to defend the Prince in Cornwall,' he declared, clasping a blood-sodden kerchief to his face, 'and my exhausted horse are no match for these Roundhead cavalry.'

When the magnitude of the disaster to his forces had been assessed, he wrote a despatch to the Council of the Prince and sent for Nicholas. 'Major Skelton, it is meet that you should carry this report of the battle at Torrington to the Council of the Prince, at Pendennis. Please read it, that you may better respond to any questions they may put to you. We have lost 60 slain, 600 prisoners and 1,600 weapons and I fear we have witnessed the destruction of the Cornish foot. But Lord Capel and I will continue to do our duty as the King's loyal subjects and await the Prince's further instructions. Tell His Royal Highness that!'

Nicholas galloped south with mixed emotions - sadness at the death and maiming of more of his fellow Cornishmen, admiration for the noble Hopton and Capel, and relief that he had survived the battle and remained free. But, most potently, there was satisfaction that he might now endure what was to come beside Juliana and the Arundells. When, sick with fatigue, he arrived before the Pendennis gatehouse, the sentry stepped forward, his pike presented. 'I am for Chancellor Hyde from Lieutenant-General Hopton.'

He was ushered into the guardroom of the keep and joined, shortly, by Hyde and Culpeper. 'What news, Major?' Hyde demanded, anxiously.

'Parlous ill I fear, Sir Edward, as General Hopton's despatch will reveal.' He presented the red-sealed document to the Chancellor.

Hyde read the narrative with Culpeper peering over his shoulder. When he looked up his face was drawn and grave. 'I will convey these tidings to His Royal Highness. You may then give us your own account.'

With the departure of the two councillors, Nicholas perched on the heavy table of the guardroom and looked at the panelled walls. He was very tired, but his mind wandered back to those so-distant days when he had supped with the Queen of England in a room above - a buoyant young man he hardly recognised. Footsteps sounded and Culpeper reappeared to beckon him up the stairway into a small room of the royal apartments. Hyde stood at the side of a tall, dark, olive-complexioned boy of about 16, with blunt features and a fleshy nose. He wore purple velvet. Nicholas swept a deep obeisance to Charles, Prince of Wales, Duke of Cornwall, heir to the Stuart throne.

The prince regarded Hopton's messenger, the exhausted eyes, the hollow cheeks and dishevelled locks, the battle-stained doublet and mud-plastered boots. 'You have brought us ill news, Major.'

'I fear so, Your Royal Highness!'

'And what say you of events?'

'I fear that Lord Hopton's forces are in tatters, while he is opposed by disciplined, well-equipped troops flushed with victory. But he and Lord Capel declare themselves at the service of your royal father and Your Highness.'

'Would there were more of such calibre! What should we do now, Chancellor?' He turned to Hyde.

'Order Lord Hopton to stand with the horse at Stratton, Sir, until the French troops promised by Her Majesty the Queen and Lord Jermyn arrive. Send him what horse we have and despatch muskets from Truro to reinforce him.'

'Quite so! Then let us so instruct secretary Edgeman.'

As Hyde departed to find his secretary, Nicholas saw defeat shadowed Culpeper's eyes. Seeking to divert their minds from Hopton's chilling report, the Prince said, 'You seem young to hold your rank, Major. Have you seen much service?'

'Nigh on three years, Your Royal Highness, substantially as a staff officer under Sir John Berkeley, but I was at Lostwithiel and the second battle of Newbury, besides Torrington.' He smiled inwardly; he would not mention Sourton Down and Stratton.

'Do you believe our cause lost in the west?' Culpeper interjected.

Nicholas looked cautiously at the Prince. This was clearly not a discourse to his liking. 'It must be conceded, my lord, that General Fairfax is more able than his predecessor, the Earl of Essex. His force is also more deadly and his policy of magnanimity in victory has won many to his standard.'

'Methinks, our prime hope lies in a treaty with the Scots, Your Royal Highness,' Culpeper declared. 'If Fairfax advances further, our horse will be trapped and, without cavalry, we cannot continue the fight.'

'I care not for this converse, Culpeper.' The Prince's dark face was stern, as Hyde returned to say that the orders to Hopton were being drafted. 'You have served us well, Major,' the Prince continued. 'Go, take your rest.'

'There will be work for you here, Major Skelton, arming and victualling the western forts.' Hyde added.

Outside the apartments, Toby Herrick waited to escort him to his quarters. Seeing his condition, he asked, 'Do you have any other apparel?'

'My servant followed me and should be here, shortly, with my portmanteau,' Nicholas told him.

Herrick showed him to a small chamber in the officer's quarters. Summoning his last reserves of energy, Nicholas dragged off his boots, divested himself of his stinking clothes and laved his face, before collapsing into the cot, utterly spent.

The door latch clicked softly and the hinge creaked. He opened his eyes. It was daylight and Juliana was looking down at him. Behind her, Meg bore a tray of food and drink. She bent over him, smoothed his hair from his face and kissed him. 'You have slept for 12 hours and must be very hungry.'

He reached up to take her hand and brush it with his lips. 'Aye, I am,' he declared, 'but for more than food.'

Juliana put a finger on his lips. 'Eat now!' While he drew himself into a sitting posture, she continued, 'Are you truly unharmed?'

He laughed. 'Quite sound, praise be to God.'

As Meg placed the tray before him, her pale cheeks darkened a shade. 'Good day to you, Major, what joy it be you have come to us safe from the Roundheads.'

Juliana could not remain silent while he ate, and pressed him with questions regarding events since their parting at Antony. As her maid removed the tray, she said, 'My guardian believes that the departure of the Prince for the Continent is imminent.'

'I think not imminent, yet it cannot be long delayed.' She grasped his hand. 'You must go with him!'

''Nay, my place is with you and your family.'

'No, you must go, for you are a marked man.'

'That is not certain '

The door creaked again and John Arundell stood in the tiny room. Seeing Nicholas' bare shoulders and chest, he observed, 'What is this, Juliana? In an officer's bed-chamber and he half-naked. Father Ambrose will require amends for such wantonnesss.' Nicholas was not certain if the eyes twinkled beneath the craggy brows.

'I will gladly pay penance, dear guardian, for the Lord has sent Nicholas safe to us.'

Arundell regarded him sternly. 'You have endured Torrington without hurt. Would you now defy Fairfax with us?'

'Do you propose to defy him, sir?'

'Yes, by God, I do!' Arundell was evidently astonished that anyone should doubt his resolve.

He held this old man in deep respect, for was he not one of a special breed, like Hopton, Capel, Bevill Grenville? He was 70 years of age and his eldest son had fallen in the cause, yet here he was still breathing fire, still exuding loyalty. With Fairfax a few miles to the north, it was no time for empty words, hollow sentiment. He, himself, may not comprehend their inspiration, but he had caught its essence at Stratton, for Bevill Grenville was its personification, the Golden Griffin its symbol. Gold! Pure metal, immutable in fire! James Chudleigh had succumbed to it and died one of them.

Before the power of Arundell's gaze, his soul was as naked as his body beneath the blankets. 'Will you stand with us, Nicholas?' he asked, again.

He had yearned to live among the Arundells and he would gladly die with them. 'Aye, sir, I will.'

▗▖▖

On 25th of February, Fairfax reached Launceston. By 2nd of March, he was at the gates of Bodmin and the Council of the Prince could delay the departure of their charge no longer. Nicholas stood near Juliana and the other Arundells as their royal guest took his leave, en route for Land's End. Grouped around him were Hyde, Culpeper, Sir Richard Bassett and others and, behind, some 300 souls who made up his household – cooks, barbers, launderesses, scullions. With farewells and loyal huzzas, the procession began to move. Soon its tail had passed through the gatehouse and disappeared from sight. After the sound and bustle, the silence was oppressive.

A brisk sea breeze blew across the open ward. 'I fear for Lady Anne Fanshawe, particularly, on the voyage,' Juliana said.

Nicholas nodded. They had been his own thoughts as he watched the pregnant woman, wife of Sir Richard Fanshawe, secretary to the Council, climb into one of the coaches. 'She should properly be abed, with her waiting-women in attendance, not seaborne to the Scilly Isles, this night.'

Juliana shivered. 'Let us go inside.'

As they walked towards the huddle of buildings beside the gatehouse, Nicholas observed, 'There has been neither sight nor sound of the Duke of Hamilton, since I returned here.'

'He was removed three months since to St. Michael's Mount.'

'Then, you are deprived of your close companion?'

She took his arm. 'Yes I have missed him, but I am amply compensated.'

He glanced at their entwined arms. 'I fear a penance will be demanded for this intimacy,' he said, lightly.

She halted, releasing his arm. 'Then we must formalise our betrothal!.'

This was the moment he had been dreading for, with his resolution to stand with the Arundells and acceptance of the possible consequences, had gone another decision. 'Hinny, we know that I may suffer death or imprisonment, if I am taken by the Roundheads.' He paused, searching for words. 'I cannot bind you to me.'

She gazed, unwaveringly, at him. 'None of us will be taken. Has my guardian not made that clear? Let us be joined, that we may better endure what is to come.'

'I cannot believe that the Colonel will countenance the death of the womenfolk, in his resolve. You must remain free.'

A storm was gathering in her face. 'Do you love me?' she demanded.

'With all my heart.'

'Then we will be betrothed!'

For a long moment he was silent, before forcing himself to say, 'Upon my honour, I cannot do it!'

Her face stiffened and two spots of colour rose in her cheeks. 'I have waited three years to be bound to you.' Her voice was breathless, intent. 'I have given myself to you as only a wife should. I have prayed to the Holy Mother that you be preserved from dangers, and my prayers have been answered. She has brought you to me at this time of trial, and now you would deny me. By Heavens, you shall not toy with my love so!'

Throwing her cloak about her, she turned on her heel and flounced into the apartments and up to her chambers, where she gave way to a fit of weeping, till exhaustion overwhelmed her and the tears came no more.

Chastened by the power of her passion, Nicholas stood, uncertainly, at the doorway, before making towards the landward walls of the fortress. Was this not the age-old problem of the warrior in love? Should they grasp at happiness, before the dark clouds closed about them, or should their love remain unfulfilled till fate decided whether he should live or die, be maimed, lie prisoner, or flee into weary exile? Once he would not have hesitated, but now he loved her more than life itself and she must remain free.

Fairfax would even now be turning towards this last, Royalist bastion in the west and he would not be long in coming.

CHAPTER 20

Rivalry Resolved

On 5th of March, a messenger from Hopton cantered across the castle ward to the office of the Governor, demanding to see Sir Edward Hyde. Arundell received him. 'What is the substance of your message?'

'General Hopton was obliged to evacuate Bodmin and is encamped on open moorland by Castle-an-Dinas, near St Columb. During a Council of War, he was pressed by the officers of horse to treat with General Fairfax, for they regard further resistance as futile. Lord Hopton refused to negotiate without the authority of the Prince of Wales and I am come to obtain it.'

'I regret that His Royal Highness, his Council and entourage sailed in the ship, *Phoenix*, for the Scilly Isles three days since,' Arundell informed him. The officer's shoulders drooped despondently. 'What are General Hopton's intentions regarding Pendennis and the other western forts?' Arundell continued.

'He refuses to treat for them, regarding them as not subject to distress. His Lordship, likewise, refuses to discuss the surrender of the infantry.'

Arundell suddenly felt very tired. Poor, gallant, dogged Hopton. He looked at the spent soldier before him. 'I can do nothing to help him, for 'twill be too late ere he even learns that His Royal Highness has departed. You had best take some refreshment and rest.'

▣▣▣

The next day, Fairfax sent a personal letter to Hopton, urging him to surrender, to spare more bloodshed and offering his own intervention with the Parliament, on behalf of his adversary, 'whom we honour and esteem above any other of your party.' Officers and men would be free to depart overseas and all troopers surrendering their horses and weapons would receive 20 shillings.

Other events were conspiring against Hopton. Two days earlier, Hugh Peters came to Bodmin with Royalists prepared to treat for the surrender of Mount Edgcumbe. As a consequence, letters of recommendation on behalf of these Royalist Commissioners, which eliminated any danger of a rising in East Cornwall, were sent to the Parliament. Further, from letters captured in a ship at Padstow, Fairfax learned of plans to transport thousands of Irish to England, to fight for the Royalists. When Peters declaimed these plans to a gathering of Cornish people, at Bodmin, the Royalists were much vilified for this intention.

Under these pressures, Hopton agreed to meet the Parliamentarians, at Tresillian Bridge near Truro, and there yielded up his cavalry. But he would not give up the foot.

Shortly after these events, Arundell sent for Nicholas. 'Come with me and you shall see a sight to leaden the heart.' The old man led him across the ward and through the gatehouse to the approach road.

They heard the creak and rumble of waggons, the lowing of oxen, the clip-clop of horses and the desultory rat-tat of a single drum, then the shuffle and scuff of exhausted men, as Hopton's infantry came into view. The column wound its way up from the sea and merged into ragged order, as it passed through the gatehouse and into sanctuary.

Some of the men were without weapons; filthy hose hung about their ankles; blood-stained rags hid their wounds. The women walked beside carts loaded with wounded, once-white aprons and black skirts soaked and muddied. They were like another broken army that had trekked along Cornish roads, towards their homes in the eastern counties, victims of Essex's folly. The wheel had turned full circle.

They drove some cattle, but pitifully few relative to their numbers, which Nicholas estimated to be about 900, with many senior officers among them. To feed them! Their own troops were already mutinous, for want of pay, and supplies were barely adequate even to sustain them.

Arundell's voice broke through his anxious reverie. 'I have authority to transport their remaining stores down-river from Truro, if I can find boats. Go quickly, commandeer every craft you can lay your hands on, and bring in everything that is moveable!'

Nicholas hurried away and Arundell was joined by Juliana. She did not stay long, but went to organise Meg and the other women into caring for the sick and wounded. For the next two days, she laboured to wash and bandage, comfort and pray with Hopton's men. When, at last, she felt able to leave them in other hands, she straightened, brushed dank hair from her face and sought her bed. Restored, she began the implementation of her plan to persuade Nicholas to reverse his decision, regarding their betrothal. Dressing carefully, she had Meg arrange her coiffeur so that no hair was out of place, then she went to pay her morning respects to her guardian, knowing that Nicholas was with him. He was preparing to leave as she glided close past, exuding a fragrance of orange water, but she paid him no attention and he departed, smarting and hurt. Worse followed. She renewed her friendship with Toby Herrick and they were to be seen, regularly, walking on the seaward walls or standing atop the keep, looking across the Roads. Nicholas' coolness towards Toby, stemming from the belief that he was the voyeur in the stables, turned to bitter jealousy.

Arundell observed the rift between his ward and her suitor with mixed feelings. Juliana was showing every sign of forming an attachment with Captain Herrick and his orthodoxy led him to hope that this most eligible young man might seek her hand, for it would be a propitious union. But, other more pressing matters required his attention.

On the 12th of March, Hannibal Boynton offered to treat for the surrender of St. Mawes Castle, with its 13 guns, on the eastern side of the Falmouth Haven. Six days later, the Dennis fort, at the mouth of Helford River, capitulated. The previous day, Fairfax had effectively stopped off access to Pendennis, by stationing two regiments at Pennycomequick. They arrived just in time to prevent Sir Henry Killigrew from firing his home, Arwenack House, to deny it to Fairfax.

Within the circumscribing walls of the castle, the Arundells and the varied humanity under their charge, were well aware that their ordeal had begun. On the day that St. Mawes and the Dennis fort capitulated, Fairfax summoned Arundell to surrender, giving him two hours in which to reply. This was more than enough time for the intrepid old man, who wrote to Fairfax declaring that his decision needed but two minutes and avowing that the castle had been committed to him by his lawful King and he was honour-bound to keep that trust, or be branded a traitor.

The insurgent generals, knowing Arundell's resolution, prepared for a long siege. Leaving the castle blockaded by the Plymouth regiment of horse and three other troops, Fairfax made for Bodmin, to arrange for the settlement of the county.

At the end of the month, Sir John Berkeley was faced with a similar ultimatum, at Exeter, and agreed to treat. On the 13th of April, he surrendered. The terms of the Treaty of Exeter were very favourable to the defeated Royalists. Berkeley's troops marched out armed and accorded the honours of war; the cathedral and churches were spared and the Cavaliers permitted to compound at two years' value of their estates, with no further impositions.

When the news of this clemency reached the beleaguered castle, Nicholas was constrained to hope that they might, similarly, escape retribution and, in the fading light of the evening, he walked to the walls, deeply thoughtful. There, he resolved to beg Juliana to go with him to Arundell and ask blessing for their betrothal. In conversation with Herrick, in an embrasure of the walls, Juliana watched the meditative figure turn and walk purposefully in her direction. When the alcove was visible to Nicholas, she pressed up to Herrick and kissed him. Unaware of Herrick's surprise at this turn of events, Nicholas watched him slide an arm around Juliana's waist and draw her close to him. Overwhelmed by jealous rage, his new-found resolution withered on the instant and he sprang towards the man who had supplanted him. Drawing his sword, he presented it to his rival's throat crying, 'By God, Herrick, I'll brook no more of this.'

Shaken by his passion, Juliana grasped his sword-arm, while Herrick stepped around her, unsheathing his own blade and standing on guard. 'Then let us settle the matter, now,' he responded, fiercely.

Juliana threw herself, boldly, between them, 'Stop this!' The clear command, the fragile buffer, sobered them.

'God's teeth, Juliana, are you mad to bait men so?' Nicholas regarded Herrick. 'You are right, the matter must be concluded, but not here. You shall hear from me.' He turned and walked abruptly away.

Without attempting to hide her dismay, Juliana left her new suitor and went to the walls, where she remained watching the sea frothing on the rocks below. Toby spoke, but she did not reply so he moved away and stood, like her, contemplating the restless waves, aware now that he had been a pawn in a game of love.

After a while, she called to him, 'Toby!' He affected not to hear and she came towards him, in the dusk. 'Toby, please forgive me!' Her voice was low, for they were within a few yards of the sentries.

'I fear that you will take chill in the night air, Mistress Arundell.' His tone was icy and she cursed the demon which had driven her to that act.

'Hear me, I pray! I have behaved unforgiveably and do not merit your regard, so do not hazard your life on my account.'

'I have little use for it!'

'Than give it to the King. Know that I love only Nicholas and it was to provoke him into asking for my hand that I committed such heartless folly, but let Nicholas and me be your friends.'

The wind flicked at his fair locks. 'The challenge will come from Nicholas. I am content to accept it.' He was almost as tall as Nicholas and, despite his boyishness, had the same hard look of the seasoned soldier. She felt a tremor of fear for her beloved. With a stiff bow he turned, descended the steps from the walls, and began to cross the ward. Then he paused and turned back to her, while she waited expectantly.

'I beg you, do not dally there. Remember the Roundheads are wont to give us a few shots, at this time of the day.'

She did not move until he resumed his walk and entered the officer's quarters, then she went to Nicholas' door. 'May I come in?' she asked, as he opened it in response to her soft rap.

'As you wish.'

Inside the cell-like room, she closed the door and sat upon the cot, while he looked down at her. 'I have been foolish,' she said humbly. 'Please believe that Toby has no place in my heart.'

He had known Juliana in many moods – proud, angry, arrogant even – but Juliana penitent was a new experience, and he was immensely relieved by her admission.

But he was not quite ready to succumb to her. 'Then why did you buss him, like a trollop?'

'To excite your jealousy. To goad you to change your mind. To make you think that you might otherwise lose me.'

'You still believe me wrong?'

'I do, I do!' She took his hand. 'Let us be bound, together, regardless of what lies ahead. Our love is all of life, what more is there?'

He raised her up and took her in his arms. Had he ever truly doubted her? If not, why, in the name of Heaven, had he allowed mere pique to drive him to challenge Toby Herrick? As if guessing his thoughts, she drew away. Will you promise that you will pursue your quarrel with Toby no further?'

'Jamie has already borne a note to him demanding satisfaction.'

'Then you must withdraw it!'

'That would impugn my honour.'

'A pox on your honour! You have caused a young cornet to carry a challenge to a duel and obliged a subordinate officer to met you. What must the

Governor do, when he learns of it?'

'He need not. I do not have to kill Herrick, a slight wound would suffice.'

'Are there no bounds to your arrogance? Toby Herrick is a gentleman, trained in arms since childhood. You would hazard your life trifling with such a man!'

'Was it a gentleman who crept behind us into the stables?'

'I maligned him in that matter. Shortly afterwards a groom was flogged for molesting a maid, there, and he confessed to other, like offences. All the evidence points to him. It is beyond reason that Toby would spy upon us so.'

She saw, with despair, that her defence of Toby and her demand for an abject retraction of his challenge had antagonised Nicholas, as swiftly as her contrition had touched him. How could she blame him, for she was the cause of the quarrel and she must resolve it. Turning from him, she said, 'I see that you will not be influenced by me, but I will not have your blood, or Toby's, on my hands.'

He did not move as she opened the door and departed. No one in this affair was blameless, least of all Juliana, but he would stand surety for her impulse with his life, if needs be. There was a tap at the door and he opened it to find Jamie Ross waiting to present him with the reply to his challenge. He opened the note and read: 'Captain Tobias Herrick will be pleased to afford Major Skelton the satisfaction he demands, with the sword, and proposes a meeting on the foreshore of the Carrick Roads, beneath the castle, at dawn tomorrow.'

Of a sudden, there was a series of loud booms and, moments later, cannon shot began to rain into the ward. Nicholas leapt towards the window, to see the partly-constructed chapel, which Prince Charles had proposed for the worship of the garrison, topple and fall in clouds of dust. Then, in the flashes which lit the sky, he saw Toby run from the doorway, below, towards the quarters of his gunners.

As he sprinted across the open grass, another salvo straddled the area and he staggered and fell. A fire was burning near to where he lay, as the wind from the sea drew and encouraged the flames. Nicholas was galvanised into action as he realised that the burning building was a small powder store, from which some rampart guns were served. He raced down the stairs and ran towards the recumbent figure. As he bent over it, the sparks crackled and spat and he smelt the singeing fabric of his doublet. Grasping one of the extended arms, he drew the body of the powerful young man across his shoulders and staggered back the way he had come. As he reached the door arch, an immense blow struck him in the back and he was pitched through the doorway and flung against the far wall of the vestibule. His ears sang as he lay where he had fallen, dazed and bruised. Opening his eyes he looked up at the vaulted ceiling, still bedizened with Tudor roses, but cracked and devoid here and there of its plaster. Nearby, lay the inert body of Toby, a bloody gash on his forehead. Nicholas drew himself into a sitting posture and put his head in his hands.

'Zounds!'

The voice came from far off. Toby was beginning to stir. Gingerly feeling his head, he examined the blood on his finger tips and groaned again, 'Zounds!'

Despite the shock of the explosion and their antipathy, Nicholas laughed with relief and amusement at his companion's soot-streaked expression.

'I last recall being in the ward,' Toby remarked, tentatively.

'We left it in haste.'

'Did you bring me here?'

'Aye.'

Toby gave a weak grin. For two or three minutes there was silence, while their faculties returned, then Toby looked towards his rescuer. 'Studied you logic in the schoolroom?'

'Not that I mind!'

'As I thought, for I see little in your action.' He waved his hand towards the plaster fragments littering the flags. 'Not 10 minutes gone you saved me from being blown to pieces. Within hours we are to determine who of us may live and who die. The issue could have been resolved without risk to yourself. What became of logic?'

'I vow, 'twas absent.'

'Then let us be pragmatic and abandon this course, for there can be no proper conclusion to it. How might I live, if I thrust my sword between your ribs? And would you save my life, today, only to take it tomorrow?'

'It is a palpable argument.'

'Then give me your hand on it.'

Nicholas rose, painfully, and helped Toby to his feet as the guard captain entered, four musketeers crowding in behind. 'Thank God, I find you sound, gentlemen.'

'Has the bombardment ceased?' Nicholas wiggled a finger in his ear.

'It has. It was another delivery from the two batteries of ordnance north of Arwenack.'

'Whatever we may want for, powder and shot are plentiful and I will return them full measure, tomorrow, with permission of the Governor,' Toby vowed. ''Twill be more profitable than my previous engagement.'

'In the meantime, you must come with me to the chirurgeon – I will then put Juliana's mind at rest, for she is much troubled regarding us.' Herrick's face clouded at the reference to Juliana, but he said nothing.

By morning, Nicholas's hearing had almost recovered from the shock of the explosion and he repaired to a logistics meeting with the Governor. Arundell gave him a sheet of paper. 'We have but six weeks of provisions left,' he told him. 'These are the supplies we need and I am informing the Prince of Wales of our parlous state.'

Nicholas smiled grimly. 'With respect, sir, it is optimistic to describe a small quantity of tainted beef, a little bread, and the dregs of the wine as six weeks' supply for over 1,500 souls.' He looked at the long list – clothing, surgeons' chests, medicines, beef, butter, oatmeal, herrings, sugar, spice, vinegar, wood, wine and biscuit, sea-coal, needles and fish-hooks, 2,000 lb of tobacco and twenty gross of pipes, match and munitions, shot and bullets, firelocks, granadoes, swords for the officers and three months' pay for all ranks. 'Gad, just to read this mouth-watering list is a penance.'

Arundell smiled, 'Aye, but a worse one for lusty young bloods. We old ones do not have such an edge to the appetite. Albeit our bellies are empty, we are blades of the right stamp, here, as yon Roundheads shall discover.'

On 17th of April, Colonel Hammond, commanding the investing forces, summoned Arundell to surrender. His reply was a flat rejection.

□□□

Toby hailed Nicholas, one morning, as he was walking to his quarters. 'We are preparing a postscript to the Governor's letter. Would you care to witness it?'

'Gladly!'

'Then come to the keep.'

Nicholas followed him over the drawbridge to the octagonal gunroom, on the first floor, where the great culverins were already manned and cleared for action. Their crews stood or knelt about them, stripped to the waist and undeterred by the draught of crisp air which drove in through the splayed gunports in the wall. The men were already showing the first signs of malnutrition and the thin light, which came through the smoke vents above, drew dark shadows beneath their ribs.

'With 94 pieces of ordnance in the castle, 'twould be neglectful not to show the Roundheads our spirits and powder stocks are high.' Toby declared.

'Would that we could transform some of those powder barrels into casks of wholesome salt beef or manifest a few cheeses from that pile of shot,' Nicholas replied.

Toby shook the sagging front of his doublet. 'Do not speak of food.' He advanced to the middle of the room to relay orders through his master gunner. Five-and-a-half inch iron shots were loaded into the muzzles of the cannon, then powder was scraped into each breech and closing tampions inserted. When all was ready, he bawled, 'Give fire!'

A great roar wracked Nicholas' ears, acrid smoke soured his nostrils and the ordnance whipped at the restraining tackle. Then the heaving, grunting task began again, to prepare the monsters for the next salvo. After the recent assault upon his hearing, Nicholas found the clamour unbearable and signalled to Toby that he was leaving. From the greensward, outside, he looked back at the spouting guns. The bombardment was a splendid defiance, but the field of fire permitted by the embrasures and the number of culverins which could be deployed, in any direction, from the round keep, were limited. The ramparts were the only place from which to hammer the Roundheads.

Juliana appeared in the entrance to the main accommodation block and he hurried towards her. Their privations had exaggerrated the fine bone structure of her face and her beauty was almost ethereal. Since the dangerous provocation of her two suitors she had not mentioned their betrothal and had devoted her time and energy to caring for the increasing number of sick in the castle. He enquired of her charges. 'They need more food,' she told him. 'Mothers are depriving themselves of what little there is so that their mites may have more.'

She led him, through a vestibule, into a long bare room lit by shafts of light from windows high in the walls. A row of cots lined each side of a central aisle – about 40 in all – close-packed and containing mostly, children, but here and there, a woman. Attendants moved quietly among them, their white caps bobbing as they bent to smooth a sheet or murmur a word of comfort. A child began to cough and Nicholas went to it. The contorted face was almost as pale as the pillow, the skin translucent, the lips colourless. Brown hair clung, dankly, to the forehead. As the racking cough subsided, Juliana took a damp cloth and brushed back the encroaching locks. 'They need wholesome food,' she repeated.

An old woman, in the next bed, overheard her, 'And that goes for you too, milady, and the young gentleman, I'll be bound. 'Tis hard for soldiers to keep their spirits up when their bellies be empty. What would ye give, sir, for a pastie or some hog's pudding and apple pie, washed down wi' a quart of ale?'

Nicholas swallowed the saliva her tantalising picture had induced, 'My pay for a year, mother, if you can produce it.'

The weatherbeaten furrows deepened and she gave a low laugh. 'Bless ye, sir, nothin' I'd like better. I've raised five sons, girt big boys – two drowned at sea, one slain on Bradock Down. The Lord keep t'other two safe, here, for there's nought their old m'am can do for 'em now.' She turned away and closed her eyes.

They left the oppressive infirmary for the sunshine outside. For the second time that day, Nicholas had turned from scenes of a castle under siege, frustrated and inadequate. Juliana took his arm. 'Thank you for coming to see.'

He placed a hand on top of hers. 'War is most cruel when it involves women and children. Would that I could do something.' He kissed her hair and she returned to her duties in the hospital, while he went to stare, thoughtfully, at the Roundhead entrenchments around Arwenack. Then, he rejoined Toby in the now-silent gunroom, where he was making an inventory of ammunition expended. On the table before him lay a spyglass.

'Bring your glass to the walls,' Nicholas said. As they walked, he continued, 'I have just seen the most pitiable sights – women and children succumbing to starvation, because every attempt to get provisions into the castle has been thwarted by Batten's ships and barges blockading the roads. Does not logic dictate that we should seek relief from the land?'

They circumvented a body of drilling pikemen. 'What have you in mind? The peninsula has also been sealed off by Hammond and Fortescue!'

'We might capture some of their own stores and bring them back to Pendennis!'

'You are an audacious fellow! What is your plan?'

'I haven't one as yet. Let us first observe.' They were climbing the steps to the ramparts as Nicholas continued, 'Keep your head down, but look where the undergrowth grows to the walls. At night, a party could be lowered into the trees and could work its way to Smithick quay. There will be stores, there, I'll be bound.'

Toby was cynical. 'And the Roundheads will never notice the rumble of wagons or the clop of pack-horses returning in the night.' He raised the spyglass to his eye and, for a full minute, leaned motionless against the stonework, studying the distant beach. 'Look you, at yonder figure beyond the scrub,' he said, at last.

Nicholas raised the glass and picked up a stationary cart with a thin doleful horse betwixt the shafts. Beside it was the tall, powerful figure of a man, stooping to gather kelp. As he watched, the man turned and, from the cover of the cart, looked towards the castle. His large shapeless hat was turned up at the front revealing the face beneath – ruddy and red-bearded. 'I swear it is Robin! What is he doing there?'

'I think we should find out.'

'Then, you will come?'

'Aye, but on a reconnaissance only.'

'Then let us take our plan to the Governor.'

They found Arundell looking through the narrow window towards Falmouth Bay. Before they could speak, he said, I am watching a fellow who must be desperate for seaweed. I feel I know him – something about his movements.'

'We believe it is Major Smythe, sir.'

Arundell slapped his thigh. 'Of course! But what is he doing there, taking such a risk?'

'And why do the Roundheads allow him there, sir? He must spread the kelp locally, on Killigrew land.'

'Aah!' Arundell's contemplative sigh died as he opened the door and instructed the orderly outside. 'Request Henry Killigrew to come to my office!'

Killigrew joined them, shortly. He was cast in the same mould as Grenville and Arundell and had fought with Hopton from the earliest days of the war. 'Henry, look you at yon figure on the beach out there.' Arundell handed him Toby's spyglass and aligned him with the distant beachcomber.

Killigrew raised the glass to his eye. 'So, he has arrived,' he said, thoughtfully.

'What mean you?' Arundell's tone betrayed displeasure.

'Forgive me, John, but I was charged to keep close certain intentions, till the proper time. Would you ask Captain Herrick to withdraw, before I disclose them?'

Arundell nodded to Toby. As the door closed behind him, Killigrew continued in his quick, resolute voice. 'Before I abandoned Arwenack, Prince Maurice sent orders that I was to assist Major Smythe to contact Major Skelton. If the military situation made this difficult, Smythe was to be absorbed among my estate staff and I instructed my steward to designate him as a kelp gatherer, so that he might move, unremarked, about the peninsula. Now, he is here – for what purpose I am not acquainted.'

Arundell looked curiously at Nicholas. 'You had best devise your own plan for a rendezvous. Be assured of my full support.'

'Thank you, sir. By chance, Captain Herrick and I came to see you with a plan to forage for food from the Roundheads' own stores. Given Sir Henry's local knowledge and influences, we may effect both objectives. Have you a plan of the castle and its environs, sir?'

Arundell nodded and went away, to return, shortly ,with a roll of parchment and accompanied by Toby. Chairs scraped, as they settled around the table, and the two senior officers looked to Nicholas. 'The seaward blockade and the close investment on land have frustrated all attempts to supply us,' he reminded them. 'I have no plan to remedy that situation, merely to bring some relief to the sick women and children.'

Killigrew's eyebrows contracted as he looked, challengingly, at Nicholas. 'Very commendable, Major, but what is its military value?'

'It would, assuredly, boost the spirits of the garrison, sir.'

Arundell unrolled the parchment. 'Describe your plan.'

'It is to descend into the woods, by night, from the western ramparts, where the angle of the bastion hides us from the main gate, and make our way to Smithick quay – the Parliamentarians must be supplied from the sea. Having established what stores may be taken, I had proposed to lead a raiding force the next night. Since I am to rendezvous with Major Smythe, I propose that Captain Herrick lead the raid, while the major and I create a diversion, before we set about whatever other business may be required of us.'

Arundell was pensive. 'The risks are high and the only way to bring back enough supplies to justify them is by sea. Five boats rowing into the Roads around Pendennis Headland would meet the need. But it is about a mile and a half each way – a formidable row for hungry men.'

'Given our sorry state, sirs, my gunners are strong fellows in the shoulder and could form the boat crews,' Toby suggested.

'While the raiders are drawn from the families of the sick,' Nicholas put forward.

Arundell glanced at Killigrew, who nodded. 'Siege warfare is not to my taste. I endorse this initiative.'

'As do I,' said Arundell. 'The usual fires to guide relief vessels will not be lighted. Go now, recruit your force, check the tides and be sure the moon will not betray you.'

'Meantime, I will effect contact with Major Smythe,' Killigrew said.

CHAPTER 21

The Reconnaissance

At ten o'clock that night, Nicholas and Toby were lowered down the western ramparts, wearing grey doublets, breeches and hose and dark fishermen's caps, with two pistols and a knife thrust in their belts. Reaching the base of the walls, they slipped free of the ropes and listened, intently, but the only sound was the distant lap and surge of the sea. The night was moonless. From the woods below rose the smell of damp earth and foliage, while, above them, the claustrophobic castle hovered like a great black raven.

As they moved into the trees, the stillness was shattered by the roar and spurt of cannon from the ramparts, lighting their descent through the woods to the coastal path above the rocks. At the wood's fringe they waited, till the brief artillery onslaught ceased, before setting off towards the Parliamentary lines at Arwenack. It was not long before they heard the tramp of infantry and Nicholas held out a restraining arm. Moving quickly back behind a clump of furze, they waited while a foot patrol passed by, barely seen.

'We must give their positions a wide berth,' Nicholas whispered, 'and that means a dip in the sea.'

Toby shivered. 'Twill be a mite chill this time of the year. Maybe we can find a boat?'

'Then it needs be small for us to handle.'

Emerging from their sparse cover, they headed cautiously across the neck of Pendennis Point towards the shoreline of the Carrick Roads. At the water's edge, they searched among the small boats on the pebbles and found a coracle-like craft with a paddle lying within it. Launched on the flooding tide, they paddled hard till the outline of Smithick quay showed vaguely, inshore.

'Let me reconnoitre, for I am to lead the raid and one of us must stay with the boat,' Toby whispered.

'We go together.'

Overhead, a brief exchange of conversation and retreating footsteps were audible. As the craft glanced against the pier, the thin reflection of lanterns revealed a stair leading to the decking above. They mounted the steps. A lone sentinel kept indifferent watch, his attention on the tavern lights of Penryn, while the two raiders melted into the shadows between the lanterns.

'It is dangerously quiet,' Nicholas murmured. As if to resolve the problem, the Parliamentary ordnance fronting Arwenack House opened up on the castle, its reverberations rumbling, ponderously, on the night air, its brilliance revealing an open-sided warehouse in a cobbled yard, sealed from the coast road by a wall and a gate. Moving along the jetty, they reached the store, to find several barrels, some piles of shot and boxes which probably contained muskets and bullets. At its far end, were other barrels, sacks and a hoard of cheeses.

Toby made a small slit in one of the sacks. 'Grain!' he whispered, exultantly.

Nicholas stooped over the muslin-wrapped cheeses and sniffed. The once-familiar aroma stung his nostrils and the urge to carve out a wedge and cram it into his mouth was almost overwhelming.

Toby was rocking one of the small barrels. 'Beer or wine, I wager.'

Nicholas peered at the lid of one of the larger barrels, in the flickering light of the cannon fire, and made out crudely formed letters, applied with a thick paint: B.E.E.F.. 'We've seen enough! He beckoned Toby to follow him.

The sentinel was standing at the head of the stairs, watching the now -desultory bombardment of Pendennis Castle and blocking their escape route.

'The tide turns in an hour and will draw us out to sea. We need half that time to row beyond the Roundhead lines and come ashore,' Toby whispered.

'We will wait,' Nicholas replied and Toby breathed impatiently. 'Twill be the end of the enterprise if we have to slay him,' he added, to steady his friend.

'Twill soon be the end of us, if we do not.'

Two more rounds of ordnance were discharged, before Toby stood erect and slipped the knife from his belt. But there was no more firing. For a few moments the sentinel remained looking eastward, then he walked to the far side of the jetty, allowing them to scurry to the stairway and slip down out of sight. Stepping into the boat Nicholas loosed the painter, as Toby silently deployed the paddle and eased away from the jetty. Now, they were exposed and vulnerable, but the sentry did not move and soon a bank of fog obscured them. When they judged that they had passed the flank of the Roundhead lines, they beached the craft and dragged it a few yards from the water's edge, before collapsing, spent, upon the foreshore. After a few minutes, Nicholas rose and urged on his companion. Re-entering the treeline, they groped blindly up the slope, each snapping twig sounding like a pistol shot in the silence. Breaking from the woods near the base of the walls, Nicholas felt for the rope by which they had descended and gave three sharp tugs. There was an immediate response. Securing the rope about Toby, he jerked, again, and his companion ascended, slowly, and disappeared. The rope slithered down towards him and, a few moments later, he was hauled through an embrasure and pulled to his feet, inside the castle.

Among the small knot of soldiers stood Juliana and Meg. Juliana grasped his hand. 'Thank God you are safe. My guardian is being roused from his bed.' She took his arm. 'Why did you not confide your plan to me?'

'Would you have approved, had you known?'

She thought of her ailing patients, the old woman, the consumptive child, all of them. 'No,' she said, quietly.

Leaving her with Toby, Nicholas went to the Governor's office, to find Arundell at the head of his council table, with Killigrew on one hand and, on the other, Robin!

'Please be seated. Sir Henry sent one of his estate workers in the garrison to Arwenack, to bring back Major Smythe.'

'Then it is possible to penetrate the enemy lines?'

Arundell glanced towards Killigrew, 'It is possible to pass under them,' Killigrew said, enigmatically. 'I will confide to you a secret Major Skelton, if you will take oath not to reveal it to anyone beyond these four walls.' Steely eyes held him.

'I so swear.'

'A tunnel runs from the castle to surface near Arwenack Drive. With the house and grounds occupied by the Roundheads, it will not serve as supply route, but, with the right guide, it suffices as a communication link with loyal members of my household.'

'Tis a mite low for tall fellows,' Robin pressed his hands into the small of his back, 'but it has spared me another day of gathering that damned seaweed.'

Killigrew's contracting brows cut short the banter. 'The passage through the tunnel takes too long. Tonight you will go overland.'

Nicholas looked to Arundell. 'What of the sortie to Smithick quay, sir? I consider it feasible.'

'Then it will go ahead under Captain Herrick.' Arundell brought in Toby and spread out a large map of the area. 'Give us your appraisal.'

'In order to succeed, our force must reach the warehouse jetty undetected,' Nicholas told them. 'A diversion would assist that aim.'

Killigrew leaned forward. 'Such as firing the great barn at Arwenack.' Arundell glanced, sharply, at him. 'You would agree to that?'

'Aye! I could not deny the Roundheads my house, but that would, at least, rob them of fodder for their horses.'

'Nicholas and I could attend to that, ere we depart,' Robin proposed.

'Capital!'

'We have not been idle,' Arundell informed them. 'Five boats now lie hidden among the rocks at the foot of the castle, on the eastern side.'

'And I have 30 volunteers to man them,' Toby replied.

'Good!' Arundell turned to Robin and Nicholas. 'You will leave the castle, shortly, and make for the barn, where Robin will feign sickness during the day, while you lay hidden, Nicholas. You will fire the barn at' – he glanced around the table – 'say midnight?'

The group nodded. 'The fire shall signal the bombardment of the Roundheads before the house and the attack on the jetty. While you lead the attack, Captain Herrick, I advise that your second-in-command remain with the boats. Who is he to be?'

While Toby hesitated, Nicholas said, 'Might I suggest Cornet Ross, a young fellow anxious to prove himself.'

'Aye, 'twill blood the boy,' Arundell agreed. 'What provender may we expect from this sally?' he demanded.

'About two ton of grain, five barrels of salted beef, some cheeses, beer and wine, sir.'

When Jamie arrived, Nicholas felt a pang of remorse for involving the boy. Sudden arousal from sleep had left him pallid, but his locks were smooth and he was fully accoutred. As he came smartly before his grizzled commander, even Killigrew's piratical countenance wrinkled into a smile. But Arundell did not patronise him, as he gave him his orders. When he had concluded, Jamie said, 'Thank you very much, sir.'

It was Arundell's turn to smile, grimly. 'Do not thank me, Cornet, for I do you no favour. Now, away to your beds, for you will not see them this coming night.'

When the others departed, he dismissed Robin and Nicholas. 'You must begone within the half-hour or dawn will find you in the middle of Arwenack park.'

Nicholas hurried after Toby and Jamie. 'God grant you success and a safe return,' he told them.

'And you, likewise,' Toby replied. 'I would be a true friend of Juliana and yourself, Nicholas,' he added.

'So you shall be,' Nicholas replied, embracing him. He beckoned to the young cornet. 'Come with me, Jamie.'

They hurried to his room, where he penned a note to Juliana, which he handed to the boy. 'Please give this to Mistress Arundell, in the coming day, and do your duty.'

When Jamie had gone, he threw off his torn clothes and damp hose and exchanged them for black doublet and breeches, trimmed with silver braid, and the rose-red sash of the Cavaliers. He drew on black thigh boots, buckled a belt about him and slipped a baldrick and sword over his shoulder. He was conspicuously a Royalist officer and that is how he would die, if must be.

At the ramparts, Robin was waiting with Thomas Hughes, Killigrew's man, and the soldiers handling the rope. Nicholas smiled at the troops. 'You have sufficient strength to lower Major Smythe safely, I trust?'

The soldiers chuckled, softly. 'We've allowed that the Major ain't been starving like the garrison, sir,' one of them replied, grinning diffidently at the big man.

'Well, don't hold that against me, when I'm dangling on that rope,' Robin replied, genially. 'Let us to it! I will go first, while your strength lasts.' Looping the hemp about his waist, he tested the knot before climbing into the embrasure. As the rope was paid out, he disappeared into the darkness below. Nicholas followed, then Thomas Hughes. For a moment they huddled together, at the foot of the ramparts.

'I will lead the way down through the trees.' Nicholas whispered.

'Well, hurry, 'twill soon be dawn,' Robin answered.

When they had slithered blindly down the slope to the path, Robin moved Thomas Hughes in front and they set off towards the outbuildings of Arwenack mansion. Hughes advanced quickly and confidently, and soon they were clear of the brooding presence of the castle and moving through sand dunes. Feeling a breeze caress his cheek, Nicholas hoped that it would sift the dry sand over their tracks, before first light.

Suddenly, a subdued laugh and a mutter of conversation halted them. Ahead, a copse showed against the sky and, after a few minutes cautious waiting, Hughes led them into a shallow defile which cut through the trees. It brought them to an area of pale light, cast by a lantern over a gateway in a wall. Skirting the pool of light, they ran noiselessly into the shadow of the wall and followed it till it led to a massive building. Hughes eased the latch of the postern gate and swung it open on well-greased hinges. They were inside the great barn of Arwenack.

'I must return, straightway,' their guide said. 'for 'tis nigh on dawn.'

'Thank you, good Hughes.' Robin closed the door, soundlessly, behind him, before leading Nicholas up a ladder to the straw-stacked loft, above. 'We can lie soft here, with ample cover, till evening. Killigrew's bailiff will bring food.' He drew aside some bales of straw and motioned Nicholas into the confined space, then he repositioned them allowing Nicholas room to stretch out.

But sleep eluded him and, gradually, the grey light of dawn filtered into the great stone barn. He heard a cock crow and a blackbird began to sing, in a tree nearby. There was a distant cry of wheeling gulls where, less than a mile away, Juliana would be preparing for morning prayer. Soon she would have his note and would know that, once again, fickle fate had denied their betrothal. From the yard below, came the sound of marching men, harsh words of command – then the smell of bacon cooking! Cramp gnawed his belly, saliva filled his mouth.

Robin had yet to tell him what he must now do for the great cause. Why did they continue? The Prince, Maurice, Hopton, Hyde, Capel had all departed. Cornwall, except for Pendennis, had surrendered. What was happening, elsewhere? Was the King defeated, captured? What was he doing hiding in a barn close to the enemy, when men like Berkeley had gained honourable terms of surrender? They had all sworn to serve this arrogant, feckless King, who signed away the life of his loyal minister, Strafford, for the sake of expediency; who had sought to rule as an autocrat, divinely appointed!

He knew the answer. Like Berkeley, he had served the King loyally, and could lay down his arms without disgrace, but in doing so he would forfeit that which he held most dear – Juliana's respect, if not her love, and the esteem of the Arundells – of Jack-for-the-King, of Sir John of Lanherne, of Colonel Richard. For these men, this family, above all for Juliana, he would endure.

He lapsed into an uneasy sleep. 'Nicholas, wake up! 'He opened his eyes to see Robin and a tall, broad-shouldered man he did not know standing behind. 'This is Sir Henry Killigrew's bailiff, demanding to know why his idle kelp-gatherer is still abed.'

The man smiled. 'I would not drive a fellow to the beach who complains of fever and pains in his belly. He had best lie here, today. Mayhap, you will take his food.'

'Food!' they both said. 'Food!'

Nicholas came to his feet. Bread, cheese and an earthenware jug stood upon the floor. 'Come, eat,' said the man.

'But do not overtax your shrivelled belly,' Robin warned.

With all the self-control he could muster, Nicholas began to eat, starting with the cheese and savouring its oily texture, tasting its strong bite on his tongue. He poured and drank the cool, dry cider from the earthenware jug, letting its apple-sharp tang caress his throat. Even the rye bread that he might once have eschewed was food fit for the gods. Robin and the bailiff watched him, approvingly, then Robin joined in the simple repast, as the bailiff began to descend the ladder murmuring that he would return later.

As his head disappeared from view, a colic-like pain gripped Nicholas' bowels and his belly began to distend until his pistol belt became an insufferable constraint. He abandoned the food and stood up, releasing the buckle, but the discomfort was so intense that he could not stand upright. His friend eyed him, concernedly. 'Eat no more for the time being,' he advised, 'but fart, vigorously.'

Nicholas smiled wryly, 'Without the food, I lack the vigour.'

'Perhaps 'tis as well, for you have within you the capacity to bring every trooper in Arwenack to the alarm and we must keep yon' roof intact till we fire it tonight.'

Gradually, the griping pain subsided, but Nicholas made no further attempt upon the food and, eventually, he was able to settle down to sleep, to be awakened by unaccustomed noises from the floor below. Wondering where Robin might be, afraid to move the bales of hay, he held his breath. After an eternity, the sounds subsided, then the bales were eased back and Robin looked down at him. 'A work party of cavalrymen, gathering hay for the stables,' he murmured, anticipating Nicholas' question. 'Will you take some more food?'

Nicholas nodded and Robin handed him two wooden platters, the earthen jug and a pot. He noted that the previous fare had been augmented with slices of beef. By taking small portions, at intervals, he avoided distress. The tantalising process complete, he felt restored and ready for the night's work.

Robin had informed the bailiff of Sir Henry Killigrew's intention to fire the barn and, in the early evening, he brought in four barrels of tar, which they opened and placed at the conjunctions of the roof supports with the walls. Then they piled straw over them. When the bailiff departed, Robin directed Nicholas back to his hiding place and perched himself on a bale of hay.

'This is the plan,' he muttered, conspiratorially. 'Just before midnight we light these piles. Hopefully, they will remain undetected for a few minutes, but, once the thatch ignites, the roof will burn like tinder. In the interval, we make our way through Smithick, along the road behind the foreshore. There, we rendezvous with Geoffrey, who will be waiting with horses for us.'

'What is our purpose?'

Robin leaned forward. 'We three are charged to hide and preserve a copy of the records of the agents and Royalist sympathisers which we established in London. Further, we are to be acquainted of those supporters of the King in the West Country who would remain loyal, if His Majesty were finally defeated.'

'Whence came these records?'

'Geoffrey brought them from Edward Gilbey's house, just before Fairfax arrived and was desperate for a place to hide them. He came to me and I asked' – he hesitated and looked searchingly at his friend – 'I asked your father to hide them under the floor of his cottage.'

Nicholas rose and stood over him. 'You have involved my father in this struggle? God knows what penalty he might pay for such an act. And at this stage! He has played no part in the war!' Nicholas had raised his voice and Robin grasped his arm and drew him down, listening for any sounds from below, before continuing.

'Your father was more than willing. He is proud of your service to the King and, in his way, would make amends, on behalf of the Carews, for Sir Alexander's aberration. He doubts not that Lady Jane would approve.

'But she must not know!'

'Quite so! Do you swear to keep this information close to you?'

'I swear.'

'Then we will mount up and ride hard, by night, for Antony, when Geoffrey is met.'

'Twould not be proper that we should be at Antony without Her Ladyship knowing.'

'Of course! It is only the matter of the documents that we shall keep secret. There are codes to be hidden as well,' Robin added. 'Come, this is a dangerous place for such talk, let us be silent till it is time to go.'

'And then let us go quickly, for I have no fancy to be here when the Pendennis gunners give fire.'

'Amen!'

CHAPTER 22

The Raid

Father and son looked up at the sky. It was very dark, as on the previous night, but there was no mist, nothing to muffle sound and provide pockets of cover for the 30 men and two officers of the raiding party. 'Batten is a vigilant fellow,' John Arundell commented. 'Besides his warships at sea, he has barges patrolling in-shore. Please God I am not sending these men to their deaths.'

They walked along the ramparts and satisfied themselves that the guns which dominated Carrick Roads were manned and cleared for action. An earlier inspection of the cannon facing towards Arwenack had reassured them that all was ready in that quarter. Richard drew his cloak about him, 'The night air chills my bones,' he said.

'It will not for long, Richard, for I promise you a hot engagement, this night.'

At the sally-port, they found Toby and Jamie with their crews, darkly-clad, their faces smeared with earth. Each man was armed with a sword and pistols, while some also carried a musket and bandolier. A small keg of gunpowder stood on the ground at Jamie's feet. Arundell pointed to it. 'What is the purpose of that?'

'To disconcert any pursuers along the jetty, sir, and aid our withdrawal.'

'Then, I trust you have properly devised the fuse length.' He looked at the tense, waiting men. 'May God Almighty go with you and bring success to our just endeavours. God save the King!'

The men, heartened by the old warrior's voice, doffed their caps and checked an involuntary cheer. Arundell turned to Toby. 'I shall go to the watchtower of the keep and, at first sign that the barn is alight, will fire a pistol. It shall be the signal for both the cannonade on Arwenack and your landing. Go now and time your journey well. Be silent and watchful, till the attack.'

'Aye, sir!' Toby opened the door and slipped out, the raiders filing out behind him, with Jamie at the rear. Richard secured and barred the door, then followed his father to the keep, up the spiral stairs and on to the roof of the watchtower. Behind them there were brisk, light footsteps and Juliana appeared in the doorway. Before Arundell could frame his protest, she took his arm. 'My patients are the reason for this enterprise. I must be part of it.'

Arundell covered her hand with his own, gently squeezing it, conveying his understanding. Gratefully, Juliana moved to an embrasure and stood motionless, while they waited for the signal to fire upon Arwenack. The chill night breeze penetrated their worn apparel, seeking the pared, spare frames beneath. She shivered, from cold and apprehension. If she had not invited Nicholas to visit the hospital that day, would 30 brave soldiers be hazarding their lives tonight? And where was he who filled her anxious thoughts – waiting to fulfil his part in this endeavour? There had been no opportunity to embrace and say God Speed or call upon the Holy Mother to protect him, only his note to say... She saw a tongue of flame pierce the blackness where she stared. 'Look!' she cried.

Arundell had seen it, too. Drawing a pistol from beneath his cloak, he fired into the air. Juliana started at the sudden breaking of the silence. Thin traceries of light appeared along the landward ramparts, as matches were brought to the glow and presented to powder. Then a hoarse shout and 20 pieces of ordnance roared brazen-throated, into the night. The flash was blinding, the noise stunned her. She blinked, then saw that the distant flame was blending with a second and the sky was aglow.

Before the guns spoke again, she heard the crisp rattle of small arms from well to the right of the flames. There was movement, behind her, and Killigrew joined them to watch, tight-faced, the further destruction of his inheritance. Again the ordnance roared, joined this time by the demi-culverins in the keep below. The watchtower shook, the floor heaved, and pungent smoke wafted upwards and caught her throat, as the great shot began to rain down upon the environs of Arwenack.

The muskets and pistols cracked again towards Smithick. She pictured Toby and his men tumbling out of their boats and racing up the stairs of the jetty, swords in one hand, pistols in the other, and boy Jamie preparing to cover their retirement. She imagined Nicholas' tall figure beside Robin, running the gauntlet of the Parliamentarians as they retreated from their night's work at the house. Then, as the guns thundered again and their angry roar engulfed her, she felt the nape of her neck tingle and tears of pride start in her eyes. She was an Arundell among Arundells – on the most exposed point of Pendennis Castle. The Prince of Wales and his advisers had fled, the Royalist cause was in tatters but, everyday, from the jackstaff of this tower, the Union flag fluttered defiantly.

A salvo of Roundhead shot fell into the greensward, below, and fragments of metal and stone thrashed the granite walls. The stench of burnt gunpowder was overwhelming, and her view of the incandescent sky almost obliterated by smoke, as the demi-culverins fired again. 'Juliana, go below!' Arundell commanded. 'This is no place for you.'

He was right, her place was in the hospital. She descended the stairs to the guardroom, crossed the drawbridge and was halfway over the greensward when the Parliamentary ordnance struck again. Dropping to the ground, she buried her face in the grass, until the firing ceased. Then, rising, she ran, her lungs rasping from the foul air. Inside the building, frightened children were crying; women lying in the truckle beds about the walls were white-faced, wide-eyed and she saw one of the nurses cowering in a corner of the room. She had work to do.

⊟ ⊟ ⊟

Toby and his men were up the stairs and halfway down the jetty before they met the first opposition. The shouts of the fleeing sentry brought out the six-man guard, who strove to present and discharge their muskets, but the raiders cut through them, without a backward glance. Toby ran on to the shed where the provisions were stored. The scene, obscure last night, was lit by the glow from the fire and he found that the food stores had been depleted, but there were still 10 sacks of grain, three barrels of beef and some cheeses remaining.

Behind an arc of musketeers, the bustling men grasped the sacks and cheeses and loaded the barrels of beef on to a handcart that stood nearby. At the end of the jetty, they laboured, desperately, to carry their prizes down to the boats. Two of the barrels were successfully transferred, but the third pitched into the water and was lost, when one of the men lost his footing on the treacherous stairs. They were still loading the grain and cheeses when there was a shout from the direction of Arwenaek, and a party of musketeers came pounding towards them, silhouetted against the orange glow of the fire.

Toby's men fired and some of the Parliamentarians fell, but the others came resolutely on, to present their cumbersome weapons at the Royalists, now withdrawing along the jetty. Their volley struck men down, amongst the precious grain, which had spilled from a broken sack, and they advanced again with drawn swords, till the Royalists halted them with a round of pistol shot at point-blank range.

When the rearguard reached the head of the stairs, Toby saw that two sacks of grain lay in each boat with the cheeses packed around them. A solid phalanx of Roundhead pikemen and musketeers ran on to the jetty and he knew that the six survivors of his rearguard would not halt their impetus with the one volley that time would allow. There was no sign of Jamie, so he yelled to the sergeant who commanded the boats, 'Cast off!'

The enemy were halfway along the jetty when a crisp command halted them. The musketeers came to the front and he knew that his meagre force was about to be annihilated, while a small cannon being manoeuvred to fire on the retreating boats would blow them out of the sea. They were finished!

A tremendous explosion rent the air, sending bodies, equipment, pikeshafts, muskets, planking and baulks of timber hurtling skyward, as smoke obscured the scene. Toby was spun around and flung on to his face, while a cascade of debris fell about him.

As the sea breeze thinned the smoke and revived him, he focussed on a gaping hole that had been blown in the jetty. A narrow way remained around each side of it and enemy reinforcements were approaching, the leaders already bunching to circumvent the obstacle.

'Into the sea beneath the jetty!' he shouted at the dazed Cavaliers.

The men hesitated and he swept the two beside him over the edge and into the chilling water, 20 feet below. As they surfaced, the nearest man began to beat water, frantically, and he grasped him and drew him under the jetty. Securing his grasp around one of the slimy piles, he looked around for the other man, but he was beneath the sea. Summoning his last reserves of strength, he dived, hands blindly extended until he felt the man's loose doublet. Grasping it, he kicked upwards. As his head broke the surface, he looked up at an officer leaning over the side, pistol in hand. There was a bright flash, the crack of exploding powder and Toby was repossessed by the sea, a bullet between his eyes.

Jamie Ross had a tenuous hold on the slippery timbers of the jetty. Having waited until almost the last second, he had plunged into the sea, while the suicidally-short fuse burned to the keg of powder, which he had lashed beneath the decking. His worm's-eye view had afforded scant perspective on the events above, but he had timed the explosion well.

Bodies struck the water in the fading light of the fire and four men swam past him. Three more bodies plunged in and he witnessed Toby's struggle to save his men, ending in his death.

Nearby, a soldier was clinging to a pile, his blood staining the water, and Jamie beckoned to him. But the man did not move, so he struck out towards him. 'We must get to the shore. Float on your back– trust me.' The soldier released his grip and rolled over, arms akimbo, while Jamie towed him landwards to join his comrades. 'Our task is done and we have no choice but to surrender,' he told them, laying the wounded man upon the beach.

The Roundheads were scrambling over the pebbles, towards them, as he called 'We surrender to the Parliament.'

Rough hands dragged them up to the road, where a captain waited. 'I am Cornet James Ross and these men are under my command,' Jamie told him.

The Roundhead looked down at him. 'A pretty havoc you have wrought. Was this the work of a mere boy?'

'Not entirely.'

'Well Colonel Hammond will have the truth of it from you at Arwenack.'

◻◻◻

With Sir Henry Killigrew and Richard, John Arundell watched the fire dying and heard the sounds of conflict abate. 'Our party must be pulling back and they will soon be in need of our support,' he said.

Killigrew sniffed the wind, 'There will be no call for them to row, for the breeze favours them.'

'But Batten will surely intervene, and 'twould be unforgiveable to fail them now,' Arundell responded, briskly. 'Go you, Richard, and have the seaward gunners bombard the area where he may be lurking, then let us go and watch for our boats.'

◻◻◻

Within the hospital, Juliana had restored order and calm. The seaward bombardment made little impression on the weak and exhausted inmates, but she conquered the urge to abandon them and rush to the walls. Instead, she walked quietly between the rows of cots, waiting for news of the returning raiders.

◻◻◻

Geoffrey had not failed his friends. When Nicholas and Robin crossed the dunes behind the foreshore and entered the trees abutting Smithick village, they heard the faint clink of bits and came upon him holding the heads of three mounts. As they edged cautiously from cover, a heavy explosion drowned the other sounds of combat coming from the jetty. The confused cries which followed signalled the moment to break out and ride for Anthony.

Meg hurried to where Juliana bent over a child's cot. Her hasty arrival said all and Juliana followed her out into the night. Gathering up their skirts, they ran to the walls above the sally-port, to join the Arundells and Killigrew. She leaned through an embrasure to see a sailing barge bearing down upon a knot of small boats heading for the castle.

The sally-port door was already being opened and Arundell was urging a party of musketeers down the rocky slopes towards the sea's edge. Richard shouted an order for the fires kept in constant readiness on the ramparts to be lighted and the well-primed combustibles flared in seconds. The light of the fires picked out the hull of the barge as it struck the leading boat with a splintering crash. The shattered craft keeled over, as breached planks surrendered to the sea, and the barge turned broadside on to the musketeers among the rocks. They raked it with fire while it completed its turn and headed out to sea. The small boats were well inshore in the shallow water, and safe from further attack. Richard was calling together a party to recover them and unload the stores and Juliana hurred to join them, Meg at her heels. Scrambling and slipping over the rocks, they waded into the sea and laid hands upon the gunwhale of the first boat to beach. The exhausted crew were helped ashore, slack-mouthed and blood-spattered. Next, the absurdly-small cargo was brought out and Juliana made an eager tally of the supplies, as three other boats were run up on to the rocks and unloaded.

Was this all of it, one barrel of beef, seven sacks of grain and nine cheeses? She returned to the water's edge, as another man was carried ashore, one stocking soaked in blood, teeth bared in pain. Holy Mother, what a price to pay! Where were Toby and young Jamie? She grasped the arm of the sergeant commanding the last boat. 'Where are Captain Herrick and Cornet Ross?'

The man looked at her, eyes bleared with fatigue. 'I don't rightly know, lady. Methinks the Captain was shot in the water.'

Juliana's face drained. 'And Cornet Ross?'

'Perished likely as not, when the pier blew up. He surely saved us by that deed.'

She sat down upon a rock, the restless water swirling about her feet and looked towards Smithick quay. In her mind's eye, she saw the sturdy young man with fair locks who had embraced her and declared his love. She had used him, tantalised him, and now she had sent him to his death. And what of the eager boy who had vowed at Antony to protect her with his life? Had he, in truth, sacrificed it for her? Hot tears started to her eyes and ran slowly down her cheek, but she did not notice them; nor did she feel the chill creeping stealthily up her legs, for she was already numb. What of her beloved? Did he also feature in this night of disaster.

Meg came to her. 'Milady, the soldiers are asking where the provisions are to be taken. There will be knives into the cheeses, if you do not hurry!'

Roused from her morbid reverie, Juliana took Meg's arm. 'Aye, I am forgetting my duty. These brave men shall be fed, for they have risked all.' Calling to the commander of the musketeers to remove the supplies to the hospital cellars, she picked her way back up the rocks and through the sally port into the castle. Then she went to allocate rations to the returned raiders, the sick women and the children. The lot of the young and the ailing would be improved for a while, at least.

❖❖❖

The horsemen reined in on the high ground above Truro. 'We must skirt the town and ride on,' Geoffrey told them. 'I have paid a farmer at Grampound to hide us during the day, but we must find one more resting place before the final leg to Antony.'

'I have thought on that,' Robin declared, spurring forward.

They drew rein again at cock's crow, within sight of a farm nestling in a valley. 'I will go ahead and speak with the yeoman, while you wait to see how I am received,' Geoffrey suggested.

Robin took a carabine from his saddle and sighted it on the front door. A stocky man answered Geoffrey's knock and they crossed the yard to a barn and disappeared inside. Moments later, Geoffrey emerged and beckoned and they cantered into an interior, dry and sweet with hay.

The farmer gave them a gap-toothed smile. 'I fought fer the King, at Bradock Down, gentlemen, so no harm will befall ye, here.'

Robin smiled. 'Thank you, good yeoman. Will you bring food, before we rest?'

'Gad, but I tire of barns!' Robin declared as they unsaddled and watered their horses. 'Had I known how much time a soldier spends in them, methinks I would have become a cleric.'

'A vocation for which you are singularly unsuited, lacking both piety and self-denial.' Geoffrey turned to Nicholas, 'Do you not agree?'

The farmer returned with a wholesome, young woman, wearing chopines upon her feet, against the mire of the yard, and bearing a tray of food and drink. When they had eaten, Robin contemplated the hindquarters of the woman, as she retreated through the postern. 'Nicholas, remember you that lovely creature who served us wine, in the Ship Inn at Fowey?'

'The night we rode over from St. Blazey? That I do.'

'Her face has haunted me since, for she was the personification of aristocratic beauty, dark and proud. Yet she never spoke. How many times have I tried to imagine her voice. I would see her, again!' he added, longingly.

'How will you compass it?'

'The inn shall be our stopping place, this evening.'

'Do not set your heart upon seeing her, Robin – much time has elapsed since our visit.'

Robin looked at him strangely, but did not reply.

'Can we even be sure mine host and his wife will not betray us?' Nicholas continued.

'Yes!'

'How do you know that?'

'I swear you were right – they are Catholics and will have no love of Roundheads.'

Nicholas said no more. Having armed and hidden themselves among the hay, they slept till the yeoman and the girl aroused them with more victuals. This time the light was fading with the approach of evening. They ate the food, quickly, and were soon on their way through St. Blazey, passing Menabilly, devastated home of the Rashleighs, on the headland to their right, then into Fowey from the hills above.

Robin was now firmly in command. 'Leave it to me to seek mine host, while you two attend the horses. Be on your guard!'

'We could press on to Antony, if needs be,' Nicholas commented.

'It is 20 miles away and I have another reason for pausing here – not connected with the innkeeper's daughter,' he added, seeing Geoffrey's amused lift of the eyebrows.

At the hostelry they waited, while Robin disappeared inside. In a few minutes he was back with two ostlers, who took the horses. His companions followed him into the inn and up the stairs, where the landlord was waiting to conduct them to the chamber in which Robin and Nicholas had previously supped. Sconces of candles had already been lit and a newly-lighted fire crackled in the grate. The dark panelled room was snug and welcoming. 'There is a large bed and a single cot in the next chamber, gentlemen. It is the only accommodation I can offer tonight.'

'Twill serve well, landlord. Pray send in some wine and, when you have prepared food, I beg you return, for I would speak with you.'

A few minutes later the daughter of the house came in with a flask of wine and three goblets. 'Good evening, gentlemen. My father believes you will find this claret palatable.' The voice was low and rich.

Robin's eyes followed her as she crossed to the table in the window alcove. When she had served the wine, Robin jumped to his feet impulsively and raised his cup, 'To beauty!' he proposed.

She smiled again. 'Thank you.'

'Is that lady not a superlative creature?' he demanded, when she had gone.

'Aye, it must be said,' Geoffrey agreed. 'I see now what drew you back – jet black hair, golden skin and the grace of a cat.'

'And that voice,' Nicholas added.

'But I did not bring you here merely to indulge my fancy.'

The innkeeper reappeared to announce that supper would be served, soon. 'You wish to speak with me?' he looked towards Robin, who stood with his back to the kindling logs.

'I do. Do you recall when my friend, here, and I last supped with you?'

'Indeed. We were honoured to have a senior officer as guest.' There was a hint of a smile. 'And you are not a gentleman to be readily forgotten.'

'Then you will recall that we wore the Royalists' sash. Where stand you, landlord, touching the King's affairs?'

'With respect, where stand you?'

Robin studied him for a long moment. 'We remain the King's loyal servants! Now what say you?'

'My wife and daughter are of the Catholic faith,' he replied, cautiously.

'Then you will not welcome the rule of Parliament?'

The innkeeper bowed his head in a minute gesture of acquiescence, but said nothing.

'But would you serve the King?'

'I would, for he is the anointed of God.'

'Good! I should like to know that I could obtain a boat and crew to sail to France, should the need arise.'

'What would you pay?'

'A fair price.'

'I know not what that may be in these dangerous times, but I will see that a vessel and trustworthy crew are available, as you may require.'

Robin went to the table and recharged his goblet. 'God save the King.' He raised the cup to his lips.

'Amen!' the innkeeper replied. His wife and daughter brought in the food. 'We have goose and some cheese for you and there are a few more flasks of the claret – recently brought from the Continent,' he added, pointedly.

'Splendid, and the meal by grace of your ladies.' Robin bowed, extravagantly.

The trio sat to an excellent meal, but Nicholas, plagued by guilt, compared his situation with the company at Pendennis. When he confessed his unease, Robin was short. 'Your conscience is altogether too delicate a flower, my friend. Do not ask us to share your remorse. Conditions at the castle are not of your making. Indeed, you have risked life to relieve them. In this war you have endured pain, cold and fear, not seeking to impose them on others. Tonight, you are in credit. What of tomorrow or the day after? Best contrive life a day at a time.'

'He is right,' Geoffrey added.

When the innkeeper came back, Robin eyed him, hopefully. 'Our contentment would be complete, could you furnish a bottle of brandy. And we would take it most kindly if your daughter would join us for a little discourse. We have been much in one another's company, of late, and yearn for gentle society.'

'She shall bring a bottle.'

'Our thanks. May we know your name, friend?'

'Abraham Tresidder.'

Seeing Robin's pleasure as Tresidder agreed to his request, Nicholas hoped that he was not setting his cap in vain. The daughter came in with brandy and a guitar and Robin applauded at sight of the instrument. 'Come sit by the fire, while I charge the glasses. What will you take?'

'A little wine, I thank you.' She took a goblet from a court cupboard and handed it to him, before sitting with the guitar hung across her shoulder. Robin snuffed the candles while her fingers idly caressed the strings. The sound was warm, deep and evocative, like her voice. She began to play a slow, haunting melody, as the big man slid silently into a chair opposite her. The mood and tempo of the music changed – faster, stranger, as she plucked swiftly at the strings and rapped the case of the instrument. Now she sang. The melody relied much upon repetition of the note, upon melodic decoration and cadences unfamiliar to the ears of Nicholas and Geoffrey, but their senses thrilled to the sensuous throb of the guitar. The light from the flames shimmered across the slim, vigorous hands and accentuated the fine bone structure of her face. Her eyes had closed and she appeared oblivious to their presence, lost in a world where the sun was hotter, the earth drier, the senses sharper than she was wont to know. The song ended with a final flourish on the vibrating strings, but the group remained silent, transfixed. Then Robin cried, '*Olé!*'

'*Gracias!*'

'It was *cante jondo* was it not?' he enquired.

'*Cante flamenco*, precisely, from Andalusia – the music cf the gypsies,' she told him, smiling, impressed by his knowledge.' I had not expected to be so appreciated.'

'A soldier of fortune tries to bring back more than scars from his Continental adventures. Tell me, Mistress...?' His head cocked, questioningly.

'Katherine.'

'Mistress Katherine, how comes it that we are entertained by the music of Spain on an April evening in Cornwall?'

She gave him an amused glance. How often she had excited the curiosity of strangers and how often had she told her tale. Well, she would tell it again. 'It began with King Phillip's great enterprise.'

'The Armada?'

'Yes. The Duke of Medina Sidonia, commander of the fleet, had anchored in the lee of Dodman Point and sent off pinnaces to determine the whereabouts of the English fleet. My grandfather was an officer aboard one of these. He had climbed into the shrouds to search the horizon, when the ship was struck by a squall, as dusk gathered. He lost his footing on the wet ropes, pitched into the sea and was lost to sight from the ship. He contrived to discard helmet and cuirass, but cold and exhaustion overcame him. When he was near the end, he was picked up by the crew of a fishing smack returning to Falmouth Haven, after their capture and interrogation by the Duke.'

She paused to study her absorbed audience. 'When he in turn was interrogated, and it was learned that he was a minor nobleman, a ransom for his return was demanded. For whatever reason it was not forthcoming and, eventually, he was released to fend for himself. He made his way to Fowey and, being an accomplished musician, found favour with families like the Rashleighs and the Mohuns and their kinsfolk, the Trelawneys of Pelynt, the Courtneys, Arundells and Carews, who came to Hall – across the river at Bodinnick. He lived in this inn and married the innkeeper's daughter. My mother was their only child and she, in due course, married my father – a seafarer who had grown weary of roving.

'My grandfather died before I was born, but he instilled in my mother a love of music and skill with instruments – a little of which I have inherited. 'She smiled, deprecatingly.

'Indeed you have,' Robin assured her. He glanced at his companions, then back to Katherine. 'Forgive my lack of courtesy if I introduce my friends only as Nicholas and Geoffrey. I am called Robin.'

Nicholas smiled acknowledgement. He studied the dark, golden woman in the firelight. She was older than Juliana, about 25 years of age, and had poise and maturity quite inappropriate to her station. Clearly, the blood of her grandsire ran strong in her veins. He imagined her life at the inn, kept from the taproom by the father and confined to waiting at table upon sea captains, merchants and an occasional gentleman, admired, exotic, but remote. A merchant might seek to win her, but their ambitions were frequently directed towards union with the gentry. The dark eyes and full lower lip suggested passion and her interpretation of the music confirmed it – not a woman for the affected or the foppish, yet vulnerable, defensive. The man who possessed her must be both strong and loving.

She was requesting to be excused, to be about her duties, and Geoffrey was saying, 'You have a great gift and fine voice, Mistress Katherine . Grant we may be further entertained, at some future time.'

'But not this visit, I fear, for we must be gone at nightfall, tomorrow,' Robin interjected.

'I know not what business you are at, but I will ask God's protection for you.'

Robin took her hand and kissed it. 'I for one will take no risks, that I might enjoy the delight of your company and music, again, sweet Katherine.' Geoffrey and Nicholas swept her a bow as she crossed the room with Robin's eyes following her, till the door closed behind her. 'And so to bed and dreams, gentlemen.'

He was at the door connecting the room with the bedchamber, surveying the beds. 'It would be best if you, Nicholas and Geoffrey, slept upon the four-poster and I will take the cot. It would be unwise to discard other than weapons and boots, so I will be thankful to lave myself under the pump, before daybreak.'

Geoffrey shivered. 'Methinks, a friend of the family, like yourself, might arrange for hot water to be brought to us.' Robin laughed and pushed Geoffrey on to the bed, as Nicholas told him, 'Geoffrey is right – my starveling body is not yet ready for such exposure.'

◻◻◻

Early the next evening, Katherine leaned from her lattice to watch their departure. She waved goodbye to them all, the elegant man with the white, reckless smile, the tall, dark, very handsome younger man, and the big man with the red beard – but it was the broad back of the big man that she watched as they disappeared into the darkness, to a late crossing of the River Fowey over Bodinnick ferry, arranged by her father.

CHAPTER 23

The Provider

It was well before dawn when they arrived at the gates of Antony and hammered upon the lodge-keeper's door. He appeared, complaining bitterly, till he recognised Nicholas. 'Will you swear to keep our presence here close, Samuel, for 'tis what Her Ladyship would wish?' Nicholas demanded of the old man.

'Aye, I will, Maister Nicholas. Ye can be sure of that,' he promised, pulling open the tall gates.

The three men cantered over the soft turf of the parkland, till they came to the cottage of Skelton senior. He admitted them to the parlour and stirred the embers of the fire into life. While he went to prepare food and drink, Nicholas found temporary shelter for the horses in an outhouse. As they ate, Skelton questioned his son regarding events since their last meeting. Then Nicholas became inquisitor. 'Does Lady Jane know of the records that you hold?'

'She does not and it sorely troubles me to so endanger her.'

Robin interrupted them. 'Then, Mister Skelton, will you pray take us to her before the household is astir and we will acquaint her of the facts. Geoffrey, pray stand guard upon the drive and warn us of the approach of anyone, whomsoever.'

While Geoffrey rode towards the gates, Skelton led Robin and his son across the park , through a back door into the library, and bade them wait. Jane Carew appeared, wearing a nightcap and swathed in a fur robe. 'Lady Carew, I offer my profound apologies for so incommoding you,' Robin began.

'I am sure the matter must warrant it, Major Smythe,' she replied, calmly.

'It does, Your Ladyship,' He paused, carefully framing his words. 'I doubt

227

not you remain the King's true servant?'

'Be assured of that, Major.'

'Then you should know that Mister Skelton recently took possession of secret records for the cause.'

'So I am aware, Major, for I enjoy the confidence of Mr Edward Gilbey.' She went to the door and admitted the lame spymaster, likewise clad in night attire.

'Good morning, gentlemen! I commend your dedication, for I had not expected you before we broke fast.'

Nicholas's half-reproachful glance at his sire prompted Jane Carew to say, 'Your father was sworn to conceal the presence of Mr Gilbey and his daughter.' She smiled, enjoying the surprise this last revelation evoked.

'Letitia is with me to copy the records,' Gilbey explained. 'Sir Edward Hyde requires duplicates to be taken to the Prince of Wales, at Elizabeth Castle, in Jersey, which brings me to the second purpose of my visit – to select a courier.'

Jane Carew intervened. 'Mr. Gilbey, think you this matter could wait upon daylight? Methinks it might best be dealt with over breakfast.'

'Of course, Lady Carew.' Gilbey inclined his head, apologetically.

'Then please be my guests in one hour, gentlemen.'

'We will keep the presence of your daughter and self a secret from Geoffrey,' Robin told Gilbey, 'Twill make a pleasant surprise.'

▣▣▣

Breakfast was enlivened by the presence of Letitia, as ever the fresh spring flower. Her silvery laugh was much in evidence, as Geoffrey amused her with an account of their stay in Fowey.

'How stand our affairs?' Robin enquired of Gilbey.

'The King lies at Oxford in some despair, I fear, uncertain as to a course of action. He pleads with the queen to send troops from France and even entertained the idea of striking south-east, at one of the Cinque Ports, to gain a point-of-entry for them. Bad news is his regular fare, so many of his strongholds have fallen – Belvoir, Ashby-de-la-Zouch, Lichfield, Corfe. Yet he manages to preserve some semblance of style at Court, I am told. He also draws hope from divisions among the religious factions. While the Independents are in the ascendancy in the House of Commons, the Presbyterians dominate the Assembly of Divines in the City of London, and there is much animosity between them.

'The Frenchman, Cardinal Mazarin, has, it seems, sent an ingenious young diplomat, Jean de Montreuil, over here to restore the old relationship between

France and Scotland and to draw the King into an alliance with the Scots against the Parliamentarians. I know not what will become of that endeavour, but, methinks, His Majesty is unlikely to be deceived by the Scots Commissioner's vague promise of an alliance, if he will concede a little on the religious issues.'

Noting that all present had finished breakfasting, Gilbey leaned across to Jane Carew and asked for the servants to be dismissed. He looked around at the three Cavaliers. 'My friends, following the appearance of a fleet of Parliamentary ships off the Scillies, the Prince of Wales was obliged to move on to Jersey, where he is safe in the care of Sir George Carteret, governor of the island. His advisers must know who they may still trust, in the West Country, and Sir Edward Hyde has charged me to supply that information. To that end, Letitia will spend the day copying our records and I will then call upon one of you to sail, forthwith, with this intelligence. Who shall it be?'

'It would seem that I am best equipped for the mission,' Geoffrey volunteered. Letitia's grip tightened on his arm.

'What gallantry, Geoffrey, so soon to desert your love. 'Tis better I should go,' Nicholas interceded.

'Aye, I believe it would be,' the spymaster replied, 'for I have need of Geoffrey for other matters touching the King's affairs.'

'Then 'tis settled.'

'Aye,' Gilbey nodded.

'And I shall find you a boat,' Robin contributed.

'Well said, my gallants!' Gilbey beamed, benignly. 'Now, will you join me in congratulating Geoffrey, upon his promotion to Major.' He passed a document to his prospective son-in-law, before reaching across the table and shaking his hand. Letitia kissed his cheek.

'Many believe our cause to be lost,' Gilbey went on. 'Those of us who continue to serve must do so clandestinely, and we will be in danger of execution, as spies, if caught. The three of you, if captured, must declare that you are soldiers of Pendennis garrison, on detachment. Letitia will go to work, now, at Mister Skelton's cottage. We will all depart at nightfall and cease to be an embarrassment to Her Ladyship.'

'I also serve the King and am content,' Jane assured him. As she went to summon servants to clear the table, her attention was drawn to a detachment of Roundhead cavalry crossing the park, an officer at their head. 'See!' she cried to Gilbey, pointing through the window.

Robin was on his feet following her pointing finger. 'We have horses stabled at the cottage.'

'Nothing can be done about them,' she said, 'But you must come with me, quickly!' She paused at the door and called to Skelton senior, who was crossing the hall, 'Please have the baggage of Mr and Mistress Gilbey brought to the library.'

Jane Carew swept her guests across the hall and into the book-lined room. Closing the doors, she crossed to the fireplace and turned one of the decorative knobs featured in its design. A section of shelves rotated, silently, exposing a black void beyond. She hurried to the tables, struck the tinder and lighted a sconce of candles, which she gave to Nicholas. 'This priest hole is no secret to you, but please God it is to those who approach. Wait at the bottom of the steps!' Nicholas hesitated, reluctant to leave her alone. 'Hurry, your father shall be my support.'

Nicholas led the way through the narrow aperture and down a flight of stone steps, as the Gilbey baggage was thrust into the hideaway and the section of library wall slid shut. Robin drew his sword and crept noiselessly back up the steps, listening for sounds from the house. Nicholas looked about at his still companions, at the cobwebbed walls lit by the flickering candles. He had not been in the old priest hole since he was a boy and had almost forgotten its existence.

Jane Carew hurried back to the room they had vacated, and was directing the clearing of the breakfast table, when the front-door bell clanged through the hall. 'Hurry away with these things,' she urged the scurrying servitors, 'and bear yourselves loyally, I pray you.'

The bell jangled again, accompanied, this time, by the hammering of a sword-hilt on the door. 'Open in the name of the Parliament!'

Skelton tugged at his doublet and strode, purposefully, to the front door. On the step stood a Roundhead captain, sword in hand. Observing Jane Carew, he pushed, unceremoniously, past the steward and confronted her. 'Who am I addressing?' he demanded.

'I am Lady Carew, widow of Sir Alexander Carew.'

'You were a mite tardy opening your door, lady!'

'I do not rush to welcome visitors with naked swords, Captain. What is your business?'

The officer glanced down at his blade and returned it to its scabbard. 'A fellow at Antony reported seeing horsemen passing through the village before dawn this morning.'

'Travellers heading for the Tamar crossing, no doubt.'

'I think not, for we have checked that possibility. There are precious few places for them to go on this neck of land.'

'Nonetheless, it seems a poor reason for this intrusion. By what authority do you enter my house, without invitation?' Jane regarded him steadily.

The Roundhead was nonplussed by her fortitude. 'I have no formal authority, only my orders to investigate. Do you harbour any strangers in this place?'

'None.'

'With your permission, I will satisfy myself.'

'You will not, sir! If you have no authority, you will not!'

Colour rose in his face. 'You are imprudent, lady.' He glanced over his shoulder at the sound of his cornet's footsteps on the flags. 'There seem ample horses in the stables for a widowed lady and her family, sir,' the officer reported, 'including one fine mount suitable for a gentleman.'

'What do you say to that?' the captain demanded.

'My eldest son is a good horseman and has outgrown the smaller animals He is presently learning to master the Arab of which you speak.'

'Are you for King or Parliament, lady?'

The question undermined Jane Carew's composure. Hers was a tainted household and she would, joyfully, have proclaimed that she was four-square for Charles, her annointed King, but that would be folly. 'I am for peace and the wellbeing of my family. But know you that my husband served the Parliament and his step-brother, John Carew, is one of its most faithful adherents.'

'I had heard on't.' For a moment he was silent, then he bowed and turned for the door, beckoning the cornet to follow. At the threshold he paused. 'I trust 'twill not be necessary to trouble you further, Lady Carew.'

The steward closed the door behind them and turned to his mistress.

'It is alright! Go, find John Gendle and send him to the gate. He is to be sure the Roundheads have left. Upon his return, I will bring forth my guests.'

Returning to the breakfast room, she watched her head groom canter across the park, to return shortly. Hat in hand, he entered the room where she still stood. 'All's well, milady, they'm all gone.'

Jane dismissed him and went to open the secret panel. 'You are safe, now,' she assured them.

Robin brushed a cobweb from his sleeve as the section closed behind them. 'We must be more circumspect in departing than in our arrival,' he said, when Jane had told them of the informant at Antony village.

'Indeed we must,' Gilbey agreed. 'Now, there is much to be done ere darkness falls.'

◼◼◼

Just outside St. Germans village, John Gendle reined in. 'This is the road to Liskeard, as ye well know, Major Nicholas. God speed.'

'Thank you, John. God keep you and yours safe.'

'They'll be fine once I'm married to Janet Salter, Major, for they'll 'ave a mother again.'

Nicholas glanced at Robin, who showed no concern at Gendle's news, but smiled broadly at the groom. 'You are a lucky fellow, John Gendle,' he declared. Raising their hands in farewell, the Cavaliers spurred away into the darkness, towards the port of Fowey.

□□□

Robin and Abraham Tresidder, with Nicholas behind them, stood at a window in the inn, considering the sturdy fishing smack lying at the quay's edge. 'And we can rely on the crew's discretion?' Robin enquired.

'I am a good judge of seamen, having been one myself,' Tresidder replied. 'And it would not be in their interest to betray you, after part-payment of such a goodly sum – even if they were so inclined, which I doubt.'

'Then tell them to make ready to sail, as soon after nightfall as wind and tide dictate.' The innkeeper left them, to reappear below as he crossed the quay and went aboard the smack.

'What will you do while I am gone?' Nicholas asked his friend.

'I shall work here, ostensibly as a cellarer. 'Twill provide healthy exercise, keep me out of the mainstream of activity and permit me to earn my keep, instead of being a drain on His Majestys dwindling revenues.'

'And make better acquaintance with the fair Katherine?'

Robin grinned. 'You read my mind, Nicholas. I have quite set my heart on't.'

'Then I wish you well.' Nicholas patted his friend's broad back.

In a short while, Tresidder returned. 'Everything is arranged,' he informed them. 'I will take you to the boat at seven o'clock and it will sail, forthwith.'

□□□

Nicholas stood beside the weatherbeaten figure of Eli Walsh, skipper of the smack, *Lanteglos*, as he steered her through the moored ships riding the dark waters of Fowey harbour. Behind the thin cloud there was a promise of a moon and, against the pale sky, Polruan Castle appeared on the port bow and slowly fell astern. The lights of the town faded and he felt the breeze freshen, as they left the mouth of the river and sailed towards the open sea. Westward lay Gribbin Head with the Dodman beyond and, yet further, well beyond sight, stood the fortress of Pendennis.

'Are we in any danger from Batten's squadrons?' he asked.

'I shouldn't be surprised if somebody don't come and have a look at us,' Eli replied. 'But they'm used to us coming and going. What they'm really interested in is anything approaching or leaving Falmouth Haven. 'Tis that stubborn old devil, Colonel John Arundell, they'm out to thwart. Can't help admiring him, though,' he concluded with a grin.

Still in the lee of the Dodman, Eli swung the wheel and bawled orders to his crew to trim sails. Now they were set on a course east-south-east, to the Channel Islands, a 100 miles out across the dangerous sea. They had been running before a stiffening wind for about half an hour, when the white sails of another ship appeared on their starboard beam and a voice hailed them out of the darkness. 'Ahoy, who goes there?'

'The fishing smack *Lanteglos*, out of Fowey,' Eli bellowed.

'Oh, 'tis you Eli, you old pirate. On your way and good fishing!'

'Thank ye, kindly.' Walsh looked at his passenger. 'Pirate is it – chance would be a fine thing. 'Tis many a moon since pirates sailed out of Fowey. Nowadays, we poor mariners have to be content with the pilchards, herring and hake.'

The horizon was still tinged red by the setting sun when they approached the island of Jersey, the next evening. They were sailing due south, passing the great curve of St. Ouen's Bay on the port side, then rounding Corbiere, while overhead the gulls wheeled and screamed. They swung about Noirmont Point and, as night closed in, the sails were furled and they rode at anchor before the small port of St. Aubin.

Already, a pinnace was putting out from its quay. A standing figure called for the captain and Walsh moved to the bulwark. 'Stand by, I am coming aboard'. To Nicholas' relief the light of the deck lantern showed that the officer coming over the side wore the rose-red sash of the Royalists. 'You are strangers. What is your business?'

Nicholas stepped forward. 'I am Major Skelton, in the service of the King. I have papers for His Royal Highness, the Prince of Wales.'

The officer inspected him, carefully. 'I will take you to Elizabeth Castle.' He turned to Walsh. 'Meanwhile, this ship is impounded.'

'But I must get back to Cornwall. Every hour away puts me and my crew in greater danger.'

'Your ship will be freed as soon as we are satisfied regarding your passenger.'

Nicholas climbed into the pinnace. Ahead, the bulk of the great castle loomed out of the darkness, on the far side of the bay. It reminded him of his approach to St. Nicholas' island, on that fateful night. The craft beached and he stepped on to a shingle spit. The officer led him along a narrow dog-leg of land to the guardhouse of the castle, then under a semi-circular arch and up a flight of steps, closely pent-in between the stout walls. They passed by a gun platform, through another arch surmounted by the royal arms of Elizabeth and up a further flight of steps lit by a lantern. They were in the upper ward of the castle, with massive barbette emplacements to the left, a modest house and a sturdy, more imposing residence to the right, overshadowed by a squat keep.

Admitted to the larger house, they were conducted to a long, low room, with great brown beams and a grey, stone fireplace at the far end. Bright tapestries formed a backdrop to the elegant figure awaiting them. 'I am Sir George Carteret, Governor of Jersey.'

'Major Skelton of the garrison of Pendennis Castle in Cornwall, sir, with documents for His Royal Highness, the Prince of Wales.'

'I regret that the Prince is not on the island, Major. Following his recent sea voyages His Royal Highness has evinced an interest in navigation and has gone to St. Malo to commission the building of a yacht.'

'And what of Sir Edward Hyde, sir?'

'He accompanied him. I anticipate that they will be absent for two days. Should this be a matter of urgency, I will send for him.'

'The matter is confidential, but not urgent, sir. With your permission, I will await their return.'

'Of course! Captain Moignard, you will arrange accommodation for Major Skelton.'

'I came by fishing smack out of Fowey. The skipper fears to be long absent from port, so I beg he be released, as soon as possible.'

'See to it, captain.' Carteret gestured towards a tall-backed chair. 'Please be seated. The Prince arrived from the Scilly Islas on the 16th of this month, in the ship *Proud Black Eagle*, with his Council, the Governor of the Scillies, Francis Godolphin and a retinue. They are now in my care.' His manner and speech marked him as a dynamic, autocratic man, clearly master of his island. 'Tell me your news.'

'You will know, sir, that St.Michael's Mount has surrendered, but Pendennis holds firm.'

'His Royal Highness and the Council are deeply troubled at their failure to relieve it. Sir Edward Hyde is even now arranging a further dispatch of stores from France. It occurs to me that you could offer valuable guidance to a captain running the blockade, for you must know artillery dispositions, tides, and hazards?'

'I would gladly do so.' Nicholas responded, eagerly.

'You would welcome some supper and bed.' Carteret summoned a servant and he was taken to an adjoining room, where he took an impromptu meal. As he was finishing it, Walsh was brought in.

'Eli, I am obliged to remain here, but I know your concern to be gone. Tell Abraham Tresidder that, as soon as I return, he shall know of it.'

'Aye, aye, that I will, sir.'

'Go with my thanks, Eli, and in God's keeping.' With the departure of the fisherman, he was smitten by a sense of isolation, alone among strangers, beyond the shores of England, separated by the hostile sea from his beloved and those friends with whom he had shared so much. Morosely, he poured another cup of wine.

Carteret would not permit him to leave the castle until his papers had been delivered to the Prince and ratified. So, for two days, he roamed the walls, occasionally glimpsing a lone figure or group of people who looked familiar. During low tide, he made his way across to Hermitage Rock, lying beyond the castle's western walls, to view a natural cavity within the outcrop, where St. Helier had lived as a hermit during the sixth century, till pirates found and decapitated him. He walked upon Raleigh's yard, the gun platform he had noted the evening of his arrival, and looked down upon the decaying, monastic priory below. Mounting to the top of the keep, he gazed about at the beautiful island to which he was denied access. So this was what life was like for the Duke of Hamilton, during his confinement in Pendennis. At least, he had the friendship of the Arundells to sustain him.

As he looked seaward, a ship entered the bay from the east and, soon, a pinnace appeared from the harbour below and headed towards the approaching vessel. He continued to watch as the ship grew large and the Royal Standard become visible at its masthead. Sails were furled and he heard the anchor drop into the sea. The pinnace came alongside and bright colours splashed the ship's weathered hull, as its passengers descended to the boat. Leaving his lofty viewpoint, he hurried to the lower ward.

Perhaps more than coincidentally, he was joined by Captain Moignard as he came to the Iron Gate leading into the ward. 'The waiting is at an end,' Moignard said, as they walked towards the harbour.

'Princes take their own time,' Nicholas replied, 'but at least this one has returned.'

From the outer walls, both men watched the royal party disembarking from the pinnace. Nicholas recognised the thickset figure of Sir Edward Hyde, at his master's elbow, and Culpeper following behind – with an auburn-haired youth.'

'Who is that with Lord Culpeper?' he asked.

'Sir John Grenville.'

His spirits soared. He had never met this Grenville, whose parents had shown him kindness, but he was a Cornishman, one of his own kind among these high-born personages. The party was drawing near and both soldiers swept their King's son an obeisance. The eye of the Prince dwelt on Nicholas for a moment, as if seeking recollection, but he passed on.

That evening, Nicholas was summoned to the governor's house and taken to the room where he had met Carteret. It was occupied by the Prince, Hyde and Grenville. The Prince greeted him. 'Good evening, Major Skelton. I am reminded by Sir Edward that we met, briefly, when I was at Pendennis Castle.'

'Yes, Your Royal Highness. It fell to me to bring you Lord Hopton's report on our defeat at Torrington.'

'I pray that you are not about to report another calamity?'

'Indeed not, sir. I bring, among other things, a list of those in the West Country who pledge their continuing service to His Majesty and yourself.'

'Good. Sir Edward commissioned this list, for we see Sir John Grenville as a future rallying point for our loyal subjects in the west.'

'Mr. Edward Gilbey has the original, which he has taken to his home,' Nicholas told the Prince, as he drew a red-sealed package from his doublet and passed it over.

'How go affairs at Pendennis?'

'Colonel Arundell and the garrison remain resolute, sir, though there are some desertions. They are greatly straitened for lack of food and provisions, though stocks of powder and amunition are high.'

'Their plight lies heavily upon us,' Hyde interjected. 'While in France, I arranged that supplies be purchased for disposition among small transports, so that some part, at least, may get through. But it will not be for some time, I regret. We must first show the French that we have the money to pay for them and, for that, we depend much upon Her Majesty the Queen and Lord Jermyn. Then ships and crews must be found. I doubt 'twill be before June.'

'But, sir,' Nicholas turned to the Prince, 'the garrison are starving and sickness is rife. I do not know how they may endure so long.' His voice was too charged, his gestures too dramatic for such company, but he did not care. Pendennis must have food!

'We can do no more, Major,' the Prince told him.

'Your pardon, sir, I do not doubt it.'

'I will write, myself, to Mr Gatford, the chaplain, when there is a firm prospect of despatch,' Hyde added, reassuringly.

'Sir George Carteret suggested that I sail with the ships, Your Royal Highness.'

'An excellent suggestion. In the meantime, enjoy your stay in our haven, for you, likewise, can do no more.'

John Grenville addressed the Prince. 'I would be glad to learn from the Major how matters stand in the county, sir. I take exercise walking the coastline, Major Skelton – perhaps you will join me when opportunity permits.'

'With the greatest pleasure, Sir John.'

Released, Nicholas went to a corner of the ramparts and leant upon one of the great guns pointing north-west. Out there, far beyond its range, was where he should be. But for the moment he would take Robin's advice and live for the day. He looked forward to exploring the island in the company of John Grenville. Now it was time for bed.

Next morning, Moignard tapped on the door. 'You are free to go, as you please, about the island. A horse will be at your disposal.'

'That is good news, for I find castles uncongenial.'

'I understand. I sometimes long for wider horizons than Jersey offers.'

Nicholas grinned. 'I must live with that problem for a while. What sights do you recommend?'

Moignard laughed. 'I suggest a quiet canter around the coast to Gorey. There, persuade a fisherwife to cook you something from her husband's catch. You will, again, be confronted by a castle, but a magnificent, medieval one, Mont Orgueil, which dominates Gorey.'

'If the scenery and food warrant it, I will endure the castle.'

'May I advise a Cornishman about fish?'

'Do! Since my confinement in Pendennis, food has become an obsession.'

'It is a little early in the season for many fish. Ask the goodwife for bass, for it is a fighting fish and has crisp, firm flesh, or mayhap red mullet. If mullet is your choice, tell your cook to leave the liver in the fish – it is considered a delicacy. Shall I go on?'

'That will suffice for today.'

'I will requisition some French white wine for you. Immerse it in the sea, awhile, before drinking it.' The Jerseyman was altogether more relaxed and friendly than before his audience with the Prince.

Moignard had provided a good horse and he rode it, slowly, along the island's southern coastline, so different from the rugged grandeur of his native Cornwall. The tide was low and hundreds of rocks projected above the water, like the decayed teeth of a shark, dark and dangerous. He smelt the tang of the sea, felt the spring sun already warm, on his face. Today, for the first time since he could remember, he was free – free of fear and free of duties. There was no cause to be on guard against Roundheads sallying from the rising ground, for despite a strong Puritan element in the Channel Islands, Carteret ruled his domain with a strong hand.

Before him was the outdated, but still noble, fortress of Mont Orgueil and the little fishing village of Gorey, nestling into its grassy skirts. Later he would ride to it, but for the moment the dunes drew him. He dismounted, tethered his horse in a sparse clump of trees and tramped into the dry, shifting sand. It may not be Cornwall, but the gulls were wheeling and crying and the sea was beginning to run in. He threw down his cloak, hitched up his sword and dropped to the ground. Overhead, the sky was a very pale blue, with small wisps of cloud sailing slowly across it. He tilted his hat over his face, closed his eyes and was soon fast asleep.

CHAPTER 24

The Heart's Truth

Throughout May, Nicholas waited for the ship that would bring relief to Pendennis. Chafing at his inability to hasten the day, he tramped the island with John Grenville, and caroused with Moignard and Sir Henry Mannering, the rascally old seafarer who had brought the Prince of Wales from the Scillies and who regaled them with tales of his days as a pirate on the West African coast. On one occasion, he drank the night away with Mannering and Lord Ruthven, Earl of Brentford, a soldier with 25 years' service in the Low Countries' wars, now lapsing into a drunkard.

He also encountered Sir Richard Fanshawe, Secretary to the Council of the Prince, whilst taking a turn about the ramparts. Fanshawe recognised him as a companion of Juliana, with whom his wife had a blossoming friendship. 'Ah, Major Skelton is it not?' the Secretary greeted him. 'I hear that you brought sombre news concerning the plight of Pendennis Castle. Pray, tell me for I will do all I can to help.' He listened, attentively, while Nicholas rendered his account and soberly shook his head when he had finished. Nicholas enquired if his wife had been safely delivered of her child. He replied, 'I rejoice to say she has, but lately. You must come to us and see the baby. She would welcome a visitor from the mainland and news of Mistress Arundell.'

Within a week, the Fanshawes had invited him to dine at their lodgings in St. Helier. He arrived in the town a little before midday and paused beneath the chestnut trees, heavy with candelabras of blossom, which ringed the market place. Spring sunshine splashed their leaves gold and translucent green and cast a crochet of shadow over the awnings and the cobbled ground. Sir George

Carteret had decreed that only the Prince's people were to be served before noon and there were still a few servants and lower members of the entourage about the stalls and in the open centre of the square. In the far corner, his host was in discourse with Lord Ruthven and his family but, even as he stepped forward, the little knot broke and the Brentfords came towards him. As he doffed his hat, the Scotsman, now a sober and solicitous husband, returned a perfunctory greeting, but his daughter and wife, a lady in her own right, acknowledged him graciously.

Behind him the local people were beginning to move into the square, chattering amiably, taking their turn to buy. There seemed to be plenty of produce left for the islanders, no doubt an indication of the parsimonious lifestyle of the exiles – despite Carteret's generosity. One stall was festooned with Normandy fowls, capons and goslings. On another, overlaid rows of bass, mullet, sole, turbot, plaice, whiting, mackerel and lobster stared reproachfully at him. Everywhere there were flowers in abundance. Further on, a butcher had posted his prices on a slate: best mutton at 3 sou the pound, lamb at 3 sous 6 deniers, veal 2 sous 3 deniers, beef 2 sous 6 deniers, pullets 2 sous the couple. Then there were stalls laden with crocks of butter, cheeses, vegetables and fruit.

Nearby, a clock struck the hour. Behind the trees, where he had last seen his host, he found the stocking – merchant's shop where the Fanshawes were domiciled. Inside it was dark, after the bright sunlight, and smelt of silk and lisle. Standing before the displayed hose was a woman in widow's weeds who obviously expected him. She led him through a curtained arch, between a group of sewing women and up a narrow staircase. He was admitted to a small room and welcomed by his host, petite Lady Anne, and her sister.

The simple meal was enlivened by Lady Anne's cheerful account of their experiences since fleeing from Pendennis, with the Prince. 'We were robbed of all our possessions, by the seamen you know, ere we reached the Scillies and scarce knew how we might shift for our next meal, during our stay,' she told him.

'You seem in happier circumstances, now,' Nicholas observed, eyeing the modest room and listening to the sounds of the market.

'Indeed we are, thanks to Sir George Carteret, who sustains the Prince's entire household. 'Tis a heavy financial burden, which he assumed unexpectedly. He has housed the gentlemen-in-waiting in the castle, but many others of us – Sir Edward Hyde and Lord Culpeper included – are lodged here in the town. You, yourself, are much privileged to be afforded accommodation at the castle.'

Nicholas laughed. 'I occupy a small cell above Raleigh's Yard. Perchance, I was given it because I was an object of suspicion when I arrived, and was not permitted to leave the castle.'

'And what think you, now, of Jersey? My husband and I are much taken with it, but I think that his service as Charge d'Affaires in Madrid has made us, anyway, adaptable.' She bubbled merrily on, not pausing for his reply. 'We have seen peacocks at Trinity, swans at Samares and St. Ouens, and an abundance of red-legged partridges throughout the island.'

'The sheep have most intrigued me,' he interjected, while she drew breath. 'Some have six horns, three on each side of the head. In each group, one sweeps forward towards the nose, the second stands upright, while the third inclines towards the neck'.

'Capital!' she cried, clapping the palms of her small hands and leaning forward in her chair, as fascinated as he by the strange creatures. 'Capital,' she repeated thoughtfully. 'La, I have made a pun.'

He laughed again, enchanted by her bright femininity.

'Come, Major Skelton, you must see my new babe – born in adversity, I fear.'

'But its mother in no way downcast, I observe. I would be delighted.'

She took him into the next room, smaller even than the other, which just accommodated a bed and an improvised cot containing a cooing, bonneted infant. As he watched the contented child, he envied the Fanshawes, enduring exile and adversity together.

'And now you must tell me how it goes with the Arundells and that gallant company,' she said, her face growing serious. 'Truly, the King has no more loyal subjects.'

When they had talked further, Lady Fanshawe said, 'On Sunday, the Prince goes to service, yonder.' She indicated the town church, its tower visible above the trees. 'You shall accompany us, for 'twill be quite an occasion for our small community, I promise you.'

He should have told her that he was a Puritan and eschewed the High Anglican rubric, but he had not declared it before midnight mass in Christ Church, at Oxford, and he had no wish to do so, now. 'That would be a great pleasure,' he replied.

So he found himself among the crowd that rode behind the Prince, as he crossed the sands of St. Aubin's Bay – 100 horsemen before him and 300 musketeers behind, drums beating.

Within the orange, granite walls of St. Helier's Church, he stood diagonally left of Charles, who sat before the pulpit, his knights and gentlemen about him. The Prince's books lay on a table covered with rose petals and a cushion had been provided for his elbow, when he knelt. Carpets had been spread on either side of him and scented herbs scattered around. At the table stood Dr. Poley, ready to find the psalms for him and to turn up the biblical texts quoted by the preacher.

Nicholas' eye ranged over the squat, round pillars supporting the plainly-plastered ceiling, through a spur-shaped arch towards the altar, at the stained-glass window, which rose above it. But he did not see the small, sharp-featured man with domed forehead and thinning hair who sat in another part of the church. With an eye at least as perceptive as his own, he watched the ritual of the service, observed an unusual procedure for receiving the offertory and, more particularly, noted that the communicants did not go to the table to receive the sacrament, but waited in their seats, contrary to the custom in Jersey. All that he registered was recorded in surreptitiously-scribbled notes. The man was Jean Chevalier, a Jerseyman, whose diary of this period – augmented by reports from his son, at whose home Culpeper lodged – was to inform and entertain men long after those about him had returned to dust.

Nicholas was a spectator at another event involving the Prince. Carteret had ordered all males, between 15 and 70 years of age, to march in their parish groups to St. Aubin's sands, there to be received by His Royal Highness. Charles rode between the ranks and raised his hat, as the throng shouted, 'God save the Prince and the King!' He then knighted the Seigneur of St.Ouen – Sir Phillipe de Carteret. When the Prince had watched various maneouvres, the officers present knelt and kissed his hand, while he sat his horse. Finally, he distributed gifts of money to the troops – borrowed from his universal provider, Sir George Carteret.

So the days, and then the weeeks, slipped by. For a while, Nicholas dragooned himself to draw a veil of half-forgetfulness about him, to close his mind to the deteriorating situation on the mainland. But as his tall frame filled out, again, and the clean air and exercise restored him to peak vigour, he found the waiting and uncertainty becoming intolerable. Now, every day and latterly by the hour, he pictured Juliana's beauty fading, her pert breasts withering, as the tainted provisions were exhausted and the needs of the growing numbers of sick bore in upon her.

When he could bear it no longer, he haunted the environs of Carteret's office, until finally that worthy Cavalier agreed to see him. Before he could complete his protest, the Governor raised a peremptory hand. 'Tonight, you will be aboard one of my ships when it sails for St. Malo. There you will transfer to a man-of-war, already stocked with provisions and munitions and waiting to sail for Falmouth Haven. I need not tell you of the perils you will face on the voyage – how you must pass through Warwick's fleet and hazard the Roundhead shore guns.'

'It is what I have waited for these past weeks, sir.'

'Then may the Lord be with you all, for I know not when and if Sir Edward Hyde or I can muster further relief.'

Outside, Nicholas went to the walls facing north-west, for the last time, and looked towards Pendennis, before climbing to his cell to assemble his few belongings.

That evening in the company of Sir Thomas Hooper, he returned across the bay to the little harbour of St. Aubin, where he had first arrived. To starboard, lay the three miles of sandy beach which he had walked with Sir John Grenville. Grenville had asked searching questions concerning the personalities on the list he had brought to the island, and it had become clear that he was no fair-weather Royalist and that Cornwall could look to his leadership in the time ahead, as once it had to his father. Despite his impatience to be gone, he felt a certain sadness to be leaving Jersey. Like the Fanshawes, the varied aspects of life on the island had delighted him and he recalled with pleasure his first sight of tulips – a novelty in Western Europe – and the many other flowers which grew in such profusion. It was apparent that the higher echelons of island society, the seigneurs and their families, were cultivated, elegant people. He had particularly admired one of these gentlemen's apparel, a suit of olive green trimmed with satin ribbons and worn with gold-fingered gloves and sky-blue stockings.

His reverie was abruptly broken as their pinnace came alongside the ship that was to carry them to St. Malo. Aboard and installed, he came on deck to find a mist moving sluggishly in from the sea, slowly blurring the outline of coast and castle. But a strong breeze soon carried it away and the bustle of setting sail began.

For a second time, the familiar outlines of the island were obscured, as darkness fell with the freshening wind. The anchor slithered up from the sea bed and the deck tilted, gently, beneath his feet, as the sails filled and the small vessel turned towards the south-east extremity of the bay and France. He was facing the Vintaigne de Noirmont, the high, tree-clad land behind St. Aubin, which sheltered the eastern end of St. Brelade's Bay beyond. Crossing the deck, he watched St. Helier's rock and the squat outline of Elizabeth's keep show briefly and fall away. Now, they were into the open sea, the bow probing the darkness towards St. Malo. For a while, he listened to the sea hissing along the waterline and the yards creaking against the pull of the sails, then he went below to find what rest he could on a rough truckle bed, alongside Hooper's.

Hours later, they were aroused from uneasy sleep and came up to find that they were anchored amid a vaguely perceived forest of masts, below the granite ramparts of St. Malo, the corsair's lair.

Across the harbour, the *Doggerbank*, a ship of about 70 tons, awaited their arrival. Captain Thomas Diamond, the master, welcomed them aboard. 'We are anxious to be away gentlemen, though I fear this freshening wind augurs ill. Nonetheless, we will take our turns. We are a full complement, having another knight and others of quality aboard. There are also some Irish soldiers going to join the Pendennis garrison.'

'Do not tarry a moment, then, Captain,' Hooper said. 'I am commanded to give you your commission from the Prince of Wales and letters from the Prince, Lord Culpeper and others, for the Governor.'

Diamond gave orders to set sail, before conducting his passengers to a minute cabin lit by a lantern swinging from a beam. Pushing some navigation instruments aside, he opened his orders and spread a cargo list on the table. Nicholas read:

10 Barrels of Beef.
6 Chaldrons of Coal
65 Hogs cut up, and salted
10 Tun of Cyder
3 Fat of Peas
100 Weight of Match
1 Cask and a half of Bread
1 Barrel of Candles
1 Barrel of Mustard Seed

'Twill do well enough,' he said.

Diamond picked up the manifest. 'Then let us pray the design succeeds. I must return on deck, for I fear the force of the wind.'

□□□

Two Parliamentary frigates, *Warspite* and *Increase*, beat towards the French coast, under their captains, Henry Southwood and Thomas Faulkner. On their way down the west coast of England, towards their station in the Channel, they had been driven by ill weather to take shelter, after rounding the tip of Cornwall. This circumstance had afforded a meeting with Vice-Admiral Batten aboard his ketch, *St. Andrew*, and he had required them to be watchful for any Royalist ships making for Falmouth Haven. But they had seen nothing, for there had been no abatement of the foul weather, since, and visibility was poor. It was the morning of the Lord's day, 7th of June, as they made out the entrance to the Breton port of Peroes Guirec on their port bow. They steered towards it, gratefully.

Pitching at anchor, outside the port, lay the *Doggerbank*, for Diamond had been obliged to turn back for shelter from the storm outside. Nicholas leaned on the starboard bulwark, gazing disconsolately towards the westward horizon, obliterated by squalls of rain. Two ships were approaching. He wiped the rain from his eyes and looked again. They were men-of-war! He ran aft, calling the alarm, and met Diamond, who paused for one long look before declaring them to be Roundheads.

Diamond cut the cables while his crew strove, desperately, to raise sails, but, before he could gain control, the *Doggerbank* was aground. The Parliamentarians sailed within pistol shot, dropped anchor and began to pour fire into them. The gunners of the stranded vessel and the Irish soldiers soon returned a hot exchange, while Nicholas and the other passengers lined the bulwarks, adding their own shots to the battle, amid the choking smoke and splintering timber.

A ship's boat, with six-man crew, was put out to try to draw the *Doggerbank* seaward, but water was flowing fast into the harbour and the canting deck levelled. Diamond hoisted sail and they began to move. The two frigates weighed anchor and came towards them, intent on boarding and the ship's boat had to be abandoned, as she sailed close inshore among the dangerous rocks. The deafening thunder of guns and the crack of shot continued and the air sang with the whine of flying metal. A falling block struck Nicholas painfully on the shoulder, robbing him of the use of his right arm. They had made about three miles along the coast when the deck lurched, violently, and he was thrown off his feet. The ship had, again, run ashore and, this time, there was no escape. Diamond succeeded in loosing off his cannon once more, but now they were being pounded with case shot from the frigates' guns and plied with small arms fire. The air was lethal and, all about them, rigging, sail and yards crashed to the deck. Ropes snaked over the side and grappling irons thudded into the bulwarks.

The first of the enemy boarders were swinging out of the shrouds and others scrambled over the side, swords drawn, pistols in hand. Diamond's men and some of the Irish began to leap over the shoreward bulwarks, only to be shot or drowned.

As Nicholas stood, helpless and uncertain, a small sliver of metal scourged his cheek and, a moment later, he was engulfed in canvas, as more sail and yards came tumbling down. He lay still, while running feet beat the deck, listening to the shouts and cries and the clang of sword on sword. Soon the turmoil diminished, to be replaced by the rattle of small arms fire from the shore. A further exchange, shouted orders and he felt the ship begin to move. Presently, he heard grunting and felt the sail being pulled off of him.

'Another one here!' a voice called, as he was dragged to his feet. 'Been hit in the face, by the look of it.' Nicholas raised his hand to his cheek and felt the raw edge of flesh, the congealing blood. 'Best get that dressed. Take him aft.'

He walked, with a seaman grasping his arm, to where a chirurgeon was working with bandages and ointments. When his turn came, the wound was painfully drawn together and covered.' Put him below, in the gun room, with the others.'

In the still acrid area between decks, he made out Diamond and his companions of the voyage, except Hooper, who had left the ship, before the engagement, to go about some business in Morlaix. 'That is the end of it, then?' he said to Diamond.

'I fear so, despite assistance from the population on shore.'

With the weather improved and the wind set fair, the little flotilla put to sea. A day later, the tossing ship steadied and the captives heard their anchor splash overboard. They were brought up on deck and Nicholas looked about him. Their ship lay in the Carrick Roads off Smithick, just outside the range of Pendennis' guns. He looked towards the outline of the castle, on its promontory. Nothing had changed; he had come full circle and had brought not one ounce of succour to the beleagured community within.

The knot of prisoners was put into a boat and brought alongside Smithick quay. Nicholas climbed the familiar stairs and walked down the jetty, noting the new planking towards the seaward end. No news had reached him of the raid and he wondered, as he had many times before, how it had fared. An escort fell in around them and they set off down the coast road to Arwenack House. Nicholas found himself confined in what he surmised had been a wine cellar, with Captain Diamond as companion.

Diamond was first to be interrogated. As he returned, Nicholas was marched up to a great room which looked along Arwenack drive. Waiting for him was Colonel Richard Fortescue, commander of the besieging Parliamentary forces. 'Well, Major,' he began, 'our frigates have scotched another gallant, but futile attempt to relieve the castle. You know, it would be much easier, for all concerned, if someone like yourself – for we believe you have influence there – could persuade Colonel Arundell to abandon his defiance.'

'I would not be party to such an approach, Colonel.'

Fortescue was thoughtful for a few moments. 'We further believe that you were party to the attempted subornment of Sir Alexander Carew, on 19th of August, 1643, while he served as Governor of St.Nicholas' Island and you were a commissioned officer of the Parliament. Nicholas's heart sank and a sour fear turned his belly. So they had not forgotten! He remained silent. 'Do you not wish to comment on that?' Fortescue demanded.

'I am an officer of the King.'

'Very well, Major, but earlier misdemeanours might be forgiven were you to assist in terminating this siege. Think on't.'

Nicholas's bandaged face remained impassive.

'Return him to his cell,' Fortescue commanded the guard.

Fortescue appeared content to play a waiting game and left him alone. He passed the time in conversation with Diamond and established a particular rapport with one of his jailers. When he felt it propitious, he asked, 'Was there not a sortie from the castle, to capture provisions, some two months since?'

'Aye, a rare night that were – the great barn ablaze, the jetty blown up, but it availed 'em little. We shot their commander dead in the water, and three of 'is men.'

Grasping the bars of the door, Nicholas hung his head. So, Toby had died doing the work he, himself, had resolved upon. 'What of the second-in-command?' he asked, anxiously.

'Oh, a game young lion that one. We had 'im prisoner in this very cell for a time, but 'e was released and 'as gone back to 'is 'ome, for all I know.'

'Then he was unharmed?'

'Aye, safe and sound, though lucky not to have blown 'isself to kingdom come.'

Praise be to God that I do not have Jamie on my conscience, as well, he thought.

After a few days, the wound in his cheek knitted and was inspected by John Haslock, Surgeon to Vice-Admiral Batten. Haslock handed him a mirror and he viewed his countenance for the first time since his capture. A raised pink wheal, about two inches long, ran under his cheekbone, on the line of his beard.

'Whatever did that must have been very thin and very sharp,' the surgeon told him. 'Time will do much to improve your appearance, but I fear you will always be scarred.'

A week later Diamond was released and he was left alone. Towards the end of June, Fortescue sent for him again. 'You might wish to know, Major Skelton, that Oxford surrendered to General Fairfax on the 24th of this month. Were it not for that stubborn old Cavalier up there, on the hill, we might soon return to our homes, for the King's cause is lost.'

'He will never accept that.'

'You are in a unique position to persuade him that he has no prospect of relief and would be well advised to surrender. By the bye, we are now in no doubt of your part in the affair of St. Nicholas' Island and expect small difficulty in proving the charge.'

Nicholas regarded Fortescue, evenly. How he wished he might acquiesce with honour – to end old Arundell's pointless resistance, the suffering and the misery, which must now be rife. To ensure that his own life was not forfeited – that it might be lived out, in happiness, with Juliana as his wife. 'I am an officer of Pendennis garrison – it is not meet that I should subvert my commander from his duty, as he sees it.'

Fortescue snorted in exasperation. 'I vow Arundell has put his mark on all of you!'

On 27th of June, the Governor made his last bid for supplies. A Guernsey barque left Fowey laden with slates, casks of corded wool, oil and various other commodities. Aboard was a one-handed colonel from Pendennis, carrying a latter to the Prince, declaring that they were now poorly clothed and sickly fed upon bread and water, and had come to the last. The letter, written in cypher on cambric, was too late, for Charles had yielded to his mother's wishes and sailed for France – without Hyde, Capel or Hopton, who refused to accompany him.

Fortescue continued their private battle for Nicholas's will, taking him, personally, on a tour of inspection of the entrenchments and artillery, which sealed off the peninsula. Back in his cell, he acknowledged, in a lonely soliloquy, that his opponent controlled all factors but one – Arundell's indomitable will. But the old man was a realist who did not need endorsement of his grim appraisal of the situation; it was honour which bound him to keep faith with his King, at whatever cost. Notwithstanding, the Roundhead believed that he represented a card that he might play to undermine the Governor's determination. He was, thus, spared from being despatched to London, as Alexander had been, to stand trial – with the attendant possibility that the purpose of his activities, in the capital, might be uncovered and supporters of the King endangered.

Fortescue tried, again, in late July. 'Reports from deserters say they are eating horse-flesh in the castle, he told him. Yet again, on an early August night, he brought him up to see the fires burning on the Pendennis ramparts, a vain guide to approaching relief ships. But there were none, only one small boat-load of supplies having reached them. There was no shortage of munitions, though, and for three days Nicholas listened to the thud of cannon and counted 200 shot fired.

In the second week of August, Fortescue broke him. 'I trust there is no one in the castle for whom you care deeply,' he asked, almost casually, as he studied one of Killigrew's paintings.

There was silence while Nicholas struggled with a sense of foreboding, 'Why do you ask?'

'Plague has broken out.'

Nicholas half-vomited. Hearing the strangled sound, Fortescue turned to face him, surprised at the intensity of his reaction.

'What do you wish of me?' his prisoner murmured.

'Return to your cell. Paper, quill and ink will be brought to you. Write a plea to the Governor, begging him to capitulate – for whatsoever reason you feel will weigh with him most.'

Nicholas nodded. He cared nothing now for his life, nothing for Arundell's regard, only that Juliana should be brought from that festering place. Back in his cell, he drafted and redrafted that letter. Conscious of Arundell's iron code, he sought to strike the old man in his weakest spot - his love for Juliana and his natural compassion. He begged him to surrender for her sake and that of the women and children, for the sick and wounded. He told him that honour had been satisfied and that there was no more to be gained from futile resistance.

When he had finished it, he lay on his cot, sleep eluding him. He watched daylight creep through the small barred aperture, above, and waited for Fortescue's summons. But none came. Rising, he prowled backwards and forwards like a caged animal, looking at the letter, cocking his head for any sound, without. At about midday, there were footfalls, turn of key, and he was climbing the cellar steps. Emerging into the hall, he found a group of eight Parliamentary officers standing in earnest discussion – two full colonels, three lieutenant colonels and three others.

They barely glanced at him, as he passed by and was ushered into Fortescue's presence. Without waiting for the Roundhead to speak, he proffered his letter. Fortescue read it and slowly refolded it. 'May I ask the identity of the lady mentioned, herein?' he asked, quietly.

'Mistress Juliana Arundell, the Governor's ward.'

Fortescue returned the letter, his stern, soldier's face softening a little. 'I would not, knowingly, have laid siege to a man's reason. The gentlemen outside are Parliamentarian Commissioners. Colonel Arundell has indicated his willingness to treat, simultaneously, with Vice-Admiral Batten and myself. It would seem that your letter may not be required.'

249

Nicholas was overwhelmed with relief. Please God it was not too late! He glanced down at the shameful compilation in his hand and crushed it.

'I am not the final arbiter in the matter of Sir Alexander Carew's subornment, as you may judge, but I think it unlikely that you will be called to account for it. General Fairfax's policy is one of clemency and reconciliation and, methinks, our superiors have more pressing business than the arraignment of deserters.' Again that feeling of a great burden lifted from his shoulders. 'Go now. You will be kept informed of developments.'

On the evening of the next day, 16th of August, he was visited by Captain Walter Maynard, in his cell. 'You will be pleased to learn, Major Skelton, that I, with others, have today signed a treaty with the Governor of Pendennis Castle and certain senior officers for the formal surrender of the castle, tomorrow.'

For a moment, the constriction of his throat did not allow him to speak, then he said, 'I am most obliged for the courtesy you have shown me, Captain.'

At about midday on the morrow, he was brought up before Fortescue, on whose desk lay his sword and baldrick. 'Major Skelton, your imprisonment will be terminated within the hour and you will be free to meet your lady, shortly afterwards. It is proper that you should do so wearing your blade, for you and your confreres have not been dishonoured. Indeed, I understand that it was the intention of some officers to blow up the ordnance, so that victor and vanquished might perish together, but this design was foiled by a mutiny of their men.' He passed the weapon to him. 'A barber, and fresh linen and hose await you in your cell. I hope that we may never confront each other, again, as enemies.'

'And I thank you for your kind consideration, Colonel Fortescue'. He bowed. 'Your servant, sir.'

When his beard and locks had been trimmed, he looked, anxiously, at his face in a mirror and was encouraged that the scar was less livid than before, though still conspicuous.

Maynard walked with him to the main gates of Arwenack House and bade him '*Adieu.*' He turned to his right and began to walk along the road at the shore's edge. Almost immediately, he came upon a thickening crowd of people, all making their way to the foot of the castle approach, tense, excited, curious – burghers, fishermen, tradespeople, off-duty soldiers, even perhaps the families of the reprieved garrison. A square had been formed about the approach, by pikemen and musketeers, the crowd at their back. A troop of Plymouth horse was stationed within the hollow square, well back from the slope. At the front of the cavalry, a lieutenant colonel, Richard Townsend, he understood, waited to take the surrender. He eased his way through the crush of bodies, until he was standing where the slope blended into the flat ground. It was warm and the smell of humanity lay heavy on the air. Beside him, stood a young women holding a large sheaf of mauve and white valerian.

'Do you know anyone in the castle?' he asked her, indicating the flowers.

'No, sir, but somehow I thought I ought to bring these along, as a sort of welcome to them, you might say.'

'May I buy them from you,' he asked, producing some coins. 'I would like them for a very personal welcome – from both of us,' he added as the girl eyed the money. She handed him the flowers.

It was now two pm. High above, kettle drums rattled, trumpets blared, and from the gatehouse issued the survivors of the Pendennis garrison. At their head marched the ravaged figure of John Arundell, looking somewhat like a tortoise – scraggy neck protruding above an oversize corselet. But his casque was topped by a bright plume and his hand was on his sword. Immediately behind were his familiars – son Richard, Mathew Wise, Lewis Tremayne, William Slaughter, Charles Jennings, Nevill Bligh and Joseph Lane among them, but Killigrew notably absent. Following came the band, then musketeers and pikemen, seemingly overburdened by their weapons. But the musketeers wore their bandoliers with the '12 apostles' and powder flask; their matches were lit at both ends and each held a bullet in his teeth. Their ragged standards fluttered in the light breeze from Falmouth Bay, the colours of Hopton's regiment prominent among them, as they passed by, tramp, tramp, tramp...

The measured tread of the soldiers have way to the broken steps of the women and children. Leading them was Juliana, wearing her best gown, her lace spotless. But the garment hung, shapeless, from the shoulders of her shrunken figure. A small child walked each side of her, one holding her hand the other encompassed by her protecting arm. At her heels was the inseparable Meg, her normally-thin features almost skull-like.

Nicholas' throat constricted and a tear slid, slowly, down his scarred cheek. 'All thanks to thee, Lord God. She is safe!'

The tail of the column, comprising the pitiful litters of the sick and incapacitated, was now level with him. He wondered where the victims of the plague were and shuddered.

About 900 souls, in all, had passed by, adding their own aroma to the crush of those about him. They had entered the hollow square and were forming up behind Arundell, facing the now-dismounted Roundhead colonel. The band played out its theme and was silent. Arundell stepped forward to conclude this least abject of surrenders, jaunty and heroic!

Nicholas' eye strived, desperately, to keep sight of Juliana and, when a stentorian voice bawled, 'Parade dismiss,' and the orderly ranks of men wavered and dissolved, he jostled his way towards her. She saw him and, handing the children to Meg's care, came to him eyes bright with joy and relief, 'Nicholas! Nicholas!' She threw her arms about his neck and the flowers fell to the ground, forgotten. He held her and held her, till she could scarce breathe. 'One of the Commissioners gave me a message, yesterday, that you were well and would await me.'

'That was Colonel Fortescue's doing.'

'Tis the first news I had had of you these four months'.

'Fortescue told me there was plague in the castle.'

'It is true and there is much to be done. But come with me to Arwenack park – they are going to feed us.' This last was said with feverish intensity. As he released her, she caught sight of the scar and ran her fingers gently over it. ' There is so much to tell,' she said. Then, seeing how anxiously he watched her, she added, 'You look like one of Sir Henry's buccaneers.'

She had contrived to dress her hair in some semblance of style, but it was lifeless, its metallic burnish gone, and he saw that her complexion was blemished. Her body had felt thin as a taper in his arms. Remembering the valerian, he stooped, picked them up and presented them to her. 'Dear Mother Mary, how beautiful they are!' She looked about her, seeming scarce able to believe she was free.

He took her hand. 'Come, let us find you food. But remember, take a little only, at first, or you will rue it.'

The famished garrison and their families were making all haste towards Arwenack, to end their long fast – some to forfeit, through indulgence, the lives they had so slenderly preserved. John and Richard Arundell were left almost isolated and the reunited lovers hurried towards them. Seeing their entwined hands, Richard gave a haggard smile. 'I declare their union is ordained and should be denied no longer, father.'

The old man nodded as he observed their flawed faces. 'I agree, for we shall never be nearer the heart's truth than this day.'

They greeted Nicholas cordially and, after the felicitations due to the occasion, Arundell asked, 'Do you still love Juliana and would you have her as your wife?'

'With all my heart, sir!'

He reached for their hands and laid Nicholas' over his ward's. Encompassing them, he declared, 'Take her and cherish her, with my blessing.' Juliana gave a little cry and leaned forward to kiss him, then she slipped her arms around Nicholas and wept quietly with happiness. His own eyes misty, her guardian avowed, 'Whatever may befall my estates, you shall have a dowry that will not shame an Arundel!'

Nicholas tilted Juliana's chin and kissed her. 'And I give you my whole life.'

CHAPTER 25

The Constant Cavaliers

Painful as another parting was, Nicholas' duty drew him to visit his father, while the three Arundells journeyed, quietly, back to Trerice. He resolved to call upon Robin, on the way. Abraham Tresidder welcomed him with uncharacteristic geniality. 'Something special is called for to celebrate the hero's return,' he declared. ' You will find Robin in the cellar. Do not emerge till you have sampled its contents, liberally.'

Scarcely had he begun the descent into the cellar when a large form stepped from among the barrels into the morning sunlight pouring through a grating in the wall. Robin, arms bared, was wrapped in a leather apron, his red hair haloed by the sunlight – a biblical toiler transcribed from a stained glass window. 'Is that you, Nicholas? Oddfish, I feared never to see you more!' He strode forward and embraced him. 'You have been in the wars!'

'Aye, 'tis true, but first we have *carte blanche* from mine host to make free with his cellar.'

'Then let us to it. As ever, I shall be your mentor.' He laid a hand on one of the barrels. 'We will begin, here, with this good burgundy. Know you that Abraham Tresidder is my prospective father-in-law?' he asked, as he filled a cup. 'Lovely Katherine and I are betrothed.'

'Then I drink to your health and happiness, joyfully.'

'Furthermore, Abraham is minded to foreswear a publican's life and Katherine and I are to take over the inn – a dowry·cum-inheritance, one might say.'

'Tresidder has shown himself a true judge of men.'

Noting the amused twinkle in his eye, Robin said, 'But I am a changed man, my friend. Granted, I take a little wine – for my stomach's sake, you understand – but you could not now describe me as a toper. Sit you here and we will review our lives these past months.'

Hours later, surfeited with wine and food, Nicholas climbed into the saddle, bemused and unsteady. The three Tresidders and Robin had entertained him, royally, and he was left in no doubt of the bond between the big man and their daughter. With a last wave of the hand, he rode for Antony.

Now sober, he received his second embrace of the day, from his father and an anxious enquiry regarding the scar. 'Her Ladyship has begged me to forego the pleasure of supping with you, my son. You are invited to join her, that she might discuss a matter of business with you.'

He and Lady Jane ate alone, then she conducted him back to the solar and they sat at the window, watching dusk creep over the grassland and the tall trees. 'The wonderful news of your betrothal lends extra point to what I would say to you,' she began. 'Penalties laid on my late husband's estate oblige me to realise a sum of money. I believe I may best do this by the sale of Trewhella Barton and, knowing that you once loved it, I decided to mention it to you before proceeding. Demands upon the estate require regular payments, until a full penalty has been exacted. It would, therefore, be appropriate if an initial sum were forthcoming and the residue of the purchase price, at intervals, coincident with my obligations.'

As if embarrassed by her drift, she went on to surmise that life would become more difficult and unpleasant as the droves of minor paid agents, appointed by the Parliamentarian committee administering Cornwall, went to work. While he listened, he weighed the portent of what she had said, and the more he thought on it the more excited he became – no longer tenant, but landowner. 'Lady Jane, I gather that you are offering me first option on the Barton?'

'If you so wish,' she smiled, sensing his enthusiasm.

'I do so, but I must first determine my position. Meantime, pray accept my grateful thanks.'

Early next morning, his mind abuzz, he set out for Trerice, where he had been invited as guest. Everything depended on what Arundell might muster as Juliana's portion. He rode hard back to those few square miles of the Pyder Hundred in which he had lived and worked till Charles Stuart raised his standard to signal the start of the Civil War and the transformation of his life. He spurred his big, black mare up a long slope and reined in as they breasted the rise. Below, the land stretched towards the Camel, where it wound its way to its sandy estuary and the Atlantic. To the south, he saw the Barton, a thin plume of smoke rising straight from the kitchen chimney towards the overcast sky. Faintly, on the still air, came the lowing of cattle from the byre. It was, still, exactly as he remembered it, timeless – the triangular pediment poised on the two round columns of the porch, the nine leaded windows looking to the meadow, beyond. Against the buttressed walls of the barn lay several implements. It was harvest time. He had a great urge to call, but he would not surrender to it until he had made it his own.

His gaze turned west again, to the damp haze that hung on the horizon, then gathering his cloak about him, he heeled the horse forward, down the gentle slope ahead. Shaking the reins he urged it to a gallop, for they were approaching the dry-stone wall, behind which he had come upon Juliana, as a child. In response to his cry of encouragement, the mare rose in a soaring arc and landed, sure-footed beyond the wall and ditch. He patted its glossy neck. May he surmount all obstacles towards possession of the Barton with such ease.

At Trerice, he was accommodated in a guest chamber overlooking the front lawns, from which the daisy-scent of chamomile rose to the open casements. On the gravel beneath, scavenged three peacocks with moulting plumage, like courtiers fallen upon hard times. How well they symbolised the condition of this household.

A little before noon, he left his room and followed the gallery to the staircase. Below, John Arundell stood with his back to the empty fireplace, surveying the hall with a proprietorial air, his pleasure at being home touchingly evident. 'Ah, Nicholas, I have found a few bottles of malmsey in the cellar – it seems to have improved with keeping.' He smiled. 'Yet, everything seems better than I remember it. Do you know, we have held this land since the 14 century and my father built this house some 80 years ago. See, his initials and those of my mother and his sister are on the ceiling.'

Taking the glass Arudell handed to him, Nicholas looked up at the scrolled characters among the lozenge plasterwork. 'Long may you enjoy your ancestral home, sir, content in duty well done.'

The old man's brow contracted. 'Tis not done and will not be till Charles Stuart is secure upon his throne. As for my house and lands, I know not how long they may be mine under the Parliament.' He paused as Juliana and Richard joined them, then he stood back and looked at his family arms, fretted in the massive overmantal. 'Yes, we are an ancient family which honours its kin. Soon you will be one of us, Nicholas, and shall be like a second son to me, now that John is gone. United, then, we shall fight on.'

Nicholas felt Juliana's hand slip into his. Her presence and Jane Carew's proposal filled his thoughts and he had spared none, of late, for Charles Stuart. Had it not ended then – with the surrender of Pendennis? Was not even Arundell's honour satisfied? He squeezed Julian's fingers and felt their reassuring pressure in response.

They sat to board, where the light flooded in through myriad panes of glass. Scissors and thread had been used to good effect, while he had journeyed to Antony, and the Arundells' gauntness was not as apparent as at the surrender. Juliana was dressed in her green brocade, while Richard, cast in the same mould as his sire and now greying at the temples, was content with simple russet. The old man, at the head of the table, wore the grey velvet Nicholas remembered when they were last together in this room, over six years since. Even now, the portrait of the King looked down on his most loyal subects and the great table exuded its aroma of beeswax. But, now, the Arundells had accepted him as custodian of Juliana's happiness – and he was well content.

When they had finished the simple meal, Arundell said, 'Take a turn with me, Nicholas!' He led the way through the library to the steps giving on to the garden from the semi-circular tower. For a moment, he revelled in the sunshine, before they set off to the great barn, flanked by stables and a mill. The old man looked ruefully at the water-wheel, silent, still and green with slime. 'I loved to stand here and listen to its rumbling and splashing and the gurgle of the leat, when Trerice and the family were mutually sustained. But the grain has not been sown and gathered since I took the workers from the land, to garrison Pendennis, and this is the consequence.'

He pointed to the double doors of the barn. 'In winter, I would have 20 men threshing grain, in there. With these doors and the pair on the far side open, the dowse would come fluttering out in the cross-current, hazing the winter sunshine.Winnowing is back-breaking work, but I made sure there was plenty of cider to clear the dust from their throats.' Nicholas followed him to the middle of the cobbled courtyard – to the circular trough in which apples had once been pulped, by a granite roller, turned by a patient horse.

'And how has the bowling green fared, I wonder?' They climbed the steps, on the north side of the forecourt, to what had once been a smooth rectangle of emerald turf. Now, it was daisy and dandelion strewn and burned by the summer sun.

'You see, Nicholas, there is much to do. Richard and I will shoulder the burden, but you are assured of a home here, and your particular knowledge of husbandry will be of value to the work.'

Nicholas was silent, framing his reply, glad that he need not burden the old man with his presence for long. 'You are most kind, sir, but I must tell you that Lady Carew has made me a proposition. It seems that she must sell Trewhella Barton, to pay the fines upon her estate. Knowing my attachment to it, she has offered me the first option to buy and would be content with a lump sum and incremental payments.'

Arundell stroked his grey beard for a moment. 'Then tell Jane Carew that Juliana's portion shall match the down payment. And before we set about restoring Trerice, the Barton shall be made a fit home for you both. I doubt not the Parliament will turn a baleful eye on me, 'ere long, and I would see you settled first.'

Turning his penetrating eye upon Nicholas, he continued, 'One other matter must engage us. Tomorrow is the Sabbath. Juliana will go to worship with her Catholic kin of Lanherne, while Richard and I give thanks for our deliverance at God's house, yonder.' He gestured towards Newlyn East Church. 'What will you do?'

'I must go with you, sir.'

◻◻◻

Juliana and Nicholas were married three months later, in the private chapel of Lanherne. Such was the standing of the Arundells, in the county, that few were inhibited by their religious conscience from attending the ceremony. Arundells, their Royalist intimates and other prominent families in the county, filled the left-hand pews. Notably absent was Sir Henry Killigrew, who had died at St. Malo from a self-inflicted wound, sustained when he exuberantly fired a pistol, at the end of the siege.

Jane Carew, foregoing her place among Arundell kin, sat with her children and her faithful steward. Staunch Puritan that he was, Skelton senior was prey to conflicting emotions – joy for his son, admiration for his beautiful bride, but uneasy in this ornate temple.

Foremost among the guests on Nicholas' side were Sir John and Lady Berkeley, and Geoffrey and Letitia, he newly ennobled by the death of his father and the succession of his eldest brother to the earldom.

Mr and Mrs Edward Gilbey were there and the three Tresidders, and that gallant sprig, Jamie Rose, who had ridden from his family home near Helston. And, at the elbow of his beloved friend, stood Robin Smythe, magnificent in a new plum-velvet suit with a sash of blue satin tied in a great bow. Nicholas, no less splendid, but half a head shorter, awaited his bride at the high altar.

Juliana came to him, her radiance reflected in the faces of those who turned to watch her enter the chapel. Her mother's veil floated about her head and shoulders and over a white silk, embroidered gown, caught with clusters of tiny pearls. He felt his throat constrict, for she was so beautiful.

From the transept, the household and estate workers of Lanherne and Trerice, and the little community from Trewhells, made what shift they could to witness the ceremony, between the fluted pillars and lofty arches of the nave, and over the heads of their betters.

The marriage service was short and simple, the forbidden Mass unobserved. Afterwards, Sir John and Lady Katherine Arundell provided a sumptuous wedding breakfast, in the old house with the wolf's head crest above the door, while musicians in the gallery filled the great hall with joyous sound.

As the three boon companions, their brides and Katherine Tresidder, were in animated discourse, a young man with auburn hair emerged from the crowd of guests and joined them. His sudden appearance, at the centre of attention, brought a spontaneous cheer from those nearest and he turned to acknowledge the acclaim. Nicholas was the first to speak. 'Sir John, I had not thought to see you here!'

'Was I not invited?' Grenville responded, mockingly.

'You were, and welcome,' Nicholas greeted him.

'And where better to meet with true Cavaliers than an Arundell nuptial feast?'

Nicholas smiled with the others at his gallantry, while thinking that even their wedding day was not free from political intrigue.

'I wish you happiness and healthy issue,' Grenville continued. 'Methinks, there were moments on Jersey when you doubted you would witness this happy day.'

'Aye, Sir John, and many another, but the Lord is good!'

'Amen to that. Know that my remembrances of those times will not fade, and that I am a true friend, whatsoever may befall.' With a bow to the ladies, he melted back into the crowd.

Robin murmured in Nicholas' ear, 'I doubt not such friendship is to be valued, but the price of it is continuing service to the King.'

◻◻◻

Nicholas brought his bride home to the Barton, a very different place from what he had left. The worn and cracked flags had been renewed and the smoke-stained parlour cleaned and refurbished. Brocade curtains hung at the windows and Arundell furniture graced the low room – a court cabinet, a sturdy refectory table and carved chairs with backs and seats upholstered in the same material as the curtains. Portraits of Juliana's parents hung on the wainscoted walls, while blue Delft china brought colour to window ledges and dark corners. Upstairs, their bed chamber was graced by a draped, four-poster bed and much evidence of Juliana's elegant taste. Behind the farm, a piece of meadow had been encompassed by a high wall and, soon, it became a garden full of hollyhocks, lavender, hellebore and many sweet herbs.

Nicholas took up the challenge of the seasons again, while Juliana set about winning the hearts of house servants and farm workers. Last to succumb was Dorothy Crabtree, for had she not once been virtual mistress of the Barton, deferring only to a youth who had gone to war – and come back a man?

Meg and Dorothy were never easy with one another, for Meg's position, as Juliana's maid, was unassailable and the relationship between the two women gave rise to occasional flashes of temper, to which Juliana applied a soothing balm.

The first two harvests were poor, but then times were hard for all, as the price of tin continued to decline and plague took 500 in St. Ives alone. There was much to do, for the ravages of war must be repaired and paid for, and the cost of the troops quartered in the county met from revenues. The worst fears of Jane Carew and John Arundell were soon realised. Like many other Royalist delinquents, they were subjected to constant demands from agents of the County Committees, collecting assessments from their sequestrated estates. Those who failed to pay had their stock and possessions sold and distrained, and anyone suspected of undervaluing their estate was examined under oath and sometimes imprisoned. Informers made a steady living.

The Arundells, still resolute for the cause, were sustained by hopes of a Royalist revival – with scant justification. In January, 1647, the Scots handed the King over to Parliament. At first he was held at Holdenby House, Northamptonshire, then given over to the army, at Newmarket. In November, he fled from his domicile, at Hampton Court, to the Isle of Wight and there signed an engagement with the Scots Commissioners. In February, 1648, with the Scots massing in the north and the populace restless under their burden of taxation, the country erupted.

One day early that spring, Nicholas came from the byre to find Richard clucking over his new-born son, while Meg, now appointed nanny, hovered nearby. Juliana was at his side, smiling fondly. Seeing Nicholas, she said, 'It seems that the war has broken out again, in Wales, and has spread to London and East Anglia. Richard says that Sir Hardress Waller has arrived in Exeter, as commander of the Roundhead forces in the west and governor of Pendennis Castle.'

Richard took up the story. 'Such is the feeling against the army that Waller has been forced to withdraw all but two companies of his troops, from the city, and billet them in Tavistock. We must be ready to take every advantage of the situation.'

Nicholas regarded his wife and son. His life was hard but satisfying and he had no wish to become embroiled, once again, in danger and death. Yet there could be no escape. 'What do you propose?' he enquired.,

'I am on my way to sound out Royalist opinion in the county. Meanwhile, we must keep in close touch with events. My father asks that you journey to Exeter, to see, for yourself what passes, there.'

He tried hard to read Juliana's face. There was concern for him and the disruption of their lives, but also acceptance of the call. 'I will be gone within the hour,' he assured Richard.

▣▣▣

The once familiar figure of the landlord was directing a pot-boy to a rowdy group of troopers when he entered The Ship. At sight of him, the innkeeper greeted him, warmly. 'Major Skelton, 'tis good to see you!'

'I had best be plain Mister in this company,' he cautioned, calling for a pot of ale.

'Aye, 'twould be wise. We could do without their custom, I'll be bound. There have been some rare goings on 'twixt their general and Mr. Bennett, the Mayor, for the people are stubborn against them. If Waller had had his way, he'd have quartered 600 men on us, but we obliged him to put them in the churches and churchyards, by shutting our shops and houses against them. This lot forced their way in here.'

'Can nothing be done?'

'I think not. When the Mayor protested to the Parliament, Waller seized the keys and arms of the city. But he's got his hands full in Cornwall, too, for it seems the troops' pay is in arrears and a Colonel Fortescue has refused to surrender his governorship of Pendennis Castle, till he receives further orders from the Parliament.' As he regarded the noisy soldiers in the corner of his taproom, the innkeeper warmed to his narrative. 'Then there's problems with the commissioners appointed to raise money for the relief of Ireland, as well as rumours that the Royalists are rearming.'

Seeing Nicholas' empty pot he refilled it, waving aside the proffered coins.

When Nicholas was satisfied that he had gleaned all available information, he said, finally, 'Well, I must make tracks for home.'

'Beware of highwaymen, for they abound on lonely roads!' the landlord warned.

He rode straight for Trerice, where he found a conference of local Royalists under way. Around the table, in the great hall, were John and Richard Arundell, Sir John and Jonathan Trelawny, Sir Arthur Bassett, Colonel Robert Harris and Sir Charles Trevanion of Caerhayes. They listened carefully, as he enumerated Waller's problems. When he had finished, John Arundell said, 'It would best serve our design to engineer a rising led by those less prominent than ourselves – 'twill create confusion and, should it succeed, we may move against strategic points in the county.' This view met with general approval.

Their voices rose to the musicians' gallery, where the servant who had once betrayed Juliana listened intently. Soon, the Sheriff of Cornwall had wind of their intentions and he duly informed Waller. 'These malignant gentlemen speedily mean to disturb the peace of the county.'

Waller responded by arresting numerous leading Royalists, among them some who had foregathered at Trerice. He was further warned by Antony Gibbs, a Penzance shopkeeper, that he might expect trouble locally. The Arundells, to their surprise, were not arrested and continued to plot. The old man, alert now to unseen listeners, sent for Nicholas and led him to the solar. 'I am informed that a number of Royalist officers, Major Thomas Grosse of St. Buryan chief among them, have amassed some 200 rebels and plundered Penzance. Athough this may be the prelude to a general rising, I like not the calibre of these men and fear that the Parliamentary Committee's agreement to parley with them, over alleged grievances, may be to gain time, till more troops arrive. I wish you to determine whether we should fan the flames or remain aloof. Observe, but do not become embroiled!'

He rode back to the Barton, much troubled. Despite the harsh rule of the Parliament, their 18 months of marriage had been deeply happy. Juliana had recovered well from the ordeal at Pendennis and had made Trewhella a haven of warmth and comfort. Six months since, she had borne him a fine son and her breasts and hips had grown full with motherhood. Each night, they lay together in the four-poster bed, snug in down and feathers. Yet there was a price to be paid for his happiness.

Juliana was also uneasy, when he told her of his mission, and he wondered how much their marriage had blunted her resolve. 'Do not take your own horse and be as unobtrusive as possible,' she advised. 'Should anything go awry, and we have unwelcome visitors, I will tell them that you have gone to Truro to buy stock.'

He travelled south across uplands strewn with gorse and dead bracken, through sunken lanes and over bridges which had echoed, for centuries, to the clop of pack horses. On Monday, 22nd of May, he arrived in Helston. At the inn where he took a room, a local told him that a strong force of cavalry and foot had seized Penzance from the rebels, two days before, and he concluded that the uprising was over. But, minutes later, someone shouted in at the door that Mullion had risen and the Mayor of Helston was calling for volunteers, to augment the town guard.

His informant laughed, cynically. 'He can't trust the ones he's got already,' he commented. But there was a general exodus to homes or arms and soon he was alone in the taproom.

Fearing that he might miss some important development, he went to lie on his bed, listening to the shouting below and watching the light of torches flickering on the ceiling. The Mayor and Justices of the borough were clearly resolved not to be taken unawares, and kept the watch. Next morning, he ventured abroad, to learn that a sizeable force of Royalists was advancing over Goonhilly Down. While he waited for his horse to be saddled, he watched a small band of Parliamentary horse assemble behind the Mayor. When they rode from the town, he shadowed them, through hedge-shrouded lanes, until they encountered the rebels and withdrew, fearing an ambush.

He took the opportunity to contact the Royalist scouts, in a lane leading down to the Helford river, unaware that the Mayor and his troopers had proceeded on to join with Roundhead reinforcements coming from Penzance. The scouts took him to their commander, a Captain Pike, and Nicholas sat with him on the churchyard wall, in Mawgan village to discuss developments. The wooded slopes above the river had dimmed to a green-black haze when the Mayor and his augmented force came at them, through the huddle of houses before the church.

Scrambling into the saddle, Pike shouted, 'Make for the Gear! Follow me!' They reached the ancient earthwork, in which his men were entrenched, and looked back on the advancing cavalry supported by foot. They were in a commanding position, some 200 feet above the creek, and might hold off the enemy, but he carried only a pistol and his orders were clear. Behind them, in the dusk lay Goonhilly Down and St. Keverne. Wheeling his horse, he made off at breakneck speed across the unfamiliar ground, but had not gone far when his mount stumbled and he hit the ground with a sickening thud. Angry white lights flashed in his head and he lay face down in the turf, until the first of the fleeing rebels aroused him. Struggling to his feet he looked about. His horse was nowhere in sight, but all around men were running and he staggered forward with them. When it seemed that his legs would bear him no further, the men ahead halted at the cliff edge. At first there were despairing shouts, then an eerie silence, as they listened to the pursuit. Someone shouted and several men joined hands, ran forward and disappeared from sight. Others followed, himself included.

Closing his eyes, he launched into space and plummeted down, with the wind whistling in his ears. With a stinging impact he hit the sea and a dark void closed over him. His feet struck its pebble floor and he thrust upwards, but water was entering his thigh boots and, for a terrifying moment, he thought he would not rise. Then he broke surface and breathed, frantically, before the waters closed again. But he had seen a rocky outcrop, only yards away, and fought his way towards it. A knee struck its jagged contours and he reached out, blindly, clawing his way back to the life-giving air.

A clatter of small-arms fire raised angry splashes on the water. Putting the rock between him and the cliff top, he struggled for breath, while he noted that the coastline to his right ran north. Thrashing along the rocks, he touchd bottom and came ashore on a narrow strip of shingle. As yet, there was no movement on the cliffs above. Struggling out of the impeding boots, he disposed of their soggy contents and groped his way up a bracken-strewn path from the beach. Keeping the sea on his right and watching the fitful moon, he loped northwards, until the Helford river barred his way. From the cover of its tree-clad banks, he searched until he found a small rowing boat. Daylight found him a few miles south of Penryn, confronted by a shallow stream. Falling on his face, at its edge, he slaked his thirst, laved his face and lay prone, too weary to move. He was at least 30 miles from home, horseless and without sustenance.

A soft drumming of hooves startled him and he rolled over, as a horseman broke from the nearby trees, a slim youth on a fine roan.

'Jamie!' he called eagerly.

The young man rode towards him. 'Major Skelton, is it you, sir?'

He got to his feet. 'Aye, and glad to see you. How come you by, so opportunely?'

'There is news of a Cavalier rising to the west and I was on my way to learn what passes. I was minded to join it, but, with my father a month dead, I fear to distress my mother more.'

'Keep away, for all is lost.' He waved feebly, indicating his distressed state.

'Up behind me, then, sir, and we will away to my home. 'Tis only two miles.'

They came to a substantial old house standing in a park. As they hurried inside, a woman emerged from a room off the hall and came, anxiously, towards them. She was probably not yet 40, but pale and drawn.

'Mother, this is Major Skelton.' Good breeding overcame surprise as Mrs Ross greeted him. 'The Major needs fresh linen and a suit. With your permision, I will attire him with something of father's, but we shall need Elizabeth's expert help.'

'Of course I will find her.'

Thanks to his sister's needlecraft, Nicholas was apparelled more than tolerably. While she worked, he recounted his recent adventure. 'So you see, I am in some difficulty,' he concluded.

'It is necessary that I visit Lostwithiel, about my father's business with the Stannary Court, and tomorrow would be as good a day as another,' Jamie responded. 'We will travel together, as far as Truro. From there, it is not a difficult journey home.'

'Pray that I arrive there before the Roundheads. For sure, my relationship with the Arundells will bring us a visit.'

'What is to be done, if your absence is discovered?'

'It will be a poor story I fear, but Juliana will say I have gone to Truro, on business.'

'Then you shall rest now and, later, we will enter the town separately, ostensibly to negotiate the sale of some of my father's stock.'

'Excellent, but there remains a problem of dates. I have been absent since Saturday – it is now Wednesday.'

'You have an old friend in Fowey, an innkeeper and wine importer. You visited him, first, and left an order written in your own hand. In a forgetful moment you also left your ring.'

'How is that to be contrived?'

'When I arrive at Lostwithiel, I will have a messenger go to Fowey, with the articles and an explanatory letter.'

'Jamie, such plotting would carry you high among the Cavaliers. It is not flawless but, methinks, it will suffice.'

☐☐☐

Nicholas patted the bay he was riding. 'Your father had a fine eye for a horse,' he said. 'I would dearly like to negotiate one genuine purchase – this beauty – for Juliana.'

Jamie looked fondly at the creature. 'It is true, I cannot keep it and would like nothing better than it should pass to that lovely lady.'

'Then it is agreed.'

Within sight of Truro they separated and Nicholas rode in first. Each took a room at the same inn and made themselves conspicious, discussing business, publicly. The next morning Nicholas set out for home, full of gratitiude to his young friend.

□□□

As soon as the Barton came into view, it was apparent that trouble awaited him. Six Model Army troopers sat their horses around the front door, while a riderless horse stood tethered to the portico. He rode into the yard and dismounted, exuding a confidence he did not feel. Inside, he found Juliana confronting a tall, Parliamentary officer.'

'What business have the enemies of the King in my house?' Nicholas demanded.

'The servants of the people seek the malignants behind the rising in the south,' the Roundhead responded, aggressively.

'What should I have to do with that?'

'Your wife tells me you have been to Truro.'

'That is true and I have learned of these events, but they were centred around Penzance, Mullion and Helston, were they not?'

'How long have you been absent? Your wife seems oddly vague on the matter.'

'Six days.'

'On a journey to Truro?'

Nicholas feigned exasperation. Ignoring the Roundhead, he turned to Juliana and sighed. 'I had a surprise for you, which this blundering fellow obliges me to reveal. I went to Truro to buy a horse to replace Bellerophon, but, first, I visited Robin, to order wines for your birthday. And sadly, I have lost the ring you gave me.'

Juliana took his hand and looked at the naked finger. The Roundhead, irritated by his indifference, demanded, 'Do you deny complicity in the events I referred to?'

'I have stated the purpose of my travels, and I will tell you the names of those with whom I have been in contact'. He gave the officer details of Jamie and Robin.

The Roundhead slapped his gauntlet against his boot. Be sure you tell the truth, Cavalier, or you will, yet, rue it.' With a curt bow to Juliana, he made for the door. It slammed and they listened to the sounds of the horsemen departing.

Juliana sat down, her face pinched. 'Nicholas, it is only a matter of time before they learn the truth.'

He took her hand and raised it to his lips. 'Part of the truth stands outside, as you shall see. Of the rest, be assured all is arranged and your ring is safe.' Still, holding her hand, he led her into the yard. The bay whinnied at sight of its new master.

Juliana clasped her hands to her face. 'Oh, he is beautiful! Is he truly mine?' She went to the horse and murmured endearments into the sleek ear, while the creature nuzzled her hand. They were instant friends. She turned to Nicholas. 'My birthday is not until September.'

'I doubt it matters.'

She ran to him and he caught her in his arms.

▪▪▪

The Gear Rout, as the episode on Goonhilly Down became known, was a minor setback for the Royalists compared with Cromwell's decisive victory over the invading Scots, at Preston, in August of that year. Yet the dismay of the Cornish Cavaliers was relieved, the following month, by Sir John Grenville's recovery of the Scilly Isles.

Within Parliament, two groups duelled for power, the Presbyterians and the Independents. During a period of ascendancy – with Cromwell absent in the field – the Presbyterians sought a peace treaty with the King. But he, devious to the last, would agree nothing, and once order had been re-established in the country, the Army demanded that he be brought to trial.

CHAPTER 26

Kiss of the Axe

Lady Anne Fairfax peered through the eye-slits of her mask, at the extraordinary scene unfolding below. Westminster Hall was awash with people. There were crowds cramming the steep galleries, along the east and west walls, where she sat, and milling about the floor area right up to the wooden barrier which divided the public from the court. Beyond the barrier was an island of quiet.

She looked up at the massive, hammer-beamed roof and towards the south window, below which stood rows of tiered benches covered in red baize, ready to accommodate the commissioners who were about to try their King. A raised chair had been placed in the middle of the front row of benches, with a reading desk and scarlet cushion before it, where the Lord President of the court would take his place. In front of this arrangement stood a table covered in a rich Turkey carpet and two chairs.

It was shortly after two o'clock when the 68 Commissioners entered the Hall, preceded by a party of halberdiers. Three men, in black barristers' gowns, took their places centre-stage, the remainder, sober-suited and solemn, filled the benches. The sword and mace, which had been carried before the procession, were placed on the table. Anne Fairfax searched for Oliver Cromwell, as the guards formed bristling lines around the court.

One of the two clerks rose and read out the preamble, which purported to empower the court to its purpose. The Lord President, John Bradshaw, then ordered the royal prisoner to be fetched, while the commissioners responded to a roll-call. As each rose to his name, Lady Fairfax became more agitated and, when the name of her husband, the Lord General, was called, she cried out, 'He has more wit than to be here!' But her voice was partly submerged by the clerk's and by the movement of the commissioners.

Then she saw the King enter, surrounded by soldiers. He wore black; around his neck hung the jewelled George, on a blue ribbon, and his cloak was emblazoned with the great silver star of the Garter. Looking neither to right nor left, he walked quickly to the red, velvet chair, which had been placed facing Bradshaw, and sat down. Beneath the tall black hat, his hair hung, grey, to his shoulders.

While observing the impassive face of the King, she thought yet again of the Prebyterian ministers who continued to denounce the army, Cromwell and the subservient Commons, from their London pulpits. Forty-seven of them had reprimanded her husband for allowing the army to seize power, and had urged him to remedy the evil purpose that was being enacted here, today. She and her mother, Lady Vere, both women of strong opinions, had added their voices, but Tom, though much distressed by their rancour, did nothing. Both women had received a pamphlet from another London minister, John Geree, arguing that the generality of the people of the land abhorred the idea of trying their King. Dear God, could she do nothing!

The Lord President had begun to speak. 'Charles Stuart, King of England, the Commons of England, assembled in Parliament, being sensible of the great calamities that have been brought upon this nation, and of the innocent blood that hath been shed...'

When Bradshaw had completed this claim to the legality of the court, John Cook, the prosecutor immediately began to read the indictment from a parchment scroll. While declaring, 'I do accuse Charles Stuart, here present, of high treason and high misdemeanours...,' he turned to glare at the prisoner.

'Hold a little,' called the King, but Cook continued to read. Raising his cane, the King tapped him on the arm, to attract his attention, and the silver head of the cane fell off. Anne Fairfax looked aghast at the horrid symbolism of this incident.

Bradshaw would brook no interruption. 'Sir, the court commands the charge to be read. If you have anything to say afterwards, you may be heard.'

The charge, which was not lengthy, alleged that Charles had been trusted with a limited power to govern and according only to the laws of the land, but had taken to himself an unlimited and tyrannical power, overthrowing the rights and liberties of his people. He was, further, accused of traiterously and maliciously levying war against the Parliament and people, and of procuring invasions from foreign parts. After his defeat, he had renewed the war in the sole interest of himself and his family, and was impeached as a tyrant, traitor, murderer and implacable enemy of the Commonwealth of England.

The intensity of his ordeal seemed, strangely, to have eradicated the King's speech impediment and throughout his trial he was fluent and clear. He now demanded, 'I would know by what power I am called hither. I would know by what authority, I mean lawful.'

Lady Fairfax strained to hear the rest of this opening, but it was lost to her, because of the noisy arrival of more spectators, at the lower end of the Hall.

Bradshaw's response was a repetition of Cook's phrases and a demand for the King to answer, 'in the name of the people of England, of which you are elected King.'

To suggest to Charles that England was an elective Kingdom was an error and Bradshaw was duly admonished. The King continued, 'I do not come here as submitting to the Court... I see no House of Lords, here, that may constitute a Parliament... Let me see a legal authority..., warranted by the constitution of the Kingdom and I will answer.'

Unable to stand his hectoring eloquence, Bradshaw endured a further lengthy speech, which he, finally, curtailed by ordering the removal of the prisoner.

Charles rose and, as a parting shot, looked towards the table where the charge now lay. 'I do not fear that!' he said, dismissively.

The next day, the Sabbath, was kept by the Commissioners as a fast and they were delivered of three sermons. In one, Joshua Sprigge, chaplain to Fairfax, revealed that he shared the doubts of the Lord General by an ambivalent declamation, 'He that sheds blood by man shall his blood be shed.' Another army chaplain declared, 'Judge not that ye be not judged.' Only Hugh Peters expressed doubts in his text, 'I will bind their Kings in chains.'

Monday morning found the Commissioners considering their dilemma in the painted chamber, in the environs of Westminster. How should they proceed, if the King would not acknowledge the court? How to reconcile their unprecedented action with English Common Law?

In a case of treason, they could treat the prisoner as guilty, if he failed to plead, but then they could not demonstrate the King's guilt by calling witnesses and prove him guilty.

Seventy Commissioners assembled in Westminster Hall, that afternoon. It was apparent that Lady Fairfax's intervention had made some impact, because a proclamation was read, which warned that anyone causing a disturbance would be instantly arrested. The King entered the chamber, with his usual dignity, and took his seat. Cook, the prosecutor, was taking last-minute legal advice, but

Charles would brook no delay and gave him a sharp poke with his cane, to Cook's fury. But the prosecutor opened with a motion '...that the prisoner be directed to make a positive answer, either by way of confession of negation, which if he shall refuse to do, the matter of the charge may be take *pro confesso* and the court may proceed according to justice.' Bradshawe then declared, uncompromisingly, that the court were fully satisfied with their authority and that the whole kingdom, the King included, must be satisfied with it, likewise.

In his penetrating response, Charles asserted that, for himself, he would be content with his previous protestations on the legality of the court, but his concern was for the freedom and the liberty of the people of England. For if power, without law, may make laws, may alter the fundamental laws of the kingdom, I do not know what subject he is in England that can be sure of his life, or anything that he calls his own.'

When Bradshawe found opportunity, he interrupted the King with, 'Sir, you speak of law and reason – it is fit there should be law and reason, and there is both against you.' In fact, what was against the King was his own abuse of law and his resort to arms, which brought about the Civil Wars. But how to prove it if he would not answer the charge? But against the King's charge that Parliament was indeed a court, whereas the House of Commons alone was not, the Lord President could only bluster and reiterate the call for the prisoner to answer.

So the second day ended on an uncertain note.

On the third day, the Commissioners attended in the highest numbers to date, though they were a little over half the number appointed.

The King maintained, at length, his dogged disdain for the legality of the court, but Bradshawe took an opportunity to counter Charles's asserted concern for the privileges of the people. 'How far you have preserved the privileges of the people your actions have spoke it, but truly, sir, men's intentions ought to be known by their actions. You have written your meaning in bloody characters, throughout the whole kingdom.'

Recognising their desperate difficulties, the Commissioners repaired to the Painted Chamber, at close of the day's proceedings. The fact that Bradshawe had been obliged, three times, to order the removal of the prisoner by the soldiers, in order to silence him, was ample proof that the force of the army prevailed, not law.

In the shadow of this tyranny, the King's was less apparent, particularly without witnesses to stand against him.

And Fairfax must be persuaded to come to Westminster Hall for the next session!

But the Lord General was subject to vigorous pressure from the other directors, even within the army. A Major White had published an open letter to him: 'The King and his party being conquered by the sword, I believe the sword may jointly remove the power from him, and settle it in its original fountain, next under God, the people.' Because he did not believe the King could justly be killed, he proposed he be kept prisoner. This would debar his son – young, free and, therefore, infinitely more dangerous – from claiming the crown. Use the sword with all tenderness, he entreated Fairfax.

The Presbyterian clergy, in London and the country, also maintained remorseless pressure and the Scots Commissioners published a robust remonstrance. William Prynne, who had denounced the army in Parliament before the Purge, published an expanded text of his speech.

Fairfax did not move. Various excuses were made for him – pressure of other business, fear that he might be thought ambitious for the throne, among them.

Despite their inability to call their witnesses, the Commissioners took depositions from them, which confirmed the King's active participation in the war and his intention of continuing it, even during the recent treaty negotiations, and published them in some newssheets.

On 27th of January, Anna Fairfax, in the company of her friend, Mrs Nelson, took her place in the galleries for the last time. Both ladies were masked, against recognition, and, below them, the Lord President was robed in red, as evidence of the solemnity of the occasion.

Charles' entrance was greeted with cries of 'Justice!' and 'Execution!' from the soldiers and some onlookers. He was calm and purposeful and demanded he speak before Bradshawe opened the proceedings. Only when he received an undertaking that he might speak later was Bradshawe able to begin his address:

'Gentlemen, it is well known to all, or most of you here present, that the prisoner at the bar hath been several times convened and brought before the court to make answer to the charge of treason and other high crimes exhibited against him in the name of the people of England...'

Leaning forward, Lady Fairfax cried, 'Not half, not a quarter of the people of England! Oliver Cromwell is a traitor!'

Colonel Axtell, who was responsible for security, unaware that he was referring to the wife of his Lord General, shouted, 'Down with the whores.' and ordered his soldiers to level their muskets at the two ladies. Anne Fairfax stared defiantly into the menacing barrels, but those about her were anxious for her to be gone, and she was bundled out.

So she went from Westminster Hall, out into the biting cold, to her house in King Street, to the husband who remained silent while their sovereign was illegally tried and sentenced to death.

How many times had she conjectured what were his true thoughts, as she looked in on the tall, dark figure at his desk, bent over some new missive to discomfit him. No doubt Oliver Cromwell's iron will and Henry Ireton's contumely bore heavily upon him, for he seemed to be ever in their company. Well, she had done what little she could.

The Prince of Wales was no more successful. His letter to Fairfax, imploring him and Cromwell to restore their sovereign to his just rights and the country to peace and happiness, was set aside without answer.

Thenceforward, matters moved inexorably. Charles, a greying careworn figure, was brought into Westminster Hall for trial. He challenged the legal authority of the court, reminded them that he was their hereditary King and declared his respect for the peace of the Kingdom and the liberty of the subject. He succeeded in exposing the dominant power of the army and showed that force, not law, prevailed. What he failed to show was that he had protected his people in return for their subjection to his divine kingship.

So, he was sentenced to death and, on 30th of January, 1649, stepped from a window of the Banqueting Hall of Whitehall palace on to a black-draped scaffold. There, his head was severed from his body by a heavily-disguised executioner, possibly Richard Brandon, 'Young Gregory', who had despatched Sir Alexander Carew.

□□□

Shortly after the King's death, Nicholas took his evening place at the fireside and Juliana reached for a pile of newspapers and pamphlets beside her chair. 'Richard is returned from London and has brought these across, for our perusal. If you cannot read them all, select *The Moderate* and its supplementary pamphlet, *A Perfect Narrative of the Proceedings of the High Court of Justice in the Trial of the King*.'

He opened the broadsheet and held it towards the candles. When he had digested the content, Juliana said, 'Secure in our own happiness, we have tacitly accepted the inevitable, like most of the populace. Neither has protest from abroad been notably vociferous. Now it is done. Yet, the King remained unyielding, convinced of his divine appointment. Even on the scaffold, his plea was liberty and freedom of the people and for the law which ensured that their lives and goods be their own. He simply believed that their welfare and

Government were his God-given responsibility. Now they have murdered him and discarded his values. And what shall we have in his place – a Republic!'

Nicholas shook his head. It was hard to assimilate these events, so distant from their world. After so much bloodshed, so many sacrifices, that it should end like this! And what must still be endured? What lay in the future for their son? He looked across at Juliana and she smiled bravely. They had survived so many vicissitudes, already, and together they would go on, the bond between them growing ever stronger.

In March, they were further saddened by the execution of the Duke of Hamilton. His ineptitude as a military commander was confirmed when he met Cromwell, at Preston, with a force of Scots nigh on three times the strength of the Parliamentarians and committed the cardinal sin of allowing his regiments to scatter, while his opponent held his own in tight check. The captive Hamilton had made a last obeisance to his royal master, in the mud, as he passed through Windsor on the way to his trial, before following him to the block. How prophetic had been his words to Nicholas at Pendennis, 'Who knows when the courtier will feel the kiss of the axe!'

But there was also joy in the year. In September, Juliana bore him a daughter.

CHAPTER 27

The King Returns

1649 was a year of alarums and excursions. The ravages of the Royalists' privateers increased; every port was watched and travellers closely questioned about their business and destinations. In September, Charles II returned to Jersey, raising hopes among the Cavaliers that the Channel Islands might become a springboard for troop landings in Cornwall.

By early 1650, men were increasingly receptive to the King's agents, inspired by their traditional loyalties and religious sentiments, and restless under the burden of taxation. Distinguished persons came and went in the county. Even the eminent Presbyterian, Lord Robartes, was not above suspicion of corresponding with the King. But Cromwell's victories in Ireland helped to persuade Charles to seek a treaty with the Scots and, before embarking on the final negotiations, he sent a Colonel Keane into the West Country. Inevitably, he found his way to Lanherne, where young Sir John, Richard and Nicholas received him. 'I come, gentlemen, to determine what support His Majesty might expect from his loyal subjects, were he to land forces in the county. He also invites you to specify your conditions for raising troops to assist this endeavour.'

Sir John responded, 'Please assure the King that we remain his loyal servants, Colonel. We are prepared to raise 3,000 foot and 300 horse, within a month, provided that Sir Richard Grenville lands from the Scillies with 1,000 foot, 40 barrels of powder, and arms for our own force.'

Keane's eyebrows lifted. 'Sir Richard is disgraced!'

Arundell smiled dryly. 'Do not underrate the standing of a Grenville, in Cornwall. It is our condition. His Majesty must establish this presence before we would venture to put troops in the field. To act in anticipation would place us in unacceptable danger, for our every move is watched. Already this year, arms have been discovered at Sir John Grenville's house, at Stowe, and Sir John Berkeley and Colonel Slingsby have been apprehended at our neighbour Trevanion's home, Caerhayes.'

'Very well! Is there more?'

'We seek personal assurance from His Majesty that, should God restore him, he will permit freedom of worship, particularly to those of us of the Catholic faith.'

'These matters shall be conveyed to the King.'

'I fear that he may be hard put to it to guarantee this last,' Richard remarked, 'for, methinks, the Scots are resolved to impose Presbyterianism upon our people.'

Keane was silent.

'You run no small risk penetrating this far west, Colonel,' Nicholas remarked.

''Tis true. There is a race meeting at Salisbury, in the second week of April. I ask you to meet me, there, for the King's response.'

▣▣▣

Sir John of Lanherne returned from Salisbury, brimming with enthusiasm. 'The King pledges us ease and liberty of conscience, agrees to reinstate Richard Grenville and permits us to take the Engagement to the Commonwealth, as an expedient.'

Richard remained dubious. 'I do not see how he may reconcile these undertakings with the commitments which the Scots will demand from him,' he responded slowly. He was right. Charles bound himself to establish Presbyterianism in England, swore to the Covenant and undertook to implement the laws which placed penal constraints upon the Catholics. His action was bitterly condemned by many of his most devout adherents – Hyde among them – and by Henrietta Maria and his brother, the Duke of York. Others paid with their blood. The most distinguished of them, James Graham, Marquis of Montrose, the King's Lieutenant-General in Scotland, was executed and dismembered by his new allies.

Nicholas angrily confessed his disillusionment to Juliana. 'I sometimes questioned the logic of supporting the Stuarts, until you spoke of the beliefs to which the first Charles was faithful. Since his death, we have endured a military dictatorship and been bled by taxation, and my confidence in our cause has grown. Now, this duplicity. John of Lanherne has given form to our disillusionment, by seeking licence to journey to London in order to compound for his estate.'

Juliana avoided a direct reply to his bitter words. 'Poor Colonel John despairs of ever obtaining his discharge,' was all she said.

The ailing old man's spirits, further taxed by John Grenville's loss of the Scillies, rallied briefly when his King, crowned by the Scots at Scone, marched into England at their head. But his elation was short-lived, for Charles was defeated by Cromwell at Worcester and fled, ignominiously, back to the Continent. His most loyal subject lived on to witness the installation of the victor as Lord Protector of the Commonwealth.

❖❖❖

Juliana glanced from the four-poster bed to her husband's broad back, as he stood at the window of Colonel John's bedchamber in the manor house of Tremadart, looking towards the village of Duloe. He, too, had loved the old warrior, whose last days had been blighted by a fine of 10,000 pounds on his estate, so crushed that he had petitioned Cromwell for partial exemption.

Despite the Protector's acknowledgement of the Articles of the Treaty of Pendennis, he had been forced to pay in the end. Now he who had given so much had surrendered his last possession.

'Nicholas!' she called quietly, and he came to her side. They looked down upon the still figure, the jaw supported by a cloth about the head, the eyes closed, hands folded peacefully upon the coverlet. She made the sign of the cross and he took her hand to lead her from the room.

❖❖❖

Sir John Grenville returned to Stowe and gave the Cavaliers their rallying point, as Cornish representative of the Sealed Knot. This organisation, centrally controlled by seven men and dedicated to restoring the monarchy, was in close touch with the King, Hyde and the Marquis of Ormonde. Grenville's task was to collect arms and horses and give the signal in the event of a rising, before seizing Plymouth. Now, all was intrigue and hope again. Jonathan Trelawny, in conjunction with Grenville, Sir John of Lanherne, Richard Arundell and Nicholas, acted as messenger to the King in plans for an uprising. Robartes had assured Sir John Arundell of his support, and disaffected Levellers and Anabaptists entered into the intrigues with him.

Yet again, it came to naught. The Sealed Knot concluded that the Army, purged of its disaffected officers, could not be relied upon to rise against it leaders And they were further constrained when the county leaders were arrested and flung into jail – among them Sir John Grenville, incarcerated in Plymouth. Nor could the local populace be induced to rise, as Richard Arundell admitted to his faithful associates, at a meeting in the solar at Trerice.

'It would be folly to attempt an insurrection,' he told them. 'Sir Joseph Wagstaff and John Penruddock have tried and Penruddock is captive in Exeter. Nor do I trust the weaponry sent to us from that city and am determined to have it inspected by the blacksmith.'

The arms were discovered in possession of the smith and all those involved counted themselves fortunate that they were not arrested. Penruddock and his associate, Colonel Grove, did not fare so well and were beheaded at Exeter. Other executions and regressions, and the appointment of 10 major-generals, to maintain order throughout the country, subdued even the Cornish gentry.

Cromwell seemed invincible. He was even offered the title of King, but declined, fearing the opposition of the army. But on the 3rd of September, 1658, he died and was succeeded by his son, Richard. Obliged to call Parliament, so that money could be voted for the troops, he issued writs for an election. As a result, Sir John Grenville and his kinsman, William Maurice, were returned.

And another rising was engineered. Sir John Grenville and Jonathan Trelawney, aided by the Arundells and the Presbyterian Boscawens, planned to take Plymouth and Pendennis Castle. But there was treachery within the Sealed Knot and the rising in Devon and Cornwall was paralysed by the arrest of Grenville. Although he was twice examined by the Council of State, and his home searched for papers and arms, nothing was found.

One day, while Nicholas was working in the little room that served as office and study, Juliana appeared in the doorway. 'John Grenville's steward is here to see you, though he is somewhat reticent about his purpose.'

'Show him in.'

She brought in the tall, taciturn man long known to her, who Nicholas had encountered on rare visits to Stowe. He handed Nicholas a letter, sealed with the golden griffin crest. It read:

8th July, 1659

'My dear friend,

I doubt not that even you have been dispirited by our adversities and hope that you might find a spell in London, as my guest, agreeable to you. I beg you not to disappoint me. John Phillips will give you details of the arrangements.

Yours truly,

John Grenville.'

When he had finished reading, Nicholas passed the letter to Juliana, giving Phillips his cue to speak. 'My master requests that you return to Stowe with me, prepared for an absence of at least one month.'

Nicholas looked questioningly at Juliana. How could he leave the farm; there was too much to do? But something in Phillips' manner could not be denied. Reading his mind, Juliana nodded. 'The farm will survive in Isaac Tremain's hands and Meg will care for the children.'

She was right. Isaac, the son of his old cowman and Janet's younger brother, would manage, for he and Juliana had been at pains to render him literate and numerate and he was a reliable stockman. Regarding Meg's custody of the children, nothing need be said, for she was devoted to them.

'If you would care to enjoy the garden, awhile, Mister Phillips, we will set about our preparations.'

They followed the same route that Juliana had taken when, fearful of her love's safety, she had visited John Grenville's mother. But, they turned aside at Kilkhampton and Phillips led them to a vicarage, beside the church, where they were received by Nicholas Monck, Grenville's chaplain.

'I fear that I cannot resolve the mystery of Sir John's invitation,' he said, apologetically. 'He proposes that we travel in the Grenville coach to his lodgings in London, believing that such a group, in possession of his letter of invitation, will appear in no way conspiratorial, if challenged.'

'Is there, then, some conspiracy afoot?' Nicholas demanded.

Monck hesitated. 'I know only what Mister Phillips conceded. Sir John regards your presence as affording me protection, against what I cannot say.'

'Then we must contain ourselves till all is revealed,' said Juliana, brightly, savouring an adventure.

'I recall hearing that you are brother to General George Monck, commander of the Parliamentary army in Scotland,' Nicholas commented.

'That does have interesting implications, to be sure,' the chaplain answered, reflectively. 'Now I am as intrigued as you.'

The Grenville coach, with the griffin's head crest upon its doors, rumbled heavily towards London, progressing at about 30 miles each day. Shaken and jolted, its occupants were always intent upon reaching the next stage, where the stop to change horses afforded an opportunity for food and rest. A week after setting out, they drummed over the cobbles of Lincoln's Inn Fields, where Grenville lodged with fellow Royalists.

'Thank you for coming so promptly.' With a courtly bow, Grenville kissed

Juliana's hand. 'I would not have imposed upon you so, were it not a matter of the greatest moment.' They had entered an ornately-ceilinged room, with windows overlooking the spacious Fields beyond, and Grenville carefully closed the doors. Nicholas realised that it was the house where he and Robin had sat at supper, that night when they had fled with Geoffrey into the stews of Southwark.

'Is this not a fine house?' John Grenville enquired. 'Stowe is a splendid habitation and my father would have embellished it, further, had he lived, but my fancy is to rebuild it, along these lines, for parts of our home are very ancient and damp. However, to my purpose! Know you that my chaplain is of an old Devon family and brother to General Monck?'

'Yes.'

'The King believes that the general might be influenced to support the restoration of the monarchy.'

This was news indeed!

'He is understandably circumspect in the matter and I propose to send Nicholas, your namesake, to carry a letter from the King and to sound out his brother. Need I say that it is not only a delicate mission, but one fraught with difficulty and possible danger for a man of the cloth. He needs a companion with a cool nerve and a trusty swordarm. Will you do it?'

Nicholas knew he need not look at Juliana. 'How will we travel?'

'By ship to the Firth of Forth, then up the river Esk to Dalkeith.'

''Tis a long voyage, beyond the strength of one man to keep constant vigil.'

'Then name another to go with you – one you would trust with your life.'

He replied without hesitation, 'Geoffrey Knollys, Earl of Thurston.' He caught Juliana's eye and she nodded.

'An excellent choice,' Grenville responded. 'He inherited the title, but lately, upon the premature death of his brother, did he not?'

Nicholas nodded.

'The family home is Thurston Park, near St. Albans, some 20 miles north of London,' Grenville reflected. 'We have three days, while passages are arranged. Sound him out.'

Nicholas set off alone, next morning, across the waterlogged clay of Islington and northward, until he arrived at Geoffrey's country seat, to see the great house for the first time, as he crossed the park with the lodgekeeper at his side.

Thurston Park was a perpendicular slab of a house, with flanking towers topped by cupolas. Mullioned windows broke the severity of its line and the July sun lent a roseate glow to the brickwork. A wide flight of shallow steps led to the front door, which was surrounded by an ornate stone arch. High above, a fretted parapet hid the roof. Nicholas was a little overawed by its grandeur.

Geoffrey's and Letitia's welcome could not have been warmer, and he felt a pang of guilt regarding his self-imposed mission, when their two small children, a boy of 11 and a girl of nine, were presented to him. His own continuing service to the Royalist cause was obligatory, but Geoffrey had no such commitment. Recognising that there was a serious purpose behind his friend's visit, and once news of families and old friends had been exchanged, Geoffrey led him up an elaborately-carved staircase to a room on the first floor. 'I perceive that something weighs heavily with you, my friend.'

'Aye, and I hardly know how to broach the matter, for 'twas my suggestion to involve you in an enterprise of great moment and, mayhap, some hazard.'

Geoffrey cocked an eyebrow and smiled. 'Then let us have it!'

He told his comrade of Grenville's initiative and their proposed involvement in it. When he had finished, Geoffrey walked slowly to the window, above the front door, beckoning Nicholas to follow. Outside the park stretched flat and green, abundant with English oaks.

'My brother died earlier this year, without issue, broken by the struggle to redeem our estates from the tyranny of the Parliament. Thanks be to God, he succeeded and we are the beneficiaries of that sacrifice. It is my sacred trust to keep our inheritance secure.'

Nicholas's heart sank. 'I understand. It was wrong of me to ask this of you. '

'You misunderstand. Restoration of the monarchy is our veriest guarantee for the future. Should I be instrumental in that great purpose, I would assuredly have kept faith with him.' Geoffrey's white teeth showed in a smile. 'I am your man!'

On the road back to London, there was much speculation about their impending mission to Scotland, but Nicholas had few facts to call upon, and soon the talk turned to Robin.

'Does he thrive?' Geoffrey wanted to know.

'Hugely! The inn at Fowey is but a small part of his enterprise and serves chiefly as headquarters for his wine-importing business. Can you imagine a man more suited to the trade? He distributes throughout Devon and Cornwall, and along the coast of Dorset, and into Somerset, and his judgement is almost infallible. He has become quite a wealthy man, even investing in an occasional merchant venture to the West Indies.

'He idolises his daughter, Anne. She promises to be as beautiful and accomplished a musician as her mother, but it is a great sadness that his son was stillborn. It would seem unlikely that Katherine will bear him more children, for Anne is already 11 years old.'

'Would that we had the rascal with us on this coming enterprise!'

'Had I known what John Grenville would ask of me, before we left Cornwall, I would assuredly have brought him along.'

Arrived at Grenville's lodging, they waited till he bustled in from the Commons. He called in Nicholas Monck, immediately, and proceeded to explain the enterprise. 'The King cherishes hopes that George Monck might be the instrument for restoring the House of Stuart to the throne. As you know, the general served His Majesty's father in his second war against the Scottish covenanters, and in Ireland, until he was captured by the Roundheads in Cheshire. Monck refused to turn recusant and was held in the Tower for over two years. Upon his release in 1646, with the King a prisoner of the Parliament, he joined the Roundhead army and took command of their forces in Ulster. I will not burden you with details of his subsequent career – suffice to say that he has been a general on land, and at sea against the Dutch. Having finally defeated Tromp, he was sent back to Scotland, which he has ruled for the past six years.

'Now to the nub of it, gentlemen. Monck was loyal to the Protector and, when he died, declared his allegiance to Richard Cromwell as his successor, but he did not move against Fleetwood and Desborough, in April, when they overthrew the Protector or, more recently, against Lambert, when he and the Republicans re-established the Rump Parliament. The King, therefore, requires me to sound him out and I have chosen brother Nicholas as my emissary.'

Grenville glanced around at the enthralled faces. 'I need not tell you that we are making history.'

He stood up. 'Our host tells me that arrangements have been made for your sailing, tomorrow, through the network you Cavaliers established these many years gone. Do this service for your King and honour and glory shall be ours!'

▫▫▫

They sailed up the North Sea, hugging the coast, until, emerging from early morning mist, they made out the mouth of the Firth of Forth. Then it was up the River Esk to the granite houses and mean thatched cottages of Dalkeith. As Nicholas watched the once-familiar process of furling sail and dropping anchor, he wondered what sort of man, the brother of his namesake would be. Perchance, they would not even meet him, for John Grenville had made it clear that they were escorts, not emissaries, and that, anyway, George Monck was a very cautious man. He smiled. Grenville fervently believed that they were making history, but he doubted that history would even record their presence.

A message was sent to the general and, soon, a man in civilian clothes came aboard, greeting Nicholas Monck familiarly. 'I'm Thomas Clarges, General Monck's brother-in-law,' he informed the two Cavaliers, in a strong London accent. His appearance occasioned no surprise; both he and his sister, Mrs Monck, were secret Royalist sympathisers and it had been his own suggestion that Nicholas Monck should visit his brother. 'Lodgings have been found in the town,' he continued, 'where the general asks you to wait till he may see you.'

Nicholas Monck was absent for long periods during the several days they spent in the town. When he returned, he spoke, openly, of their discussions. 'My brother will commit nothing to writing, nor will he even declare himself, despite the King's offer of £100,000 if he will restore him to the throne.' He gave a slow, self-satisfied smile. 'But I have been working upon the sympathies of Anne Monck and Price, my brother's chaplain, and I doubt not that we have allies, there! We are, by the bye, invited to family supper this evening. '

'So we are to meet Scotland's overlord, after all,' Geoffrey murmured.

They came to the Parliamentary headquarters a little after six o'clock. George Monck was 50 years of age, with a fleshy face and strong, rounded chin. He wore his hair long and affected a thin moustache, but no beard. Heavy eyebrows and a slighty petulant set to the mouth gave the impression of a forceful, strongly-opinionated personality. Indeed, Nicholas Monck had told them that his brother occasionally resorted to physical violence, when displeased, and cited an incident when the Under-Sheriff of Devonshire had proposed to arrest his father, for debt, as he prepared to receive the King at Exeter. George, then 16, bribed the Sheriff to delay the arrest, but he, nevertheless, took Sir Thomas Monck before the King arrived. Whereupon, young George went to his lodgings and thrashed him, soundly, for his perfidy.

The general presented his wife and brother-in-law and chaplain Price and led them to table. During the meal, the Cavaliers were much intrigued by Anne Monck. Her origins were of the humblest, her father having been a farrier. She was also married to a farrier, in the service of the Prince of Wales, when she had met Monck in the Tower, while serving as his laundress. She became his mistress and then his wife, on her husband's death. Like George she was not averse to violence, and had been known to slap him when angered. She was attractive, and clearly, a woman of character, and there was no doubt of the general's attachment to her. Unlike her circumspect husband, she made little attempt to disguise her sympathies, prompting Monck to chide her. 'How oft must I repeat it, wife, "he who follows truth too closely upon the heels will, one time or another, have his brains kicked out."

She laughed and chose another subject, but her cheerful cockney chatter continued to amuse them.

As they prepared to leave, the general said, 'I would like it widely known, brother, that I am devoutly Presbyterian. Let there be no doubt in the mind of your pricipals of my persuasion.' At this first intimation of his concern for religion, delivered with no trace of fervour, Nicholas Monck and chaplain Price exchanged looks of amused cynicism.

Aboard ship, Nicholas Monck and his two companions leaned on the bulwarks, watching Dalkeith disappear into the mists. Out in the Firth, isolated shafts of light penetrated the lowering cloud, transmuting the dark waters into pools of liquid silver, the only relief in the monochrome landscape. As the Scottish coast became a smudge, Nicholas Monck looked sidelong at Geoffrey. 'You are well acquainted with affairs in the capital, my Lord Earl, what make you of my brother's intentions?'

Geoffrey cast a cautious glance over his shoulder. 'Were it meet to wager with you, Parson Monck, I would lay odds that your brother will support the King, in the long term. But he is a shrewd man and knows that the time is not ripe, nor will be while Major-General Lambert can enter the field against him, should he march on London.'

'Methinks, the general's mind was revealed in two particulars,' Nicholas interjected. 'Firstly, in his concern that his religious persuasion should be known - surely another expression of a political stance – and, secondly, in advising the King to declare a general pardon, settle the arrears in soldiers' pay and declare for religious tolerance. Nor should we ignore the influence of his wife and brother-in-law and the chaplain – there seems little doubt where their sympathies lie.'

Geoffrey laughed. 'Aye, our journey has been worthwhile, if only to meet that redoubtable lady. In truth, were not some of us blessed with the inestimable advantages of birth, I doubt the social order would be what it is.'

Nicholas watched the lightening horizon, thinking that in that sentiment lay the foundation of the mutual regard between himself and his friend.

□□□

When Nicholas Monck and his companions gave an account of their mission to Grenville, he confessed himself baffled by the general's response to the King's overtures. Only one thing was clear – that the time had not yet come for Charles Stuart to claim his inheritance.

When Geoffrey returned to Thurston Park, Juliana and Nicholas travelled with him and spent several happy days with the Knollys family, before returning to Cornwall, there to follow events as best they could.

Geoffrey had been right in forecasting that Lambert constituted a problem for George Monck. On 13th of October, the handsome Roundhead forcibly debarred the Speaker and Members from entering the House and established the army as the ruling power. Then, Lambert marched north to Newcastle, where, reluctant to provoke more civil strife, he agreed that he would proceed no further, provided his adversary remained north of Berwick. But time was on Monck's side. With the advent of winter, Lambert's army, unpaid and disaffected, began to desert and Fairfax seized York for Monck. Lambert, more stylish than many a Cavalier, but resolved in his principles, returned to London and threw himself on the mercy of the Rump Parliament.

It was Monck's hour. Braving the snow and ice of a severe winter, he set out from Coldstream, just south of Dalkeith, on 1st of January, 1660, and crossed the frozen Tweed. Between Durham and York, he rode through the passive remnants of Lambert's army straggling south, and, on 3rd of February, entered London. Taking up residence within the walls of Whitehall Palace, no longer illuminated by Titians, Rembrandts and Carravegios, he repudiated the authority of the Rump and called for elections.

Still he did not declare himself, and the numerous Republicans and Independents who called upon the all-powerful and newly-convinced Presbyterian ran the gauntlet of abuse from the redoubtable Mrs Monck, who continued to leave no one in doubt where her sympathies lay.

The freely-elected Parliament was strongly supported in the West Country and the Cornish gentry helped to secure Pendennis Castle in its name. Grenville, that vital link between Monck and the King, visited the general, in a further attempt to understand his position, before proceeding to his royal master, at Brussels. Monck's advice that the King should offer a general pardon, confirm sales of land during the war, pay the soldiers and declare for liberty of conscience, formed the framework of the Declaration of Breda. When this was presented to the Parliament, the two Houses begged Charles to return with all speed, and he stepped ashore at Dover on 25th of May, to be received by Monck on his knees.

Monck was created Duke of Albermarle and John Grenville became Earl of Bath, Viscount Grenville of Lansdown and Baron Grenville of Bideford and Kilkhampton. Retribution followed for others, principally the regicides – those who had signed the King's death warrant. Notable among them was

John Carew, still staunch in his belief in a republic and in his God. Making no attempt to escape, he was arrested, tried and subjected to the appalling fate of hanging, drawing and quartering.

CHAPTER 28

Reward and Retribution

On a mild March day, four years later, Nicholas approached the Barton. It had been a tiring journey, but well worthwhile, for he had become an associate – albeit in a small way – of the Killigrews, in their plans to develop Smithick into the port of Falmouth.

Two horses were hitched to the porch and he found Richard Arundell and his son, John, with Juliana. His own son, James, hovered near the window, anxious to be included in the family group about the fireplace. Juliana was in a state of suppressed excitement. 'Hinny, Richard has come from the King and has news for us.'

Seeking to disguise his satisfaction, Richard told him, 'I have been granted the patent of Baron Arundell of Trerice, in recognition of my father's services to the Crown.'

'Would that he were here to witness this day,' Juliana sighed.

'Amen!'

'And in recognition of your own service to the Stuarts, I doubt not,' Nicholas told him, for Richard had fought at Edgehill and Lansdown, as well as defending Pendennis and conspiring for the King's return.

'So His Majesty was pleased to say.'

'This calls for a toast – pray, excuse me.' Nicholas went off to the cellars and returned with two bottles of best claret, supplied by a well-known importer of Fowey. When glasses were charged, he looked around the little group. 'To the master of Trerice, and the memory of your heroic father.' Skeltons toasted Arundells. 'And may you two, young John and James, know peace all your days.'

Richard put an arm around his kinswoman. 'Still, it is an unjust world. Nicholas Monck made Bishop of Hereford, John Robartes Lord Privy Seal and Deputy-Lieutenant of Ireland, yet Richard Vyvyan, Master of the Mint during the war, must content himself with the governorship of St. Mawes Castle and Gentleman of the King's Privy Chamber. A poor reward for nearly £10,000 spent in the royal cause. And for you, my dear relatives, not even that!'

Juliana had been watching Nicholas while Richard spoke, 'We are content for you,' she said.

'But the county is yours,' Richard continued. 'You are a Justice of the Peace, Nicholas, and well regarded. Why not bid for a seat in the Commons? You would have powerful supporters, not least John Grenville up there in his new house at Stowe. Say but the word and I promise you will not be disappointed.' He bent to kiss Juliana and extended his hand to Nicholas. 'God go with you both and with you, young James. Come across to Trerice, this afternoon – I have a new falcon for you.' He cocked an ear, as the music of the virginals came to them from somewhere in the house. 'And my love to your beautiful daughters.'

As they stood beneath the portico and watched the departing Arundells, Nicholas reached for his love's hand. 'Let us walk awhile.'

They crossed the yard into the meadow, and climbed the gentle slope, till they looked down on the Barton. This was the view he had when he sat astride the black mare, that day he rode over from Antony, with Jane Carew's proposition churning in his mind, 18 years gone.

Juliana held his arm and looked up into his face, at the ivory thread of the scar, half-hidden in his beard, at the suspicion of grey at the temples. He was still strong and hard, but the old uncertainties were long departed, the thrusting ambition spent. 'Are you much disappointed to have been passed over?'

In the courtyard below, James was harnessing his horse, watched, admiringly, by his younger sister. Meg came from the house and, in response to the child's demand, lifted her into the saddle. 'I am as receptive to honours as any man, yet I am only truly ambitious for you and the children.'

'But Richard is right, you are widely regarded and could be more so, were you to sit in the Commons.'

'Mayhap, but then I must rely on James to manage the Barton and my dearest wish is that he should go to Oxford, to Exeter College. And how might I contrive without you, all those miles from home?' He pressed her head to his breast.

'Or I you, except for the honour due to you.'

Spring sunshine broke through the thin cloud, bringing the first hint of summer to come. Soon, the honey-sweet scent would rise from the meadow and the bees begin their quest for nectar from the clover, as they did season on eternal season. In the far distance, where the Gannel met the sea, the horizon would shimmer in the heat. 'We shall see,' he told her. Harkening to the thin notes of the virginals coming from the open windows of the farmhouse, he added, 'Our eldest daughter is becoming a passable musician.'

Lightning Source UK Ltd.
Milton Keynes UK
UKOW040615140712

195979UK00001B/2/P